Legends Untold

Avily Jerome

LEGENDS UNTOLD
Published by Dragontail Press
P. O. Box 54550
Phoenix, AZ 85078

ISBN 979-8985204414
Copyright © 2023 by Avily Jerome
Cover design by Robert Mullin

Available in print from your local bookstore, online, or from the author.
For more information on this book and the author visit: www.avilyjerome.com

Brought to you by Avily Jerome

Library of Congress Cataloging-in-Publication Data
Jerome, Avily
Legends Untold/Avily Jerome 1st ed.

Printed in the United States of America.

For my dad, who loved this story enough to keep pushing me to publish it. Thanks, Dad, for all your support of my books over the years. I love you.

Chapter One

Four-inch, saliva-drenched fangs glistened orange in the setting sun.

The man covered his face with his arms and stumbled backward as the creature swooped toward him, its immense wings thundering as they beat the air. Searing pain sliced through his shoulder and sucked away his breath before he could scream.

Gravity, only a moment before anchoring him to solid earth, failed. The field and his sheep dropped away beneath him as the pressure in his shoulder pulled him heavenward.

Above him, the dark scales that lined the creature's underbelly blocked his view of anything else. Instinctively, he thrashed against the claws gripping him, but that only intensified the pain.

With a rush of wind, the creature shot into the sky, and the man's body jolted. As his arm jerked upward, a popping sound, like dried twigs cracking underfoot, sounded in his ears. Pain like nothing he'd ever felt radiated from the torn ligaments in his shoulder.

Higher and higher they soared, until the man skimmed the tops of the tall jungle trees and the branches carved deep slashes in his legs and torso.

The creature flew onward, toward the cave-riddled cliffs high in the mountains.

Desperate for freedom, the man used his free hand to claw at the monster's leg, but instead of releasing him, the talons dug deeper into his flesh.

An agonized moan escaped his lips. He grasped for the knife he carried at his waist.

With one flurried motion he pulled the knife from its sheath and plunged the weapon into the soft skin between the creature's claws.

Fire erupted from the creature's mouth, intensifying the warmth in the spring air, and a screech split the dusk. The grip on his shoulder released.

Wind whipped around the man as the treetops rushed up to meet him. Bones and branches snapped as he plummeted through the foliage, thumping and cracking against every branch for what seemed like hours.

At last his momentum slowed and he came to rest, sprawled across a web of thick limbs, still thirty or more yards from the ground.

Anguish stabbed every particle of his body. He called out, but his voice choked out little more than a squeak. Again, he pushed air through his vocal chords, but the motion sent his body into spasms of torment. He scarcely possessed the energy to breathe, let alone the power to call for help.

As the night enveloped him in darkness, he prayed to whatever spirits might be listening that somehow, someone would find him.

***

"Come on, Randi. You're going to miss your flight." Meg's voice echoed off the stone walls of the narrow passageway.

Randi jumped, almost dropping her tool kit. "One more minute. I think I found something." Randi brushed at the crack in the ancient stone wall. "Come check this out. I think this is hollow back here."

"Great. I'll take pictures and email them. If you don't get going soon, you'll miss your flight and you won't make it back in time for class on Monday."

Randi brushed the dust from her watch and pointed her light at it. She grinned at her supervisor-turned-friend. "If I leave in half an hour, I'll still be fine. Come help me with this."

Meg pulled her hand-brush from her tool belt and shined her flashlight on the crack next to where Randi worked. The glow cast eerie shadows on the carved walls of the dim tunnel.

"I agree. It's very similar," Meg snorted, her tone dry. "Who would've figured the theme would be consistent on different parts of the same structure?"

"Thanks for your confidence in my archaeological skills. Seriously, check this out. I think this indicates a sacred space. Like some sort of inner holy place, the spot in the very center of the temple where the most sacred idol would have been. I think they worshipped this creature."

Meg grinned. "Which one of us is the professional archaeologist, and which one is just a budding historian who's lucky to even be here?"

Randi cleared a warren of dust bunnies from the crack and returned Meg's smile. "I do appreciate the opportunity, Yoda. Not many students get the chance to work on a real dig."

"You're welcome. You could come back if you were studying archaeology instead of history." Meg brushed a lock of short, dark brown hair behind her ear.

Randi shrugged. "I just felt like I clicked better as a history major. I'm better at book research than field research. Besides, if I didn't, who would keep all your facts straight for you?" Her fingers found a bump in the fissure. "Ah!" She felt around the edges of the bump. "I'm beginning to wonder if I made the wrong choice. I think I found the catch to open it."

"Hold this." Meg thrust her flashlight into Randi's hands. "Point it there while I try to open this. Be careful. The sidekick is the one who always gets mauled by the inevitable booby trap."

Randi focused the beam of light on the area where Meg's fingers worked against the stone. "What makes you think I'm the sidekick?"

"Because," Meg paused to peer into the crack. "If it weren't for me, you'd be spending spring break doing something boring, or something you'd regret, like getting drunk on the beach, or—got it!"

Click.

"Step back!" Meg planted her hand on Randi's chest and shoved her back against the opposite wall.

Rock grated against rock, and metallic scraping echoed through the chamber. Slowly, a foot-square piece of the wall slid away and revealed a small opening into a dark chasm beyond.

"Light," Meg demanded.

The beam played across stone walls at the other end of a small chamber. Something gold stood on a pedestal in the center, its gleam muted but distinctive.

7

"What is that?" Randi asked.

"It looks like an idol. I think you may have been right. Probably something these people valued very highly. Some sort of deity, maybe."

"Can you tell what it is?" Randi peered past Meg's shoulder, focusing the beam on the gleaming, two-foot-high object sitting on a marble pedestal.

Even hundreds of years of dust couldn't disguise the splendor of the statue. A serpentine head with ruby eyes twisted above a sturdy gold body. Bat-like wings, encrusted with precious stones, stretched up from the back of the body, as if the creature would take off in flight at any moment.

Meg pulled on rubber gloves and stuck her arm through the opening. "I can't quite reach it. You're a little taller than I am—you try."

Standing on her toes, Randi stretched her arm toward the artifact. Her fingers brushed against the cool metal. "Almost there."

She strained to get closer and grasped again, closing her fingers. Instead of the chill of smooth, hard gold, however, the feel of something soft and leathery squished beneath her fingers.

Before she could release whatever it was she'd grabbed, needles pierced her glove and sent fire from the base of her thumb through her veins. She dropped the thing and yanked her hand out.

"Ow!" The echo of her voice in the closed quarters took on a surreal, haunting quality.

Burning agony throbbed in her hand, pulsing up her arm.

The dim light in the tunnel swirled in a fog around her head, dizzying, rushing around her eyes, nauseating her.

Meg's voice sounded far away. "Randi? Are you okay? What happened?"

"I think—I think—" The words felt like mush around her thick tongue. "I think something bit me."

Her head cracked against cold, hard stone just before the darkness overtook her completely.

***

Beep.

Beep.

Beep.

The steady rhythm of monitors, accented by the ebb and flow of high-pitched, terse voices, pulled Randi back to consciousness. She blinked against the harsh glare of fluorescent lights. "Meg?"

"I'm here, kiddo."

"Where am I?"

"Local hospital. Here are your glasses."

Randi shoved her glasses on her nose and took in the dingy, checkerboard linoleum and ancient medical equipment. A second glance revealed a sardine can-like room. Patients of every size huddled in chairs and on beds while doctors and nurses buzzed around the room. The odor of sickness—blood and pus, medicine, and unwashed bodies—wafted around the entire room, not just her bed.

Randi suppressed a shudder. "Did I miss my flight?"

Meg chuckled. "You got bitten by a venomous snake. You could have died, and you're worried about your flight?"

The throbbing in her hand blurred Randi's thoughts. "Snake—what kind of snake?"

"They aren't sure. The pattern of the fangs is different from anything they're familiar with. The venom doesn't seem to have done any lasting damage, but since you did pass out, you should get tested when you get home."

"Am I okay?"

"Well, despite the almost-nineteenth-century condition of this hospital, yeah, you're going to be fine. We have to wait a couple of hours, but it will work out."

A cockroach skittered down the far wall. Randi shuddered and turned back to Meg. "I still need to get home."

"I already called the airline and got you a stand-by ticket, so you can leave on the next flight after you get released from here."

Randi leaned back against the bed and the stench of sweat and antiseptics stung her nostrils. "Am I going to be home in time to shower first?"

Meg chuckled. "At least you still have your sense of humor. That's a good sign. I think. Anyway, it's not you. It's the hospital. That's what you get for getting injured in a remote part of Cameroon."

"Great. How long did you say I have to stay?"

"Just until the doctor is sure you won't have any lasting effects from the bite."

"Wonderful. Okay, take my mind off of it. Tell me about the artifact. Did you get it out?"

Meg cocked her head and gave Randi her trademark mom-glare. "After you were bitten, did you really think I'd stick my hand in there? Besides, I came here with you. I didn't have time."

"I appreciate that, by the way. You will email me with anything you find out, though, right?"

"Of course."

She closed her eyes, trying to picture the statue. "Can you get me a piece of paper and something to write with?"

"Sure. Why?"

"I think I'm coming up with a theory, but I need to map it out a little."

Meg returned a few moments later with a pad of notepaper and a pen.

Pain cramped Randi's hand when she clutched the pen, but she gritted her teeth against the ache and began to sketch. In a few quick strokes, she duplicated what she remembered of the etchings on the temple wall.

"Okay, look at this one here. I think this symbol represents the statue. Didn't you tell me once that most of the ancient gods had roots in actual things people saw, like the sun and the moon, or lightning, or wild beasts?"

"That's right."

Randi sketched again, outlining the shape of the statue. "Well, if we're right and this is one of the most sacred idols, then what if it was a glorified snake or something in real life?"

She added shading and the gems encrusting the wings to the picture. "Something powerful enough to make the people fear and worship it."

"Randi, do you know what you're saying?"

"I've been saying this for months. This is just the kind of evidence I need to put in my thesis."

"Your thesis? You mean, you're going to use this—"

A scream split through the emergency room. Keening wails drowned out any sound from the other patients.

Randi stared at the man being brought in.

Blood oozed through the bandage on his shoulder. His arm and one leg flopped over the side of his stretcher at awkward angles. Viscera spilled from a slash in his abdomen, and wounds mottled the man's skin.

A doctor shouted something, grabbed supplies from a nearby nurse, and put pressure on the gashes covering the man's stomach and chest.

"What are they saying?" Randi asked Meg.

"I thought you spoke French?"

"Not when they're talking that fast. Anyway, I read it better than I speak it. What's going on?"

"He needs to get to surgery immediately. The doctor wants to know what happened."

Panicked voices jabbered at one another over the man's tormented screeching.

"What is it?"

"That man—" Meg's voice came out as a hoarse whisper. "They found him over a hundred feet up in a tree."

"How did he get into a tree with those injuries?"

"They don't know. They think he was being chased by something."

The man yelled something unintelligible.

"Now what's he saying?" Randi looked from the man to Meg and back.

Meg shook her head. "I'm not sure. Something about a monster—a flying monster? He must be delirious. Maybe he was dragged into the tree?"

"What kind of creature would be powerful enough to drag a grown man a hundred feet up in a tree? Wild cat of some kind?"

A doctor injected the man with something, and within moments, he slumped against the gurney, his eyelids drooping.

A string of words spewed from the doctor's mouth.

"They're taking him to surgery," Meg interpreted. "They don't know if he'll live."

The doctors wheeled the rolling cot in Meg and Randi's direction.

Blood and saliva seeped from the man's drugged lips as he muttered something.

"He's saying something about being dropped," Meg explained to Randi.

One of the nurses said something in a firm, clipped tone.

11

The procession stopped only a few feet from where Randi's gurney sat shoved up against a wall. The nurse disappeared around the corner.

The man on the stretcher stared at Randi, his eyes dull with narcotics. His gaze dropped to the bandage on her hand, then drifted to the sketch in her lap.

Fire sparked his glassy eyes to life. Hysteria-laced squawks poured out of his gaping mouth. White-knuckled fingers gripped the rail of his gurney and his one good leg thrashed as though trying to propel him from the picture.

Jumbled syllables tumbled from his slack mouth.

Meg's eyes appeared to be only a fraction away from bursting out of her head entirely.

"What is it? What did he say?"

Meg's lips opened and closed a couple of times before any sound escaped. "He said—he said, 'That's it! That's the monster that attacked me!'"

Chapter Two

The agent, carrying flowers, winked at the nurse behind the desk. "Can you tell me where the farmer who was attacked is?" he asked in flawless French.

"You a reporter?"

"No, just an old friend."

She eyed him suspiciously, but handed him a clipboard. "You need to sign in."

He signed the name that matched the passport he used to enter the country and smiled at her.

"Down the hall, last door on the left. He's in the middle."

"Thanks." The agent strutted down the hall to the room where the man lay, his gurney sandwiched between two others, separated from the other unconscious patients by nothing more than a tattered curtain.

Drug-induced slumber kept the patient quiet, his chest rising and falling at even intervals.

Monitors beeped rhythmically, echoing off the dingy linoleum and stark walls.

The agent smiled at the primitive setup. This job would be far more difficult in a hospital in the States. Not that he couldn't do it—he already had on plenty of other occasions. Still, it was refreshing to have such an easy assignment. He clamped a pillow over the man's face. Just before the monitors attached to the man started beeping, he nudged one with his foot, unplugging it from the wall. When he was certain the man was dead, he replaced the pillow, then stepped out into the hall.

"Ma'am, can you come here?" he called down the hallway.

The nurse ambled down the hall. "What's going on?"

"Look," Rob said, pointing. "He doesn't look right."

The nurse took a step closer to the patient.

"Good lord, what happened?"

The agent shrugged.

The nurse noticed the unplugged monitor and plugged it back in, to be met with the sound of flat-lining. "Damn it, they're going to give me hell for this," she muttered.

She turned to the agent. "Out. Now. He was dead when you got here."

The agent nodded and stalked down the hallway to the exit.

Once outside, he called the Director. "It's done."

"Good," the Director's voice crackled. "And the story?"

"Taken care of. Tomorrow morning, tucked away in the back of the paper, will be a story about an animal attack. Big cat dragged the man into the tree, then ran away when rescuers arrived. He died from his injuries at the hospital."

"Excellent. You've done well."

***

Los Angeles, Califorina
Three weeks later

"Mom, what's this?" Randi carried the picture to her mom in the kitchen.

"What's what, honey?" Her mother, Jean, wiped her hands on her apron. Randi showed her the grainy photograph.

"I have no idea. Where did you find it?"

"It was in the pile of Dad's mail in his office."

"Randi, you shouldn't be spending the last day of your weekend going through your dad's old stuff."

"And you can't leave it in there forever. He's been gone two years. Somebody has to deal with it."

Her mom pulled her reading glasses out of her front pocket and examined the picture. She turned it over and read the inscription. "Dr. Ross, I received your inquiry. I hope this helps. –T. S." She looked at Randi. "Where did this come from? Who is T. S.?"

"I was hoping you knew." Randi took the picture back and stared at it. "It's postmarked Potsdam, Brandenburg, in Germany, but there's no return address, no letter, just this. But Mom, did you see it? Do you know what this means?"

Jean shook her head firmly. "No. There's no point in going down that path. You can't tell anything from that photo. You have no idea where it came from or what it's supposed to be."

"It's obvious. Dad was looking everywhere for this. Who knows if this could've been the piece of evidence he was waiting for? Maybe he wouldn't have—"

"But he did." Her mom clipped her words, her tone hard. "He dedicated his life to grasping at straws, and when he ran out of straws, he gave up."

Randi took a deep breath. "I understand, Mom, but if this is out there, then maybe there's more. Maybe it just needs to be found."

"Miranda, don't do this. Your father had so much potential that he just wasted. You have a promising career ahead of you. I already lost your father to this crazy obsession. I don't want lose you, too."

The pain in her mother's eyes stabbed Randi's heart. Her mom was right. It was foolish and fruitless. But if there was even the slightest chance her father was right...

"Mom, I promise I won't turn into Dad. I will finish my degree and I'll be a good, proper historian. But, I can't promise not to follow where the evidence takes me."

Her mom clutched at her apron, her knuckles white, but she nodded. "Only the evidence. You can't follow hearsay or whispers or your own heart. And you can't do it exclusive of everything else. I want you to have a real life."

Randi smiled and squeezed her mom's hand. "Deal."

"Okay, then. Will you please set the table? The Carvers will be here in a few minutes. Is Nik coming?"

Randi stuck the envelope in her bag and began arranging the plates and utensils. "No. He had a date or something."

"That boy. When will he realize you're the perfect girl?"

Randi rolled her eyes, even though her mother couldn't see her from the kitchen. "We're friends, Mom. That's it."

15

When she finished setting the table, she ran out to her mom's garden and cut an array of flowers and arranged them in a vase in the center of the table.

"Oh, honey, that's beautiful. You always make everything look so nice. Are you sure Nik can't make it?"

Randi was saved from further debate by the doorbell. "I've got it." She opened the door.

"Oh, Miranda, don't you look lovely? I can't believe how grown up you look!" Mrs. Carver planted a wet kiss on Randi's cheek and bustled in, followed by her morose husband. "Those flowers are lovely. Are they from your garden, Jean?"

Randi's mom smiled and set the roast in the center of the table. "Yes. Randi arranged them. I keep telling her she could have gone into Interior Design, but she's got too much of her father in her."

Her mother smiled as she said it, but Randi still heard the resentful edge to her voice.

Randi smiled at Mrs. Carver. "It's a nice hobby, but at heart I'm a researcher. I prefer to dig into a good book rather than a furniture store."

She smiled and chatted through dinner with her mom's oldest friends, but her mind kept drifting back to the photograph in her bag. Was it really what she thought it was? What her father thought it was? T. S., whoever he was, knew something, and if he knew it, then other people knew it, too. The truth was out there. Despite her promise to her mother, Randi knew she couldn't just let it go.

After dinner, she taped the picture into her notebook, next to the sketch she'd drawn of the idol in Cameroon. It couldn't be a coincidence. If there was even a chance her father *wasn't* wrong about everything, she had to find out.

***

Coffee?

Randi smiled at the text from Nik. *Sure*, she texted back. *Campus Coffee @7:30?*

See you there, Nik responded.

She put the final touches on her makeup and went to the kitchen to grab a granola bar for breakfast. Her roommate, Kelly, sat at the table drinking coffee and checking email on her phone, her usual pre-work routine.

"Have a good day," Kelly said as Randi went past.

"Thanks," Randi said as she hurried out the door.

Nik beat her to the campus coffee shop. By his side sat a petite girl with short black hair. Randi stuffed down the resentment that welled up at the sight of the other girl and sat at the table across from Nik.

He pushed a coffee toward her. "Cream, shot of sugar-free vanilla. Just like you like it."

"Thanks."

"Randi, this is Lissa."

Randi smiled. "Nice to meet you."

"How's your paper?" Nik asked.

Randi took a deep breath. "I have a good feeling about it. How about you? Are you actually graduating this time?"

Nik grinned, his quirky smile lighting up his face. "I think so. I can't have you matriculating without me. Plus, I've got my lucky keychain, so I have no excuse." He held up his keys, displaying a keychain shaped like a license plate from Connecticut bearing his name—she'd had it custom made when she went to visit her grandparents three summers ago, with the correct spelling.

"You still have that thing?"

"Of course." He brushed a lock of hair from her face. "Why wouldn't I?"

She scooted back from the table a little bit. "I guess I just didn't expect you to keep it this whole time." She turned toward Lissa. "How do you two know each other?"

"So, Lissa just transferred in from Boston College. She saw me sitting here, and since she doesn't know anyone yet, she asked me to show her around. Her major is… what was it again?"

"Women's Studies, emphasizing in Women in Politics."

Randi took a sip of her coffee. "That's really cool. What year are you?"

"Junior. You?"

"Finishing my Master's in June." Randi touched her bag where her notebook was stashed. "I have a little bit of tweaking to do on my thesis, but it's primarily going to focus on the role of mythology in ancient cultures."

17

"Mythology?" Lissa chirped. "How quaint. I suppose you'll join the women's suffrage movement in your spare time?"

Randi blinked at her, then turned to Nik. "She's adorable. No wonder you adopted her."

Nik's face turned red and he took a big gulp of his coffee.

Randi turned back toward Lissa. "Actually, a culture's myths and legends play a huge part of how that culture develops and evolves. Myths influence religion, politics, and even the day-to-day function of a society, and those societal rules form the basis for modern cultures. Our government, our morals, everything is based in ancient mythos. Your Women's Studies wouldn't even exist if not for my myths." She stood. "I need to go. I don't want to be late for my first class. Thanks for the coffee, Nik. I'll see you later."

Nik stood as well. "It's time for me to fly, too. See you later, Lissa."

Shaking her head, Randi grinned. Nik never said "goodbye." He always just repeated that line from a song he liked. He walked with her part of the way until she turned to go toward the history building and turn in her final paper to her thesis advisor.

***

Dr. Lupkin's eyes flickered to the bottom of the page. Only one more paragraph.

Good.

> *In conclusion, dragons have been a part of the history and mythology of many different cultures throughout the world. There is evidence to support the theory that what our myths and legends refer to as dragons is based in cultural realities, and that these folk tales are indeed historical facts. Dragons were actual creatures that roamed the earth during ancient and medieval times, and their factual existence cannot be separated from the other historical tales that are the basis of modern societal mores.*

Dr. Lupkin set the sheaf of papers on his already cluttered desk and straightened his back. It ached from being hunched over as he read the Master's thesis that he was supposed to be evaluating. Although his tiny window faced west, the sun had almost set, leaving his office dim, with only the pale glow of the lamp on his desk to light it. Sighing, he leaned back, almost touching the stark, white wall with the top of the reclining, swiveling office chair. The chair was the brilliant find from an office supply store closeout, and he'd paid a lot for it, even at the reduced price. It was worth the investment, however, considering how much time he spent in it.

Taking his glasses off, he set them on top of the papers and rubbed the dents on the bridge of his nose. He often had a hard time with the things Miranda Ross turned in. She was a bright student—brilliant, even—but she possessed some wild ideas. Always, she did her research, and her papers were well thought out and intelligently written. Although her subject matter tended to be somewhat... controversial, he always gave her good grades, because she met the requirements to the letter. He had not expected her to do *this* for her thesis, however. As her advisor, she'd discussed with him that the topic would be the role of mythology in history, and how it shaped culture. Even her outline had pinpointed the role of many different mythos in the creation of religions and laws and moral ideals within any given culture. She'd hinted toward the various mythologies involving dragons, and how certain cultures used that symbolism to portray good and evil, but nothing she'd said to him in any of their meetings had indicated that her entire thesis would be about the historical *reality* of dragons rather than contain that *possibility*.

Perhaps he should have expected it—he knew her well enough—but still, for her Master's thesis? He'd expected something more... conventional. He shuffled through the papers until he found her introductory paragraph. Adjusting his glasses back on his nose, he began to read.

Many of the folk tales and legends that we today think of as fantasies and fairy tales are based in real, historical occurrences. Ancient rituals and ceremonies, triggered by historical events, have been passed down through the ages and have developed into religious practices and ceremonies that people around the world

*still use today. One thing that seems to have gotten lost
in the realm of fantasy, however, is the existence of
dragons. There are many evidences to suggest that
dragons were real creatures. One example is the
existence of related animals, such as dinosaurs and
great lizards. Another example is the existence of
extensive mythology regarding huge, fire-breathing
lizards throughout many cultures all over the world.
Finally, there are many places throughout the world
where native people still believe in creatures that we
would describe as dragons.*

Randi went on to meticulously describe and cite examples of her premise.
She had done her homework—that much was obvious. Each of her points
was thoroughly researched, documented, and cited, and she had reasonable,
compelling arguments. The paper was flawless. Eighty-three pages of
academic superiority, from a technical standpoint.

But really, dragons? What in the world could she be thinking? What next,
a doctoral paper on unicorns? A Time-Life series on leprechauns? Was Time-
Life even still relevant? He felt like he was aging exponentially.

He rubbed at his temples and took his glasses off again with a sigh. The
fact was, she could not expect to present this thesis before a committee.

Perhaps he could talk her out of it. A brilliant student, she would make a
fine historian, if she would focus and work on things that were a little more…
well, a little more realistic.

Dr. Lupkin pressed the button on his intercom.

"Tracy, send a message to Miranda Ross. Tell her to make an
appointment to come see me immediately."

No answer. Tracy must already be gone. He'd tell her in the morning.

He glanced back at the paper before him with a sigh. Redoing her thesis
was the only option Randi had if she wanted to graduate.

Chapter Three

Dr. Lupkin says your thesis is unacceptable. Please schedule an appointment immediately.

Randi frowned at the email on her phone, sending her glasses slipping down her nose. Dr. Lupkin's TA didn't mince words.

Adjusting her glasses, she pulled her bag up higher on her shoulder and pushed on toward her next class. A knot formed in her stomach as she considered the consequences of the message.

Well, she might as well get it over with. She called Dr. Lupkin's office and scheduled the appointment for later that afternoon, after her classes finished.

Still hurrying down the hall, she maneuvered through the phone's menu until she found her schedule and inserted the time of her appointment.

Her shoulder collided with someone's arm. "Excuse me," she said, looking up.

Not just someone's arm. Nik's arm. Despite her best efforts, her heartbeat sped up a notch.

"Hey, Randi." Warm, hazel eyes twinkled down at her.

"Good morning, Nik." She stuck the phone back into her bag.

"So. Distracted much?"

She finger-combed her hair back from her face. "Kinda. What are you doing in the history department?"

"Looking for you, actually."

"You could've texted."

"Yeah, but you always take, like, three hours to get back to me, and this is urgent. What are you doing later? Want to get some coffee or something this afternoon?"

She raised an eyebrow at the urgency of coffee, but before she could agree, she remembered the meeting she'd just scheduled. "I can't. I have a meeting with Dr. Lupkin."

He leaned forward, a lock of reddish hair falling over his eyes. "What about?"

The knot tightened in her stomach. "He didn't specifically say, but it's something about my thesis."

"Oh, Randi, you didn't!"

Randi gave him a wry smile. "I'm afraid I did."

"What were you thinking?"

"I was thinking that I've studied hard and have come to my own conclusions. Dr. Lupkin told us to write about something we're passionate about, so that's what I did."

"What if he doesn't accept it?"

Anger burned in her cheeks, the suggestion a little too close to her own fears for comfort. "He can't not accept it."

"Well, then, what if the board doesn't approve it?"

She took a deep breath and shrugged her shoulders, hoping she sounded more confident than she felt. "I don't know. I'll cross that bridge when I get there."

"You should've just written something you knew they would accept, and done the dragon thing on your own time. Your outline was amazing, and you could've rolled with that and probably gotten published."

"I'm not going to just say what people want to hear. I'm not about that."

"I know." Nik brushed a lock of hair out of her face. His fingers lingered a moment on her cheek. "Because of your dad. That's one of the things I like about you."

Her pulse spiked, and she stepped back, lowering her eyes. "Nik, don't."

Nik sighed. "I know. I'm sorry. Just friends."

Her face tingled where his fingers brushed against it. "I have to run. I'm going to be late."

"Okay," he said. "It's time for me to fly, too. But call me when you get done with Dr. Lupkin and I'll take you to dinner."

"All right, bye." Randi waved as she left.

***

The professor in Randi's last class droned on about what would be on the final, but she barely heard. The clock behind his head told her class was almost over. Then she had to face Dr. Lupkin.

What if Nik was right? What if her thesis was rejected? What if Dr. Lupkin was finally fed up with her and recommended she be denied her degree? Even if she wanted to, she didn't have time to write another thesis. Unfortunately, she didn't want to. She couldn't seem to help it. Once she got an idea in her head, all she could do was run with it.

At last, class let out and she made her way up the stairs to the History Department offices. She glanced at the empty chair behind the TA's desk as she passed, and went on toward Dr. Lupkin's office. Her stomach did a backflip as she knocked on the door.

"Come in."

Scents of stale coffee, pipe tobacco smoke, and peppermint candy pervaded Randi's nostrils as she pushed open the door.

Dr. Lupkin looked up from behind the mounds of papers on his desk. "Ah, Miss Ross, I'm glad you're here. Sit down."

She eased herself into the small chair in front of his cluttered desk.

"Do you know why I asked you to come in?"

Randi nodded. "Yes, Dr. Lupkin. My thesis."

Dr. Lupkin nodded. "It's very well written, very clear and concise. It's just—somewhat unorthodox."

Somewhat unorthodox? That was a generous statement. "I understand."

Dr. Lupkin's eyes flickered to the bottom of the page he held. "It doesn't match what I was expecting based on your outline."

Dr. Lupkin set the paper on a sheaf of pages on his already-cluttered desk and straightened his back. He set his bifocals on top of the papers and rubbed the dents on the bridge of his nose. "Miss Ross, you're a good student and a good historian. You push the envelope and make connections most people wouldn't. I am always impressed by the depth of your research and the way you connect ideas. I did not expect this for your thesis, however."

Randi smiled, hoping to lighten the mood. "I thought you knew me better than that."

Dr. Lupkin returned the smile, but it seemed halfhearted. "This is your Master's thesis, Miss Ross. The fact is, you can't expect to present this before a thesis review committee."

"I understand." Despite her current nervousness, she felt comfortable and welcome in the worn chair across from the desk. She always had. As if it were a place where learning happened on its own, and she could absorb it just by being there.

Dr. Lupkin sighed. "I'm not sure I'm getting through to you. You're one of my best students, and I don't want to see you fail because of this." He tapped the pages in front of him with the edge of his glasses. "Therefore, I've decided that if you wish to write your thesis on something else, I'll grant you a continuance."

Randi's stomach churned.

Yes. She desperately wanted to start over.

An image of the staid and proper board members laughing at her and ridiculing her flashed through her mind. Dr. Lupkin's offer dangled in the air, taunting her, tempting her.

She closed her eyes and paused. "Thank you for your consideration, but I won't be rewriting my thesis."

"I see. Would you care to explain why not?"

"Because I believe it would compromise my principles, and I believe it would undermine my education."

Dr. Lupkin furrowed his bushy eyebrows. "Would you care to expound on that?"

Good thing she'd skipped lunch, or she'd be in danger of losing it. "Well, I came to school to learn. I've studied hard in all of my classes and done mountains of research. My research has led me to certain conclusions, and I've made an effort to be true to those conclusions. If I were to start over and write something else, it would imply I'm only here to get a piece of paper stating I have a degree, not to deepen my knowledge."

Dr. Lupkin's eyes bulged.

What had she gotten herself into? Tension gnawed on her insides. Too late to stop now. "Besides, if I were to change the topic of my thesis just to please the board, it would mean I'm ashamed of my beliefs and the conclusions I've come to, and that would be contrary to my character."

Dr. Lupkin took a deep breath. "You do realize you'll probably be the laughingstock of the historical and academic communities?"

She bit her lip to keep it from trembling then faked a grin. "I like to think I'm just ahead of my time."

Dr. Lupkin raised an eyebrow. "Meaning?"

"You always tell us not to be afraid to think outside the box and that most of the greatest thinkers were scoffed at until long after their deaths. I intend to prove my thesis, somehow, and even if I'm laughed at now, someday the truth will come to light."

Dr. Lupkin chuckled. "I suppose I can't very well argue with my own advice. If that's your decision, I'll turn this into the board immediately."

The bottom dropped out of her stomach. He was letting her turn it in.

It wasn't too late to change her mind. She could still do something else if she wanted.

She didn't. "Thank you, Dr. Lupkin."

***

An Undisclosed Location in the United States

The Director examined the report, brow furrowed. It was always a pity to have to dispose of a good agent, but once they were uncovered—well, the integrity of the Syndicate demanded complete anonymity. The work they did wouldn't get done if all the freedom of information advocates wrapped red tape all over every endeavor the Syndicate backed. Still, someone else would have to take over the post at the dig site.

A comprehensive file gave the Director all the necessary information on half a dozen trusted agents.

This one would do. This agent was loaded with potential, and practically begging for the opportunity to move up in the Syndicate. Yes, this would work.

A short phone call later, and a new agent was established at what the Director suspected might be the greatest paleontological find of the century.

***

25

Randi was just finishing putting on her make-up when she heard the knock at the door.

"I'll get it," Kelly called. "Hi, Nik," Randi heard her say.

"Hey, Kelly. What are you up to tonight?"

"I've got a date. Where are you guys headed?"

"China Dragon."

Randi smiled to herself. Nik knew Chinese food was her favorite, and the name of the restaurant seemed somewhat apropos, considering. Nik had likely gotten a kick out of that. She came out of her bedroom and pulled on her coat, though it was warm enough now that she didn't really need it.

"You look nice," Nik said, squeezing her hand.

She scrunched up her nose. "Not really."

He gave her a little thump on the back of the head.

"Ow!"

"That's what you get for insulting my best friend," he said.

Randi glared at him and gave Kelly a hug. "See you later."

"Bye," Kelly grinned, giving her a knowing wink.

Randi rolled her eyes. Kelly was constantly trying to convince her to give Nik another chance. Advice Randi robustly ignored.

The restaurant wasn't far. It catered to students, with an upscale vibe but reasonably priced menu options.

Randi sat across from Nik at the elegant table in the dimly lit restaurant and sipped at the hot tea the waiter placed on the table before gliding away to give them a chance to peruse the menu.

She tried to ignore the wistful look Nik gave her, but it was hard. It was all she could do not to return it. She took another sip of her tea, and studied the menu, even though she already knew what she would order.

"So," Nik said finally, "what did Dr. Lupkin have to say about your paper?"

"He said it was very well written and clear and concise."

"And?"

She scrunched her nose. She hated that he knew there was an '*and*'. "And unorthodox. He offered me a continuance if I wanted to write something else."

"Thank goodness!"

"I didn't take it. I'm sticking with my original paper."

"Randi, as your best friend, I feel it is my duty to tell you that you're absolutely insane."

"I know. But I'm honest. I could not, in good conscience, write something that I don't believe in just to get a good grade."

The waiter came by, and Nik ordered cashew chicken and shrimp, while Randi ordered sweet and sour pork.

"One of these days I'm going to make you order something else," Nik said.

Randi grinned. "Good luck."

"So, you're not taking the continuance. You're not even going to think about it?"

Randi sighed. "I can't say that. I *did* think about it. I thought about it a lot. But this is my paper. It's what is inside of me. Nothing else I could write would be as good, because it wouldn't be mine. It would be somebody else's thoughts coming out with my words, and it wouldn't be real."

Nik looked at her with a crooked smile. "You're nuts."

"That's why you love me," Randi quipped.

Nik grinned. "You're my favorite crazy person, Babe."

"Thanks," Randi said with a mock pout. She almost told him not to call her Babe, but decided it wasn't worth it. He hadn't listened the other million times she told him. And she couldn't help it that she liked the way it sounded coming from him.

Randi changed the subject, not wanting to dwell any longer on the meaning behind his casual words. "What did you find out about your internship?"

"I won't know for sure until next week, but I'm pretty well guaranteed a spot at the Palmer Lab."

"That's awesome! The Palmer Lab is really prestigious."

"Thanks. It's a little intimidating."

"You're going to do great." Randi smiled.

Their food arrived, and conversation stalled while they ate, except for Nik filling her in on some of the other students competing for the internship, and why he was pretty sure he was the one who would receive it.

"That's amazing. I have absolute confidence in you."

"Thanks. You gonna finish that?"

"Nope, go ahead." Randi pushed her plate toward him. "How can you eat like that and never gain weight?"

Nik shrugged as he shoveled another forkful into his mouth. "I'm blessed with a good metabolism," he said through his food.

Randi laughed. "That's disgusting! Finish your bite before you talk."

"Huh-uh," Nik grinned at her. "I have to do something to offset my natural appeal, or women just fall all over me. I wouldn't want you to have to sit there while I was surrounded by all those other women."

Randi tossed her napkin at his head. "You're a dork."

The waiter came with the check and two fortune cookies.

Nik broke his open and pulled out the paper inside. "Hmm… just as I thought."

"What?"

"It says 'Your best friend is powerless against your charms'."

"It does not."

Nik nodded. "'Fraid so, Babe."

She held out her hand. "Let me see."

"I can't. It's classified."

She glared at him and opened her own cookie. "'You're hanging out with a lunatic.' Wow, I never thought these things had any truth, but obviously I was wrong."

Nik laughed as he threw the napkin back at her. "It's getting late. You about ready to head out?" He stood, offering Randi his hand to help her up.

He didn't let go as he led her toward the exit.

Chapter Four

Dr. Lupkin shuffled the papers around on his desk in a mild attempt to clean up before leaving for the day. He didn't need to hurry home, but he was ready to be out of the office for the day. He popped a peppermint in his mouth to save his breath from the pipe he had just finished—despite the university's strict no-smoking-indoors policy—then closed the window and reached for the lamp switch.

There was a knock at the door.

Before he had time to answer, the door opened and a robust, balding man came in.

"Frank," Dr. Lupkin said in surprise. "What brings you here?"

"Evening, Peter. I was in the neighborhood and I finished a meeting early, so I thought I'd stop by. You busy?"

"Not at all, I was just getting ready to leave."

"Excellent! Is Maggie expecting you?"

"No, Maggie's at her sister's. Do you want to get some dinner?"

Frank rubbed pudgy hands together. "I was about to suggest the same thing."

"Excellent." Dr. Lupkin pulled on his coat as he headed for the door, then turned and grabbed the stack of papers from his desk. "Listen, I'm glad you're here. I have something I want you to read."

"Oh? What is it?"

"It's the Master's thesis for one of my students."

"History isn't really my cup of tea, Peter."

"I know, but I think you'll be interested in this one. It will fit in with your Sasquatch theories and mumbo-jumbo."

Frank thumbed the suspenders that stretched over his expansive belly. "Oh? What kind of history paper do you think would be of interest to me and all my mumbo-jumbo?"

"Just read it. You'll understand. I'll bring it along. Where do you want to go?"

"Chinese food okay?"

"Sounds good to me." Dr. Lupkin clicked off his lamp and followed his friend out the door, locking it behind him.

Following Frank down to the parking lot, he got into his battered old Toyota Camry that was parked in his reserved parking space.

"I'm on the other end," Frank said. "I'll meet you at our regular spot?"

"Sure," Dr. Lupkin answered.

Frank was already at the restaurant when Dr. Lupkin arrived. He always did drive a little more recklessly than Dr. Lupkin found safe.

They sat at the table and ordered their food, and as they ate, Frank perused Miranda Ross's thesis.

Frank leaned back in his chair and set the sheaf of papers down. "It's very good."

"I thought you'd be impressed," Dr. Lupkin said.

"I am. Very much so, actually. This girl is obviously bright. I've heard theories like this before, of course, but never so well thought out and documented. I'm intrigued. Who is she?"

"Just another of a thousand students I see every year."

"She's not just another student, Peter, or you wouldn't have wanted me to read her paper. What is it about"—he flipped to the title page—"Miranda Ross that has you so confounded?"

"I offered her a continuance if she would write something else, something that the board would be more likely to accept, and she refused. She said it would undermine her education to write something she didn't really believe just to get a good grade."

A hearty laugh erupted from Frank's belly. "I like her already."

Dr. Lupkin snorted. "I guess the thing is, I admire her because of her academic integrity, but I don't want her to fail because of it, so I find myself wanting her to compromise the very thing that I admire, so that she will be able to pass with honors. She has the ability to become a very fine historian, if she would only be a little more conventional."

Frank rubbed his chin. "It sounds to me like she has no interest in becoming a very fine historian. She wants to dig deep, to find facts, to uncover the things that no one else wants to uncover for fear of being considered a joke, or a not-so-fine historian."

"Exactly," Dr. Lupkin said.

Frank grinned. "It sounds to me like she would make a very fine cryptozoologist."

Dr. Lupkin snorted. "I don't think that she would be interested in that. She's interested in history, not zoology, and especially not cryptozoology."

"Perhaps not. I'd still like to meet her, though, if you wouldn't mind introducing me."

"I suppose that can be arranged," Dr. Lupkin said. "I'll send her a note and set up an appointment with her."

"Thank you," Frank said.

The two finished their meal and got up to leave.

They were walking toward the door when Dr. Lupkin stopped. "Frank, she's here."

"Who?"

"Miranda Ross," said Dr. Lupkin. "She's coming this way, with the redhead."

"Well, introduce me," Frank demanded. "There's no time like the present."

Dr. Lupkin hesitated a moment, then decided it couldn't do any harm. He intercepted Randi and her friend, who were also leaving the restaurant.

"Good evening, Miss Ross," he said.

Miranda looked up, her bright blue eyes wide behind a pair of trendy glasses, her small pink mouth open slightly in surprise. She pushed a lock of light brown hair behind her ear and adjusted her glasses. "Good evening, Dr. Lupkin."

"It's interesting that I should see you here," he said. "I have someone who wants to meet you. I let him read your thesis, and he was very intrigued by it. Miss Ross, this is Dr. Frank Lengel. He is a doctor of cryptozoology."

Miranda disengaged her hand from the boy's and extended it. "It's nice to meet you, sir."

Dr. Lengel took her hand and pumped it up and down. "It is *very* nice to meet *you*, Miss Ross."

"Thank you. Please, call me Randi."

The red-headed boy coughed.

Randi glanced from the boy back to Dr. Lengel. "Oh, this is my friend, Nik Gary."

Dr. Lengel pumped Nik's hand, as well, but not as vigorously as he had Randi's.

"They have a doctoral degree in cryptozoology?" Nik asked.

Dr. Lengel let out a good-natured guffaw. "Some of them do. And what are you studying?"

"I'm in the doctoral program for biology," Nik answered. "I find it somewhat more lucrative than science-fiction."

Dr. Lupkin winced. Frank hated when people undermined his field, despite how often it happened.

Frank still smiled, but it may have been slightly less good-natured than before. "Cryptozoology is more than just Sasquatch theories and science-fiction mumbo jumbo. It is a very real and fascinating science."

He very pointedly turned from Nik and back to Randi. "Miss Ross, I don't want to take any more of your evening, but I would be honored if you would grant me an interview sometime in the near future. I would like to talk to you about your thesis."

"Yes, sir," Randi agreed with a grin.

"Excellent. Let me give you my card. Call me when you have some time to meet." He already had one ready, and handed it to her.

Randi glanced at the card, on which were stylized pictures of sea monsters and Bigfoot creatures, and the name *Frank P. Lengel, Cryptozoologist.*

"That will be great. Thank you, sir."

"Oh, and one more thing, Miss Ross—may I make a copy of your thesis, to have for my own reference?"

Randi nodded. "Of course."

"Thank you. I hope to hear from you soon."

Dr. Lupkin couldn't help but notice the giddy grin that split his friend's face as they left.

***

Nik gaped at Randi. "I can't believe you just made an appointment with him. Cryptozoology isn't even recognized in most circles. He just wants to use you to make his own goofy theories sound more plausible."

"That's where we're different, Nik. I believe in giving everyone a chance. Besides, he's the first person who has actually *liked* my thesis. I've gotten nothing but criticism from everyone else, including you. It will be nice to talk to someone who takes me seriously for a change."

"I'm sorry, Randi, I didn't mean to criticize…"

"It's okay, Nik. I'm not offended."

She squeezed his hand, and then drew it away quickly, not wanting to give the impression that she was trying to hold his hand again. "We think differently, and I know that. But I am interested to see what Dr. Lengel has to say."

***

Randi grabbed her drink and joined Nik at his table in the courtyard.

"Hey, Randi, I'm glad you could make it. You know Dawn?" Nik's hanger-on today was a girl Randi recognized but didn't know well, other than to remember she was Nik's best friend Trent's fiancée Lacey's best friend, and she had more breast tissue than personality.

Randi smiled anyway. "Of course. Hi, Dawn."

Dawn pressed a little closer to Nik. "Hey, Randi."

Nik looked past Randi and waved. "Trent and Lacey are here. Hey, guys."

Trent and Lacey approached. "Hey, Randi. I didn't know you were coming. How's your last year of school treating you so far?" Trent asked.

"So far, great. I just turned in my thesis." *Just turned in* was a bit of a stretch. It had been two weeks, and she still hadn't heard anything from Dr. Lupkin. She knew these things took time, but every moment was like torture. That was the primary reason she'd agreed to come out tonight—so she'd have something to do other than sit around wondering whether she'd graduate.

"What's it on?" Lacey asked.

Moment of truth. If she was going to do this, she had to own it. "The historical evidence for the existence of dragons."

33

Lacey's eyes widened, but she smiled politely.

Trent, on the other hand, almost choked he started laughing so hard. "You know dragons are made up, right?"

"I'm trying to prove they're not. My research has shown that many cultures, some of which aren't even very far past, have stories about them. It's impossible to have that much documentation on something that isn't real, and once you eliminate the impossible, whatever remains—"

"Yeah, yeah," Trent interrupted. "Just don't say I didn't warn you when everyone ends up thinking you're delusional, Rand. Ha—that sounds good together. Randelusional."

Randi's face burned.

Nik stepped between them. "Okay, you two. We're here to have fun. Where should we start?"

Randi glanced at the group. "Is this everyone? No one else is coming?"

"This is it," Nik said. "Rides or games?" He started to walk in the direction of the giant rides that towered over the small, pop-up carnival.

The others followed.

Randi stopped, a few feet behind. "Nik, a word?" She smiled at the others. "We'll catch up in a minute."

They walked on and Nik came toward her. "What's up?"

"You invited me along on a double date?"

"That's not what this is. It's just a bunch of friends hanging out."

"No, it's two couples, plus me. As if this day wasn't going to be awkward enough, now I get to be the fifth wheel? At least if I'd known, I could've invited Kelly. I think I'm going to go."

Nik grabbed her hand. "Don't leave. I don't even like her. Lacey invited her. Besides, you already paid to get in. I didn't think about it being awkward, I just wanted to hang out since I've hardly seen you all semester."

She pulled her hand away. "Dawn doesn't want me here, and Trent definitely would be happy to see me go."

"They don't matter. I want you to stay. Please?"

Randi sighed. "Fine. But if Trent says anything else about my thesis, I can't guarantee I won't punch him."

"So, what about me? Do I get to say anything?" His eyes twinkled and the corner of his mouth twitched.

She glared at him. "Best-friend rights grant you a little bit of leeway, but only a little."

"Fair enough. Come on."

They hurried to catch up with the others. Dawn shot Randi a dirty look as she intertwined her fingers with Nik's. Randi sighed. It was going to be a long night.

Randi stood on the sidelines on the rides that were two-seaters—which was most of them. Why had she agreed to stay, again?

Nik and Dawn came stumbling off one of the rides.

"That was awesome," Nik said, at the same time Dawn said, "I don't feel so good."

"Let's take a break and walk around," Lacey suggested.

They wandered toward the rows of carnival game booths.

Dawn held her stomach. "I'm going to run to the little girls' room. I'll find you guys in a minute."

Trent found a baseball throwing game. "What do you think, Lace? Is my softball arm good enough for this?"

It wasn't, and after a few tries, he gave up and they moved on. A few booths later, they found a booth lined with giant, plush dragons for prizes.

"There you go, Randelusional. That's the one for you. Be careful, though. They might be real." Trent laughed, his tone mocking, and he and Lacey moved on down the row, leaving Nik and Randi alone.

"Actually, I think he's right. You need one," Nik said. "It's a sign. If you can win one, it means you should go forward with your idea."

"Brilliant. I'll base my entire future on my basketball skills. That'll end well."

Nik laughed. "Okay, then, how about this. If I can win one for you, I get to tease you as much as I want."

She laughed. "Deal."

Nik stayed at the booth, spending far more money than he could afford, trading up little by little, but at long last he earned the biggest prize.

Randi picked out a bright purple one with a green chest, and the attendant handed it to her with a grin, presumably well pleased with his earnings for the evening. She hugged it. "It's perfect. And even though you won it, I'm still taking it as a sign."

Nik brushed her face with his fingertips. "It doesn't count." He leaned toward her, his lips dangerously close to hers.

She put her hand on his chest and took a step back. "What are you doing?"

"Nothing, I just…"

"We've been down that road, Nik. It didn't work. Let's not risk our friendship by trying something futile. Anyway, thanks for the dragon."

"It's fitting. But I still think you should reconsider."

"What, and go into Interior Design, like my mom wants? That's not going to work for me."

"Better that than ending up like your dad."

The words hung in the air for a long moment.

"My dad didn't fail," Randi said at last. "He was right all along, and I have proof."

"Proof? What kind of proof?"

Just then, Dawn came back from the bathroom. She eyed the plush dragon. "What did I miss?"

"Nothing. I was just about to head home." Randi looked at Nik. "I *will* prove it."

Chapter Five

Dr. Janice Peterson held the distinguished position of chair of the board that consisted of six other members, all distinguished in their fields and respected professors at the university. To have made it this far in their studies, the candidates were all accomplished enough that the board rarely had reason to refuse awarding a student's degree. Janice believed this might be one such case, however.

She was the first to read Miranda Ross's thesis. She considered herself a *serious historian* and had worked herself into an outrage over the mythological drivel Miss Ross had presented in her paper.

She'd intentionally placed Miss Ross's thesis at the bottom of the pile, so there'd be plenty of time left at the end to discuss it.

The other members sat around the massive mahogany table in the spacious conference room, chattering about classes and schedules and summer plans.

Janice tapped her fingers on the table, waiting for the conversation to wind down. "Let's move on. Last on our list of students to consider is Miranda Ross. I think it's clear this student has no place graduating from this institution."

Someone coughed. She looked up. Dr. Jones was usually a fair, logical man. His opinion would go far in proving her point.

"Yes, Dr. Jones?"

Dr. Jones rubbed the stubble on his chin. "Well, while I don't personally agree with the conclusions reached, it seems the requirements for the paper have been met. There have been a number of theses over the years I didn't personally approve. Regardless of the subject matter, however, it's my duty to see that certain standards have been met. They have been. In my opinion, this is an acceptable thesis."

"I disagree, Dr. Jones," someone else said. "History should be kept to historical facts. While I agree the arguments presented were logical, and even convincing, they haven't been proven, and therefore the thesis does not meet our specifications."

"That's what I think, too," a third chimed in. "This is not a document describing history. It describes a fantasy."

"Pardon me."

Janice narrowed her eyes at the man whose hand was raised. He was a bit of a dreamer. His specialty was in medieval history. She didn't really want to know what he thought, but protocol insisted she let him speak. "Yes, Dr. Black?"

"Well, I must admit, the idea of dragons intrigues me. However, aside from my personal opinions, I have to agree with Miss Ross that, even if the conclusions are a bit speculative, the legends and myths of a people are a part of what makes them unique, and are therefore absolutely relevant to history. I approve this thesis."

Janice frowned. She hadn't expected anyone to take Miss Ross's side. Not everyone had voiced an opinion yet. The odds still might be in her favor. "Dean Palmer?"

The dean of sciences, Dr. Alice Palmer, steepled her fingers. "I can see both sides of this argument. I think we can all agree the subject matter is a little strange, but merit ought to be given for the effort involved. I'm undecided."

That was of no help at all.

"Dr. Keating?"

"Well, I'm leaning toward the fact that a historical paper should contain historical facts, but she did her research, and plenty of it. I agree with Dean Palmer. She should be given credit for all her hard work. Besides, there are plenty of instances where a theory was posited based on theory and speculation, but time either proved or disproved it. I'd hate to see her fail because her subject matter is, *as yet*, unproven. I, too, am undecided."

Janice composed her features and kept her voice calm. "Very well. I suggest we invite Dr. Lupkin in to discuss both the thesis and the general qualifications of the writer. Any objections?"

She glanced around the room. "Good. I'll send someone to retrieve him."

They took a short recess while Janice's TA went to go find Dr. Lupkin. Fifteen minutes later, he joined them at the conference table.

Janice smiled at the nervous look on Dr. Lupkin's face. He probably wished he'd had more time to prepare his argument.

She drummed the table with manicured nails and waited for the rest of the board to be seated. "Good afternoon, Dr. Lupkin. We're all here today to discuss the thesis of one of your students, a Miss Miranda Ross."

Dr. Lupkin nodded.

"What can you tell us about Ms. Ross?"

"Well, she's a brilliant student. She's thorough. She has a passion for learning and particularly a passion for history."

There were a few scoffs around the table at that, but Dr. Lupkin didn't seem to notice.

"Are all of her papers on such outlandish subjects?" Janice asked.

"Well, naturally, I'm not her only professor, but I believe she has written a number of papers on all different subjects."

"Yes, but have you seen any sort of pattern, any sort of trend in her subject matter?"

"Miss Ross tends to choose topics that are not already deeply researched. She has said she came to school to learn, not just to get a degree. She tends to find topics that require intense research and that have the potential to be groundbreaking ideas in time."

A few heads bobbed and brows furrowed.

Janice scowled. Dr. Lupkin had said the right thing. All people in search of real knowledge appreciated in others the deep desire to learn.

"There is a bit of controversy among the board over this thesis," she went on matter-of-factly.

"Yes, Dr. Peterson, I thought that might happen."

"Did you mention this to your student?"

"Yes, ma'am."

"What was her response?"

"She felt it would demean her academic integrity to write something else.

In her words, again, she came to this school to learn. She did her research, and her research led her to certain conclusions. She felt strongly enough about those conclusions to make them the subject of her thesis, and she said she wouldn't compromise her intellectual ethics by writing something about which she did not believe, just to get a good grade."

The other board members looked around the table at one another. Dean Palmer cocked her head slightly, her face unreadable. Even Dr. Willoughby and Dr. Irons nodded.

Janice's jaw tensed. "I see. Well, Dr. Lupkin, there are those among us that feel the study of history should remain just that—the study of *history*. Facts. Not suppositions or fantasies. What do you have to say to that?"

"Well, I feel my personal opinion is irrelevant. However, if I may speak on behalf of Miss Ross, as she posited in her thesis, myths and legends are a part of history. Such things have a direct impact on our anthropological development, and they deserve as much study as anything else."

"Thank you, Dr. Lupkin, but while you may not find it relevant, I think the board would like to hear your personal opinion."

Dr. Lupkin took a deep breath. "I would have to say I believe there is no aspect of human history that isn't worth our study, myths and legends included."

There were nods all around the table.

"I don't think any of us would disagree with that, Dr. Lupkin," Janice said. "However, Miss Ross has concluded that these stories are *not* myths or legends, but actual facts. It is there the disagreement arises. She is supposing the existence of dragons is fact, while the historical community agrees it is fiction. Now, do you personally feel she is correct in her assumptions?"

Dr. Lupkin paused. "No, I don't," he sighed. His voice seemed to echo in the silence that followed his statement.

Janice followed his gaze as he looked around the table at the brows furrowed in thought, the chins being rubbed, and the fingers being tapped in concentration.

"However..." The silence in the room broke. All heads turned in his direction. "After having read her arguments and examined her sources, I do believe her suppositions are not unfounded, and her conclusions do hold weight."

Janice shot him a glare. "I see. Do you believe she will actually be able to prove dragons did, in fact, exist?"

"Well, ma'am, I don't know about that, but I believe she ought to have the chance to prove herself wrong."

Janice's eyes narrowed. "Thank you, Dr. Lupkin. Does anyone else have any questions?"

Silence thick enough to wade through reigned in the room.

"That will be all, Dr. Lupkin."

Dr. Lupkin stood and left the room.

Janice looked around the room. "Shall we vote?"

***

That evening, Janice poured herself a glass of champagne and sat on the leather couch in her living room.

Rob took a beer from the refrigerator and plopped himself on the coffee table facing her. She tried not to wince at the magenta slash, just beginning to transition from a wound to a scar, running down the side of his face. Hazards of the job, he told her. She never asked what he meant by that. He always told her she didn't want to know, and she believed him.

Despite being in his fifties, Rob kept in remarkably good shape. His muscles rippled even twisting the lid off his beer bottle. "You gonna tell me what's wrong?"

She combed her fingers through her hair. "Nothing, really. There is just this student—she wrote a paper that is very disturbing."

"Disturbing how?"

"Well, she has a thesis that is utterly absurd, and totally beyond the realm of possibility. The thing is, she is smart and has a way of writing that makes it sound believable. If her work were made known, it could be potentially embarrassing."

Bubbles tickled her throat as she swallowed a sip of her beverage. "We denied her thesis."

Rob reached over and clasped her hand. "Then what do you have to worry about?"

Janice sighed. "She strikes me as one of those people for whom adversity makes them push harder. The type of person who gets Netflix shows that call into question everything we know to be true, creating a network of…

alternative facts so the public doesn't trust actual facts. It undermines everything I've spent the last thirty years building."

Rob shrugged. "Well, like you said, the chances of her being noticed are so slim, it really isn't even an issue."

"But she's young, idealistic, and full of charisma. Like that woman, what's-her-name, the senator? There are still news stories about how she made her own party embarrassed to associate with her. That's how this student is. She won't stop until she proves what she has set out to prove, and she will make herself get noticed. Worse, she'll bring the rest of us down with her."

"Even if she does, will it matter? You said her thesis is beyond the realm of possibility. If that's so, then she'll only make herself look like an idiot."

Janice took a deep breath. She needed to consider the possibility she didn't want to consider. "What if she's right? What if there was some way she could prove it?"

"So what? New discoveries are made every day. You could even use it to your own advantage, as one of her professors."

"No, you don't understand. If her thesis is correct, it will change the entire course of our history. And not just history. Geology, science, biology— it would shake the foundations of everything we have come to accept as fact. It would create a scandal that would wreak havoc on our entire world!"

Rob's eyes narrowed. Janice knew all too well what he thought of people who stood out, despite how he tried to hide that side from her.

True to the role they both knew he played, he continued with his encouragement. "If it were true, wouldn't that be a good thing?"

She looked at him, trying to convey with her eyes how serious she was. "No. The world couldn't comprehend something like that. It would unravel the very fabric of our society."

"Do you think this girl is trying to accomplish all this on her own?"

Janice sighed. "No, I don't think she's trying at all. I honestly doubt she has any idea of the ramifications of her actions. I think she is trying to make her mark upon the world, to do something no one has done before, and I don't think she has any concept of the possible consequences."

"What are you saying, then? Are you just venting, or do you want something done about her?"

Janice blinked slowly. "Are you suggesting what I think you're suggesting, Rob?"

Rob gave her a wry smile. "You know better than that, Jan. I'm not suggesting anything. But you know all you have to do is say the word."

Janice regarded him a moment, considering. Finally, she exhaled. "No. At least, not yet. I'm just worrying."

Rob stood and planted a kiss on her forehead. "In that case, I'm going to bed. Are you coming?"

"I'll be in soon. Good night."

***

Later that night, Janice lay in bed, lying still so she wouldn't disturb Rob.

Rob got up. Apparently she hadn't needed to worry about waking him. She almost got up with him, but he seemed to think she was sleeping and walked out on the wrap-around porch.

He had his phone. Who was he calling at this hour?

Janice crept from the bed and walked toward the sliding glass doors, still open a crack.

"I need to speak to the Director," Rob said.

A pause. "There's a new player in the game. Randi Ross. Nothing serious yet, but I believe it merits observation. Maybe more."

Another pause.

"What would you like me to do?"

Janice inched closer, hoping to catch the other side of the conversation.

"Done."

Rob dialed one more number.

"What?" a deep voice on the other end answered.

Good, she could hear this one.

"It's me," Rob said. "I may have a job for you."

"You know I'm on assignment right now."

"That's fine. It's not urgent."

"The target?"

"None yet. Just a head's up. I'll contact you if there are further developments."

"Yes, sir."

Rob closed the phone. Janice darted away from the door and plopped into bed, working to make her breathing sound deep and normal. Rob climbed in beside her, but she didn't move. She couldn't afford to let him know she'd heard anything. She already knew too much.

Chapter Six

"*Denied?*" Randi sat across from Dr. Lupkin in his office. Her heart felt like it had dropped through the bottom of her chair and exploded on the floor.

"I did warn you this might happen."

"I know, but... I guess I never really thought it would."

Dr. Lupkin smiled sympathetically. "It's just a matter of revision. Change your thesis to reflect the historical role legends and myths play on a culture, like your outline suggested. Discuss how cultures and religions are shaped by local myths. You're smart enough. You can rewrite it and graduate after fall semester."

"So prostituting my paper is my only option?"

"Well, not your *only* option. You could pick a new topic and start over completely. Or..."

Randi looked up, suddenly hopeful. "Or?"

"Or prove that you were right all along." He smiled, but his eyes suggested he didn't think that was a great idea. "In the meantime, rewrite your thesis."

Randi left Dr. Lupkin's office and sat in her car in the parking lot. A whirlwind of emotions went to war inside her, until she couldn't think.

She did the only thing that occurred to her in that moment. She called Nik. "They denied me my degree until I rewrite my thesis."

"I knew it. I warned you this would happen. You should've listened to me in the first place."

"I don't need 'I told you so' right now."

"Well, what do you want me to say?"

"How about 'I'm sorry. I know how hard you worked,' or 'those jerks don't know what they're talking about,' or something even remotely supportive?"

Nik's voice softened. "I'm sorry and those jerks are stupid. Better?"

Randi scowled at the phone. "Marginally."

"So, what are you going to do?"

She ran her fingers through her hair. "I don't know. I need to think about it. I hate the idea of ripping apart my life's work and recreating it into a bastardized shell of what it should be just to pander to a bunch of academics, but I don't want to have to start over from scratch, either."

"Couldn't you use pieces of your current paper as a base? Write something about mythology in ancient cultures, so you don't have to waste all that research."

"It wouldn't be the same."

"So what? Is it worth it to stand on principle or is it better to do what they told you in order to get your degree?"

Randi ran her finger over the scar on her arm from the snake bite she'd gotten in Cameroon. "There is another option. I can prove it. Then I wouldn't need a new paper."

"What if you can't? What if you spend years searching and never find anything? Not only will you not have anything to show for your work, you won't have a degree to fall back on."

He didn't have to say it. She knew he was thinking it. *Like your father.*

"Maybe you're right," she sighed.

"Hey, I have another call. Let's talk about it later, okay?"

Randi stared at the phone long after Nik hung up.

The facts were there. The board was a bunch of idiots if they thought her work didn't prove that. Somehow, she had to make them see she was right about this. She called the school and found the head of the history department. Dr. Peterson was able to schedule her for that afternoon, so she grabbed coffee and hung around on campus until it was time for her appointment.

"Good afternoon, Miss Ross," Dr. Peterson said. "Have a seat. I understand you want to contest the board's decision on your thesis?"

Randi nodded. "I met the requirements of the paper. I cited my resources and came to a logical conclusion based on my research, so I'm not sure why the board felt I should be denied my degree."

"Miss Ross." Dr. Peterson's whole demeanor screamed of condescension. "The mythological drivel you presented in your paper was like a slap in the face to anyone who has spent their lifetime studying real history, as I have. This was not a paper about history, it was a long rabbit trail of fantasy."

"I have to disagree, Dr. Peterson. If you'll take a second look at my sources, you'll see they're firmly grounded in historical documentation."

"Documentation about legends and myths," Dr. Peterson insisted.

Randi gripped the arms of her chair. "The legends and myths of a people are a part of what makes them unique and are therefore absolutely relevant to history. But again, if you'll take a closer look, you'll see the facts."

"Miss Ross, are all of your papers on such outlandish subjects?"

Randi bristled. "I've written a number of papers on all different subjects."

"Yes, but do you tend to lean toward the fantastical?"

"I'm an avid researcher. I tend to choose topics that are not already deeply researched."

"Perhaps you would do better in a different field. History is about facts, not science fiction."

"This is not science fiction." Randi's voice was louder than she'd intended, but she couldn't stop now. "There is real, credible evidence that dragons were historical beings, but you refuse to crawl out of your preconceived ideas long enough to even acknowledge it."

"Watch your tone, young lady," Dr. Peterson warned.

"Don't patronize me. I have done more research into this topic than you've probably done in your entire life. You're as dry and dusty as the books you hide behind."

Dr. Peterson stood and glared at her. "That's it. I'm done humoring your childish tirade. The board made its decision."

"The board is filled with people as stupid as you are."

"I gave you a chance," Dr. Peterson said through clenched teeth. "You're expelled, effective immediately. Get out of my office."

Randi gaped at her.

"Out!"

Randi stumbled backward out of the office. How had things gotten so out of hand? *Expelled?*

She drove home on autopilot, her mind whirling. She'd contest the expulsion, of course, but she'd effectively killed any chance of getting anyone on her side. Even if they let her back in, they'd never allow her thesis. And they might just block anything else she tried to write.

She thought about calling Nik again, but decided against it. She couldn't face the way he'd look down on her for this. Not now.

Instead, she called Dr. Lupkin. News of her outburst and subsequent expulsion was already all over the school.

"What do I do?" she asked, fighting tears.

"Honestly?" Dr. Lupkin sounded resigned. "Leave with as much dignity as you have left. Apply somewhere else and finish your degree as well as you can. I'll write you a recommendation, but only under the condition that you play by the rules and don't embarrass me."

Randi hung up the phone. Maybe she should apply to another school. But that would require starting so many things over, when she'd already put in so much work.

There was another option. The one Dr. Lupkin had mentioned suggested earlier.

Prove she was right all along.

***

"Meg? It's Randi." Randi sat in her bedroom with just a lamp on, trying to keep her voice low so she wouldn't wake Kelly in the next room. It was the middle of the night her time, which was when she had the best chance of getting through to her friend and former mentor.

Meg's delighted squeal hurt Randi's ears. "When are you coming out to work with me again?"

"Funny thing, that's actually why I'm calling. I was wondering if you maybe had room on your team for an unofficial historian?"

"Unofficial? What does that mean?"

Randi rubbed the scar on her arm. "Interesting story. I... uh... sort of got expelled."

"You what?" The excitement in Meg's voice suddenly waned.

"Basically, I have to prove my thesis before I can go back. And some of the artifacts in the dig you're at I think would go a long way toward that goal, so I was hoping I could come join your research and document your findings."

"Listen, Randi, you know how much I enjoy working with you, but without credentials there's not much I can do. I'll see if I can pull any strings, but I don't have a lot of hope."

Randi sighed. "I understand. Thanks. Let me know if anything changes."

"I will," Meg promised.

Randi rolled over in bed and stared at the wall. What was she going to do? How was she supposed to prove anything without a degree, any real connections, and spending all her time waitressing just to pay the bills?

Her gaze landed on the business card she'd stuck on her dresser.

Dr. Frank P. Lengel, Cryptozoologist.

It wasn't ideal, but maybe he'd have some advice, or could point her in the right direction.

First thing the next morning, she called the number on the card and set up an appointment for later that afternoon.

***

Randi squealed her car into a parking spot outside Dr. Lengel's office building.

She glanced at her watch. Her appointment should have started eight minutes ago. "Story of my life," she muttered.

She took the stairs to the second floor two at a time and found the number on the door. Under the number was a sign.

American Cryptozoological Society
Dr. F. P. Lengel
Dr. J. R. Bryant

A bell jingled as she pushed open the door and entered an office waiting room that reminded her of a jungle. The carpet was plush, dark green, and worn slightly where the bottom of the door scraped against it. A dark cherry wood rail separated forest green paint on the bottom half of the walls from tan on the top. Cherry framed pictures featuring the Loch Ness Monster, Bigfoot, winged dinosaurs, and fossils decorated the walls.

The tiny waiting area contained a few chairs and a small table with magazines strewn across it. Another door led to the back part of the office, and a window, like the kind in a doctor's office, revealed a small receptionist's space. A bored-looking woman in her late thirties sat clicking away at a computer.

She looked up when Randi walked up to the counter. "May I help you?"

"My name is Randi Ross. I have an appointment with Dr. Lengel."

"Just a moment." She pressed the intercom button on the telephone. "Dr. Lengel, there's a Ms. Ross here to see you."

Dr. Lengel's voice buzzed back on the speaker. "Show her in, please."

The woman stood up and opened the door. "This way." She held the door until Randi entered, then led her down a hallway to the door with a sign reading "Dr. F. P. Lengel." She knocked once, but opened it without waiting for an answer and waved Randi inside.

Dr. Lengel stood up from behind a desk that was laden with neat stacks of files, a fountain pen with a dragon head etched into it, and a paper weight in the shape of a unicorn. On the windowsill behind him was a framed photo of a young woman about Randi's age.

Dr. Lengel extended his hand. "Welcome, Miss Ross. I'm glad you could make it. Have a seat."

She shook his hand and sat in a high-backed chair upholstered in a blue paisley pattern across from the desk. "Thank you, sir."

The door clicked shut as the receptionist left, and Randi sat facing Dr. Lengel, not sure what to say.

"Well, Miss Ross, just to clear the air, Peter—that is, Dr. Lupkin—told me what happened. I'm very sorry. That must be very frustrating."

She nodded. "Thank you."

"Their loss, however, is my incredible gain!"

Randi couldn't help but smile at his infectious grin. "Okay, I admit it, I'm curious about what you do here."

"Of course you are. I'll explain in a moment. First, tell me, what do you know about cryptozoology?"

"Not much," Randi shrugged. "Of course, I ran across a little when I was doing research for my paper, but I tried to stick mainly with historical documents, not conjecture."

Dr. Lengel nodded encouragingly. "Go on."

"I know that cryptozoology is the study of creatures which have not been proven by science to exist, such as Bigfoot, the Loch Ness monster, or things like that."

"Exactly," Dr. Lengel said. "But it's so much more than that. There's so much out there that can't be explained by science, but cryptozoology helps fill in some of the gaps. So, I imagine you have some idea why I was intrigued by your thesis."

Randi nodded.

His hands reminded her of inflated doctor's gloves, but red, as he rubbed them together in front of him. "What I don't understand is why a brilliant student with so much potential for a serious career would risk it all by publishing a paper of this kind."

Randi paused. "Well, there are several reasons. First and foremost, I am interested in the pursuit of truth. In my undergrad studies, I came across so many references to dragons, giant lizards, and other unexplained creatures, that I came to the conclusion that those creatures must have existed in human history. Eventually, I made the study of such creatures my main pursuit during my master's studies."

"But why dragons and not something else?"

"There are literally thousands of experts in things like Renaissance art, Egyptology, American history, and so on. I didn't want to specialize in something that has already been done thousands of times over. I want my work to be new."

Dr. Lengel gave a nod.

Encouraged, Randi went on. "People think they know everything there is to know about history and science. Especially in archaeology, I've seen so many things that are glossed over because they don't fit the accepted timelines and paradigms of accepted human history. I don't want to be a sheep and just go with the flow. I want to discover something that hasn't yet become accepted as fact. Dragons, or dragon-like creatures, seem to appear in nearly every culture, so I found lots of sources to work with."

He grinned at her. "I see. May I make an observation about you, Miss Ross?"

"Of course."

"You seem to want to do more than just make a discovery. It appears to me that you have a deep desire to prove something to the world, or to someone in particular. It seems that you want to go against the flow as a personal mission to perhaps prove a point. Am I right?"

Randi felt the heat rise in her cheeks. "Maybe a little."

Dr. Lengel grinned again. "Do you mind if I ask exactly what it is you're trying to prove?"

She paused, carefully thinking through what she wanted to say. "My father was a scientist who believed a lot of the historical record to be... shall we say... *inaccurate*. I grew up hearing all these competing theories. A few years ago, he was at a symposium with a lot of really well-respected scientists. He brought up some discoveries he had made that he felt disproved several tenets of accepted human history, and he was laughed off the stage. A few weeks later, he committed suicide."

She adjusted her glasses. "I didn't start out on a mission to prove anything, but the more I studied, the more I found that was intriguing, and I started to realize maybe there *was* proof of what my dad was trying to show people, not just in biology, but in all the sciences."

She leaned forward. "My feeling is that if I can prove that dragons or related creatures, such as, for example, dinosaurs, have been alive and in existence during what we know of human history, that people will have to rethink the entire fossil record. They will have to admit that science has not proven everything there is to know about human history or animal history or anything else. I feel like if I could do that, I might in a small way help vindicate everything my dad died for."

Chapter Seven

Dr. Lengel leaned back in his chair, chuckling. "I see."

"What?" Randi asked. She crossed her arms, embarrassed at her own excitement. She wished she were better at reading people—she had no idea what he might be thinking.

Dr. Lengel folded his hand under his chin. "I think you would make a fine cryptozoologist, Miss Ross."

"Why's that?"

"Because you're not afraid to go after the truth, despite criticism. In some ways, I, too, am on a mission to prove the world wrong."

Randi raised her eyebrows.

"The thing I'm trying to prove, Miss Ross, is not that certain theories are *wrong*, but that they are *incomplete*. There is so much we don't know about our world and the life in it. Bigfoot may be a missing link. The Loch Ness monster may be an ancient being that has inhabited the depths of lakes and seas for millions of years, or it may be a highly evolved species that we have yet to uncover. These creatures are not myths, but are facts that are waiting to be uncovered."

"That is a good way to look at things."

"Thank you," Dr. Lengel smiled. "So, Miss Ross, let me ask you something. Based on what I have learned about you, I assume, despite no longer being a student, you are planning on pursuing the topic of your thesis further? Finding proof?"

Randi nodded.

"How?" he asked.

"Excuse me?"

"How are you planning to do that? Are you independently wealthy? Do you have a grant? Do you have connections?"

Randi laughed. "No, no, and no. I had scholarships and a part-time job, so other than some student loans I don't have any outstanding debt. I'm free and clear as far as that goes. I certainly don't have any *extra* money, either, though. My current plan is to pick up more hours at work, or maybe find a second job and save up for a couple of years. I'll do research for now, and then, when I have enough money, I'll take some trips abroad. Ideally, I would like to join an archaeological dig somewhere, and study art or writings that refer to dragons or dinosaurs or things of that sort."

"Mmm-hmm," Dr. Lengel said. "That's it?"

Randi shrugged. "It's not like I have a lot of options at the moment."

Dr. Lengel nodded. "Very well, then, Miss Ross, you're in luck. I'm going to propose to you."

Her eyes widened. "I beg your pardon?"

Dr. Lengel laughed. "I'm going to offer you a job, Miss Ross."

"A job? Doing what?"

Dr. Lengel grinned. "What else? Searching for dragons!"

Randi's mouth dropped open. "Are you serious?"

"Miss Ross, one thing I never am is insincere."

She blinked for a few moments, trying to wrap her mind around the concept. He wanted to pay her to do what she was most passionate about doing? "What would it involve?"

"Well," Dr. Lengel rubbed his hands together. "Basically, you would do whatever my partner or I tell you to do. You would do the research we ask you to do and go to the places we send you. We have people who are contractors for us, who are paid based on pictures they capture, fossils they find, and so on, but what I'm offering you is more of a junior partnership. I want you as a permanent part of the team."

Randi forced her bottom jaw back to its rightful position.

Dr. Lengel grinned. "Of course, your primary focus can be your search for your dragons. You will be expected to help research other things, too, but I have no problem with you making the search for dragons your priority."

"That's really generous, but—um, I'm sure you have plenty of other work to do. Why would my pet project be more important than your things?"

"Well, for one thing, the idea intrigues me. Most people think of cryptozoology very narrowly. They think of Bigfoot and the Loch Ness monster, both of which are very important to us, but which are hardly the only thing we do. I like the idea of a full-scale dragon hunt.

He cracked his knuckles, making Randi wince. "But also, because I know that people will work much harder on the things they are passionate about than the things they are assigned."

"Okay, then, why me? I'm a historian, not a biologist or a cryptozoologist. Why did you pick me?"

"I've read your thesis. I know what you're capable of, and I'm confident I can expect that kind of dedication and thoroughness as an employee. Not to mention the fact that you're brilliant and passionate about what you do. That's the kind of attitude—the kind of *person*—I want working with me."

"I don't know what to say."

"I'll take that as a solid maybe, then. I can't wait for you to meet my partner—he's on a trip right now, but you'll meet him soon. You'll like him."

Randi started to answer, but Dr. Lengel interrupted.

"Actually—well, you probably won't like him. He is an extremely intelligent man, and is consequently one of the most annoying creatures on the planet."

Randi giggled.

"He's good at his job, though. We work well together. I mainly do the research, and he mainly does the field work. I go on trips occasionally, myself, but I'm mostly too old and fat to do much but stay here." He laughed, shaking his prominent stomach.

Randi smiled.

"It works, though," Dr. Lengel went on. "We're a good team."

"So, if he is your partner, won't he have a say on whether or not you hire me?" Randi asked.

Dr. Lengel shrugged. "Technically, but he sort of already did. I called him a few weeks ago, after I spoke to you at the restaurant, and read him a few excerpts from your thesis. I told him I was meeting you today, and he gave me the go-ahead to offer you a job if I thought you'd be a good fit. Speaking of which, what do you say? Do you want to work for us?"

Randi took a deep breath. "It is a very intriguing offer."

"But?"

Randi grinned. "I didn't say *but*. I was just going to say I need some time to think about it."

Dr. Lengel visibly relaxed, a grin splitting his face. "In that case, absolutely. How much time do you think you'll need?"

"How about a week?"

Dr. Lengel rubbed his fat, red hands together. "Very well, I'll see you next week. I'll have your office ready for you."

"You seem awfully confident that I'm going to accept," Randi laughed.

"I have a sense about these things."

Randi couldn't help grinning. "I'll see you next week."

Both she and Dr. Lengel stood and extended their hands.

"Thank you for coming in today, Miss Ross." Dr. Lengel pumped her hand up and down.

"Thank you, Dr. Lengel." She left, clutching at her skirt to keep her hands from trembling.

This couldn't be happening. Not really.

Her own office? Working for someone fun who encouraged her to follow her passion? The opportunity to do what she'd always wanted?

The money wouldn't be great, she didn't imagine, but that would be the case in any entry-level position. Her mom would be disappointed—all those years of school and all she had to show for it was a position as a researcher in a virtually unknown field.

She needed some time to breathe, to really let Dr. Lengel's offer sink in. She needed to call Nik.

She felt the secretary watching her as she walked toward the door. She turned and smiled. "See you later."

"Are you going to work here?"

"I'm not sure yet. Maybe."

"Oh."

Randi waited a moment for her to say something else, but she didn't. As she walked out, the secretary picked up the phone. Something in her expression, in the furtive way she reached for the phone, left Randi feeling unsettled, but she couldn't quite put her finger on why.

***

"He offered you a job?" Nik's appalled tone echoing through the phone hurt Randi's ear.

"Yep," Randi answered, adjusting her earpiece and merging onto the freeway.

"You didn't say yes, did you?"

"I haven't said anything, yet. I need to think it over."

"What is there to think over? Despite your thesis, you could still have a real career. You can transfer to another school and be done in six months, then you could have a distinguished position teaching history in college, or joining any historical society you wanted. You could be curator of a museum, or—"

"Or, I could get paid to do something I love and am passionate about." Randi gritted her teeth, trying to keep her voice calm.

An irritated snort came over the airwaves. "So, when do you have to decide?"

"I told him I'd let him know by next week."

"That's not much time."

"No," she admitted, "but, realistically, Nik, this is a really good opportunity for me. I'm going to appeal my expulsion, and in the meantime, I get to get paid to do research on what I want. This is a good job, doing something I really enjoy."

"Does that mean you're going to take it?"

"I honestly don't know. I haven't even processed it myself yet. I guess it intrigues me. I'm definitely considering it."

"Well, I vote no."

Randi gave a short laugh. "Nicky, I hate to break this to you, but your vote doesn't really count."

"I just want what's best for you," he said.

"No, Nik, you want what *you* think is best for me. That isn't necessarily what *is* best for me."

"Right, because you've done a great job on your own. You couldn't even graduate," Nik sneered.

"Good bye, Nik," She hung up without waiting for him to say goodbye. She leaned her head back against the headrest, and sighed. Why did he have to be so difficult? And why, oh, why did she have to care about his opinion so much?

***

Mt. Hood National Forest, Southeast of Portland, Oregon

Carole McCray sat in a hunting blind she'd built in the glade by the stream, watching the pink-tinged clouds in the fading light. She slapped at a mosquito.

This was the fifth evening in a row that she'd sat in the same spot, silent, waiting. Once, she'd caught a glimpse of it, just coming out into the clearing, but the wind changed, or it sensed her—she wasn't sure which. It bolted before she even got a clear view, let alone a picture.

She swatted another mosquito away from her face. If it was coming, it would be any minute now. After adjusting the headband that kept her short hair out of her face, she picked up her camera. Lens cap off, focus for distance and low light, shutter speed for movement. She was ready as she'd ever be.

Her eyes scanned the woods for any sign of movement. The thudding of her heart echoed in her ears, and she put forth her full concentration to keep her breath coming in slowly and evenly.

Having grown up in the Pacific Northwest, she had a built-in love for stories of Bigfoot, but was sensible enough to realize that most of those were exactly that—stories.

Most of them.

She harbored a deep-seated belief that he was out there somewhere, and she was determined to find him.

The few people she told either thought she was nuts, or shook their heads and tossed her condescending glances, until she stopped telling people.

As far as anyone knew any more, she just took frequent camping trips by herself in the woods when she wasn't working her day job at the photography studio. She mostly worked weekends, doing weddings and other special events, but her dream was to take pictures of Bigfoot.

Over the years, she got some fuzzy shots even *she* wasn't sure were real, but managed to sell some of them, sometimes to tabloids, and sometimes to other buyers, like a cryptozoological society. At the time, it surprised her that there were so many people out there willing to believe in monsters, and that were so willing to pay good money for any shred of would-be evidence. Now, she recognized that there were kindred spirits out there, she just had to look in the right places. And those places weren't usually upscale photography studios.

The sun sank lower, casting long, cool shadows around the glade. A slight breeze picked up. She heard the twittering of birds as they settled into their nests for the evening, and the scraping of squirrels' claws on the bark of the trees. A deer wandered into the glade, one step at a time, its nose in the air, sniffing.

Finally, it went to the stream and lowered its head to drink.

Carole sat very still, scarcely breathing. Too bad Seth hadn't come. He would have admired the simplicity of the sight. She'd invited him along, since he was one of the few people with whom she shared her passion for Bigfoot, but he couldn't take the time off work.

They didn't always see eye to eye—Seth argued that if she did find proof of Bigfoot's existence, scientists and thousands of others would come in and rip the forest apart looking for him.

Still, they shared a love of nature and beauty, and a passion for the earth. Seth was an avid environmentalist, even more so than Carole.

She didn't agree with all his views, but they made it work—four years now. She hoped to get married, but Seth kept putting it off.

"We will eventually," he said every time she brought it up. "I just don't think I'm ready yet."

He would kiss her then, in that way he had that sent tingles down her spine, and she would forget for awhile her desire to solidify their relationship legally.

Carole glanced at the darkening sky. It was getting late, and with the darkness came cold. If the creature she sought didn't show up soon, she would miss her chance. As it was, she would have to use her flash, which meant that she'd get only one chance to get a good shot, because the moment the camera snapped and the bright light shattered the darkness, the creature would be gone.

Stifling a yawn, she realized she would have to go if she wanted to find her way back to her campsite.

Movement caught her eye just as she started to sit up and stretch. She held her breath, and slowly lifted the camera up to her eye, focusing on the bushes. A creature crept out very slowly, standing upright and sniffing the air.

She gulped back her awe.

The beast crept cautiously into the clearing, pausing and looking around between each step. Suddenly it stopped, turned, and stared directly at her. She snapped the picture before it could run.

A loud, bellowing growl that sounded like a combination of bear and wolf howls erupted from its mouth as it crashed through the underbrush in the opposite direction.

It was several moments before Carole recovered enough to realize what just happened. She'd actually seen Bigfoot, and gotten a picture of him—a *good* picture.

Her heart pounded and her breath came in ragged gasps.

Recovering her senses, she carefully packed her camera away in its case and slung it over one shoulder, hefting her hunting rifle over the other. While she didn't believe in killing things unnecessarily, she wasn't stupid, either. She knew better than to spend a week alone in the forest without any sort of protection.

It was a long hike back to her campsite—she hadn't wanted her scent anywhere near the stream where she'd determined, through long, arduous exploration, was a likely stomping ground—but she found it in good time and without any trouble. Soon, her campfire blazed, protecting her from both animals and cold with its bright embrace.

She kept her camera case around her shoulder all evening. Now that she had the picture she'd been waiting for, she wasn't about to let it out of her sight or risk anything happening to it.

After a dinner of beans and tortillas, she huddled into her tent, her camera close by her side. She snuggled into her sleeping bag, thinking about how excited Seth would be when he saw the picture.

She woke just as the sun peeked over the treetops, and began to pack up her gear. She didn't even bother to eat—she could pick something up at the gas station on the way home, and she wanted to get going.

A bright glare covered the clearing by the time she finished packing all of her gear into the back of her pickup. She opened the front door and carefully set her camera case onto the passenger side seat, then climbed in. She patted the floor under the rug until she found her keys and sat up.

Her mouth dropped open. There, standing just at the edge of the clearing, was another Bigfoot.

Chapter Eight

Another Bigfoot!

Or was it the same one? She wasn't sure—it had been dark before.

It stared right at her, lips curled up in a slight snarl. The hair on the back of her neck stood on end and her mouth went dry.

The driver's side door was still open, not that it mattered. The thing could easily break through the windows, or tear off the entire door if it had a mind to.

Taking deep breaths, she willed herself to stay calm. She didn't want the thing to smell her fear, or get spooked and attack her.

They regarded each other for a moment that seemed like an eternity.

He was much like all the stories described him, standing over eight feet tall. Possibly related to both humans and to apes, and yet he looked like neither. His eyes, positioned at the front of his face, sparked with what might be intelligence, but might be nothing more than a predatory gleam. His arms were longer than a human's but shorter than an ape's, and he had very human-like hands.

When he snarled, his teeth reminded her more of a dog's than anything else. A thick mat of dark, brownish-gray hair covered his body, even around his mouth and nose. She was no biologist, but this creature did not seem to her to be a mix between humans and apes—a missing link. It seemed like something else altogether.

Very slowly, she reached out with her right hand and pulled the camera bag into her lap, all the while staring at the creature. She pulled the camera out and turned it on. The picture would be mostly guesswork—she wouldn't have time to focus.

She knew instinctively that the moment she moved enough to bring the camera up, the Bigfoot would either bolt or attack, but she was banking on the fact that legend always portrayed him as a very shy creature, not given to random attacks.

Why wasn't he gone already? She'd never heard of a Bigfoot actually allowing itself to be seen, let alone standing and staring at someone. Was it the one she had photographed last night, come to hunt her down? Was it a young one, curious about her presence in the forest and without enough instinct to stay hidden? She had no idea, but she wasn't going to look this gift horse in the mouth, and she wasn't going to miss out on the opportunity of a lifetime.

In one swift movement, she pulled the camera up and snapped off several pictures.

At her sudden movement, the beast threw his arms up and growled, much like the growl he'd uttered the night before. He dropped to all fours and charged toward her, snarling and growling. She slammed the truck door and honked the horn, a loud, solid noise that disrupted the quiet of the forest.

At the sound, the Bigfoot turned in one fluid motion and bounded on all fours to the safety of the forest.

Carole sat in the truck for several minutes, panting, staring after the Bigfoot. The sound of her heart pounding echoed in her ears.

When she had her breath back, she checked out the pictures.

They were good. She'd spared no expense on this camera, with motion sensitivity and high shutter speed, and it paid off. A couple shots were blurry, probably because her hands trembled with the adrenaline rush, but there were a few that were downright amazing. Even better than the one she took the night before.

She leaned back against the seat, her mind whirling with the implications of what she just accomplished. To her knowledge, she had just gotten the most conclusive evidence of the existence of Bigfoot there was.

It occurred to her to get a few pictures of the tracks before she left, and some soil samples. Maybe there would be hair or something that could be analyzed.

She honked a couple of times before getting out of her truck, just to make sure that the creature would not come back, then jumped out and pulled a little trowel and some plastic zipper bags out of the storage box in the bed of her truck.

She examined the ground around the place where the creature had been standing. The tracks weren't very good. The ground was moist enough, but there was too much grass and vegetation to leave very good foot impressions. Still, she took several pictures of the best ones, including pictures of her foot next to the giant print.

There were some claw marks from his front feet, but it appeared that most of the weight was still on his back feet, so she guessed that his front feet were used mainly for balance and to help propel him forward.

Most of the reports she read were of Bigfoot standing upright, and never any citations of anyone getting a cast from the print of the front foot—or hand, or whatever it was. She concluded that upright was probably his preferred position, but he went down on all fours when he was in a hurry.

When she'd gotten enough pictures, she took some soil and grass samples from the deepest tracks. She followed the tracks to the edge of the clearing and looked at the trees. A tuft of hair gently waving in the breeze was stuck in the bark where he scraped against a tree. She turned a plastic bag inside out and stuck her hand in it, like a glove. Pulling off the chunk of bark with the hair in it, she folded the bag back over it, so the bark and hair was inside the bag, uncontaminated by her own skin or hair. Finally, she put the bags carefully in her cooler and got in her truck.

It was almost nine in the morning by the time she made her way out of the forest and onto the highway. She'd told Seth that if she wasn't back first thing in the morning, she probably wouldn't see him until late that evening, after shooting a wedding. She glanced at the clock on the dashboard. If she hurried, she might still be able to catch him before he went to work.

A grin spread across her face. She couldn't wait to show him her pictures. She accelerated just a little more, trying not to speed too much. She stopped at the Country Man in Canyon City to fill up her gas tank and went inside for a cup of coffee and a bagel while the attendant pumped her gas.

She ignored the man behind the counter whose bulging eyes scanned the area where her legs met her back and hurried back to her truck.

65

Before long, she was back on the road, the pavement flying by under her tires until she finally made it back into Portland.

She missed the morning rush hour, but even so, it was a full half hour from the city limits to her apartment complex. She pounded up the stairs to the apartment she shared with Seth.

The first thing she noticed was the unlocked door. It wasn't like Seth to leave the door unlocked overnight, and she wondered if he'd been out already that morning.

The second thing she noticed as she walked in was that the woman in the kitchen was wearing Seth's shirt, the blue one Carole gave him for Christmas. Long, tan legs stuck out from the bottom, and dark, curly hair tumbled around her shoulders. Carole met the woman's eyes, and they stared at each other for a moment.

"What the—" Carole didn't quite get the expletive voiced when Seth came out of the bedroom.

"Hey, Baby, I was thinking," he said, coming up from behind and slipping his arms around the woman's waist.

It was then that he noticed Carole standing in the doorway.

Carole stood, mouth gaping. The pieces were all there, but her brain refused to connect them, refused to tell her what she didn't want to know.

"Carole! I—I didn't expect you back yet."

It all hit her at once, the obvious, horrible truth. "Obviously," she said, unable to disguise the tears in her voice, but not taking her eyes away from the other woman's gaze.

"I'll just go change clothes," the woman muttered, pulling away from Seth's arms.

"Don't bother," Carole said hoarsely. "I'm leaving." She turned her gaze to Seth. "I'll be back later to get my stuff." She turned abruptly and walked out the door.

"Carole, wait," Seth called out, thundering down the stairs after her.

She clutched her camera bag close to her chest as she walked away as quickly as her long legs would take her.

He grabbed her arm. "Carole, listen to me."

"I don't want to hear it. I told you that I would not go through that again."

66

"Just let me explain. She just came in from out of town, and she needed a place to stay for a couple of nights."

Carole turned to look at him. "So, what, she was wearing nothing but your shirt because all her clothes got eaten by wild animals?"

Seth dropped his eyes.

"And you were wrapping your arms around her and calling her *Baby* because you think of her as a sister?"

"I know, I'm sorry." Seth traced his fingers up and down her arm. "Things got out of hand. But you're the one I love."

"If you loved *me*, you wouldn't be up there with *her*."

Seth tickled her neck behind her ear, the way he always did when she was upset. "I'm so sorry. Please don't go. Give me another chance."

"I gave you another chance!" Carole shouted, jerking away from his touch. "This *was* your second chance! I told you the last time that if it ever happened again, it was over. Do you really think I'm going to stay around and be treated that way again? I deserve better than that."

Seth stepped closer, reaching for her hand. "You do. You deserve so much better. I'm sorry, Carole. What else can I say? I made a mistake, but I love you so much! Can't you ever forgive me?"

She stepped back. "I already forgave you once. It's over."

"I don't want to lose you," he begged.

"I guess you should have thought of that sooner." She turned and tried to walk away again.

"Hey, wait a second. I want to know about your trip. Did you get a picture?"

She turned and looked at him, unable at first to switch subjects. "What?"

He nodded toward the camera bag. "Did you get any good pictures?"

She stared at him. Only a few moments ago she couldn't wait to share with him the pictures she took, but suddenly the thought of sharing any more of herself, especially her greatest triumph, with this man who betrayed her was revolting. She didn't make a practice of lying, but she knew she could be convincing if she wanted to.

This happened to be one time she wanted to. "No. I mean, I got a few pictures, but nothing more than anything else I've gotten. Probably a bear or something."

"Really? Can I see them?"

"Seth, I know what you're trying to do. You're pretending to be interested to distract me so that I'll forget about the naked woman upstairs. It's not going to work. I'll come back when you're gone and move my stuff out."

"Where are you going?"

"My mom's, I guess, for now. I'm not sure after that."

"Can I call you so we can talk about this?"

"There's nothing to talk about. You blew it. I'm done."

"I'm sorry, Carole. I never meant to hurt you."

Carole threw her head back and laughed. Seth stepped backward, looking surprised.

Carole glared at him. "That's exactly what you said last time. You know the difference? I believed you then."

"Carole, wait."

She walked away and didn't look back.

***

Los Angeles, California

Randi woke to the ringing of her phone.

"Miss Ross? This is Dean Palmer. I wonder if you could spare a few moments for a meeting with me?"

The bottom threatened to drop from Randi's stomach—right before it threatened to jump out her mouth. What on earth could Dean Palmer want with her? Obviously, it had to do with her thesis—or her expulsion—or both. But… was this about overturning the decision? She hadn't even had a chance to file her appeal yet.

But Dean Palmer had seniority over Dr. Peterson, so if nothing else, Randi might be able to make a good impression, so the Dean was more likely to look favorably on her appeal.

"Of course," she said. "When would you like me to come in?"

She made the appointment for later that day and arrived a few minutes early, determined to calm her jittery nerves before the meeting.

The waiting room to the dean's office was exactly the opposite of the waiting room at the cryptozoological society. Where the society had warm, earthy, nature vibes, this room was almost clinical, with its stark, white walls and expensive but boring black and white art prints.

"Miss Ross, Dean Palmer will see you now," the assistant at the front desk said.

That wasn't enough time.

Randi sucked in her breath and opened the door to Dean Palmer's office.

"Good morning, Miss Ross. Have a seat."

Randi sat in an uncomfortably pristine white chair. She could eat off the floor in that office, and she instinctively checked her hands to make sure she wouldn't leave fingerprints anywhere.

"I'm sure you're wondering why I asked you in here."

Randi nodded. "Yes, ma'am."

"I've been reviewing the circumstances of your expulsion. I'm sure you can understand the awkward position this puts me in. On one hand, I understand how you must feel to have been dismissed, your education and career ruined, without being given a chance to defend yourself."

"Yes."

"On the other hand, I must back my staff. I can't undermine their authority."

Randi nodded. "I understand."

"That must be terribly frustrating for you." Dean Palmer smiled in what Randi assumed was supposed to be a sympathetic way, but came across more like a lion smiling at a deer.

"I've spent quite a bit of time thinking how I could have done things differently. My behavior and attitude toward Dr. Peterson were unacceptable."

"I'm glad to hear that." Dean Palmer smiled again, but it didn't make Randi feel any more at ease.

"This may be a bit premature, but as the dean of students, I would like to come to some sort of resolution of this issue. If you're willing to write a formal letter of apology to Dr. Peterson and to the school, I think we can come to an arrangement where you can return and complete your degree."

"Wow, I don't even… thank you."

"Of course, you'd have to meet other requirements, not the least of which would be retaking the classes you didn't complete and rewriting your thesis."

69

Randi inhaled. These conditions shouldn't come as a surprise, but she still had to tamp down the rising irritation at the list of qualifiers Dean Palmer dictated.

"And, of course, you'd have to conform to the standards of this institution, particularly the history department. I cannot stress enough the importance of this."

Randi clenched her hands, thinking it through. Everyone—her mom, Nik, Dr. Lupkin—everyone thought she should just rewrite her thesis according to her original outline. It honestly wouldn't take long to do—she had all the information and source material, and she'd already written huge portions of it for her research. Switch out a little here and there to conform with the expectations put upon her, and just be done with it.

It felt so very wrong to compromise... but how could she not? She could still work for Dr. Lengel while she finished the classes and thesis, and that would enable her to continue to do her own research. But the reality was, she'd never move beyond that if she didn't finish her degree. Maybe she should take Dean Palmer up on her offer.

She had to. It was the only way.

She nodded and smiled at the dean. "Absolutely, thank you. I'll write the letter right away. Just let me know what else I need to do to get re-registered for classes."

Dean Palmer smiled, a little more warmly this time. "Good. Now that we have that settled, I have one other thing I'd like to discuss. From time to time, I come across potential job openings, and I found one that I think might suit you. The Global Archaeological Preservation Association is in need of interns. I trust you've heard of them?"

"Yes, of course."

"This internship would be more intensive, but it would also have the potential to develop into a more regular position. After you complete your degree, of course. One thing you should understand is that the Association is a highly prestigious group, and very well respected. There is no room in such a position for fantasy and conjecture. If I'm going to put my name and this school's reputation behind a recommendation, I would need to know you take it seriously. Shall I submit your name?"

Randi sat in the clinically white chair and stared at the dean. An internship with GAPA could change everything. "That's very generous of you, and it sounds like a great opportunity. I'll think about it."

Dean Palmer's smile faltered. "What is there to think about?"

"Well, I've already been offered another job."

"Oh? What sort of job?" Her eyes bored into Randi like lasers.

Randi wondered just how much to tell her. "I'd be working with a cryptozoologist."

Dean Palmer coughed so hard she almost choked. "A *cryptozoologist?*"

Randi nodded.

"Miss Ross, I can appreciate that you're young and such a career sounds adventurous and romantic, but I implore you to rethink that option. There is no place in cryptozoology for someone of your intellect and education."

Randi bristled. "I'd still be doing research. Even if it didn't work out, I would have experience and training to apply to a new position."

Dean Palmer shook her head. "I'm sorry if that's what you've been led to believe, but you are sorely mistaken. There is no coming back from a career choice of that magnitude."

Randi tried to say something but Dean Palmer raised her hand for silence. "Cryptozoology isn't a science, and no research you would do while employed in such a field would credit you in any way in the future. Quite the opposite, in fact. Any reputable museum, firm, or historical society will look at that lapse in judgment and determine you are unqualified for employment with them. And, to be honest, I'd have a hard time allowing you to return and get your degree if you're working in cryptozoology."

"I doubt—"

"Please understand me, Miss Ross. I've seen situations like yours before. Especially given that you have to overcome your father's reputation, you'd better be completely sure that this is what you want to do for the rest of your life, because once you go down that path, you will be discredited from doing any *real* work again."

Randi stifled a gasp. How did Dean Palmer know about her father? She gulped back the lump in her throat and nodded. "I'll consider it. Thank you."

Chapter Nine

Randi sat alone in her dark apartment. The sun had disappeared long since, but she hadn't bothered to turn on a light. Kelly wasn't home yet—she had end-of-the-year activities at her school that kept her out late all week, so Randi sat on her bed, alone in the dark, with the faint sounds of Yanni wafting from her speakers.

A book sat open in front of her, but she'd stopped reading a while ago. The room seemed to blur around her. She couldn't seem to focus on anything. She rested her head on the plush dragon Nik had won for her.

If she took the job with the cryptozoology society, in some ways, she'd have her dream job. Just thinking about it thrilled her. Research and fieldwork and the freedom to pursue her passion—what could be wrong with that?

On the other hand, Nik and Dean Palmer were right about it not being a respected field. Given that, her job might be tenuous. Who knew if they'd have the funding to keep her on long term? Or, for that matter, if the company would even survive?

She'd told Dr. Lengel that she would give him an answer in a week. Now, the week part was gone, with only the weekend left to think about it. She thought about her conversation with Dr. Lengel, and the one with Dean Palmer. Despite her optimism, she knew Dean Palmer was right. It was one or the other. Could she be happy in an ordinary job, doing ordinary research with ordinary historians?

The job with the cryptozoological society taunted her with its endless possibilities, while the internship with GAPA lured her with its practicality, not to mention the possibility of finishing her degree. Of course, that was just an internship. There was no guarantee she'd have a job after it was over. But she would have a degree, and a solid amount of experience to apply elsewhere.

The job at the cryptozoological society was a sure thing, at least for the foreseeable future. But could she take the risk that it would work out long term, at the expense of any notable career after that?

She wished she could discuss it with Nik, but he'd made it perfectly clear that he sided with Dean Palmer, and he refused to even listen to any other point of view. She'd hardly talked to him since they'd argued about it, and she couldn't even bring it up without him getting irate.

At least Dr. Lupkin was willing to be objective about it. They'd had a long talk earlier that day.

"Well, it is a little unconventional," Dr. Lupkin had said. "It's hardly something I would have expected from someone of your potential, but it is a legitimate job. Dr. Lengel is a good man, and very passionate about his work. The society does pretty well for itself. There's always someone willing to believe in monsters."

He began to laugh, but after a quick glance at her, stopped himself. "Anyway, the society is well established, and reputable in its own field. It would be a good job, and I think you would enjoy it. Dr. Lengel would be a good employer. I've never met his partner, but I imagine he's a decent sort of fellow, to be working so closely with Dr. Lengel. I can't say Dean Palmer is wrong about it limiting your future options, though. I suggest you don't take that lightly."

Dr. Lupkin had gone on to say, "Most importantly, I think you should consider what it is you want. Every time we've talked, it's been about your father and what he started. But suppose you never find what he was looking for. Will you be happy with how you spent your life? And if not, what is it that you do want? When you look back, thirty years from now, will you be satisfied that you did what you wanted with it?"

Randi considered his words. What *did* she want? Dr. Lupkin was right—it had always been about her father. But she wanted to finish his work because she believed he was right. She knew his research wasn't for nothing. She'd found enough evidence proving it to believe in it as much as he did.

In thirty years, even if she never found anything, would she still be satisfied she'd made the right choice?

By the time she fell asleep, she had settled on her decision. Truth might be elusive, but the pursuit of it was exactly what she wanted to do with her life, and working for Dr. Lengel would give her that opportunity.

***

Portland, Oregon

Carole had long since given up wiping the tears away and just let them stream down her face as she packed up the last box of her things from the apartment.

It had been Seth's apartment before she moved in, and his name was the only one on the lease, so she didn't really have any loose ends to tie up. She'd already paid next her half of next month's rent and utilities, so he was getting a bonus on that.

All of the things that were "theirs," like the coffee pot and the microwave and the picture frames with pictures of the two of them, she left behind. She didn't want to get in a fight over them, and she didn't really want or need them, anyway. The only things she took were her clothes and personal items, and the few things she brought with her when she moved in. She even left the big, beautiful dresser that they bought together. It wasn't worth the fight. Besides, she couldn't carry it down the stairs by herself, and she didn't really want to bring anyone else into her emotional mess just then.

"It's done. It's really over," Carole said aloud. Even as she packed everything away, it hadn't felt real. As she took one last look around the apartment, it looked empty. All the things that spoke of her presence there, the things that made it her home, were gone. It seemed naked. It was fitting, really, the apartment looking like that. It was a shell, a half-empty reminder of the last four years of her life that were consumed by Seth.

She carried the last box out, locked the door, and dropped the key through the mail slot, then went down the stairs and tucked the last box into the bed of her truck.

Leaning back against the headrest, she took a deep breath. She needed a fresh start, somewhere new. Somewhere far away from Seth, and from the memories of the four years they'd spent together in this city.

Maybe she could just move to the woods and get adopted by Bigfoot.

That was the biggest issue—she needed to be close to continue her search, especially now that she had proof. But if she stayed, Seth would always be right there—just on the edge of her existence, haunting her.

Pulling out of the apartment complex, she stepped on the accelerator.

Finally, she made it to her mother's house in a suburb half an hour away and hid in her old room. Her mom was at work, but it was the last day before summer break at the school where she taught, so she'd be home any minute.

Carole was sitting on her childhood bed crying when her mother opened the front door. "Carole?" she called out. "I saw your truck. Where are you?"

"My room," Carole called back.

Her mom shoved the door open, took one look at Carole's face, and plopped down on the bed next to her. "What is it, honey? What happened?"

"Seth cheated on me again."

"Oh, baby, I'm so sorry." She cradled Carole in her arms and stroked her hair.

They sat for a long time, her mom just letting her cry. Finally, Carole pulled herself together enough to tell the story of finding Seth with his side piece when she got home that morning.

"I think I need to move away from here," she said.

"And go where?" her mom asked.

"I'm not sure yet. I just think I need a break from Seth... even from Bigfoot."

"Well, you know I'll support you no matter what."

"Thanks, Mom." Carole glanced at her phone. "I need to get going. I've got a wedding tonight."

"Okay," her mom said. "You just let me know whatever you need, okay?"

Carole's mind churned as she got ready, and all evening as she followed her boss' instructions on which shots to get, thinking through all her possible job options, all the places she might be able to transplant to.

There wasn't much else she could do over the weekend besides plan, especially since she would be working for most of it. Plus, it was wedding season, so she would be busy a lot over the next month, but she would take that time to save up for a move, and then she would move somewhere and start over. She would make a few calls on Monday and try to get a new job lined up. And she knew exactly who she would call first.

***

Quebec, Canada

Jeremiah Bryant opened the door to his hotel room. *Something isn't right.* The maid hadn't been in yet, but things weren't quite where he'd left them when he went for his swim. His bag was slightly unzipped, though he always made it a point to close it all the way. He opened the top, fearing the worst.

Nothing seemed to be missing. Strange. Not that he wasn't glad, but he expected to have been robbed. They, whoever *they* were, hadn't taken his camera, which was worth a small fortune, or even his wallet. All of his cash and credit cards were intact.

Rubbing his chin, he looked through everything again. He was absolutely certain someone had been in his room, but he couldn't prove it.

He feared what they might have seen, if it was who he thought it might be.

He called Frank.

Frank's abrasive voice boomed on the other end of the line. "Jeremiah, it's good to hear from you. How was the lake?"

"Same as the last time I talked to you. Pretty uneventful. Made a couple of contacts. One aspiring photographer promised to send me any pictures of the monster he could get, but nothing of any real value."

He tried to keep the irritation from his voice. Wasted time bothered him. Some of the places Frank sent him were less than useless. Worse, it distracted from his true mission.

Frank didn't seem to notice. Or care. "Well, you can't win 'em all, can you? I expect to hear from Ross on Monday. Did I tell you about that yet?"

"Yes, actually—"

"Great fit for our team. I expect a yes, of course, but I don't want to be too pushy. That paper was amazing. It's all about dragons and—did I tell you about the paper yet?"

"Yes, I can't wait to read—"

"Nice kid, too. I can't wait for you guys to meet. When do you get in again?"

"My flight leaves tomorrow afternoon, but I have a couple of layovers, so I'll be in the office Monday morning."

"Excellent. That'll be perfect. You'll be just in time. Anything else I should know before I see you again?"

"Actually, yes. I think someone was in my room while I was working out. Some of my stuff was moved around."

"You're kidding," Frank said, his tone suddenly changing from jovial to concerned. "Was anything taken?"

"Not that I can tell, no."

"Well, then, maybe it was just housekeeping."

"No, housekeeping hadn't been in. I'd just arrived."

"Well, maybe they forgot something or had to finish something up for you."

"That could be."

"I'm sure that was it." Frank's voice was irritatingly cheery again. "Very well, then. I'll see you on Monday."

"All right." Jeremiah hadn't even had a chance to tell him about the man by the pool.

The man sat at one of the tables reading the morning paper while Jeremiah did laps. He'd been in the exercise room, too, taking a leisurely stroll on a treadmill.

Neither instance was out of place, yet Jeremiah felt an unmistakable gut sense that something wasn't quite right.

The man was about forty, of average height and build, slightly balding. The sort of man who blended into a crowd and disappeared without anyone having looked at him twice.

I'm not paranoid. Wariness is a rational response to past experience.

At any rate, there was nothing he could do about it now. He kicked his shoes off, thinking about what Frank had said about Randy Ross. Randy—was that short for Randall? The name sounded familiar to him for some reason, but he couldn't place it.

He showered and stood in front of the broad mirror to run a comb through his dark hair. He gave himself a satisfied smile. His tan, muscled chest and arms left nothing to be desired. He worked hard to maintain a healthy body, and it showed.

His stomach growled. He hadn't eaten since early that morning. After wrapping himself up in a plush bathrobe, he pulled the room service menu out of the desk drawer. He ordered a chef salad, with extra turkey instead of ham, and balsamic vinaigrette dressing, then plopped back on the pillows and turned on the TV. Flipping through the endless parade of vapid drivel reminded him why he didn't have a TV at home. He clicked it off.

Instead, he pulled his Bible out of his bag and read until his food arrived.

The portly woman who delivered the food reeked of stale cigarette smoke and mint gum. Jeremiah pursed his lips. Did she really think the gum would disguise the smell? He gave the woman a gospel tract instead of a tip. Clearly, she needed the Word more than money.

Chapter Ten

Los Angeles, California

The Director sat at the rich mahogany desk and surveyed the reports that lay in perfect stacks, organized first by theme, then by location, then by individual.

There were informants everywhere—in every one of the important labs and universities worldwide, in every branch of government, from national to state to city in this country, along with most of the governments in other developed nations, as well as in plenty of places and industries that were considered obscure or unimportant by other collaborations.

Most of the agents didn't understand why the Director insisted on keeping such close tabs on the more unconventional people and places, but that's where the real danger lay.

Labs were predictable, and schools even more so. They dealt in provable facts and accepted theories. Once in awhile a new discovery was made, but the Director almost always had prior knowledge to the tests that were being done and the conclusions that would inevitably be reached, and often helped those conclusions to be verified.

It was those others—the ones who dealt in alternative facts—the cryptozoologists, the fringe archaeologists, and the more radical paleontologists—who were the ones that could cause problems. Like that fellow a few years back—what was his name?—who made the TV show offering an alternate view of the historical record based on ancient sites. A different Director ran this branch of the Syndicate then. Such a thing should never have been allowed, let alone have received so much press. That mistake had cost the previous Director his position, among other things—a mistake the current Director had no intention of duplicating.

The Director's job involved more than just seeing that the right people were elected or the right scientific discoveries progressed in the right directions. It was about seeing that the wrong things never got discovered, and the wrong claims never got made.

If new evidence was found, then by all means it should be broadcast, but in the right way. People couldn't just go around making tabloid claims or offering conjecture. Civilization was an elaborate structure that needed to be handled correctly in order to preserve the world that existed. Everything from children's textbooks to the discoveries of some of the greatest minds in history were based on a set of rules that could not be challenged. The world didn't need to know everything, and it was the possession of knowledge that kept balance—the plebeians in their place, and the elite in control. It was the Director's job to see that all those things were accomplished.

So the reports came in, and the Director sifted through them, one by one, deciding which ones were important and which were of no value. Most were filed away, and few ever saw the light of day again, but there were a few that needed to be either dealt with or kept under a close watch.

Like the next report in the stack. The Director knew better than anyone what sorts of things to look for, and which people or situations might prove to be either useful or dangerous. This lead might or might not end up panning out—they'd been looking for Dr. Schleppenbach since his disappearance years ago, and now he might have been sighted in Europe. The information was sketchy, at best, but Schleppenbach was an individual who could not be allowed to resurface. The report suggested he was living the life of a retired civil servant in a remote village in Switzerland. If that was true, he could be extracted. At any rate, the report was worth following up. It might be nothing, but it might be everything.

***

Randi woke on Monday morning with a light heart.

She picked up the phone and called Nik. "Hey, it's me. Want to go to breakfast?"

"Sure," Nik answered. "What's up?"

"I'll tell you when I see you."

"Okay, when and where do you want to meet?" he asked.

"Pork and Beans in about an hour?"

"Great. See you then."

Randi quickly showered and got dressed. She knew Nik wouldn't understand or agree, but she also knew she couldn't make a decision like this without sharing it with him.

Nik already sat in a booth of their favorite breakfast and coffee joint sipping a cup of coffee when she arrived just under an hour later.

Sliding into the booth beside him, she grinned. "I've decided to take the job with the cryptozoological society."

Nik nodded, but looked disappointed. "I thought you probably would. I still don't get it, though. You could do so much better."

Randi shrugged. "That may be true, but I feel like this is where I'm supposed to be right now. There's a reason that Dr. Lengel was at that restaurant that night, and a reason we met. I feel like this is the right spot for me now. I'm not sure why, and I'm not sure what will happen, but I really believe that I'm making the right decision."

"Then I won't try to talk you out of it."

She smiled at him, peace and assurance regarding her decision enveloping her. Something told her that her relationship with him stood on the brink of something, as well—but she didn't know what lay on the other side.

Butterflies of anticipation fluttered in her stomach. Now that she'd actually made the decision to accept the job, she couldn't wait to get started.

She ordered breakfast and tried to smother the anxiety that made her stomach bubble. Around mouthfuls, she tried to talk to Nik about her conversation with Dr. Palmer, and how that actually helped to solidify her decision to work at the cryptozoological society.

He barely spoke—he sat and nibbled at his own food, and barely responded, to the point that he was beginning to dampen her excitement.

"Okay, I'm going to go." She paid her check and stood. "I'll call you later, okay?"

Nik just nodded, so she left and headed immediately to the cryptozoological society office.

She arrived at the just as the secretary was unlocking the door.

"You're back."

Randi nodded with a grin and extended her hand. "I'm Randi."

"Maria," the secretary said, taking the hand that Randi offered.

Maria appeared to be her mid-thirties, with dark brown hair that hung just past her shoulders. The dissatisfied set to her mouth seemed like a permanent fixture, and her brown eyes wore a look of perpetual boredom. She led Randi into the waiting room and waved a hand toward the chairs. "Dr. Lengel isn't here yet, but he's usually not more than a couple of minutes late. He should be here any second. You can wait out here."

Randi picked up a copy of Cryptozoology Today from the small table and began browsing through it.

She chuckled. Two weeks ago she wouldn't have dreamed that there was such a magazine, yet here she was reading it, trying to familiarize herself with the work she would be doing.

A few moments later, the door opened, and Dr. Lengel entered, wearing a loud, floral-print shirt that hugged his ample midsection. White legs protruded from khaki shorts and he pulled a pair of cheap sunglasses from his eyes.

Randi stood as he entered, and walked over to him.

"Miss Ross!" His booming voice echoed off the walls of the small office. "I didn't expect you this early."

Randi shrugged with a shy smile. "I thought that since I'd decided to accept your job offer, I might as well get started as soon as possible, if that's all right."

Dr. Lengel let out a bellowing laugh and grabbed her hand, pumping it vigorously up and down. "Excellent, excellent! Come, I'll show you your office."

She grinned. Apparently he'd been serious about having it ready for her.

He led her down the hall to the room next to his office and across from the one labeled "Dr. J. R. Bryant" and opened the door. It was painted a soft beige color, with a brown carpet covering the floor. A wooden desk with a computer and a telephone on it sat in the corner, and there were bookshelves and file cabinets along the walls.

"Feel free to change anything," Dr. Lengel said. "I'll give you a budget so you can replace anything you need to. Just let me know."

Randi nodded. "Thank you, this should be fine."

"Well, no doubt you'll find something you need to change soon," Dr. Lengel smiled. "Here are your keys. This one is for the outer door, and this one is for your office door. The only rule is that the last one to leave locks everything up. Now, why don't you fill out all the forms and whatnot so we can say you're officially an employee, while I scrounge up some projects for you to work on. I emailed you all the forms—this is your official email address and password, which you can change as soon as you log in." Dr. Lengel grinned. "I'll be in my office if you need anything."

"Sounds good, thanks." She sat down behind the desk, turned on the computer, and began exploring the desk's drawers and nooks.

She logged into the email and downloaded the forms and began filling them out.

Dr. Lengel had supplied her desk with a generous stack of new pens and pencils, along with scratch paper, a stapler, white-out, and some other office supplies. The bookshelves were mostly empty, but there were a few books. Mostly biology and fossil reference guides, but there were also a few books on various creatures having to do with cryptozoology.

A short while later, Dr. Lengel returned with a stack of files. "Whenever you have time, I want you to read through these, just to familiarize yourself with some of our current projects. We have digital backups of all these, obviously, but I'm old, and I like having hard copies." He grinned before continuing. "Feel free to do some research, and add to the files if you find anything of interest having to do with them. Eventually, you'll need to start making some contacts and things like that, but for starters let's just have you work on some of our things."

"Okay," Randi agreed.

"And, of course, since your specialty is dragons, I want you to start building a file on that. Make a list of resources and things, as well as a contact list and so on. You'll get the idea what sorts of things are in our files when you read through the others, and you can base yours on that."

Randi nodded.

"Any questions?" he asked.

"Not yet," Randi smiled.

"Good. Holler if you need anything."

"Thanks."

Dr. Lengel left, and Randi began browsing through the files.

She expected it to be a quiet day. She couldn't imagine there would be very many people coming and going, or having much to do with this sort of business.

She was wrong. The phone in Dr. Lengel's office rang continually, and the bell on the front door jingled every few minutes. Every now and then, Dr. Lengel knocked on her office door and introduced her to someone he worked with or he thought she ought to know.

"This is our new team member, Randi Ross." His chest puffed out and his voice sounded proud. Whoever it was each time smiled and greeted her politely.

She knew she would never keep everyone straight, but she smiled anyway, and as soon as they were gone, went back to her files.

The morning flew by. When she glanced at her watch, it was almost noon. An angry growl from her stomach reminded her how long it had been since she'd eaten. She was hungry, but she wasn't sure what the office lunch policy was. Not wanting to look like she wasn't dedicated to her work, she decided not to ask.

Her stomach rumbled more as the minutes ticked by. Finally, she decided she would wait another half hour and see if anyone said anything, and then she'd ask if she could run out and get a bite to eat.

***

Dr. Jeremiah Bryant woke a little before eleven, after a brief nap. He hadn't gotten in until after five in the morning, but a strict adherence to self-discipline wouldn't allow him to sleep any later.

After a quick shower, he headed to the office, arriving a little before noon.

Maria looked up from her computer, her dull eyes sparking to life. She stood up quickly and leaned over the window, her cleavage spilling out of her blouse. "Welcome back, Dr. Bryant," she simpered, extending her hand.

He stifled an annoyed sigh and briskly shook her hand. "Is Frank in his office?"

Maria nodded, her lips twisting in a frown. "The new one is here, too."

"Randy Ross?"

"Yeah."

Jeremiah made a mental note of Maria's obvious distaste. What sort of problem did she have with the new kid?

Maria opened the door between the lobby and the hallway to the offices for him, leaning in toward him suggestively.

Jeremiah went through the door, glancing back at Maria as he passed, shaking his head. As if he would ever be interested in someone like her. When would she take the hint?

He knocked on the door to Dr. Lengel's office.

"Come in."

He poked his head in.

"Jeremiah, you're back! I was just about to head out to lunch, you want to come? I was beginning to think you wouldn't be in today after all—figured you must be still recovering from your trip—but I was going to ask Randi to join us for lunch, so come on, it's time you two met."

Jeremiah smiled. Despite the way Frank managed to redefine a run-on sentence, it was good to be back. He'd actually begun to miss the constant chatter from his partner during the long nights alone at the lake. "Thanks, Frank. It's good to be back."

Frank pushed him out of the way and knocked on the last door on the left side of the hallway.

"Come in." A woman's voice.

Jeremiah paused. He thought—

Dr. Lengel pushed the door open and ushered him in.

A very young looking woman pushed the glasses up on her nose and smiled politely at him.

Jeremiah blinked a few times. "Randy?"

The woman smiled, eyes dancing with mirth at the surprise in his voice.

"Hi. Miranda Ross. Everyone calls me Randi."

She was pretty enough, with her big blue eyes, upturned nose, and dainty mouth, but he suddenly doubted a girl that young would be of any real value to the Cryptozoological Society, let alone his other project. He'd have to see about this arrangement.

"Miss Ross, I'd like you to meet my partner, Dr. Jeremiah Bryant," Dr. Lengel said.

The girl came out from behind the desk and shook his hand. "It's nice to finally meet you, Dr. Bryant."

"You may call me Jeremiah."

"Um… okay. Well, nice to meet you, Jeremiah."

"You, too." He wasn't sure he really meant it.

Chapter Eleven

Randi appraised Dr. Jeremiah Bryant. He wasn't what she'd expected. Younger, for one thing. She'd pictured a man closer to Dr. Lengel's age, but Jeremiah appeared to only be in his early thirties. Considerably better looking than she'd imagined, for another. Tall—well over six feet, with dark, clean-cut hair and piercing green eyes. She couldn't help noticing what a striking combination that made. Muscled arms folded across his short-sleeved, collared white shirt that hung loosely over a flat stomach. The one main detractor to his looks was white socks worn with sandals. Randi suppressed a giggle. Gorgeous, but with absolutely no fashion sense.

"We were just on our way out to lunch," Dr. Lengel informed her. "Would you like to join us?"

"I'd love to." Randi grabbed her purse from the top of the file cabinet and followed the two men out.

Maria gave Jeremiah a look as he walked past, longing in her eyes as she gazed at him. He, however, didn't even seem to acknowledge Maria's existence.

"Should we invite Maria?" she whispered to Dr. Lengel.

Dr. Lengel's eyebrows raised, as though the idea had never occurred to him. "I don't see why not."

Randi turned and smiled at the secretary. "Do you want to come to lunch with us, Maria?"

Maria's eyes widened in surprise. "Sure, I guess."

Randi smiled at the pleased expression that came over the secretary's face. Such a small courtesy, yet apparently no one had ever thought to extend it.

She glanced at Dr. Bryant—Jeremiah. He looked annoyed. The group dynamic at the office would take some time to navigate.

At lunch, Randi sat quietly, listening as Dr. Bryant and Dr. Lengel talked, and watching the way Maria stared at Jeremiah.

Jeremiah rambled in great length about his contact at the lake until the waiter came by to take their order.

"I'll have the chicken chimichanga, with extra cheese," Dr. Lengel said.

Jeremiah glared at him. "Frank, you know you're not supposed eat that. Don't you care about your health at all?" he demanded. "Your doctor will kill you. Come to think of it, he won't have to because you're going to kill yourself."

Dr. Lengel scowled at his partner, but a smile played at his lips, as if he were used to humoring the younger man.

"I'm serious, Frank."

"I know. But you only live once, right?" he chuckled.

Jeremiah shook his head in exasperation as the waiter shifted from one foot to the next, waiting for the next order. Randi jumped in to save the fellow from more embarrassment.

"I'll have the number five combo," she said. She shot Jeremiah a challenging look, wondering if he would say anything about her choice.

He narrowed his eyes, as if accepting the challenge. "Don't you know your body is a temple?" Without waiting for a response, he looked at the waiter. "I'll have the chicken taco salad, with salsa instead of dressing, in a bowl, not a tortilla."

"I'll have the same," Maria put in quickly.

Jeremiah's jaw clenched.

Randi bit her lip to keep from smiling. Jeremiah didn't like being challenged, nor did he like being fawned over. There was apparently no pleasing him. That would make it easy—she wouldn't bother trying. Dr. Lengel was happy with her, at least so far, and that would be enough for now.

Time would tell whether she and Jeremiah were able to come to a place of mutual respect, but she didn't have high hopes.

***

Djazani Monroe wiped the sweat off her neck with an already damp handkerchief. She surveyed the dig site with satisfaction as she mopped her forehead with the same rag. Most of the crew wore large straw hats to shade them from the sun, but even so, she could see necks and faces turning red.

Her dark skin was less prone to sunburn than some of her crew's, but she applied another layer of sunscreen anyway, hoping to stave off skin cancer.

She took a swig from her water bottle as she walked up and down, surveying the bones that were slowly but surely becoming visible. It was the finest day in her budding paleontology career—the first day she got to supervise a dinosaur fossil dig herself. It didn't matter that it was by default. The man she was apprenticed to, Administrator Schweitzer, had gotten sick, leaving her in charge.

She could have gone on all day. They all had high hopes for this dig. Based on the head shape and hollow bones, Administrator Schweitzer had anticipated that it would turn out to be Deinonychus.

It certainly appeared to be, or at least it was a very close relative, although several people had challenged that hypothesis based on the size of the head. It was nearly twice as large as the largest Deinonychus head ever found.

Her stomach fluttered with the same anticipation she had felt on her first date. Like how she felt right before the long drop on a roller coaster. She could hardly wait to see what they finally uncovered.

She would love to work the crew until the entire dinosaur was unearthed, but part of being a good leader was taking care of your crew, and they needed a break.

"Okay, people. Let's wrap it up for today," she called out.

Grateful faces glanced up at her, and bodies that a moment before had been about to collapse from exhaustion were suddenly able to scurry around and secure the dig site for the day.

She looked wistfully at the coverings that were being carefully laid over the fossilized bones. Even though they were quitting early, they had still made good progress. Another few weeks and they should be able to transport the find back to the Los Angeles Natural History Museum.

Alan Kinte came to stand beside her, his thick, muscular arms folded across his chest. "You did well today." His deep, rich voice was marked with a thick accent from his native Kenya.

She smiled, but kept her eyes on the crew. "Thanks."

"Do you mind if I ask why you're having everybody quit so early? It's not because you want them to like you best, is it?"

She turned to look at him. "You know me better than that. It's the hottest day we've had yet." She took another swipe at her forehead with her handkerchief. "We're not doing our best work because we're hot and worn out. I can hardly concentrate under these conditions, and I'm not even digging, so how can I expect anyone else to function? I figured I'd give them the rest of the afternoon off, and start early tomorrow so we can get some good work in before noon."

Kinte nodded, his expression solemn but approving.

Djazani hid her smile with a drink from her water bottle. That nod was worth as much or more than the compliment. "Once we're done here, do you want to get something to drink with me?" she asked.

"I would like that."

Kinte left to help finish wrapping things up.

Djazani waited until everyone else had left the dig before returning to her trailer. A quick shower rinsed the layers of dust and grime from her body. She dressed in a short denim skirt and pale yellow halter top, noting how much better that outfit looked than her khaki shorts and button-up shirt.

She smoothed moisturizing oil on her long, shapely legs, and slipped her feet into a pair of sandals. She dabbed on a touch of make-up, although she didn't really need much, and gave herself one final look in the mirror. Satisfied, she jumped in her Jeep and made her way into the town of Shell, Wyoming.

Kinte was already at the town's one bar when she arrived. She slid into the booth across from him.

He smiled at her, his white teeth gleaming against his lips. "Be careful. I do not want to have to kill anyone to keep them from taking you away tonight."

She lowered her eyes, looking up at him through her lashes. "I don't think that will be a problem."

They had a few drinks and danced a few dances, mingling with some of the other aspiring paleontologists from the dig.

"We should get some sleep if we want to be fresh in the morning," Djazani said at last.

"Will you stay for one more dance?" Kinte asked.

Djazani slipped her arms around his neck as they slowly circled the dance floor. She liked the feel of his warm, strong arms around her back.

She laid her head on his chest, her ear above his heart. She smiled at the way his heartbeat sped up as he drew her closer.

He leaned down and put his lips close to her ear. "You could invite me to your trailer."

She nestled a little closer. "I would love to. However, I am not going to. It is not a good idea, not here. Let's wait until we get back to L.A., and then we'll see what happens."

He sighed, but she was sure he knew she was right. They couldn't afford to be distracted. Besides, there were too many people who might see. It would make things awkward with the crew if people found out.

It was better this way. It wouldn't be too long until they were back in L.A. and could do whatever they wanted.

***

Jon Chevalet locked up the Medieval History exhibit and hobbled down the hall, his crutch clunking loudly against the marble floor. He nodded to the security guard as he passed.

It was a good fifteen minutes that he stood on the curb and waited for Shelly to pick him up. He would be glad when he could drive for himself again.

I still can't believe you broke your leg, you big dummy. He hadn't broken his leg since he was sixteen—thirty-five years ago now. Then, it had been skiing with a group of friends. This time, it was falling off a ladder while trying to patch a spot on his roof.

The cast was scheduled to come off in the morning, but then he had to transition to a boot, and it would still be awhile before the doctor gave him the okay to drive.

He was taking the rest of the week off. It was well past time he had a break, anyway. He hadn't taken any vacation days since his and Shelly's anniversary eight months ago.

A whole list of projects around the house was waiting to get done—roof chores excluded, of course.

There were a few people he needed to go see, too—some business contacts and some old friends that he hadn't had time to catch up with in way too long. Maybe after he got his cast off, he'd see if Shelly wanted to go with him to take Frank Lengel out to lunch.

The minivan pulled up, and Shelly pressed the button to automatically open the passenger side sliding back door.

Jon leaned heavily on his crutches and pulled himself into the van, stretching his cast out in front of him.

"Hey, Sweetheart, how was your day?" he asked as the door slid shut.

Shelly bit the inside of her lip.

"What is it? What's wrong?" Jon asked, suddenly concerned.

A tear formed at the corner of Shelly's eye, and she blinked it away as she turned out of the parking lot onto the street.

"Not here," she whispered hoarsely. "We'll talk at home."

They drove home in silence, Shelly weeping softly in the front seat, and Jon fidgeting in the back. The short drive seemed to last forever.

Finally, they were home, and Jon hobbled into the kitchen. Shelly sat down at the table and buried her head in her hands. Jon sat across from her, stroking her arm. He didn't press her—she would tell him whatever it was when she was ready.

At last, Shelly raised her head and looked at him through her tears.

"The cancer is back," she said.

Jon's arms dropped to his sides. The words didn't seem to make sense. They jumbled around in his ears, but refused to form into a cohesive thought. "What?" he breathed.

Shelly nodded. "It's back."

Jon closed his eyes, willing the tears away, but not before one escaped and rolled down his cheek. He took a deep breath, and opened them again.

"Okay, Sweetheart, then we'll just have to deal with it. We got through it once. We'll do it again."

Shelly shook her head. "It's worse now. And it's spreading too quickly. They can try some treatments, but the doctors don't have much hope."

Jon knew better than to try to tell her things that weren't true, like that everything would be all right, or that it wasn't as bad as it sounded. It *was* that bad.

94

"How long does the doctor think you have?" he asked quietly.

"A month or two at the most. Maybe less," she whispered.

The bottom seemed to drop out of his stomach. Months? Or less? No. That couldn't be right.

He wasn't ready.

"What—what treatments did they suggest?"

"Jon, I... I don't want to fight it this time. I don't want to spend my last months so sick I can't function. I don't want to give either of us false hope."

"But we could extend—"

She placed a hand gently on his lips. "What is the point of extending if the extension is spent in a hospital bed? I don't want to go out like that. I don't want you to remember me strapped to a bed. Let's take the time to do some of those bucket list things we always promised we'd do when you retire. I want to enjoy what time I have left with you."

Jon stood on his good leg and pulled Shelly into his arms. "I love you," he whispered into her hair as she wept on his shoulder.

***

Portland, Oregon

Carole picked up the phone and took a deep breath. She needed to do this now, or she never would.

She could hardly believe it had only been two days since she moved out of the apartment. Seth had called a few times, but she ignored her phone each time and erased his messages. They all said the same thing—how sorry he was, how he wanted her back, how if she would just give him one more chance...

She needed to make this call before she lost her resolve and gave in to Seth's pleas. She dialed the number.

"Dr. Lengel, please," she said.

A *click* as she was put on hold, a brief interlude of soft jazz music, and then another *click* as it was picked up.

"Dr. Lengel," the voice on the other end answered.

"Hello, Dr. Lengel, this is Carole McCray."

"Carole, how are you? It's been awhile. What can I do for you?"

"Well, I was actually wondering if that job offer you made is still open."

"Absolutely. I told you before, any time you change your mind, you can have a job with us."

"Good, because I changed my mind."

She heard the guffaw on the other end. "I never thought I'd see the day! How soon can you start?"

"I just gave my notice at my job, so I have two weeks left there. I'm planning to move as soon as I'm done working."

"Excellent. I can't wait to finally meet you in person, Miss McCray. Is there anything I can do for you in the meantime?"

"I'm going to need an apartment. Preferably something close to the office."

"I don't know of anything myself, but I do know an excellent Realtor. I'll give him a call. Do you mind if I give him your number so he can contact you?"

"That will be fine."

"Excellent. Anything else I can help you with?"

"Not that I can think of, but I'll let you know," she said. "Oh, and Dr. Lengel, I have a few new pictures that I think you'll be interested to see."

"I can't wait. I'll see you in a couple of weeks."

Carole hung up the phone and inhaled slowly, allowing her breathing to slow and her shaking hands to settle. She hated making new plans. She hated having to figure all this out on her own. She hated change.

Closing her eyes, she went to her calm place—a campsite in a forest, where the sounds of birds and insects were the only noise, and the sun in a blue sky warmed her. She went through the exercises to calm her mind and stave off an anxiety attack.

When the panic was subdued, she opened her eyes and allowed herself to feel.

This was a big step. And it was done. It was okay to embrace the feelings, both good and bad, but especially to allow herself to be excited about the possibilities of a different future than the one she'd planned in her head.

She'd made the commitment, now. The hard part was over. She was really going. She could feel the excitement creeping up to cover her anxiety.

A smile tugged at the corners of her mouth as she thought about the next step in her life's adventure.

Chapter Twelve

Los Angeles, California

Jeremiah looked up at the sound of a knock on his door. "Come in."

Dr. Lengel waddled in and sat in the chair across from Jeremiah's desk. "Well, what do you think of her?"

Jeremiah smiled. "I haven't decided yet."

Dr. Lengel chuckled. "Any first impressions?"

"Actually, I thought she'd be a boy. With a name like Randi. Now that I know she's not, it explains a lot. Like why you sound like you're in love with her when you talk about her."

Dr. Lengel laughed. "Maybe I am a little. At any rate, I think she'll be good for us."

"I have yet to see if she can actually do any work."

"Yes, well, I have high hopes for her. I got a call today from Carole McCray."

"The photographer?"

Dr. Lengel nodded.

"Does she have something new for us?"

"Even better. She's coming to work for us."

"Really? Last time you talked to her she made it sound like this was a job she'd never even consider."

Dr. Lengel shrugged. "Something changed her mind, apparently. She'll be moving down here in a couple of weeks. I'm giving Brian a call tomorrow to have him look up some apartments for her."

"Wow. Things are really coming together all of a sudden."

Dr. Lengel rubbed his hands together. "I know. It'll be exciting to see what we accomplish here in the near future."

"Indeed." Jeremiah hid the thoughts that churned in his mind as Dr. Lengel prattled on. These types of things were not coincidental. Someone was pulling strings—he was almost certain. And he did not trust the people capable of manipulating these events. So who were they controlling? Randi or Carole? Or both? And how could he warn Dr. Lengel to be cautious of both without revealing too much?

"Well, I'm headed home," Dr. Lengel said at last. "Don't let the new kid work herself to death her first night, okay?"

"Sure," Jeremiah smiled. "I'll kick her out when I leave."

A few hours later, he locked his office door and walked across the hall to Randi's office. Randi sat at her desk, absorbed in her reading. He tapped on the doorframe.

Randi jumped and looked up, eyes wide.

"It's just me," Jeremiah said.

"Oh." She exhaled deeply. "I thought I was alone. Come on in, Dr. Bryant—I mean, Jeremiah. What can I do for you?"

Jeremiah perched himself on the edge of her desk. "You know, you're not getting fired, and you don't have anything to prove."

She stared at him, clearly confused. "What?"

"Go home."

She glanced at her watch. "Holy cow!"

Jeremiah laughed.

"What?" she asked, her cheeks reddening.

"Nothing. I just haven't heard anyone say *holy cow* in a really long time."

Randi giggled. "That probably makes me sound about twelve years old. I just didn't realize how late it was. The more I read of this stuff, the more interesting it gets."

"It tends to grow on you, but you have the rest of your life to get into it. You don't have to do everything tonight."

Randi smiled and stood up. "Well, I know why I'm here late. What's your excuse?"

"Nothing, really. Just waiting until—" He glanced at the door. "Come on,

I'll walk you to your car."

"Waiting until someone else left so you didn't get stuck walking her to *her* car?" Randi suggested.

Jeremiah studied her for a long moment. "You're a very perceptive girl."

"I'm not a *girl*. Besides, it doesn't take a lot of perception to see Maria is completely infatuated with you."

Jeremiah snorted. "She thinks she's in love with me."

"You disagree?"

"It isn't love. She's just enamored with me because I'm the only man in California who hasn't slept with her."

Randi bit her lip. "I see."

He led her out the door and locked it behind them.

"Does ignoring her help? I mean, couldn't you at least be a little nice to her?"

Jeremiah shrugged. "It's better than leading her on. I can't help that she's attracted to me. I'm probably the best guy she's been around, but I'm not going to let her think there's a chance just so she'll feel better about herself."

"You're *so* obviously the greatest guy ever, it's no wonder she's so obsessed. And humble, to boot."

Jeremiah studied her for a moment. "Apparently you think it would be better to pretend I don't know and appreciate how I'm built. Should I pretend to be ignorant of my looks, or sorry for my brain? False humility is far worse than blunt honesty."

"That doesn't mean you have to brag."

"Well, we clearly have very different ideas of what bragging is."

Randi rolled her eyes and walked away. "Good night. I'll see you tomorrow."

Jeremiah watched her get into a car that had to be nearly as old as she was.

"You're driving that thing?"

She raised an eyebrow. "No, actually I had the floor removed. I'm just going to walk it home, Flintstones-style."

"Sorry, I just meant—"

"See you tomorrow," she called over her shoulder.

He waited until she pulled away before getting in his car. He wasn't sure he liked that girl. He might have to have a chat with Dr. Lengel if she didn't remember her place.

***

Jon's heart nearly burst at the sight of the bright face Shelly put on the next morning as she accompanied him to have his cast removed, and then on to the office of the American Cryptozoological Society. They entered the office arm-in-arm, smiling at each other.

"Is Dr. Lengel in?" Jon asked the receptionist.

"May I tell him who's here?"

"Dr. Chevalet," Jon answered.

"One moment, please."

She pressed the intercom button to announce him, and a few moments later Frank Lengel burst through the door.

"Jon, it's good to see you! Shelly, you're as beautiful as ever. Please, come in, come in."

He bustled his visitors into his office. "It's been too long. Tell me, how are things down at the museum?"

Jon launched into a diatribe about the new management, and how they claimed to want to increase revenue while doing a litany of things that were nearly guaranteed to drive away the faithful staff who kept the place running, grateful to have a topic that didn't revolve around Shelly's illness.

A short while later, there was a knock at the door.

"Come in," Dr. Lengel called.

A young woman poked her head in.

"Oh, excuse me," she said, seeing the Jon and Shelly seated in the chairs. "I didn't mean to interrupt, I just wanted to borrow a book."

"You're not interrupting at all, Randi," Dr. Lengel said. "Come in, I want you to meet my good friend Dr. Jon Chevalet. He's the head of the paleontology department at the Los Angeles Museum of Natural History. This is his wife, Shelly."

Randi stepped into the room, and shook the hands that Jon and Shelly extended.

"Head of paleontology?" Randi asked. A smile blossomed on her face. "May I run something by you?"

"Certainly. What is it?"

"I'm working on a theory having to do with the existence of dragons. My theory is that, while it is possible that some of the accounts of dragons in the

100

folklore of various people groups are exaggerated, for the most part, those legends and stories are based on factual accounts."

Jon nodded, intrigued. "Go on."

"Now, what I want to know is, from a paleontology point of view, is there any evidence that might suggest that this theory is plausible?"

"Well, she certainly doesn't waste any time, does she?" Jon chuckled.

Dr. Lengel beamed proudly at his protégé. "Why do you think I was in such a hurry to hire her?"

Dr. Bryant poked his head in the door and stood leaning against the doorpost with a self-confident air, silently listening to the conversation.

Jon gave him a polite nod—he'd never particularly liked Frank's partner, but he was good for the occasional debate—and turned back to Randi. "Well, before I get myself into trouble, I need a more specific question. What exactly are you wanting to know?"

Randi paused. "Okay, I'll break it down into two basic questions: Is it possible that some form of dinosaur-like creature could have breathed fire, and is it possible that dragons are an undiscovered species of dinosaur?"

Jon took a deep breath. He'd encountered this sort of question before, of course. The desire to believe the fantastical was common, but usually expressed by young children or the artsy type, not serious scientists. "Short answer, yes, it is possible. Long answer, well, let's see. As for breathing fire, it is very difficult to say with any certainty. The fact is that we have no animals living today that can duplicate such a feat, and so we have no way of knowing what kind of biological compounds would be necessary for such a task."

He raked a hand through his thinning hair before going on. "There are, in fact, several theories on the matter, based largely on the species that we can study, like the bombardier beetle, and various facts we know about combustion. Some of the ideas range from combustible gasses in the animal's stomach erupting when they combine with oxygen, to the friction of pieces of flint that the animal has consumed igniting organic compounds that are part of the animal's diet, and more, but there's nothing to suggest it has ever actually happened."

Randi leaned forward, her eyes intent on his face.

Jon coughed. "The final conclusion, then, is that there can be no final conclusion because there is not nearly enough evidence. Now, as for whether or not dragons could be an undiscovered species of dinosaur, I would have to say it is not probable. I won't say impossible, because there are discoveries being made every day, but the fact is we have as yet never found any fossils that even remotely resemble the descriptions of dragons. We have uncovered multiple examples of the known species of dinosaurs, but it is very, very rare anymore that we discover something completely new."

"What if there's nothing in the fossil record because it post-dates fossils? If my theory is correct and they existed during the course of human history, then it's possible they didn't exist when fossils formed."

Jon sat up a little straighter. "Now, that is interesting. If their specific adaptations developed after... It's interesting, but I would have to see a lot more evidence before getting on board with that explanation. The fossil record would have *something*, at some point, that would indicate a transitionary species."

Randi nodded, looking as though she was resigned to his explanation, but not fully convinced. She smiled and extended her hand again. "Thank you for your insight. It was nice to meet you." She found the book she was looking for on one of Dr. Lengel's shelves, then edged past Dr. Bryant and disappeared.

Jon turned to Frank. "I like her."

Frank grinned. "Me too. But enough of that—tell me, what else is going on?"

***

Near Shell, Wyoming

"Dr. Monroe, you'd better come have a look at this," José, the young paleontology student said.

"What is it?" Djazani asked.

"I'm not sure," he answered. "There's just something weird about these fossils."

He led her to the area where he had been working and pointed out the outline of the bones that he was uncovering. "Look at this, coming off the shoulder here. I was tracing my way along the shoulder, and I came across this bone protrusion here. It seems to angle away this direction, but I'm not sure how far it goes. It could be something else, something that just happened to be fossilized nearby, but it looks like it's attached to the shoulder bone here."

Djazani studied the area carefully. She borrowed the student's tools and brushed away some dirt.

"You're right. Follow it, and see how far it goes. It may be some sort of bone spur or abnormal growth. Keep trying to uncover it until you can figure out what it is."

"Yes, ma'am." José took the tool she handed back and returned to work.

Djazani walked around the site, helping here, observing there, and giving advice when asked. Her crew knew their jobs, and she tried not to interfere unless she noticed something going wrong.

After walking around awhile, she found an area near the tail to work on. After weeks of work, the outline of the fossil was now more than halfway visible, and there were lots of areas where it was excavated almost all the way through to the other side.

Djazani worked her way down the tail, hoping to find the end of it. "That's odd," she muttered aloud. "It's a little longer and thinner than I would expect on a deinonychus of this size."

Finally, she reached the tip. Another sort of bone spur, shaped almost like an arrowhead, tipped the end of the tail.

Interesting.

Perhaps this particular dinosaur had had some sort of disease, some sort of condition that caused the bone spurs to grow.

Standing, she brushed the dust from her shorts and stretched. She paused for a moment with each of the people working on the dig, mentioning the abnormalities and instructing them to inform her if they found more. She stopped next to the man who was working at the top of the dinosaur's head.

"Huh," he grunted when she had explained her findings.

"What?"

"Well, it's just funny you should mention that now. I came across some odd bone protrusions on the top of the head a little while ago. Didn't really strike me as important enough to interrupt you for, but I was going to mention it tonight."

"Really? Show me."

He pointed out the faint line he had traced around what appeared to be a large bone spike rising out of the back of the head, and another just behind it at the base of the skull.

Djazani traced her finger along it. They almost seemed like Stegosaurus spikes, only smaller, and shaped sort of like a curved knife blade.

"See how much of that you can uncover," she instructed him. "Find out how wide they are and how many there are. If there are any going down the neck try to establish a pattern—see if they are regular and naturally-occurring, or random like a disease."

"What are you thinking?" he asked.

"I'm wondering if maybe this isn't a deinonychus after all."

He nodded and turned back to his work. She watched him for a few moments until a sound overhead caused her to look up. The Bureau of Land Management plane circled overhead as a photographer tried to capture the dig site from above. He'd been down at the site taking pictures of the progress from time to time, as well.

She had seen some of the pictures at an earlier stage of the dig, but it was hard to see anything but rocks and sand and bodies of people hunched over, hard at work. She wondered what it looked like now, when so much more was uncovered.

Her thoughts were interrupted by a shout.

"Dr. Monroe!"

It was José.

She walked over to where he stood. "What is it?"

"Look at this," José shouted excitedly. "This isn't a bone spur. It's a *wing*."

A gasp escaped Djazani's lips as she followed the line of bone that rose up out of the shoulder of the dinosaur. A series of thin bones lay stacked gently across the space where the back would have been, as if the wing had been folded down in rest when the creature died.

Djazani could do nothing but stare at it for a long time.

"What do you want me to do?" José finally asked.

"Keep working. See if you can uncover the entire wing, and try to figure out how it would have unfurled, and how big it would have been." She grabbed her tools and settled in to work with him.

She stayed at the same spot for several days, until they'd uncovered enough of the fossil to get a better idea of the full picture.

A few evenings later, she contacted the Bureau of Land Management.

"Is there any chance we can get the photographer back to take more pictures of the dig site? I'd like to see what it looks like now."

"Yes, ma'am," the voice on the other end crackled.

The photographer returned the next day, circling the site and taking aerial photographs, then joining Djazani in the command tent. She quickly pulled out her laptop and set it on the desk.

"Give me your memory card. I want to see these pictures on a full screen," she said.

He complied, and Djazani began the process of downloading the pictures onto her laptop.

Her fingers drummed an uneven tattoo on the weathered wood of the desk.

37%. 54%. 71%.

Tap, tap, tap.

She bit the end of her thumb. The feeling she had earlier of anticipation multiplied a hundred fold as she waited for the pictures to show up on her screen.

86%. 98%.

At last a picture appeared on the screen. She sucked in her breath sharply as she carefully examined each picture.

"Hey, you know what that looks like?" the photographer said suddenly.

"Yes," Djazani breathed. "I do."

Chapter Thirteen

Los Angeles, California

The door to Randi's office stood open, as did Jeremiah's, and Randi heard him moving around. Ignoring the distraction, she focused on putting together the file on her dragon research, both electronic and paper copies. Dr. Lengel liked the tangibility of paper files, even though he understood the importance of backups.

Nik texted her. *How's the new job?*

She paused work to reply. *So far so good. Heading to the library in a bit.*

Cool. I have to go there today, too. Maybe I'll see you.

She didn't bother to reply. She had too much to get done. After she gathered everything she could for the moment, she went to knock on Dr. Lengel's door.

At his invitation to come in, she poked her head in the door. "I'm going to run out for a couple of hours. I need to get some stuff for my dragon file at the university library. I want to make photocopies of some of the hard copy resources I used in my thesis."

"Have fun."

Jeremiah stepped out of his office. "Do you mind if I come along? There are a few things I want to look into."

The tone of his voice suggested it wasn't really a question so much as a polite way of informing her he was coming along anyway. Randi *did* mind, but she couldn't really say anything. "Sure. Come on."

Maria practically leapt from her desk toward him. "Dr. Bryant, you have that teleconference in half an hour."

"Reschedule it for me for tomorrow, would you?" He nodded toward Randi. "I'll drive." He preceded her out of the office and held the door for her.

Randi didn't miss the glare Maria threw her way as they left. She waited until the door swung shut behind them before turning to Jeremiah. "Are you trying to make her jealous?"

"What? Who?"

"Maria. Didn't you notice how angry she looked when you left with me?"

"To be perfectly honest, I wasn't paying any attention to her at all. So no, I didn't notice."

She wanted to ask if the only person he paid any attention to was himself, but she bit back the words. "You know, if you just spent a little time getting to know her, you might not be so antagonistic toward her. You might even like her."

Jeremiah paused a moment, unlocking the car door for her, before speaking. "We have nothing in common and no potential for anything beyond a working relationship, so I don't see the value in fostering a fruitless connection."

Randi waited until he was seated beside her and began to drive. "You don't care that she's a person? I get the impression this job is all she has. She doesn't ever talk about anyone outside work, she stays late, and she clearly admires you. Who knows what kinds of things she's dealing with, and you could be someone who could help."

"If she is hurting, it is due to the consequences of her own actions, and is therefore no concern of mine. Moreover, if I try to help her, it would only succeed in either endearing myself more to her or embittering her toward me, neither of which I have any interest in doing."

Randi looked away and bit her lip. She was having trouble thinking of a comeback.

Jeremiah glanced at her sideways as he drove, a smile twitching at the side of his mouth. His expression clearly said he knew he'd won the argument.

Randi turned to look out the window. *I have never met such an ego!*

She sat in silence until they finally arrived at the library and could go their separate ways. She gathered a stack of books she'd used for her thesis and went to the photocopier to make copies of the pages she found most useful during her research, which she would then upload to her file.

Someone came up behind her and put warm hands over her eyes. "Guess who."

"Hi, Nik."

Nik lowered his hands and stood beside her. "So. It's been what, like three weeks since I've talked to you? Tell me all about the job."

"I really like it," Randi grinned. "I can't believe how fascinating everything is. I'm learning a lot, and I've found even more information on my dragons."

"Well, I'm glad you're enjoying it." He hovered near her while she made copies, occasionally asking about her job or telling her about his new internship at the Palmer Lab, but mostly just sitting quietly by her side.

After awhile, Dr. Bryant came over and touched Randi's arm. "I've got the things I need. How much longer do you think you'll be?"

Randi looked up. "Just a couple more minutes."

"Hi, I'm Nik." Nik thrust out a hand.

"Oh, I'm sorry. Nik, this is one of my bosses, Dr. Bryant. Jeremiah, this is my good friend, Nik Gary."

Dr. Bryant shook Nik's hand. "Nice to meet you. Randi, I'll be right over there. Come get me when you're ready to go."

He wandered away, and Nik spun around to face Randi. "Why didn't you tell me about him?"

"Tell you *what* about him?"

"That he's young and hot, for one thing!" Nik snapped.

Randi rolled her eyes. "Well, I didn't think you'd be interested in him like that."

"*I'm* not, but I am beginning to think *you* are."

"Well, I'm not."

"Then why did you try to hide it from me?"

Randi whipped around to glare at him. "I didn't try to hide anything. I've barely even talked to you since I started working there, and I didn't think he was important enough to mention."

"Why wouldn't a *little* detail like you working for *that* guy be important to me?"

"Wow, double-standard much? You have study dates every night of the week, but I'm supposed to not have male coworkers?"

"I do not, and I haven't been on an actual date in months. And it's not the fact that you work with him, it's that you tried to keep it a secret."

"Why do you even care?" People were starting to stare. Randi lowered her voice. "You basically told me when I said I was taking this job that you lost all respect for me and we had nothing in common anymore."

"That is not what I said. And just because we had a fight doesn't mean you should rebound with the first guy that comes along."

Randi crossed her arms in front of her chest and glared at him. "I'm not your girlfriend, Nik, so I really don't appreciate his whole angry boyfriend routine you've got going on."

Nik stepped back and lowered his eyes. "I'm sorry. I just—"

"Whatever. It's fine. But I really am *not* interested in Dr. Bryant, okay? Not at all. It will never, ever happen."

"Fine. I believe you."

"Thank you."

"Hey, it's time for me to fly, but you wanna hang out this weekend?"

"Sure. Give me a call."

"Will do." Nik strode away, his head held high.

She watched him leave, emotions she couldn't quite define tumbling around inside her, then went to find Jeremiah. One look at him and she couldn't help but laugh at Nik's assumptions. Sure, he was good looking, but *ew*. His superiority complex alone was enough to send her running without ever looking back.

***

Near Shell, Wyoming

"Okay, people, listen up," Djazani called out.

The crew of paleontologists, interns, students, and others gathered in under the awning, their attention focused on Djazani.

"I know you're all excited about what we've found, but let me stress that the evidence is far from conclusive, and we still really have no idea what we're dealing with."

110

A handful of people tossed each other significant glances.

"The anomalies we've found so far could easily be explained. It's entirely possible that we are dealing with the fossils of two completely different known creatures, somehow juxtaposed together." She raised a hand to silence the murmur of dissenting voices that rose up. "However, it is also possible that we are dealing with a yet unknown species. While it may be just an odd find, it may also be one of the greatest scientific discoveries of our time."

A cheer rose up, and Djazani couldn't help but grin in response.

She raised her voice to be heard above the voices of the others. "That being said, this is now a closed site. That means no more tourists, no more field trips, no more scientist-for-a-day groups."

Another cheer. Everyone hated the tourists that got in the way and tried to tell the real scientists how to do their jobs.

Djazani wasn't done. "It also means that everything that happens on this site is classified, so no going back and calling your partner to tell them all about it. I'm currently in the process of arranging things with the Bureau of Land Management to officially close this site and restrict access to those of us that are here right now. So, until we can get past the bureaucracy, we're going to take a break. I expect to have everything taken care of this afternoon, so take the rest of the day off and be ready to come back early tomorrow morning, so we can uncover this baby!"

A loud roar swelled at this, and Djazani knew it wouldn't be long before most of the people here were drunk.

It was a big deal. Bigger than anything most of them could have ever expected to experience in their lifetimes.

"One more word of caution," she shouted, and everyone stopped for a moment to listen. "Since this is a closed site, if any of this information is leaked out—*at all*—the person who did the leaking will be looking at an arrest, as well as a court order not to breathe another word. Thank you."

The crew wandered away, some laughing nervously at the mention of a gag order, but most of them talking excitedly among themselves. Years from now, their names could be in science textbooks as the crew who uncovered the first fossil of—of whatever it turned out to be.

***

The Director glared at the phone. There was too much to do to be interrupted by that incessant jangling. It was the agent working on the dig in Wyoming. Normally this sort of thing would be routed through a supervisor, but the Director wanted to keep close tabs on the dig. As long as the agent followed protocol, at least.

The Director answered. "This had better be important."

"There was an interesting development at the dig today."

"Interesting how?"

"Well, the fossil we're uncovering is not a deinonychus."

"Are you certain?"

"As certain as I can be without conclusive tests. The specimen is complete and intact, as far as I can tell. A fossil in such good condition is a very rare find."

"Well, if it's not a deinonychus, what is it?" the Director demanded.

"Well, that's the thing. It's not anything that's currently in our fossil records."

"What do you mean?"

"Just what I said. It cannot be identified using the current fossil record."

"You mean you don't know what it is? It doesn't look familiar to you?"

"Well, I wouldn't exactly say that."

"Then you do recognize it?"

"In a manner of speaking, yes."

"Explain yourself. What does it look like?"

"It looks like a dragon," the agent said.

The Director sucked in a breath. All the speculation, all the hopes and expectations, really hadn't been adequate to prepare for the reality. This news couldn't be kept under wraps long. The Syndicate had to take control of the information. It was vital to the Wyvern Initiative. And Wyvern was vital to the survival of the Syndicate, and its eventual rise to dominance.

No longer would their dealings be in secret. They would be the foremost authority, and this fossilized dragon was the first step. "Close that site immediately! Don't let anyone else in or out."

"Already taken care of."

"Good. Keep it that way. I'll fly out there as soon as I can."

Chapter Fourteen

The Rainforest near Ouesso, in the Sangha region of Congo, Africa

"I can't believe I let you talk me into this." Naomi trudged up the steep hillside behind her brother.

Albert turned and extended his hand to help her up the slippery path. It could hardly even be called a path. A game trail is what the French would call it. Grabbing his hand, she glared at him.

"Just like a woman—blaming me when it was your idea," Albert muttered, but with an indulgent smile.

When they were alone, they spoke in Baka, not French, although they were fluent in both. Their father, Kudabah, had insisted that all his children have a formal education. He was one of the few who could afford to send his children to the city for school, although there were several villages that had mission schools. Giving his children a Western education was a status symbol he'd worn proudly.

Kudabah had made his money guiding scientists, researchers, and tourists up to the mountain lakes in search of Mokele-mbembe, the one-who-stops-the-flow-of-rivers.

Naomi and Albert used to laugh at the stories their father would tell after returning from a "safari" or "expedition," as the Westerners called it. The large, ungainly, pale-faced people always expected to be the first to make a discovery. They tried to take pictures and videos, which of course never came out well, wanting to capture the evidence of a creature they assumed to be quite mysterious, that was really quite commonplace among the Baka people.

She had only seen Mokele-mbembe a few times, but she knew it to be real, whereas the Westerners seemed to think it a great adventure to seek the creature out. Every time she thought about it, she marveled at their arrogance—to think that they could outsmart a creature that had survived through the ages by remaining elusive. Did they really think Mokele-mbembe wouldn't know he was being tracked?

Naomi stepped across the small stream that made a squishy mud track across the trail and paused to take a breath, wondering again why they were doing what they were doing. The creature they sought was far more elusive than Mokele-mbembe. It was to the Baka what Mokele-mbembe was to the Western world—a figment, a fantasy, a tale told to children to make them behave. Most people, especially those who had been educated in Western schools, didn't believe in it at all. But Naomi and Albert knew it was real. Knew, because their father had seen it.

Kudabah came back from his last expedition wounded. He told everyone an elaborate tale about how Mokele-mbembe appeared. The rich Europeans he took frightened the creature, and it charged their campsite. Kudabah had been knocked out of the way and fell into the fire pit, scorching his leg and breaking his arm. The Europeans fled in all directions, and Mokele-mbembe disappeared into the forest. It was hours before Kudabah was able to round everyone up again and head back down the mountain. Rolling his eyes, he talked about the stupidity of Westerners—everyone else would have known not to anger Mokele-mbembe.

The Europeans returned to the city with tales of monsters and dragons.

When questioned by the many scientists and researchers, newspeople, and other curious members of society, however, Kudabah told the same story. They asked him why he thought that the Europeans would have thought it was a dragon. Falling over with uproarious laughter, he told how he had been telling the Europeans stories around the fire the night before, stories of Mokele-mbembe, and of Jengi, the Baka god, and of the many creatures that inhabited the deepest recesses of the rainforest. The Europeans, he concluded, must have let their imaginations run away with them, and thought Mokele-mbembe far more fearsome than he really was.

Although Kudabah always told this story with great belly laughs, he never took another group of explorers into the rainforest.

Then, just a few years later, when he was sick and knew he was going to pass away soon, he called Naomi and Albert to him and told them his secret. "I saw it. I saw the dragon. It is real!"

His voice was hoarse and raspy, and the sound of children shouting outside tried to drown him out, but his words were unmistakable.

Naomi and Albert gasped simultaneously.

With his dying breaths, he told his two oldest children the true story of what had happened that day, the last day he had gone deep into the forbidden parts of the forest.

We had spent almost a week at the feeding grounds by the lake, but still Mokele-mbembe refused to appear. He has gotten tired of Westerners coming to gawk at him and stays away when he knows we are near.

Finally, the Europeans promised me more money if I would take them deeper. I promised Jengi I would make atonement, but for the sake of my family, I did as they asked.

We went deeper and higher into the mountains than any of our people have gone, and finally we came upon a lake, nestled in a valley between two high peaks. The valley is guarded on three sides by high cliffs, marked with hundreds of caves in the side of the rock. We went up through the dense jungle that guarded the fourth side, following the stream that flowed from the lake at the top. I, of course, recognized the Mokele-mbembe feeding grounds, and pointed it out to the Westerners. We set up camp, and by dusk were quietly waiting for him to make his nightly feeding trip.

We saw several animals—mostly common forest animals, and some quite close to us, coming to feed and drink at the lake. Finally, our hopes were answered, and Mokele-mbembe lumbered out of the forest. The Westerners nearly jumped out of their skin in their excitement. It was all I could do to keep them quiet enough to keep from scaring him off. They tried to take pictures, but it was too dark too get any clear shots.

It was quickly becoming night, and our vision was obscured. The Westerners were focused on Mokele-mbembe. I was the only one who noticed the black shape rise up from out of one of the caves on the side of the cliff. I watched it for a few moments, thinking it an exceptionally large owl. It was coming straight toward us, growing larger as it came. Even in the darkness, it began to take shape, and in moments, it was close enough to see clearly.

I knew in an instant what it was—I recognized it from my ancestors' descriptions. It glided toward us, silently, as if not wanting to frighten its prey. Its mouth gaped open, baring long, shining fangs, and a forked tongue flicked out like a snake's. It was heading straight toward me, so quickly I couldn't even alert anyone.

I yelled and jumped out of its path, knocking over the man next to me. The beast swiveled around, moving its large body with alarming agility. Its tail lashed out at me, and I could hear the bones in my arm break.

The others had seen it by now, and we all ducked into the forest for safety, for the beast was too large to follow us into the dense undergrowth. It roared at us and sent a jet of flame in after us, scorching the trees. As I was the furthest behind, having been knocked over and injured, the flames burned me, as well. We made our way back down the mountain as quickly as we could in the dark, putting as much distance between us and the creature as was possible. I knew then that I had angered Jengi, and vowed never again to take Westerners into the sacred parts of the forest.

Kudabah died just a few hours later.

That was a little over a month ago. Since then, Albert had been obsessed with finding the creature, making plans almost immediately to leave. He hadn't told Mother, of course. She would only worry. The money Kudabah left her from his expeditions had left her comfortably settled, and she still had the smaller children to care for.

Their village, unlike many of the Baka tribes, had left behind their somewhat nomadic lifestyle in favor of settling in one place, but there was a longing deep within every Baka to retreat deeper into the rainforest, further away from civilization, living off the resources of the land. Albert used that as his excuse when he made plans to leave. He told Mother that he was going to find a place start a new village and to raise his own family, away from the infringement of Western society. He said he would return for a wife when he found a suitable location. Naomi knew the truth, however, and she insisted on accompanying him.

"What do I have here?" she'd demanded. "If I stay, my only hope is to get married, but I am already older than most girls are when they get married. I doubt any man would have me, now. I'll probably spend the rest of my life caring for the little ones until Mother is so old that I have to care for her, and when she is gone, I'll end up caring for the children of one of our sisters. I'm going with you."

Albert put his hands on his hips, the way he did when he was trying to assert his authority as the eldest. "It's too dangerous. I won't let you come."

"Then I'll tell Mother."

Albert's face fell. "I'll never be able to go if Mother finds out."

Naomi put her hands on her hips, throwing him a triumphant glance. He knew as well as she that the women in their society ruled the roost, as she had heard an American say one time. He would either have to submit to his mother's demands or run away and disgrace himself.

They both knew he would have to allow Naomi to come with him.

So there they were, trudging up the mountain, and for the thousandth time, Naomi wished she'd taken a little more time to think through this decision.

"It shouldn't be too much further," Albert encouraged. "Father said it was a three-day hike in this direction, and they arrived just before dusk. We are much faster than those Westerners, so we should easily be there by midday."

Naomi tried to find the sun through the dense branches. Wasn't it almost midday now? If Albert was right, it surely couldn't be too much more. She grumbled inwardly about her Western education, blaming her time away at school for the poor physical shape she was in.

They traveled steadily uphill, but the dense foliage made it impossible to see the top where the stream tumbled down out of the mountain lake. Finally, when Naomi thought she could not take another step, they rounded a bend and the lake came into view.

"There it is," Albert whispered.

Naomi scrambled up to her brother's side. It was just as their father had described. The clear water mirrored the brilliant blue sky. Fluffy white clouds hovered around the peaks of the jagged cliffs that rose on all sides around where they stood. Hundreds of caves nestled in the rock walls were clearly visible in the bright light of the day.

"Come on," Albert urged. "Let's climb up and check out one of those caves!"

"Absolutely not!" Naomi had to keep herself from shouting. "Are you insane? Do you remember what Father said about that thing? It could kill you in an instant, and if you climb up there, you'll have no place to run and hide."

"Yes, but Father also said it came out at dusk to hunt. It is probably sound asleep right now."

"And you don't think that you clawing your way up a cliff would wake it?"

117

Albert sighed. "Have it your way. We'll set up camp within the forest where we can still see, and wait to see if it appears at dusk. But, if we don't see one tonight, then I'm climbing up there tomorrow."

Naomi glared at him, but didn't argue. It was a fair bargain.

They set about building a *mongulu* to sleep in, and long before dusk, had a place to sleep and food roasting over a small fire.

As soon as they were done eating, they smothered their fire. Dusk came on, and they sat silently by the edge of the forest, watching and waiting for night.

Animals came to the edge of the lake to drink. After a while, Naomi saw Mokele-mbembe lumber up on the opposite side of the stream and lower his huge head into the water. Still they sat, for what seemed an eternity, waiting for the creature of legend to appear from one of the many caves in the cliffs.

***

Los Angeles, California

Randi sat in her office, browsing through one of the files Dr. Lengel had suggested might be useful in her research, the file on a creature called Mokele-mbembe. The native people in the Congo region of Africa were all familiar with the creature, which was described as something very similar to a brachiosaurus.

The idea that dinosaurs still roamed the earth intrigued her. It was fascinating to read the accounts of the local people, as well as Western eyewitnesses, some as recently as twenty years ago.

"Huh. This is interesting."

"What is?" Jeremiah asked.

Randi looked up, not realizing he'd heard her and come to her door.

"Oh, sorry, I didn't realize I said that out loud. This report I'm reading. I'm going through the Mokele-mbembe file, and I came across an interesting eyewitness report. Listen. 'Dr. Rosenbaum and I saw the creature, Mokele-mbembe. Despite the dim light, there is no doubt in either of our minds what we saw was, indeed, a dinosaur.'"

Dr. Lengel waddled in, squeezing beside Jeremiah just inside her door.

She read on as the writer described how their guide, Kudabah,

118

panicked and pushed him out of the path of a creature that flew toward them. "'It was like a flying reptile—similar to a prehistoric dinosaur—as we presumed Mokele-mbembe to be—swooping toward us like a giant bat in the darkness.' The writer and his partner escaped into the forest, but their guide was wounded."

Randi took a sip of the coffee on her desk. "Here's where it gets really weird, though. 'We immediately took the three-day journey back to the guide's village, wondering all the while if we'd taken leave of our senses. Indeed, it seems we have, for Kudabah laughed and told us we were imagining things. He told the villagers that when we saw Mokele-mbembe, we yelled and made a frightful commotion and angered Mokele-mbembe, who attacked him and knocked him into our campfire, which is how he sustained his injuries.'"

"That *is* interesting," Dr. Lengel commented. "Seems to me I must have read that at some point, but I didn't think much of it at the time."

"Let me see," Jeremiah said.

Randi handed him the article. "Do you suppose there's a way we can get a hold of the author of this? Dr. Tanner Schleppenbach?"

"Please try," Dr. Lengel encouraged her.

"Don't overwork yourself." Jeremiah said. "Let me know if you need any help."

He was probably just trying to be polite, but he sounded patronizing.

Randi smiled. "I'm sure I'll be fine."

The others went back to their offices, and Randi commenced trying to track down Dr. Schleppenbach.

She got off the phone a few hours later and came to stand in the doorway of Dr. Lengel's office. Jeremiah came out into the hall, as well.

"Something's weird," she said.

"Weird how?"

"Well, this was written just a few years ago, but I've tried to contact everyone on that team, and I couldn't get in touch with *any* of them except one."

She adjusted her glasses. "I couldn't find any trace of Dr. Schleppenbach. It's as if he completely disappeared after he wrote that article. Besides him, there was Dr. Rosenbaum and five others—two wealthy eccentrics who

119

funded the trip and three who either worked with or for the doctors."

She went into Dr. Lengel's office and sat down. "Dr. Rosenbaum died in an accident a couple years later. Of the two who funded the trip, one is dead and the other is in a mental institution. As for the three others, one is a missionary in a remote part of India and is totally out of reach, one is dead, and the third is a highly-paid professor at some German university. He's the only one I actually talked with, and he claims he knows nothing of the incident."

Jeremiah came in and sat down beside her.

She glanced at him before turning back to Dr. Lengel. "Apparently he had remained back in the city of Ouesso gathering supplies and was going to meet up with them later. They came back before he went out to meet them. They all returned to Europe, and he hasn't seen or heard from any of the team members since." She rubbed the material of her shirt in her fingertips. "I'm not one to believe in conspiracy theories, but it does strike me as very strange that no one from this expedition is alive or can be reached."

Dr. Jeremiah eyed her. "You think someone is trying to cover up what they found?"

Randi shrugged. "I don't know what to think. It seems like a big coincidence that none of these people is still around and there's no trace of their trip left. I found some articles following up Dr. Schleppenbach's article by people who went back and talked to the guide. He had the same story every time, of Mokele-Mbembe, the fire, and the runaway imaginations of two highly respected doctors. I think I need to find Dr. Schleppenbach, but I don't even know where to start."

Dr. Lengel rubbed his fat hands together. "Well, keep trying. He has to be somewhere. If you can find him, this could be huge for us."

Chapter Fifteen

The Rainforest near Ouesso, in the Sangha region of Congo, Africa

Naomi's eyes began to droop. Ready to give up all hope of seeing the creature that night, she was just about to suggest that they turn in, when Albert reached out and grabbed her arm.

She followed his gaze. A black shape, like a large bat, rose into the sky, silhouetted by the half moon shining on the valley and reflected in the clear, still waters of the lake. Its wings stretched out, thin enough to see the bones stand out from the thin membrane against the light of the moon.

Naomi stifled a cough as a smell like sulfur invaded her nostrils. The creature soared overhead, then, with astonishing speed, swooped down toward the edge of the lake. It rose up a moment later, clutching a writhing animal in the talons of its hind feet. It was impossible to make out clearly, but both Naomi and Albert knew they were seeing what their father had described.

Suddenly, out of the corner of her eye, Naomi saw another dark shape gliding toward them. She stiffened as she watched it, clutching Albert's hand. He turned to look.

The beast came closer and closer. Had it seen or smelled them? Just as they were ready to dive for cover into the forest, the beast swerved and followed the stream down. With a sigh of relief, Naomi followed Albert's gaze back toward the sky above the lake. To her astonishment, they saw dozens more of the creatures, hovering like a thick swarm of bugs above the water. Some dove into the water and came up with large fish, and others caught prey from the water's edge, but most flew silently over the peaks in other directions or followed the stream down to other lakes.

Finally, the sky cleared, all of the creatures having gone back to their caves or on to different parts of the forest.

Naomi tugged at Albert's arm. She didn't want to be there when any of the creatures returned, especially if they happened to be unsuccessful at the hunt.

"Just a minute," Albert whispered.

"Let's get inside before they come back."

"They didn't see us before. We're safe enough."

"Come on—we've been hiking for three days. Aren't you tired?"

"Sure, but I couldn't sleep even if I tried."

Naomi sat back down, looking back and forth from Albert's face to the sky. Something whooshed in front of her. She grabbed Albert's arm, digging her fingernails in.

"It's just bat," Albert hissed.

Releasing his arm, she took a deep breath. Her heartbeat began to slow, and she sat still for another half hour or so.

"I don't think they're coming back any time soon, and I need some sleep. Are you coming?" She stood and started to walk away.

Albert sighed and followed her into the *mongulu,* and she soon heard his breathing become slow and steady. Despite how tired she was, however, it was a long time before she was able to sleep.

***

Los Angeles, California

Randi laid her head on her desk. How did someone just up and disappear without a trace? And why? Dr. Schleppenbach's last known address was in Germany, but that was over a year ago. And the only reason she found that out was because he'd moved suddenly, leaving his next-door neighbor, who knew him by the name of Tanner Schrodinger, to field inquiries when he didn't pay his bills.

"What's wrong?"

The sound of Jeremiah's voice startled her. She sat up and brushed her hair from her face.

"Nothing. I've just hit about a thousand dead ends. I cannot seem to track this guy down."

"Maybe you should go there."

"Go where?"

Jeremiah shrugged. "To the last place he was seen. See if you can find anyone who knows him."

"You mean just wander around Europe until I find someone who knows him?"

"If that's what it takes. Where was his last known residence?"

"Um… Germany somewhere. Potsdam, in the state of Brandenburgh. Potsdam. Why does that sound familiar to me?"

"I have no idea, I wasn't there for that."

Randi rubbed the scar on her hand, thinking. She smacked the desk. "No way."

"What?" Jeremiah asked.

"Hold on." She swiveled in her chair and grabbed her backpack from the shelf behind her. She yanked out her notebook, pulled the picture out of it, and handed it to Jeremiah.

"This is from your thesis. The picture that may or may not be of a fire-breathing dragon."

"Look at the back," Randi said.

Jeremiah flipped it over and read the note. "I received your inquiry. I hope this helps. –T. S."

"T. S. Tanner Schleppenbach? I think he may be the one who sent this picture to my dad. Hang on." She called her mom. "Mom, do you still have that envelope, the one that the picture came in?"

"I don't know, honey. I haven't touched anything in your father's office, so it's probably still there."

"Would you check for me? It would be on the top of his stack of mail."

Randi tapped the desk with her fingernails until her mother returned to the phone.

"I found it. What do you need?"

"What does it say on the postmark?"

"Potsdam, Brandenburg, Germany."

"Thanks, Mom, you're the best." She hung up the phone and grinned at

Jeremiah. "I was right. I'm sure Schelppenbach was the one who sent this to my dad. He saw it. He took a picture of it. You're right, I have to go to Germany."

Jeremiah uncrossed his arms. "I'll put together an expense budget and help you plan."

Randi stared after him as he went back to his office. She got to go track down a person who might be able to help her, *and* the Society would pay for it?

This was shaping up to be the best job in the world.

***

The Rainforest near Ouesso, in the Sangha region of Congo, Africa

A week after their arrival at the mountain lake, Naomi sat next to the stream, dipping her toes in, while Albert paced back and forth along the water's edge.

"I'm going up there," he said suddenly.

"No," Naomi practically shouted. "It's too dangerous."

"Naomi, we've been sitting here for a week. We've learned all we can by just sitting and watching them come out to feed. We know they're sleeping all day. It's perfectly safe. I'll be back before you know I'm gone," he promised.

Naomi was neither his mother nor his wife, and as much as she loved him, nothing she said was going to make him change his mind.

She followed him out of the forest and around the lake to the edge of the first cliff.

He reached for a rock that jutted out overhead. The handholds were plentiful, and there was a cave not too far—up and over less than twenty meters away.

"I'm not diving in to get you when you fall," Naomi threatened.

Albert grinned down at her. "I'm not going to fall."

Despite her threat, however, she watched closely at the edge of the lake as he scaled the cliff, angling over toward the first cave.

It was almost twenty minutes until he finally reached it. He pulled himself up to the edge and peered inside. He disappeared inside, emerging a few moments later.

"This one is empty," he called down. "It doesn't go very deep, and the ceiling is pretty low."

He sat on the edge, his feet hanging over, and massaged the muscles in his arms and legs.

"Come on down, then," Naomi called up.

"No way. I've come this far and I haven't found anything. I'm not coming back until I see one of those things up close."

He stood and shook out his limbs, then pressed into the rock wall and continued on to the next cave, further out and higher up.

He pulled himself up into the opening.

Naomi paced along the shore, but she couldn't see anything except the dark shadow of the cave's opening.

"Albert!" she yelled. "Come back!"

He appeared at the opening and shook his head at her, putting his finger to his lips to silence her. She glared up at him, but he didn't seem to care.

Turning, he went back into the cave.

It seemed like an eternity until he came out again.

He'd stuffed something into his T-shirt, in the back, tucking his shirt into his shorts to create a pouch for whatever it was he'd collected up there.

He crawled to the ledge and turned around, slowly lowering his feet until he found a foothold.

As long as it had taken him to get up, it seemed to take twice as long for him to make any progress coming down.

The weight of the thing on his back pulled at him, threatening to throw him off balance.

He placed his right foot into a small niche and started to lower his weight onto it, when the rock he was stepping on suddenly came loose. He clutched tightly with his hands, pushing his balance to his left leg as his right leg hung freely. The rock bounced off the side of the cliff as it fell and splashed with a reverberating echo throughout the valley.

Naomi screamed.

Somewhere up above, a screech rang out, a sound more terrifying than if a pride of lions attacked a herd of Mokele-mbembe and they all screamed at once.

Albert's movements quickened as he scurried down the side of the cliff.

Naomi stood watching, powerless to help him.

A sound like the wind rushing through the tops of the trees echoed in the lake crater, and a shadow overhead blocked out the sun for a moment.

The breath left Naomi's chest as the flying beast suddenly changed its course and headed straight for her.

"No!" Albert screamed.

The creature pivoted in midair and went rushing back toward him, the talons on its hind feet extended toward him.

Its claws reached Albert, and he was ripped away from the cliff's edge, but it must not have gotten a firm grip, because Albert's body fell, time seeming to stop as it plummeted toward the lake.

Chapter Sixteen

Portland, Oregon

Carole tucked a few final items into her purse. She'd finished packing the last of the boxes into the bed of her truck the night before.

Her boss, Candace, had found someone else to replace her sooner than expected, and had told Carole that she could leave without completing her last week.

Carole was ready. Beyond ready. Now that she'd made her decision to leave and had made the necessary preparations, she couldn't wait to go.

Her mom stood at the bedroom door in her bathrobe with a cup of coffee in a travel mug, waiting for Carole to finish the last few preparations.

"Thanks, Mom." She gave her mother one last hug.

She took the coffee mug from her mother's hand and pulled the hood of her sweatshirt up, ducking her head against the drizzling rain as she ran to her truck.

"Be careful, Sweetie. Call me when you get to Aunt Esther's."

Carole waved acknowledgement and climbed into her truck. "I'll see you soon."

"Bye, baby." Her mom waved, then disappeared inside and shut the door.

Carole started the truck, then flipped through her playlists. She needed something peppy and upbeat to wake her up and get her going this early in the morning.

She looked up and jumped as a face appeared at her window.

Her heartbeat slowed when she recognized Seth and she rolled down her window. "What are you doing here?"

"Where are you going?" he asked.

"L.A. What do you want?"

"L.A.? You're kidding, right?"

"Not kidding. I'm moving there. Now, get out of my way so I can go."

Seth's face fell and his eyes widened in a pathetic gaze. "You can't leave—I... I need to talk to you."

"It's a little late for that, Seth. I'm done talking to you."

She started to roll up the window, but Seth put his hand on top, and she stopped so she wouldn't smash his fingers.

"Wait. Please. I really want to talk to you."

She rolled her eyes. "Fine. Talk. You've got five minutes until I drive away."

"That doesn't really give me time to do this justice, but okay," Seth said. "Carole, I miss you. I was stupid, and I made the worst mistake of my life, and I swear to you it will never, ever happen again. I love you, and I want to be with you and only you for the rest of my life. Carole McCray, will you marry me?"

He pulled a velvet box from his pocket and opened it, handing it to her.

Inside was a gorgeous, emerald-cut diamond solitaire engagement ring.

Carole gasped.

She'd waited for this moment for years, dreaming of it, imagining exactly what he would say, how he would look, where they would be—and now here it was, and she didn't want it.

For the last week, thoughts plagued her mind of what she would do if he came begging for her to return. She'd endured many long hours while she was packing, many long nights alone since then, to consider this moment. She thought of a life with him, married to him, and remembered that moment when she walked into the apartment and saw him with the other woman. Not just this time, either, but the time two years ago when the same thing happened. Well, almost the same thing.

Then, it had been a friend who told her. The friend saw Seth and another girl at an expensive restaurant on a night when Seth said he was going out of town for the weekend to visit an old college friend.

Carole had called Seth on his cell phone early the next morning to ask him about it, and a woman answered the phone. The story he told was true, except that the old college friend was his ex-girlfriend, Kimberly. She'd told him then that if it ever happened again, their relationship would be over.

Carole gazed at the ring, unable to form a coherent thought. The brilliant diamond glittered despite the foggy light. It had not been cheap. He was trying very, very hard.

She could take him back. He would grovel for awhile, and things would be good. They would have fun and be in love.

It wouldn't last, though. Carole knew it wouldn't. She knew Seth too well. She knew that as soon as things got rough again, Seth would use the expensive ring as leverage, trying to justify whatever he did by saying, "Look how much I love you, I bought you that expensive ring," or something along those lines.

"Carole?"

Carole shook her head. "You don't really mean it."

"Of course I mean it. I wouldn't say it if I didn't mean it."

"Oh, I know you'd go through with it, but you'd always be waiting for something better just out of reach. You'd divorce me as easily as you married me if the right opportunity presented itself."

"That's not true."

Carole swiped at a tear. "Yes, it is. That's why you never wanted to get married before."

He started to speak, but she held up a hand to stop him. "I know what you're going to say. We don't need a piece of paper to prove our commitment to each other. And I guess you're right. You already aren't committed to me, and a piece of paper isn't going to make you not a cheater."

"I screwed up. I know I did. But I love you, and I want to be with you. Forever."

Did he know how tightly he was wringing her heart between his hands? She desperately wanted to accept the ring, to accept Seth back into her heart. But she wouldn't. She was stronger than that.

She took a deep breath and handed Seth the ring box. "Two weeks ago, I would have believed you. Two weeks ago, I would have said yes. But you ruined it, Seth. It's too late now."

***

Potsdam, Brandenburg, Germany

Rob stood in the lobby of the picturesque hotel while Randi Ross consulted the map on the wall. She looked like she'd be there awhile, so he called the Director. "She's been on a wild goose chase for three days. She visited the house where he lived, which is now inhabited by a family with four little brats. She talked to the neighbors, to the merchants in all the local businesses, to old colleagues, and there's no trace of him."

"Has she seen you?"

"Of course not. She has no idea I'm here."

"Good. Keep it that way. And, Rob? You know what to do if, by some miracle, she does manage to track down Schleppenbach?"

"Of course. I'll take care of it."

Rob followed Randi when she left, his face disguised by a false beard and a shaded by a fedora. He stayed several paces behind, just close enough to keep her in sight.

She went to a small café, where presently a middle-aged woman joined her. He couldn't hear the conversation, but he wasn't overly worried. If this lead panned out, he'd soon know, and he didn't want to risk Randi seeing him.

Randi and the other woman talked for over two hours, and Randi looked pleased when she and the woman finally parted. Perhaps it was worth noting. But he didn't want to call the Director with an update unless he had something solid.

He waited until Randi was half a block up the street before following her again.

***

Los Angeles, California

Jeremiah paced his office. It was the middle of the night in Germany, and Randi still hadn't called. Perhaps it was a bad idea to send her alone. She was young, inexperienced. What if something happened to her?

130

"Jeremiah, I'm heading home," Frank called out.

"Good night. I'm going to wait a bit more to see if Randi calls with an update."

The door swung closed and Jeremiah resumed his pacing.

Maria popped her head in his doorway. "You want some company?"

"No, you should go on home. Thanks."

Maria sniffed. "Is it because of *her*?"

"Is what because of whom?"

"You don't want to be with me because of Randi."

Jeremiah closed his eyes and took a deep breath. "I didn't want to be with you long before Randi came to work here. I still won't want to be with you if she moves on. There's nothing between us, Maria. Go home."

Maria stalked down the hallway, and a moment later the door slammed. He hoped that was clear enough for her.

The phone rang and he dove for it. "Randi?"

"I found him, Jeremiah. I mean, I haven't seen him yet, but I know where he is."

"Really? That's great news. Where is he? How did you find him?"

"He's in Switzerland. I talked to a former colleague of his. I think they had a relationship, but she didn't say for sure. Anyway, I showed her the picture Schleppenbach sent my dad, to prove I was who I said I was, and she told me how to find him. I'm going to head out tomorrow, on the earliest train. I'll let you know when I find him."

"Great, I look forward to hearing what you find out. And Randi?"

"Yeah?"

"Schleppenbach went into hiding for a reason. You don't know how he'll react when you find him, and you don't know who else might be looking for him. Be careful."

***

Potsdam, Brandenburg, Germany

Randi left before dawn the next morning and took the train to Switzerland. Dr. Schleppenbbach's colleague, Sylvia Rice, had given her specific instructions on how to get to the town where he currently lived. The train took her to a small substation near the base of the Alps, and then she had to hire a cab to drive her to the hamlet, nestled in the valley between two mountains.

The village felt like a scene straight out of Heidi, with its picturesque cottages and shops against the backdrop of snow-patched mountains. Randi directed the cab to drop her off in front of the small bakery along the main road, and from there she walked along the narrow, cobbled streets to the little house right in the middle of a row.

She made her way up the stone path and tapped at the door. A man who looked to be about in his sixties opened the door a crack and looked her up and down.

"Dr. Schleppenbach?"

The door slammed.

Randi tapped again.

No response.

"Dr. Schleppenbach, please, I need to speak with you."

She waited, but still he didn't respond, so she knocked again. "Dr. Schleppenbach, my name is Miranda Ross. I have a picture you sent my father, and I need to know if it's real."

The door opened the minutest crack. "You're Dr. Ross's daughter?"

Randi nodded. "He died almost three years ago, but I've been continuing his research." She pulled the picture from her backpack. "Did you send this?"

Schleppenbach opened the door just far enough to admit her, then slammed it and turned the deadbolt as soon as she was inside.

He reached for the picture. "You got ID?"

"What?"

"Identification. Do you have some? To prove you're who you say you are?"

Randi pulled out her passport and handed it to him.

"And you're Ross's daughter?"

Randi nodded again and took back her passport. She nodded toward the picture. "I found that in a pile of my dad's mail when I was going through his office last spring."

"He never knew." Schleppenbach sounded sad, defeated.

She shook her head. "If he had, he never would've committed suicide."

Schleppenbach's head snapped up. "Suicide?"

Randi nodded.

"Hm. Well, come in. As long as you're here, you might as well sit."

Randi sat on a worn, dusty couch in the front room. The shades were drawn, and the only light was a dim lamp in the corner.

"How did you know how to find me?"

"I spoke to Sylvia."

"I mean, how did you know I was the one who sent this to your father?"

"I didn't. It was more of an educated guess. I've been carrying that picture around with me since I found it, with no idea where it came from or who sent it. Then a few weeks ago, I came across an article you wrote about your experience in Congo. I tracked down everyone referenced in your article. They were all dead or insane or knew nothing, except you. You, apparently, ceased to exist. But you signed your initials, and your story fit with the picture. It was the only lead I had."

Schleppenbach touched the photo almost reverently. "If I hadn't had my camera out and ready, I never would've gotten this shot."

"So it was real? What you wrote in your article?"

"Of course it was real. It wasn't what we were looking for, it was even more surreal. We went into the Congo looking for Mokele-mbembe, and our guide took us to his watering hole, a three-day hike out from his village, at a mountain lake. Mokele-mbembe finally did appear, but then so did the dragons."

Randi leaned forward. "What happened?"

"The guide saw them coming. We were watching the water, and they flew down from the sky. He pushed us out of the way, and the dragon blew fire at us. The guide's arm got burned. He insisted from that point on that he fell in the campfire, even though we hadn't built one."

"Why didn't you ever go back?"

"The guide refused to take us. He insisted the jungle god was angry with us, and then he made up a story about Mokele-mbembe and the campfire, so no one believed us."

"But you still wrote that article."

Schleppenbach grunted. "I never should've written it. I should've followed Kudabah's example and kept my mouth shut about what we found."

"Why? This is a huge discovery, wouldn't you want everyone to know?"

Schleppenbach glanced around the room, as though to make sure they were alone. "*They* won't let that happen."

"Who are *they*?"

He peered at her, almost looking through her. "Are you daft? Didn't you see what happened to the rest of my team? Dead. Institutionalized. Bought off." He leaned forward, almost nose to nose with her. "Were you followed? Did you lead them here?"

"Who? What are you talking about?"

"The Syndicate! They've been following me, trying to find me, to keep me quiet. No doubt they're onto you, too." He jumped up and peeked out the window through a crack in the blinds. "I knew it. You brought them to me."

Was he insane? Or just paranoid?

She joined him at the window. A bearded man wearing a low-slung hat sauntered slowly up the street. "It's just someone taking a walk," she said.

"It's one of *them*. He's watching the house. You brought them here, and now your life is in danger, too."

"One of who? You haven't told me who—or what—the Syndicate is."

"Come, quickly, out the back."

"We're not in danger," Randi insisted. "He's just taking—"

Just then, the man turned, his eyes resting on the cottage with a seemingly casual glance, but his face turned enough to reveal a scar running down one cheek.

Chapter Seventeen

Randi gasped.

Schleppenbach looked at her. "You've seen him before."

Randi nodded. "At the café, where I met with Sylvia."

The man with the scar began to walk, slowly, nonchalantly, across the street toward them.

"Come on, out the back." Schleppenbach grabbed Randi's hand and tugged.

She grabbed her backpack from where it sat on the floor by the couch, and the picture Schleppenbach had set on the end table, and followed him out the back door and through the small yard.

A crash sounded from inside the house.

Schleppenbach broke into a run. He threw open the back gate. In the alley behind the house sat an old Volkswagen bug. Schleppenbach threw open the door and crawled through to the driver's side. "Get in," he shouted as he turned the key.

Before she had time to close the door, Schleppenbach stepped on the gas and tore down the alleyway. Randi glanced around in time to see the man with the scar burst from the back door of the cottage and aim a pistol at them.

He didn't fire, though. Perhaps they were too far away, or perhaps he didn't want to draw attention to himself. Whatever the reason, he turned and went back into the cottage.

"You need to get out of here," Schleppenbach told her. "Go home as soon as possible. They'll be watching your hotel—don't go back there. Stay in public places. Don't go anywhere alone."

"What about you?"

"Don't worry about me. I can disappear. You should do the same. And whatever else you do, drop this search. It won't end well."

"I'm not going to drop it. If I prove it and publicize it, they can't do anything about it."

Schleppenbach eyed her as he drove way too fast over the cobbled streets. "Are you sure you want to do that?"

"I'm sure."

"In that case, you're going to need to go see the creatures yourself. I'll tell you how to get there."

Two hours later, Schleppenbach dropped Randi off at a train station and saw her to a train bound for Berlin, where she'd board a flight back to the States.

He shook her hand. "Don't look for me again. In fact, you never found me in the first place."

***

Near Shell, Wyoming

Djazani sat in Administrator Schweitzer's makeshift office in his trailer just outside town.

She clasped her hands together to keep from tapping her fingers as he scanned the pages of her report and studied the pictures.

"Fascinating," he kept muttering under his breath, in between coughing fits. The lingering effects of his illness had kept him from being in the field, but he was still the supervising lead on the dig.

Finally, Djazani couldn't hold in her excitement any more. "Was I right, sir? Is this an undiscovered species?"

Administrator Schweitzer clucked his tongue. "It might be. Of course, tests will have to be done, and it will have to be authenticated. I want to have a look at it myself."

A ragged cough erupted from his mouth, his body shaking with the effort, and the top of his balding head shone with sweat.

A twinge of guilt that she was glad to have been the one to make the discovery struck her, but she couldn't help it. It was an amazing find, and it would be a turning point in her career if the fossil was found to be genuine. It would mark her as a legend in the world of paleontology.

"Still, from what I can see so far, it just may be a real find," Administrator Schweitzer went on.

Djazani couldn't hide her grin. "What is it? I mean, it's not in the fossil record, so what is it?"

"If it is genuine, my dear, that will be for us to decide," Administrator Schweitzer smiled. "Djazani's Dragon, eh?"

Djazani grinned even more widely. "I like the sound of that, sir."

Administrator Schweitzer chuckled. "Listen, Djazani, I want you to do something. Put the dig on hold for a few days. I'm going to invite a few other paleontologists and some other scholars out here. If this is what we think it is, we're going to want some reputable people out here to corroborate it."

"Of course," Djazani agreed.

"Thank you. We're going to need some biologists to verify that it is, or at least could be, a missing link between dinosaurs and birds, and so on. I'm going to call the university and get a few other professors out here, too. Tell everyone to take a few days off while I get things organized, and we'll pick up where we left off then."

"Yes, sir." Djazani fairly skipped out of the trailer and ran from there to the edge of town, where Kinte waited for her between two buildings.

She gave him a hug, unable to speak because of her excitement.

He grinned down at her. "Let us go get a drink."

"He said it just might be a real find!" Djazani grabbed Kinte's hand. "He said we would get to decide what it was, because we discovered it. Djazani's Dragon—that's what he suggested!"

Djazani knew she was babbling like a child, but she didn't care. She was much too excited to worry about appearances. She'd just made the discovery of a lifetime.

***

Los Angeles, California

By the time Randi got off the plane in Los Angeles, she had pretty well convinced herself that Dr. Schleppenbach's paranoia had rubbed off on her.

She didn't know who the man with the gun was—maybe Schleppenbach owed someone money.

But a secret organization that was trying to keep her from discovering the existence of dragons… well, it was exactly as plausible as it sounded when she said it out loud.

Schleppenbach made it sound like they were in a spy movie from the seventies, without cell phones or satellite imaging or credit cards or any of the other things people could use to track someone.

And he never did give her a motive—what possible reason could a covert organization have for keeping tabs on a discovery like this one? All it would take was one local with video footage to go viral, and the word would be out anyway. There was no reason she could fathom why anyone would try to kill Dr. Schleppenbach just to keep him quiet.

Secret societies simply didn't follow people around the globe and send assassins after historians and scientists.

She wasn't in danger, and she didn't need to keep looking at everyone she encountered like they might try to kill her at any moment.

Jeremiah was meeting her at the airport. He'd insisted on being the one to pick her up, even though she could've asked her mom or Nik.

He was waiting by the exit, just outside security, and looked visibly relieved when he saw her. He took her carry-on from her and looked her up and down, as though to make sure she was all in one piece. "You're okay? No more run-ins with that guy from Dr. Schleppenbach's house?"

Randi smiled. "I'm fine. Actually, I'm pretty sure it was nothing."

"What do you mean, nothing? The man pointed a gun at you. You recognized him. He was following you."

"Was he? I mean, Schleppenbach was so hard to find, and his house was all dark and mysterious, and then he asks if I was followed and there just happens to be someone out there. Looking back, I'm sure it wasn't even the same guy. He looked vaguely familiar, because of the scar, and I got carried away."

Jeremiah raised an eyebrow. "You don't seem like the type to let your emotions run away on a flight of fancy.

"Seriously, I'm fine. I haven't seen the guy since. I'm not even sure I saw what I saw. It's just, he started talking about the Syndicate and I fell for his paranoid delusions."

Jeremiah stiffened. "The Syndicate? He said that?"

"Why, does that mean something to you?"

Jeremiah merged onto the freeway. "I'd just rather be safe than sorry. I'm going to drive you to work from now on. I don't like the idea of you being alone."

"That's really invasive and unnecessary. I'll be fine."

"It's no trouble. I'd feel terrible if something happened to you that we could've prevented with a little bit of caution."

"Nothing's going to happen to me."

"You must be starving. Do you want to stop somewhere to eat?"

Was that... did he just completely dismiss her preferences and change the subject? Did he really think she'd let him drive her to work every day? "No thanks. I'm meeting my friend Nik for dinner."

"Is that the guy from the library?"

"Yes. You're welcome to join us." She instantly regretted inviting him, but she was still flustered from his misogynistic insistence on driving her to work to keep her from being targeted by a non-existent secret society.

"Great. Where are we meeting him?"

Sighing, she told him the name of the restaurant.

"Tell me what Schleppenbach said about the dragons. The picture, it's really a dragon?"

Annoyance successfully diverted. Randi grinned. "He said the article he wrote is exactly how it happened. He told me how to find the place they went. I'm going to the Congo—I mean, if it's okay with Dr. Lengel."

"*We're* going. It's your first real foray into the field. I'll be there to back you up. And you'll need to put together a whole team."

Randi leaned her head against the headrest and groaned. "I don't even know where to start planning something like this."

"Well, you'll need about four to five people, preferably with backgrounds in related areas, like paleontology, biology, and so on, and maybe a photographer or videographer, or someone to help record your findings. It would also be a good idea to have a guide."

"I was hoping to hire a native to be our guide. If I'm really lucky, I'd like to have the same guide that led the expedition Dr. Schleppenbach and Dr.

Rosenbaum went on, because he could lead us to the same place he took them."

"I don't know if that's such a good idea. That guide insisted Schleppenbach and Rosenbaum were crazy or imagining things. If he's lying and they really did see something, chances are he won't be willing to take you to the same place. Even if he pretends to go along with what you're asking, he may take you someplace entirely different, and you'd never know the difference."

"I hadn't thought of that. Still, though, I think a local guide is the way to go."

"I agree. That's something we can arrange when we arrive. Now, do you know anyone else that might fit well with your team? If you don't know anyone, Dr. Lengel and I have some resources that would fit well. The trick is getting reputable people to go on a wild goose chase—or, in this case, a wild dragon chase—in the middle of Africa."

Randi rubbed her head. Jetlag from this recent trip was going to be killer. Who did she even know who might be up for this? Her mentor, Meg, maybe—but Meg was already an established archaeologist. Wild dragon chases weren't really her wheelhouse. Everyone else—everyone else she was even remotely connected to had severed ties when she was expelled.

Except for one.

"Nik is an aspiring biologist, but he's the only person I really know."

"I'll help you come up with some names of people to ask on Monday."

"I'd appreciate that, thanks."

"My pleasure."

They pulled up at the restaurant. Nik was already there, waiting with a table. He clenched his fists at the sight of Jeremiah, but said nothing.

"Hi, Nik," Randi said. "You remember Dr. Bryant."

Jeremiah extended his hand, and Nik gripped it, his eyes narrow and his jaw tight.

Great. She was destined for a night of Nik sitting in stony silence, Jeremiah ignoring the pointed stares, and herself doing her best to maintain the conversation. "I love this place. I'm even thinking of trying something new tonight."

Even that didn't manage to loosen the tension in the air.

"How was your trip?" Nik asked after a few moments of awkward silence.

"Good," she said. "I have a lead. I think my dad was on to something, and I have a place to start looking."

That, finally, managed to attract his attention. "That's awesome! What's your next step?"

The waiter came just then to take their orders, and when he was gone, Dr. Bryant started in with a lengthy and entirely unrelated story about how the cryptozoological society was bringing on a full-time photographer.

Maybe not entirely unrelated—he was probably bringing it up since he'd been the one to suggest bringing a photographer along on the trip—but she could tell Nik was not amused by Jeremiah dominating the conversation.

The waiter brought their food and there was a few minutes of blissful silence while they commenced eating, which was broken by Dr. Bryant again launching into a detailed explanation of what a research trip like this entailed, complete with a story about his last expedition to a lake in Canada that was purported to have a water monster akin to the Loch Ness Monster dwelling in it.

Was he just super eager to mansplain an expedition, or was he trying intentionally to keep her from telling Nik about her planned trip to Congo?

Nik was clearly irritated by the one-sided conversation, as well. He managed to disengage from his one-sided staring contest long enough to eat the rest of Randi's meal when she finished, however. "That's pretty good. You can order that again sometime."

"Thanks," she said dryly. "Sorry to cut this short, but I'm exhausted and jetlagged. We'd better get going. You ready, Jeremiah?"

Nik's eyes narrowed again. "You came together?"

"He picked me up from the airport, remember?" Randi walked away so she wouldn't have to see Nik's angry stare.

"Well, I have to go that direction, anyway." Nik, followed her out. "No sense in the good doctor going out of his way. I'll take you home."

Jeremiah paused, then nodded. "Great." He unloaded Randi's suitcase from his trunk and handed it to Nik. "Goodnight, then. I'll see you Monday, Randi."

Nik watched him drive away. "What was that about? He's not even upset about me taking over his date?"

"We weren't on a date. He just picked me up from the airport."

"I see." Nik walked stiffly to his car, Randi following behind.

She got in and crossed her arms in front of her. "Why do you care, anyway?"

"Why? How about because I haven't seen you in weeks and you brought a date on our one chance to catch up?" Nik sped from the parking lot, tires squealing.

Randi clutched the sides of her seat as the car careened around a corner. "I did *not* bring a date. Jeremiah mentioned that he wanted to go get something to eat, so I invited him to join us. You have no right to get so angry about that."

"I have *every* right."

"You need to back off. I think we need some space."

"Space? Space from what? We're not dating," Nik growled. "You've made that perfectly clear."

"Don't you dare put this on me! That was your choice, remember?"

"Yeah. I do. You won't let me forget."

Randi snapped her mouth shut, searching for the right words. Nik slowed his speed a little, and they drove in silence until they reached Randi's apartment complex.

Nik parked in one of the guest spots close to Randi's apartment, but didn't turn off the engine. He turned to look at her.

She raised her eyes to meet his. "*You* broke up with *me*," she said softly. "You weren't ready for a commitment. You wanted to see other people. You…"

"I know." Nik took her hand. "I was an idiot who didn't know what I wanted. I don't know how many times I need to apologize for that. I didn't think I was ready. But then it broke our friendship, too, and I realized…" He took a deep breath. "I have been trying for three years to get you back. I can't handle not having you in my life."

"And I can't handle always wondering if I'm one fight or one pretty face away from getting my heart broken again."

"So, what, you're just ending our friendship?"

"Of course not. You're my best friend. But that's *all*. You can't have this best-of-both worlds."

"What do you mean by that?"

"I mean, having all the downsides to a relationship—jealousies, fights, keeping tabs on me—but none of the benefits, like not seeing other people, or working toward a common goal, or—"

"Or what?" he demanded. "This?" He leaned over and kissed her. His arms wrapped around her waist, pulling her close to him, and his lips pressed against hers in a fierce, demanding embrace.

Chapter Eighteen

Nik's mouth on hers felt warm, and he tasted like the butter mints that came with the check at the restaurant.

For a moment she relaxed into his embrace, allowed his lips to move hers.

He pulled tighter, conforming her body to his.

Randi pulled away. "Nik, don't."

"Why not?" He ran his fingers through her hair. "You can't say you don't miss this."

His phone rang. A picture of a girl with black hair making a duck-lips face showed on his screen.

"That. That's what I'm talking about. We can't even have a fight without you getting calls from one of your groupies, but I can't have a male coworker without you acting like I'm cheating on you in some way."

Nik hit the ignore button. "I don't care about her. I don't care about any of them. Why can't you see that? I make one stupid mistake and you won't let me live it down."

Randi's eyes filled and spilled down over her cheeks. "I'm sorry, Nik. I wish I could believe that, but the proof is right there." She waved at the phone. "I can't go there with you. Not again."

"Why is it so hard for you to admit you still have feelings for me? Or to be open to the idea that I've grown up—changed?" He stroked her cheek with his fingertips, sending volts of electricity through her veins.

Randi closed her eyes, wishing she didn't enjoy his touch quite so much. "It's not just that."

"What, then?"

"We're going two very different directions in life. Your ambitions are just totally different from mine. I want my life and my work to mean something." She realized what she'd said as soon as it was out of her mouth, but it was too late to take it back.

"What in the hell do you think I've been doing? Do you think the internship at the Palmer Lab was just handed to me? I've been trying to prove to you—you know what, never mind."

"You're intentionally misinterpreting what I'm saying. You took this job because it was the next logical step in your career, and I supported you in that. But when I followed my convictions and it ended up costing me my degree, you acted like I was wasting my life. You can't support me through the things you don't agree with, so how can you say you'll support me through thick and thin if we're in a relationship?" Sighing, she reached for the car door handle. "I should go."

Nik grabbed her hand. "Randi, wait. You're right. I can't keep waiting for things to magically come together for us. I want to be with you. I'll make you happy, whatever it takes. And I'll support you, even if—even if you're a cryptozoologist."

Randi gazed at him, her face wet and sticky from the tears that spilled over and ran down her cheeks. He didn't get it. She didn't need him to support her *even if*. She needed him to support her, *period*. "I'm going now."

She left before either of them could say anything else they'd regret.

***

The Rainforest near Ouesso, in the Sangha region of Congo, Africa

Albert hit the water, the sound of the splash echoing through the valley.

The creature soared toward Naomi. She dove into the lake, disappearing as far as she could under the water, before the creature's claws reached her. She swam as far as she could toward the place where Albert fell.

Her lungs burned and she couldn't hold her breath any longer. She paddled toward the surface, looking through the water for any sign of her brother.

She popped her head above water and took a deep breath. The creature soared over the water, back and forth, still letting out that fearsome roar.

Naomi scanned the water for Albert but didn't see him. She dove back under the surface, pretty sure the creature hadn't seen her, and paddled onward. The next time she came up, the creature was higher overhead, still roaring, but searching from a more distant vantage point. One more dive should take her to where Albert had been.

She came up again, almost directly under the creature's cave. Above her, the creature glided into the cave and disappeared. She took a deep breath and looked around again.

The lake was deep enough that, even after going as far as she could in a breath, she was still nowhere near the bottom.

She swam as long as she could, eyes open, searching for any sign of Albert. She came up and took a breath, scanning the surface, and dove yet again. Once more, she came up empty-handed.

Her throat constricted with fear. Where was he? Was he at the bottom of the lake, or had the creature found him and dragged him back to its lair? No, she hadn't seen anything in the creature's talons when it soared into its cave. He must be somewhere in the lake.

Her eyes roved around above the surface again.

There! Something dark floated not too far away.

She struck out toward it.

Before long, she recognized the T-shirt he wore. Something round underneath it buoyed him up, pushing his face under water.

Though it seemed like an eternity, in reality it had only been a few minutes since he fell into the water. Perhaps there was still a chance.

A few more strokes brought her to his side and she turned him over on his back, wrapping her arm around his chest and keeping his head above water as she swam, pulling her free arm in long, powerful strokes and kicking her legs with all of her strength.

Soon they were at the water's edge, and she pulled Albert onto the shore. She couldn't help him with that thing up his shirt, so she untucked it and rolled it to the side.

Her eyes darted back at it. Was that what she thought it was? *No time to think about that now.*

For once, she was grateful for her Western education and the CPR course she'd taken. She just hoped she could remember how to do it correctly.

Breathe. Press down on his chest. Breathe again. Pump his chest.

She didn't know how long she knelt above him, repeating the steps, but at last his body reacted.

After giving a violent jerk, he began coughing. She turned him to his side. Regurgitated water streamed from his mouth. More than she could have imagined. Finally, he stopped and lay there, breathing heavily.

He wasn't awake, but at least he was alive. Straining harder than she could remember ever doing in her life, she pulled him up the bank and into the forest. Into their small hut.

Reluctant to leave him alone, she sat with him for awhile, but she couldn't stay for long. She had to get him dry.

After starting a fire, she stripped his wet clothes off him. There was a deep gash in his shoulder and his arm hung crooked, as if it was only attached by the skin. She'd dislocated her shoulder at school once. Fascinated by the process, she hadn't turned away when the doctor put it back. She felt certain that was what had happened to Albert.

Choking back the urge to vomit, she repositioned his arm, grateful Albert was unconscious and wouldn't feel the pain.

It took all of her strength to push it, but finally it snapped into place.

She glanced at the gaping wound in his shoulder. Infection would set in if she didn't find some herbs to make a poultice for it right away. Even so, however, he needed to get down to the village and have a medicine man stitch the wound together.

She found the plants she needed—an easy task in this lush, untouched part of the forest—and dressed the wound, then covered him up with a blanket. Her store of traditional healing knowledge was proving to be as useful as her Western knowledge of CPR.

She left him by the fire and went out to find him some food.

A patch of gourds grew down by the edge of the water, so she went there first.

Her eye landed on the thing she'd taken out of Albert's shirt. An egg. He'd stolen an egg from a monster. What was he thinking? No good could possibly come from that.

She considered throwing it into the lake or cooking it, but she discarded those ideas. Albert would never forgive her. He'd nearly killed himself trying to get that thing, and if she got rid of it he'd either kill her or kill himself trying to get another one.

On the other hand, she might be able to use it as leverage, if Albert tried to pull another stunt like the one he just did. She lifted the egg carefully. It was heavier than it looked. She carried it up into the forest, then built a nest for it behind the hut, far enough away that Albert wouldn't be able to find it, but close enough for her to check on it and know it was safe.

***

Jon Chevalet sped down the freeway, driving with one hand and clutching Shelly's hand with the other.

"We're almost there, Sweetheart, we're almost there," he muttered over and over.

Shelly had collapsed in the kitchen while cleaning up the dinner dishes.

Jon had been in the other room, catching a few minutes of late night TV, when he'd heard the crash of broken glass. Dashing to the kitchen, he found the casserole dish shattered on the floor and Shelly lying in a heap by the sink.

He picked her up easily—too easily. She'd lost so much weight in the past weeks.

After buckling her into the passenger seat, he ran to the other side, and within moments was peeling out of the driveway.

Shelly drifted in and out of consciousness as Jon sped down the street and merged onto the freeway. She was unconscious now, but Jon kept talking to her. Reassuring her that it would be all right helped to calm him, as well.

He would have loved to have a police escort just then. It seemed that whenever he was just trying to get home on time there was a police car every mile, just waiting to trap him, but as soon as he needed one, there were none in sight.

He approached the exit for the hospital and merged over, cutting off several people in his hurry to exit the freeway.

In just a few more moments, he pulled up in front of the emergency room door. He left the car running as he jumped out and lifted his wife from the seat, carrying her inside.

The woman behind the desk moved like molasses on a cold day as she pulled out the paperwork for him to fill out and put his name on the waiting list.

The hum of activity went on all around him—people wailing and crying out in pain, doctors shouting orders, machines beeping methodically, nurses' squeaky shoes shuffling endlessly across the linoleum...

No one seemed to notice that his wife—the woman who had been a part of his very soul for nearly twenty-seven years—was dying.

Several hours later, after Shelly had been wheeled away from him on a gurney, leaving him to pace the waiting room in agony, a doctor came out to talk to him.

"How is she?" Jon asked, jumping up from the chair where he'd eventually settled.

"She's stable," the doctor informed him, "but I have to tell you, it doesn't look good. You know her condition?"

Jon nodded.

"Then I don't have to tell you that there's really nothing we can do at this point other than try to make her as comfortable as possible."

Jon sat down hard in the chair, burying his head in his hands.

The doctor stood still.

At last, Jon raised his head. "Can I see her?" he asked, his voice hoarse.

The doctor nodded. "This way." He held open the door, then led the way down the hallway to a room in the ICU.

Jon sat down next to Shelly's still form, gazing at her shrunken features, holding her shriveled hand.

Eventually his eyes drifted shut, and he dozed until the nurse came by in the morning.

Her eyes told him more than he wanted to know as she gave him a sympathetic pat on the shoulder.

Jon gently stroked Shelly's hand, silently begging her to wake up so he could speak to her—look into her eyes—say goodbye.

***

Near Shell, Wyoming

Someone pounded at the door to Djazani's trailer.

She opened it, still dressed in the T-shirt and boxer shorts she slept in, and blinked at José, confused. "What's up?"

"Administrator Schweitzer wants to see you in his office."

"I'll be there in just a minute. Did he say what it was about?"

"No, sorry."

"Okay, thanks." She quickly dressed and hurried over to the administrator's trailer.

"Come in, Miss Monroe," Administrator Schweitzer said.

Djazani's stomach tightened. He never called her Miss Monroe. He always called her either by her first name, or Dr. Monroe in front of other people. What was going on?

"It has come to my attention, Miss Monroe, that you have developed a relationship with one of the students."

Djazani stared at him a moment. "I'm sorry, sir. I don't quite understand."

"Well, it seems quite simple to me. Were you not embracing a young man by the name of Alan Kinte after you left my office the other day? Were you not also dancing with that same young man in town?"

Djazani clenched her teeth, her blood beginning to boil. Who was telling tales? Who was spinning everything out of context and blowing it out of proportion?

"Sir, Mr. Kinte and I are good friends, but there is nothing inappropriate about our friendship. I danced with him at the bar, as I have done with most of the people on the crew during our off-hours. I saw him after I left here the other day. Giving him a hug was an impulsive gesture on my part due to my excitement about our find at the dig."

"Miss Monroe, the university has very strict policies about relationships between professors and students, and as my assistant, you fall under the same guidelines as a teacher."

"We do not have a relationship. We have had no other contact than those two instances you stated."

"Be that as it may, you have made the other students uncomfortable."

Djazani took a deep breath to calm herself. "I'm very sorry, sir. It won't happen again."

"Frankly, Miss Monroe, it doesn't matter whether or not it happens again, because you are being relieved of your duties as my assistant and reassigned to another professor."

Djazani gaped at him. "What?"

"I believe I have made myself quite clear, Miss Monroe."

"I haven't done anything wrong!"

"I have several witnesses who would disagree with that statement."

"So, you're just firing me?"

"No, certainly not. I'm just reassigning you. I wouldn't want this little lapse in judgment to affect your career."

"Not affect my career?" Djazani was shouting now. "You're taking me off the most important dig of the century! You're taking away *my* discovery! You're—" She stopped and sucked in her breath. "That's what this is about, isn't it? You want to take credit for my find."

The corner of Administrator Schweitzer's mouth twitched upward, and he narrowed his eyes. "This is the university's find, and as the head of the paleontology department, it is *my* find."

Djazani leaned forward, her hands on his desk, and glared. "You can't do this to me. This is *my* discovery! I'll tell the press."

"This is a closed site, Miss Monroe. If you say anything about it to anyone, you'll be arrested."

Djazani wanted to protest, but she could think of nothing else to say. She leaned back. "What about Kinte?"

"Mr. Kinte is still a student, and as such is easily influenced by those in authority over him. No formal complaints will be filed against him for his conduct, but he is to be reassigned also. After that lapse in judgment, we can't keep him on here." Administrator Schweitzer smiled smugly.

He'd won. Djazani knew he'd won, and he knew she knew. He was getting rid of her right before the site opened up to the dozens of reporters and others who had arrived for their press release, and if she said anything, he'd follow through on his threat to have her arrested.

There was nothing more she could do.

As she stood to leave, she looked Administrator Schweitzer in the eye. "You won't get away with this. I swear I'll make you sorry."

Chapter Nineteen

Los Angeles, California

Randi left early for work Monday morning. She'd hardly slept all weekend. She kept waiting for Nik to call, and he didn't.

Their fight ran through her head, tearing at her heart, over and over. The worst part, though, was that she knew she'd done the right thing. If it had all been a mistake, she could take back the words and make it right with him, but it wasn't, and she couldn't. He'd proven that, as much as he said he wanted to be with her, he only wanted her on his terms—the terms where he got to dictate her education and her career, where she played it safe and followed a pre-planned route, the way he was doing. All the baggage in their past was a side issue, the whipped cream on top of the sundae of control he needed.

The conviction that she was right didn't make it easier to stop dwelling on the things they'd both said, and it didn't make it easier to get through the weekend without seeing him. She was glad to get back to work, where she could occupy her mind with something other than Nik.

A petite woman with short blonde hair carrying a backpack stood waiting by the door when she arrived. Few people were shorter than Randi. It felt weird to actually look down to someone. Remarkably short shorts revealed the woman's tan, shapely legs. *If I looked like that, I bet Nik wouldn't have—nope. Not going there.*

"Can I help you?" Randi asked as she unlocked the door.

"I'm looking for Dr. Lengel," the woman said. "I'm Carole McCray, his new photographer."

"Nice to meet you, Carole. I'm Randi. Dr. Lengel isn't in yet, but you're welcome to hang out in my office until he gets here."

"Thanks."

Randi led the way to her office and offered Carole a chair. "So, photography, huh? What do you photograph?"

Carole raised an eyebrow at her. "Didn't Dr. Lengel mention that I would be coming?"

Randi shrugged. "Dr. Bryant mentioned we were hiring a photographer, but only briefly. I was out of town for over a week, though."

Carole nodded. "I see. Well, I used to be a wedding photographer, but I've done some freelance stuff for Dr. Lengel on the side. Some fuzzy and inconclusive pictures of Bigfoot, mostly."

"You're kidding! So Bigfoot really does exist?"

Carole laughed. "You're a cryptozoologist, but you don't believe in Bigfoot?"

Randi laughed, too, feeling an instant rapport with the other woman. "I'm not really a cryptozoologist. I'm actually a historian."

"Why are you here, then?"

"It's kind of a long story, but mainly for the dragons."

"You don't believe in Bigfoot, but you *do* believe in dragons?"

"I didn't say I *don't* believe in Bigfoot, but I have more conclusive evidence for the existence of dragons."

Carole grinned. "That's about to change."

"That's so cool. How did you manage that?"

"Lots and lots of patience." Carole leaned back in her chair, crossing one leg over the other. Her shorts rode up, exposing her toned thighs, but she didn't seem to notice. The way she sat seemed natural, comfortable. Not like Maria, who went out of her way to flaunt as much as she could.

Randi turned on her computer so she could write a report of her trip to find Dr. Schleppenbach—leaving out the part about Dr. Schleppenbach's warning against the Syndicate—then smiled at Carole. "How do you feel about Africa?"

Carole raised her eyebrows. "Why?"

"I'm supposed to be putting together a team to go to the Republic of Congo to look for dragons. I'm told a photographer would be a good addition."

Carole's eyes widened. "I—I'm not sure. I just got here. I'll have to think about it. How soon do I have to decide?"

"Not right away. We're still in the planning stages."

Carole exhaled. "Okay, thanks. I'll let you know."

A loud squeak from the front door announced someone else entering the office.

Randi got up and peeked out. "Good morning, Maria. When Dr. Lengel gets in, would you let him know that Carole is here?"

Maria smiled halfheartedly and sat at her desk.

Randi returned to her seat. "Where were we?"

"You just invited me to go to Africa."

"Right! We have a lead on where we might start a hunt for a particular beast of legend, so we have to make arrangements to get a team to a remote location, find a guide, and begin an excursion."

"Does this happen often?" Carole asked.

"No idea," Randi admitted. "I think so? When I first got hired, which was only about a month ago, Dr. Bryant was on a trip, and I just got back from a trip to locate a source, so, I guess so?"

"Huh."

Randi sensed some tension surrounding the idea of being on an international monster hunt. Carole had seemed to loosen up a little bit when she'd talked about her passion, so Randi returned to the earlier conversation thread. "My foray into cryptozoology involves me following my heart, followed by some really choice words that were totally inappropriate to the wrong person, and a couple of random coincidences. What about you? Why the sudden career change?"

"My douchebag boyfriend cheated on me so I decided it was time for a change."

"Oh, I'm sorry. That's horrible."

"It is what it is." Carole shrugged, but her shoulders tensed, and hurt, followed by anger, washed across her pretty face. "I should've known better. Anyway, I'm here now."

"When did you get in to town?"

"Saturday night."

"Where are you staying?"

"The hotel down the street from here, right by the freeway. For now, anyway. I spent most of my savings just getting here, so we'll see what happens."

"Why don't you come crash at my place? Just until you find your own apartment."

"Are you sure? I don't want to impose." Carole looked torn between being grateful and intimidated by the idea.

"It's no big deal. I mean, I'll have to double check with my roommate, but I'm sure she won't mind you sleeping on our couch for a few days."

She sat for several seconds, as though weighing the pros and cons, before the pros won. She gave a shy smile. "Thanks, I'd appreciate that."

The front door opened again, and Randi jumped up and leaned out into the hallway to see who it was. "Hi, Jeremiah."

"Good morning." Jeremiah deposited his briefcase inside his office door, then stalked into Randi's office. "I told you I'd pick you up for work. I don't want you driving alone."

"And I told you I'd be fine. This is Carole McCray, apparently our new photographer."

Jeremiah's eyes landed briefly on the legs that flexed gracefully as Carole stood up before coming to focus intently on her face. Randi pushed down the twinge of jealousy. Carole didn't even seem to be aware of how pretty she was and how her figure drew people's eyes. Randi smoothed her ankle-length skirt before turning her attention back to Jeremiah.

"I'm Dr. Bryant. Dr. Lengel told me you'd be joining us soon." Jeremiah extended his hand to Carole. "It's good to have you on board."

Carole took his hand and shook it briefly, then yanked it back, her arms wrapping instinctively around her torso.

Maybe she was aware.

Jeremiah didn't stay to chat, though. He returned to his office across the hall, and Randi and Carole sat back down to continue their conversation.

Dr. Lengel arrived a few minutes later. "Carole McCray," he boomed as soon as he'd been introduced. "It's nice to finally meet you in person. Welcome to the team."

"Thank you," Carole smiled, lowering her eyes.

"Now, I don't mean to sound impatient, but I believe you said something about pictures."

"Yes. I have a few that I took on my last trip before coming down here. I think you'll enjoy them."

"How are they? Can you see much? How'd you get 'em and where? What did you do..." Dr. Lengel was almost incoherent as he bustled Carole toward his office.

"Um... is there a restroom I can use first?" Carole asked.

"Of course, of course, end of the hall," Dr. Lengel said. "Randi, Jeremiah, you two are welcome to come into and see these, too, if you want."

Jeremiah made his way to Dr. Lengel's office, but Randi waited in the hall for several minutes until Carole finally emerged.

"You okay?" Randi asked.

Carole nodded. "Yeah. Sorry. Just needed a second."

"You need another minute?" Randi asked.

Carole shook her head. "I'm good now. Where to?"

Randi led the way and scooted in behind the guest chair. Jeremiah stood behind her, and Carole sat. She dug into her backpack and retrieved a flash drive from her backpack, then handed it to Dr. Lengel. "Also, in my truck I have some footprint casts I took and some of the grass nearby. I don't know if you can use those."

Dr. Lengel pushed the drive into the port on his computer and rubbed his hands together as he waited for it to load.

Carole didn't even try to disguise her proud, triumphant grin as her anxiety was superseded by her passion when the images came up.

Dr. Lengel let out a low whistle and clicked the button to move on to the next picture. "This is possibly the first ever full-frontal daylight picture of Bigfoot. It's blurry, but it would be hard for the naysayers to claim it's anything else."

One by one, he went through the pictures, over and over again.

"We did it," he whispered finally. "We have proof of Bigfoot. The missing link between monkeys and humans."

Randi coughed.

"What is it?" Dr. Lengel asked.

"I don't think he's a missing link."

"What do you mean? He's right there. Bigfoot, plain as day."

"Oh, I'm not saying he's not Bigfoot. I just don't think he's a missing link."

Through her peripheral vision she saw Jeremiah staring at her, but she kept her attention on Dr. Lengel.

"Why do you say that?" Dr. Lengel asked.

"Here, I'll show you. Go back to that first one."

Dr. Lengel brought up the picture and Randi pointed to the screen. "He doesn't look like a primate to me. See, there, the way his eyes are? It gives him a look more like a bear or maybe even a dog. And his teeth, see? They aren't the herbivorous flat teeth that he's usually depicted with. That looks almost bear-like there."

"Good observations, Randi." Admiration tinted Jeremiah's voice.

"That was more or less my first impression, too," Carole said, "but I'm no expert. I just take the pictures."

"Randi isn't a biologist either." There was almost a grumble to Dr. Lengel's voice.

"No, but she could have been," Jeremiah chimed in. "As a biologist myself, I have to say her conclusions are pretty accurate. I don't think this is a missing link. I think we're looking at an entirely new species."

Randi blushed, Carole beamed, and Dr. Lengel looked more triumphant even than he had a moment ago.

"A new species, eh?" he chuckled. "This seems to be our lucky day. We need to at least get the word out that we have conclusive evidence of the existence of Bigfoot."

"It's good, but it's hardly conclusive," Jeremiah said.

Dr. Lengel ignored him and pressed the button on his intercom to the front desk. "Maria, I want you to schedule a press conference for this evening. Get all the networks and whoever else will come. We have an important discovery."

He let go of the button. "Carole, you may need to answer some questions for the news. We'll have the pictures, but they're going to want an eyewitness report. Also, we're going to need some experts to verify the pictures aren't in any way fabricated. Jeremiah, get on that."

"Yes, sir." Jeremiah disappeared into his office.

Carole's face went white at the mention of answering questions for the press conference, but Dr. Lengel hadn't seemed to notice.

"Carole, you can get to work on a report. Maybe some sort of speech to give about what you saw."

Carole stared at him open mouthed. "I—I've never done anything like that. I wouldn't even know where to begin."

Randi put a hand on Carole's shoulder. "Dr. Lengel, do you mind if I help her with that? I've done plenty of speeches and that sort of thing. Maybe I can think of some of the questions she might be asked and help her type up answers to those as well."

"Good thinking. Then she doesn't have to kick Maria off her computer. All right, then, get to work!" he grinned.

Carole shot Randi a grateful look as they retreated to Randi's office.

Randi sat at the computer. "Okay, why don't we start with you just telling me everything you can remember and I'll type it out. I'll stop you if I have a question or if we need to make something more clear."

Chapter Twenty

The Director crumpled the message from Rob in a clenched fist. The situation with the informant in Portland needed dealing with. Action needed to be taken, and Rob didn't have that authority.

The Director picked up the phone and called the Portland informant. "Tell me what happened with your girlfriend."

"She broke up with me. She moved back to her mom's house, and then she said she was going to L.A."

"Did she get the picture?"

"No."

"Are you sure?"

"I'm sure. She would've told me. It's her life's dream. She couldn't keep something like that from me."

"She could've been lying. It's not as if she would have been thrilled to share that with you after she saw you with Kimberly."

"No, I would have been able to tell if she was lying."

"Are you absolutely sure about this?"

"Yes. I'm absolutely sure. I would know."

"Then why did I get a message informing me your girlfriend is going to the press with undisputable pictures of Bigfoot?"

On the other end of the line, Seth made a choking sound. "I have no idea. She never told me anything."

"Of course not, you fool. She caught you cheating on her. I expected

161

better from you, Seth. You were supposed to have this taken care of."

"I—I'm sorry. I thought—"

"I don't pay you to think," the Director hissed. "You had a job to do and you failed."

"I'm sorry."

"Let me talk to Kimberly."

There was a pause and the sound of rustling as Seth handed the phone over.

"Yes?" Kimberly asked.

"Seth is no longer useful to me," the Director said.

"I understand."

"Take care of it."

"What's happening?" the Director heard Seth's voice in the background.

"Nothing. I'm just supposed to go down to L.A. and see what I can do down there."

"What about me?"

"You're suspended," Kimberly said. "You should be thankful that's all."

"I am. Believe me, I am."

"Nice work," the Director told Kimberly. "It sounds like he believed you. I'll expect to hear from you within twenty-four hours telling me it's complete."

"I'll handle it." Kimberly's voice sounded choked, but she wouldn't dare fail.

Now to see what could be done about the Bigfoot press conference. The Director made a few phone calls to the television networks in L.A. for a little bit of damage control. The timing was terrible—the Director had arrived in Wyoming for the press release here, and therefore had very little direct oversight over what was happening in L.A. Meanwhile, Jeremiah Bryant kept drawing more allies to his side.

Something had to be done about that.

Now. Back to the problem at hand. The trip to Wyoming was turning out to be somewhat less than satisfactory. Not that the dig site itself wasn't spectacular. It was. But the Director arrived to find the agent assigned to the dig had been sent away, expelled with no more ceremony, and there was no way that situation could be remedied without causing a great deal of suspicion.

In and of itself, it wasn't a terribly big setback. The Director now had enough connections at the dig site to make the agent more or less obsolete, but it was infuriating to have been undermined, to not have things under control.

***

The Rainforest near Ouesso, in the Sangha region of Congo, Africa

Albert groaned and opened his eyes.

Naomi's heart thudded, relief overwhelming her. She hurried to his side. "Good morning."

"Where am I?"

"The top of the mountain, trying to get yourself killed."

Albert closed his eyes again, breathing heavily. "I fell. How did I get here?"

"I had to come and save you, as usual."

"What happened?"

"The creature attacked you and you dropped into the water. I swam in after you and pulled you to shore."

"How long have I been asleep?"

"Don't you remember anything? I think your fever is making you delirious. You've been in and out of it for two days."

"*Two days?*" Albert yelled, sitting up. He yelped, clutching his arm, and lay back down again. A moment later, he rolled over and vomited up the little bit of water she'd been able to force down his throat.

Naomi stood and shot him a look of disgust. "Lie still, will you? You were *attacked* by that thing! You're lucky to be alive."

"What happened to the egg?"

"You don't need to worry about the egg. You need to get better. As soon as you can walk, we're going back down to the village and we're going to take you to a doctor."

"I don't need a doctor."

"There's a hole in your shoulder, which was dislocated, by the way, and I think your arm is broken. The wound is getting infected and you haven't been able to keep any food down. Who knows what else is wrong? You're going to see a doctor."

"Tell me where the egg is or I won't go to the doctor."

Naomi scowled at him. "The egg is fine. I have it safe. I swear to you, though, I will break it and cook whatever's inside for breakfast if you don't promise me you'll go home and see a doctor as soon as you are able."

Albert glared. "All right, but if anything happens to that egg, I'll—"

"You'll what?" Naomi put her hands on her hips and towered over him.

Albert scowled and turned over.

"That's what I thought." She gave a sharp nod. "I'm fixing some food for you, whenever you're hungry."

Albert sulked awhile, but Naomi would do as she threatened, and she knew he knew it, too. Besides, despite how he tried to deny it, the pain that wracked his features every time he moved convinced her she was right about getting him to the doctor. The sooner the better.

Naomi waited outside the hut until he gave in, which she knew he'd do before long, especially if he wanted to eat anything other than broth.

"Naomi," he called out at last.

She stepped inside. "Yes?"

"Would you bring me something to eat? I'm going to need my strength if I'm going to get back down to the village and find a doctor."

"Good idea."

"I have one condition."

"What's that?"

"You have to promise me you'll take care of the egg until I get back."

"I'm coming with you. I'm not staying up here by myself. Besides, you can't make it all the way home with that arm."

"Of course I can, but I'm not going unless you promise to take care of the egg."

"Why don't we take the egg home with us?"

"No, we can't," he protested. "It's too heavy to carry all that way, and besides, what would happen when we got it home? People would wonder what it was and where we got it. The medicine man would probably destroy it. We can't take it home, and you know it."

Naomi frowned. Her brother could be as stubborn as she. Better to give in on this one than risk him hurting himself more trying to carry the stupid thing all the way home.

"All right. I'll stay here with the egg." She handed him a chunk of meat.

Naomi stalked out of the hut and went around to the back where she'd hidden the egg. What had she been thinking? Why did she ever agree to take care of the stupid thing? She could kill Albert for his stubbornness.

Still, she couldn't help feeling just a little curious. What would happen? Would it hatch, or would it just rot since it was taken away from its mother? What would it be like if it did hatch? How long would it take?

The more she thought about it, the more intrigued she became. She even began to hope Albert would heal quickly and be back so they could explore this unknown phenomenon together.

After sitting for awhile, staring at the egg, she finally went back into the hut to eat.

Albert lay on his bed of leaves, snoring lightly. She smiled, relieved he was resting well. In a day or two she could send him home. Just as soon as he was strong enough.

Something outside rustled the leaves. Naomi took the spear she'd fashioned and peered out the doorway into the deepening gloom.

Feral yellow eyes reflected the fire and something growled. Most likely a wild cat. The smell of sickness hovered around the *mongulu*. The jungle knew something was about to die, and the scavengers waited hungrily.

She yelled and threw a couple rocks, successfully convincing whatever it was that it wasn't worth the effort to come after her.

Early the next morning, she changed the poultice of leaves and mud, but the wound was deep. It worried her more than she liked to admit. He needed to have his arm set, too, before it healed in the wrong position.

Her mother taught her much about the traditional remedies of her people, but she had no idea what to do with a break as bad as her brother's.

"I can't stay here and watch the egg," Naomi told him that evening as she helped him eat the fruit she'd gathered. "There are too many predators, and you're in no shape to fend them off."

"You promised."

"I don't care what I promised. I'm not sending you back alone. We can come back when you're better."

"What if it's too late?"

She shrugged. "Then that will be a pity, but it won't be worth it if you die for this thing."

Albert scowled at her, but didn't argue any more.

"Finish eating. We're leaving first thing in the morning."

Naomi woke before dawn and gathered her herbs so she could change Albert's poultice one more time before leaving, and so she'd have enough supplies to change it along the way without having to scavenge for more.

She took her supplies to his leaf bed.

He wasn't in it.

"Albert?" she called, softly at first, and louder when he didn't respond. She checked out by the river, up by the lake, and all around the hut.

As the sun rose, she noticed a piece of bark propped up against the wall of the *mongulu*. Written on it in ash from the fire were the words, *Take care of my egg. I'll be back.*

She stared at it for several minutes. How long ago had he left? Should she try to overtake him? And if she stayed, how long should she wait for him to come back before following him down the mountain?

***

Los Angeles, California

Randi sat next to Carole at the back of the small stage in the meeting room at the hotel where the press conference would be held.

Dr. Lengel paced back and forth behind the podium, hidden from the gathering reporters by a thick, maroon curtain.

His constant motion seemed to be making Carole even more tense than she already clearly was—Carole's fingers were turning white gripping the chair's armrests.

"Are you okay? Do you need to go take a breather?" Randi asked.

Carole shook her head, though her short, quick breaths belied her denial.

Near the podium stood a forensic expert named Ben Kowalski, who would corroborate that the pictures weren't enhanced or tampered with in any way.

Carole managed a weak smile, and Randi gently squeezed her shoulder.

She could only imagine how terrified the other girl must be, preparing to be put in the spotlight and grilled like she was on trial.

She removed the teal scarf from around her own neck and draped it around Carole's. "This will frame your face and bring out your eyes. You'll do fine. Dr. Lengel will be doing most of the speaking, and I'll be right here with your notes if you need help."

Carole nodded. "Thanks."

"I'll be right back." Randi walked to the other end of the stage and pulled out her phone.

She pressed the speed dial button to call Nik.

He didn't answer. In all likelihood, he was screening her calls. She bit her lip and closed her eyes, squeezing back the tears that tried to form.

Despite the near-impossibility of the task, she attempted to make her voice sound calm and natural as she left the message she'd been debating all day. "Hey, Nik, it's Randi. I just thought you'd want to know we're going to be on the news tonight. Local stations and web stations are all here, so it should be easy to find. Anyway, I thought I'd let you know. Bye."

She glanced up as she put the phone back in her purse.

Jeremiah was looking at her.

Randi acknowledged his look with a nod, then turned away. She couldn't stop thinking about Nik. She couldn't stop replaying the horrible scene in her mind, seeing the hurt look in his eyes, or feeling his lips on hers.

Every part of her cried out with longing to be close to him again. She couldn't imagine going through every day when he wasn't a part of her life. At the same time, she hated herself for being so weak, for needing him so badly, and for wanting him despite knowing she couldn't trust him.

She sat beside Carole and tried to hide her thoughts by going over the notes.

Dr. Lengel came toward them, rubbing his hands and grinning. "We're ready to begin. Carole, are you ready?"

Carole nodded gulped, her face drained of blood, but nodded. Even her makeup couldn't disguise how sickly pale she looked.

"Excellent. You and Mr. Kowalski come stand beside me, and Jeremiah and Randi, you two stay close but slightly behind us."

Randi smoothed the lines out of her pantsuit and joined Jeremiah in the background, while Dr. Lengel stepped up to the podium, Carole by his side.

Dr. Lengel nodded to the man beside the curtain, who pulled the rope.

The curtain slowly parted, revealing a sea of faces, cameras, and recorders.

"Welcome, ladies and gentlemen," Dr. Lengel beamed at the crowd. "I'm glad you could all make it today. Please allow my staff and myself to make our comments, and then there will be a time for questions and answers."

Dr. Lengel spoke for several minutes about the American Cryptozoological Society and their work before he introduced Carole, Ben Kowalski, Randi, and Jeremiah.

He turned back to the crowd. "I know you're not all that interested in us, so let's talk about the good stuff, shall we?"

First, he gave a brief history about Bigfoot, the recent sightings and so forth. After he exhausted that train of thought, he spoke about the new pictures the Society had just gotten then proudly asked Carole to step forward.

Carole stepped to the podium, her face now flushed. She glanced at Randi, who smiled encouragingly, and turned back to the microphone.

In a tone that sounded forced, eyes glued to her notes, Carole recited her tale. Beginning with how she found that particular location, she went on to tell how often she visited it, what she used to disguise her scent, and so on. She told about the signs—footprints and other signs—that led her to believe this was a Bigfoot feeding ground, then talked about hiding in the blind, which led to her first sighting of Bigfoot at the stream, then seeing the creature again at her campsite.

Finally, she finished, and Dr. Lengel opened up the floor for questions.

The room immediately buzzed with reporters shouting, the air thick with raised hands. Dr. Lengel pointed to reporters one at a time.

"How do we know this isn't a big hoax?" one asked.

Dr. Lengel leaned into the microphone. "In a moment you'll have a chance to view the photographs taken by Ms. McCray. I'm certain the clarity of the photos will convince any skeptic of the reality of her experience."

"How do we know the photos aren't faked?" another demanded.

Dr. Lengel motioned Ben Kowalski forward to the microphone.

"I am a forensic scientist specializing in data recovery and digital analysis. I've been an expert witness in several legal proceedings for both defense and prosecution testimonies. While more tests certainly are in order, from my initial examination of the evidence, I've found no sign of tampering or falsification. It is my belief the photos are, in fact, both original and genuine."

He stepped back, and Dr. Lengel grinned with pride as he pointed to the next reporter.

"Do you believe you've uncovered the missing link between humans and apes?"

Jeremiah stepped forward. "Actually, no. We believe these photos prove there is a creature known to many as Sasquatch or Bigfoot, but we do not believe it is a missing link. Based on facial structure, eye position, and teeth, we conjecture it is something else, an entirely different species."

"Can you prove that?" another reporter cut in.

"Not at this time. But let's allow the pictures to speak for themselves, shall we?"

The press conference lasted for almost an hour, concluding with Dr. Lengel showing a slideshow of the pictures Carole had taken.

"These pictures will be published in the next issue of our magazine publication, *Cryptozoology Today*," Dr. Lengel said. "Please feel free to contact us at the number on the screen or check out our website for more information."

He nodded to the young man by the curtain.

In another moment, they were once again hidden behind the thick, maroon velvet guardian.

An excited chatter rose from beyond the curtain as the reporters compared notes and commented to each other their opinions.

Randi gave Carole an impulsive hug.

She glanced up. Jeremiah was watching her again. She walked toward him. "What is it?"

"What? Nothing."

"You were staring at me."

"Not staring. Just noticing."

"Noticing what?"

"You don't mind not being in the spotlight. You almost hide behind everyone else, yet no one else could do this without you."

"What do you mean?"

"Carole, on several occasions, looked as though she might throw up, but a glance back at you seemed to restore her. You have a calmness, a presence about you that soothes others. It's an admirable quality."

Heat rose to Randi's cheeks. "Thanks."

"Obviously that's not one of my qualities. I prefer a good debate, but too few people are able to keep up with me."

Again with that ego. Randi just smiled. "We all have our strengths, I guess."

"I didn't mean—that is, you do pretty well. In a debate, I mean. At least, better than most women."

Randi rolled her eyes. "Thanks."

She turned away and snuck a peek out from behind the curtain at the reporters still milling around, staring at the picture on the screen with the American Cryptozoological Society website prominently displayed.

A man stood at the back of the room, not talking to anyone else, not looking at the picture, but staring at the curtain where she stood.

Her heart nearly stopped. "Jeremiah."

He was at her side almost instantly. "What? What happened."

"That man. Under the exit sign on the left. I think he's the one who was following me in Germany. The one I thought I saw outside Dr. Schleppenbach's house."

Chapter Twenty-One

Jon Chevalet woke to the sound of machines blaring at him.

He'd hardly left the hospital in three days, sleeping in the chair by Shelly's bedside. She had woken a few times, but they both knew her time was short.

The machines seemed to wake her, too, for her eyes fluttered open. "I love you, Jon," she whispered hoarsely. "Always remember that."

Jon wept and held her hand, telling her how much he loved her. She lay quietly, eyes closed again, but awake and listening to him, a smile touching her lips.

Just to have something to say, he talked about the day they had met.

"I was a grad student, do you remember? You were an elementary school teacher. You brought your class in for the unveiling of a new fossil."

He stroked her hand. "I can still remember the first time I saw you. You were so beautiful! Do you remember how obvious I was, coming over to stand by you, trying to be nonchalant?"

He chuckled. "Do you remember what I said? 'I wish I had been in your class.' You laughed, and I think that was the moment I fell in love with you."

The machines continued their insistence that something wasn't right.

Jon squeezed Shelly's hand and smiled down at her. "I tried so hard to impress you with my great knowledge of dinosaur bones and fossils. I don't think I realized you were laughing *at* me, not *with* me. Something must have worked, though, because you gave me your number."

Shelly's fingers, though weak, squeezed his hand.

"Remember our wedding? Your mother kept changing everything at the last minute. The flowers had to be rearranged, and the order of the service must have changed a dozen times."

He laughed. "We were so stressed. I was ready to elope more than once. But even so, that was the best day of my life."

He recalled other instances, talking about fun times they'd had, vacations they'd taken, the exhilaration when she was promoted at work, and when he received the coveted position at the museum.

The doctor and two nurses came into the room, and one of the nurses gently guided him out of the way.

More memories overcame him, and he wept silently as he thought of all the hard times they had endured together. The frustration of trying to conceive, the pain of discovering that Shelly would never be able to bear children, then wrestling with the decision of whether or not to try to adopt.

They'd just begun the paperwork when she was diagnosed the first time and they had to put everything else on hold. She'd been so sick and miserable, but every day had put on a brave face, determined to conquer her sickness, and had been cheerful and optimistic throughout the whole painful ordeal.

Tears streamed down his cheeks. They would never again go skiing in the mountains, or spend a day on the beach; never take the Safari trip he had always promised her or the RV road trip across the country that they wanted to take when they both retired.

How could he possibly go on without her?

The beeping machines blared on relentlessly, the doctors and nurses working over his wife, their motions a blur.

He stood there, staring at them, unable to move or think.

At last, the doctors stopped. The nurse who had moved him out of the way came and put a hand on his shoulder. "It's over. Do you want to say goodbye?" she asked softly.

Jon nodded, and followed her to Shelly's side.

He took Shelly's hand. Funny, it still felt the same clasped in his as it had twenty-seven years ago, the first time he had held it, as they walked along the beach together on their second date.

Grey streaked the soft brown waves of the hair he stroked for the last time.

He kissed her lips, the same lips he had kissed every night all those years.

His tears fell onto her worn, wrinkled cheek.

He whispered into her ear, the same way he had the first time they had made love. "I love you, Shelly."

***

Randi woke to the sound of a cell phone ringing. Not hers. She stretched and rubbed her eyes. It took a moment to determine where the sound was coming from.

The living room. It must be Carole's phone.

She got up and stepped out of her room.

Glancing up, she saw the clock on the microwave.

Three seventeen.

Who would be calling her at this hour?

She glanced toward Kelly's door, but didn't really worry about her waking. She'd actually slept through an earthquake once.

She looked back toward the couch where Carole had woken and was fumbling around on the coffee table until she found her phone. She glanced at the screen before answering.

"Mom? What's going on?"

"Oh, baby, I'm sorry to call in the middle of the night, but—" A woman's teary voice from the other end, just loud enough for Randi to hear.

"What is it, Mom? What's going on?"

"There's been an accident."

Carole sat upright. "Are you okay?"

"No—I mean, yes, I'm fine, baby, it's not me. They called here because you were listed as his next of kin."

"Who?"

"Seth."

Carole gasped. "What happened? Is he all right?"

"He was driving, and it was raining. He went too fast around a corner The car flipped and rolled, and there was a truck on the other side, and…" Carole's mom's voice cracked. She was almost incoherent.

"Is he going to be okay?" Carole choked.

"I'm so sorry, baby. He didn't make it."

Carole dropped the phone.

Randi hurried over and sat beside her on the couch. She picked up the phone. "Can I have Carole call you back?" She hung up the phone and placed it back on the coffee table.

173

She put her arms around Carole in a comforting hug.

Carole buried her head in Randi's shoulder, shaking. "I didn't mean it. I swear, I didn't mean it!" she sobbed.

"Didn't mean what?"

"I wished he was dead. I was so angry at him, I said I wished he was dead, and now he is."

"It's not your fault. It's okay. It's not your fault."

She sat with Carole until she calmed down, then made her a cup of tea. "Can I get you anything else?"

Carole shook her head. "I'll be okay. The shock is wearing off. And I know I shouldn't care, after everything he put me through, but…"

"But you still loved him," Randi finished. "It's okay for you to have conflicting feelings right now. He was part of your life for a long time, and it's okay to grieve."

Carole smiled through her tears. "Thank you. You should go back to bed. We've got a big day tomorrow."

"You sure you don't need anything?" Randi asked.

"I'm good. Thank you again."

Randi went to bed, but stayed awake listening as Carole cried for a long while before falling silent.

Carole looked awful the next morning.

Randi gave her a sympathetic smile. "Did you get any sleep?"

"Not really. I thought I was done having feelings for Seth, but his death hurts as much as if we were still together. Maybe even more. I just feel so guilty about hating him."

Randi brewed coffee and took her a cup. "That's natural. Over the next few days your emotions are probably going to be all over the place. Do you want to stay home today?"

"No, I'll be fine. With enough makeup, I'll be presentable enough to go into the office."

"Okay. Let me know if you change your mind. I'm sure everyone would understand."

"Thanks. It's so weird to think we just met. After everything we've been through, working together and the press conference and then last night, it feels like we've known each other forever."

"It does," Randi agreed.

Carole gave her an impulsive hug. "Thanks. I appreciate you. You have no idea how hard this would be without you."

"I'm glad to help." Randi returned the hug, holding on until Carole was ready to let go.

***

Los Angeles, California

Djazani and Kinte got off the plane together in Los Angeles. Once they'd been reassigned, neither of them wanted to spend any more time hanging around on the outskirts, unable to even observe the dig, let alone participate. *Reassigned. Fired is more like it.*

Djazani intended to file a complaint against Administrator Schweitzer, but she knew how little that would probably accomplish. At any rate, even if he did get reprimanded, it was too late for her. By the time she dealt with all the red tape and bureaucracy, the dig would be complete, or as good as.

She'd never get another chance like that again. It was a truly once-in-a-lifetime find, and rather than share the credit, Schweitzer had decided to get rid of her. And Kinte was collateral damage. She felt as angry about that as about her own dismissal.

She spent the entire plane ride going back and forth between cursing Dr. Schwietzer and plotting revenge.

She suspected Kinte was as angry as she—this had been a career-making dig for him, too—but he was far less demonstrative in his display of emotion. Everyone there would be famous very soon, but they were sent away.

She looked at him from time to time. He didn't even acknowledge her. His eyes were fixed on the headrest in front of him, his lips closed in a firm line. What was going on behind his stoic expression?

***

The phone was already ringing off the hook when Randi and Carole got to work.

Maria sat at her desk fielding calls. "Thank you for calling the American Cryptozoological Society, how may I help you? He's on another call. Would you like to speak to one of our other representatives? Thank you, please

175

hold."

She pressed the button to put the caller on hold and looked up at Carole and Randi. "Dr. Lengel wanted to see you both as soon as you got in."

"Thanks." Randi led the way back to Dr. Lengel's office and rapped on the door.

Dr. Lengel's boisterous voice floated into the hall when Randi opened the door, and Jeremiah's subtler, but no less powerful, voice floated out as well, creating a hum of activity seldom heard in the office.

Dr. Lengel pressed the hold button on his phone and looked up. "I'm glad you're here. We're getting more calls than we know what to do with about this Bigfoot thing. I put a second phone in Randi's office, so Carole, you can work from there. Maria's answering calls as fast as she can and putting everybody she can on hold. The rest are going to voicemail. We updated the voicemail to direct as many people as possible to the website to sign up for updates, but of course everyone *must* talk to us in person." He rolled his eyes. "For now, just answer as many as you can. If people want to know more than you can answer, direct them to the website and tell them to subscribe to our magazine."

Randi took the stack of paper Dr. Lengel handed her. "What's this?"

"A loose script with answers to frequently asked questions. Jeremiah put it together this morning. Any questions?"

Randi shook her head and led Carole to her office to begin sifting through the callers that waited on hold. Almost as soon as they freed a line, another call came in.

After a few hours, Jeremiah wandered over from his office. "How's it coming in here?"

Randi finished the call she was on and smiled. "So far so good. How about you?"

He shrugged. "It's good for the society, at any rate."

Maria poked her head in the office, leaning slightly, revealing the edge of her leopard-print bra beneath her shirt. "It looks like a long day still ahead of us. Should I order in for lunch?"

Jeremiah glanced over. "Sure. Thanks."

His attention returned to Randi. "Feel free to take a break if you need one."

Maria stood there a moment longer, staring at Jeremiah. Her expression seemed to be a mix between longing and frustration. Randi felt a little sorry for her. She tried to give her a sympathetic smile, but Maria ignored her, turned, and disappeared down the hall.

Late in the evening, Randi heard Dr. Lengel's voice at the front of the office. "Maria, go ahead and let everyone else just go to voicemail. You can take care of it in the morning."

"Yes, sir."

He came down the hall and repeated the injunction to Jeremiah, then to Randi and Carole.

Randi stretched and took a deep breath, then picked up a stack of forms. "That was quite the day. Look at this—these are potential donors to the organization."

Dr. Lengel rubbed his hands with glee. "Maria, come get these."

Maria came down the hall and took the forms from Randi.

Dr. Lengel still grinned. "All these new magazine subscriptions will help pay for your dragon-hunting trip to Africa, Randi."

Maria turned abruptly. "Dragon hunting? Africa? Why is this the first I've heard about any of that?"

Dr. Lengel gave her a blank stare. "I guess we forgot to mention it to you. Does it matter?"

"Of course it matters. If you're planning a trip like that, there's paperwork to be dealt with, plans to make. There are things I need to be doing that I can't do if I don't have the information, and then you'll get upset later when it's not done."

"Calm down, Maria. I'll give you the details in the morning. Let's call it a night. Oh, and I'll be out of the office for part of the day tomorrow. I have to go to a funeral."

"A funeral? Oh, no!" Randi looked at him. "What happened? Who?"

"My friend Jon Chevalet—you met him awhile back—his wife passed away."

"Oh, I'm sorry to hear that. He was nice. I can't imagine how hard that must be for him."

"Yes, well, she'd been fighting cancer for a long while. Poor fellow. I've known him since college. Shelly was the love of his life. I don't know what he's going to do without her."

"Give him my condolences," Randi said.

"I will, thanks. See you later." Dr. Lengel locked his door and left the building.

"Let's get some food," Randi said to Carole. "I'm starving. Maria, do you want to come?"

"No thanks." Maria glanced across the hall toward Jeremiah's office, where he was still on a call. "I just have a few more things to tie up before I go. You go on. I'll lock up."

Randi smiled. "Okay. See you tomorrow then."

She left, but something didn't quite sit right with her. Maria had gotten way too upset about not knowing about the dragon trip. And staying behind instead of coming to dinner—was that just another vain attempt to get Jeremiah's attention? Or was there another reason she opted to stay behind?

Chapter Twenty-Two

Jeremiah sat bent over some papers on his desk.

Maria came into his office. "Exciting day."

"Very." He didn't look up.

"I was going to go out for a drink to celebrate. Want to come?"

"I don't drink," Jeremiah said.

"How about dinner, then?"

"No thanks. I'm going to head home."

He'd considered making sure Randi got home safely, but now that she was carpooling with Carole, he wasn't quite as worried about her. The man who'd followed her in Germany showing up at the press conference concerned him—he'd tried to go find the man and confront him, but by the time he got off the stage, the man had disappeared. But she was with Carole, so he had to trust that the agent would keep his distance. For now, anyway.

Maria was still loitering in his doorway. He got up and placed the papers he'd been working on carefully in his desk, then locked it. "I'll see you in the morning."

He brushed past her and held the door for her to exit. She sighed audibly. He ignored her.

"Good night, then." Jeremiah locked the office door. He knew Maria was staring at him, but he didn't look back. Why wouldn't she just give up? Couldn't she take a hint?

He didn't want to have to have yet another a talk with her about the inappropriateness of her behavior, but she didn't seem to grasp when he'd tried to tell her in a kind, direct way. Maybe there was some other way he could deter her from being interested in him.

I could get married. He gave a slight chuckle. *That might work. Of course, that would require finding somebody worth marrying.*

Somebody else.

His chest constricted as it always did at the thought of the woman he'd almost married.

Thoughts of her lingered as he drove home. *Why? Why couldn't it be her?*

Scenes from their relationship flashed through his mind. The way she prodded him out of his comfort zone. Randi did that, too, now that he thought about it. Or the way she always had a snappy comeback, funny and smart. Randi was one of the few women besides his ex who could hold her own with him. He appreciated how Randi wasn't so enamored with him that she fell all over herself trying to please him. He liked a woman with her own mind.

He drove half-consciously and ended up at the restaurant where he'd had dinner with Randi and her friend Nik. What was going on between those two, anyway? Jeremiah hadn't meant to eavesdrop on their conversation in the library that day, but he couldn't help hearing most of what was said. Their voices hadn't exactly been library-worthy. She'd made it very clear he wasn't her boyfriend and even made it a point to mention she'd ended any pretense of romantic involvement, yet had tried to assure him that she wasn't interested in anyone else.

Then again, that night Jeremiah went to dinner with the two of them, Nik had clearly been upset when Randi brought him along. The boy obviously thought far more of his relationship with Randi than she did. And, if he wasn't mistaken, Nik was jealous of Randi spending time with any other man.

Not that Nik had reason to worry. Just because he and Randi were at the library together, and even though Randi invited him to join them for dinner, it didn't mean he was interested in her or even cared what she did with her personal life. It was just Randi was the only person at the office worth spending time with after-hours.

But even if he *had* been interested, which he wasn't, he'd noticed the way Randi's face brightened and her eyes sparkled when she first saw her friend. In some ways, it was actually somewhat refreshing to have the reassurance that Randi wasn't interested in him. Not particularly flattering, but reassuring.

Many women were interested in him only because of his looks, so it was nice to know Randi wasn't that shallow. Also, it would be nice to be able to work together without having to avoid her because he didn't share her feelings, like he had to with Maria.

Even so, he wondered what Randi saw in Nik. Sure, he was nice looking and seemed to be reasonably intelligent. Jeremiah got the impression they'd been friends a long time, but from what he gathered, they really had nothing in common. She could do better.

***

Los Angeles, California

Nik looked at his phone a hundred times during the day. Though he knew she wouldn't, he was still disappointed Randi hadn't called. He hadn't talked to her since their fight. He'd ignored her when she called the night of the press conference, still too angry to talk to her, and she hadn't called since. She could be so stubborn.

He'd watched the news coverage of the press release, however. The segment was small, with only a few clips of the interview, but it was enough that probably thousands of people would be calling for more information. A couple clips, including the pictures, had gone viral already.

He'd watched some of them a hundred times already.

Randi looked exceptionally nice in her navy blue pantsuit. It brought out her eyes and subtly hugged her curves.

The other woman, the photographer, even with her short skirt and flawless skin, couldn't hold a candle to Randi's radiant smile and the glow that emanated from her.

He was less thrilled with the way Dr. Bryant's eyes kept returning to gaze at Randi. Randi hadn't seemed to notice. She never did believe she turned eyes.

He replayed his favorite, where the photographer looked like she was about to throw up, turned back to glance at Randi, who gave her a nod and a warm smile, then continued with her speech.

He could almost feel the encouragement from the other side of the screen. A person could accomplish anything with Randi standing behind him for support.

He ought to call her. He ought to make things right, but he wasn't sure she would answer even if he called. On the message she left, she sounded so... untouched. Not upset, or annoyed, or *anything*. From the tone of her voice he guessed she was not nearly as affected by their fight as he was.

Maybe that was better. Of course it was. Great, in fact. Superb. She didn't care a bit, and that was just fine with him. He didn't care about her either. At least she was happy.

He still jumped for the phone when it rang, eagerly checking the caller ID. Not Randi. Of course not. It was a number he didn't recognize. "Hello?"

"Nik, it's Professor Bourne."

Nik glanced again at his phone, surprised to hear from his favorite professor. "Hi, Professor. What can I do for you?"

"I arrived yesterday at a very intriguing paleontology dig site in Wyoming. Now, I know you prefer biology, but I wonder if you might consider coming out here. I think you would find this very interesting."

"I'd love to, but I'm not sure how I can. I just started my internship with the lab."

"I'll arrange for you to have a temporary transfer, and then the university will cover your airfare as well. I'll call you tomorrow and let you know your flight information."

Nik paused, thinking through the implications. Professor Bourne had been the one to give him the endorsement for the Palmer Lab in the first place, so if he was the one making the request, maybe it would be okay.

"Wow—thank you, Professor Bourne. I'm intrigued. Assuming it's okay with the lab, I guess I'll talk to you tomorrow."

Wyoming. The thought of going to work with Professor Bourne filled his stomach with eager anticipation. Almost exciting enough to help keep him from thinking about Randi.

But Professor Bourne had sounded so cryptic. Why had he chosen Nik, out of all the students at the university? And what could possibly be so exciting in Wyoming?

***

Los Angeles, California

Jon Chevalet had spent the last several days in a blur. His sister, Nancy, came in from Texas to help with the funeral arrangements, calling everyone in his address book to let them know so he wouldn't have to.

She cooked his meals took care of his house while he walked around in a daze, doing as she told him, but not really aware of his surroundings. All he could feel was a gaping hole inside his chest, draining his will to live. He walked like a zombie, responding when spoken to, but without any purpose to his step.

At the funeral, Nancy stood beside him, her arm in his, comforting and supporting him.

It was unreal—the soothing sound of the minister's voice as he spoke of *A Better Place*, the muffled sounds of sobs behind him, the squish of feet in the wet grass—all sounded muted, as if they were on the other side of a glass window.

Jon hadn't really been able to believe that she was gone, hadn't been able to grasp the knowledge fully. However, as the casket had been lowered into the ground, he felt as if half of his body had been ripped violently from him and thrown into the pit with the casket.

He desperately wanted to crawl in there with her, but his feet wouldn't move. He wanted to scream at the heavens that it wasn't fair, and beg for Shelly's life back, but his voice refused to make any sound. He longed to fall on the ground and weep, but his tears were spent.

All he could do was stand silently as the dirt piled on top of the casket, hiding his love away from him forever.

Monday would see him back at work. The museum had offered to let him take an extended leave of absence, but honestly, he wished he could go back sooner, just to keep from dwelling on the past week.

At the wake, shaking hands with everyone and accepting their endless condolences, he started to feel better. People he had known, people Shelly had known—he hadn't realized how many people they were friends with.

His heart warmed that so many had come to remember her. She had touched so many lives. Dr. Lengel was there, tears running freely down his round face. He hugged Jon fiercely, telling him how much he would miss "the missus."

Finally, it was all over, and he sat across the table from his sister.

"I have to go back home after the weekend," she told him. "Is there someone else you can get to stay with you and help you out for a while?"

Jon shook his head. "I'll be all right. I don't need anyone."

"Jon..." she protested.

"I'm going back to work on Monday. Really, I'll be fine."

Nancy gave him a skeptical glance, but was prevented from scolding him by the ringing of the phone.

"I'll get it," she offered.

Jon's head sank into his hands as she left the room. He hoped she couldn't tell how "all right" he wasn't. He was grateful for her help, but the last thing he wanted was someone else hanging around him all day every day, tending him like a sick child.

Some time alone, drowning his sorrow in his work, was all he needed.

Perhaps some good might even come of it. Who knew what he could do with his time? Maybe he would finally get around to working on that book about the Cretaceous period he'd always wanted to write.

"It's for you, Jon," Nancy said. "It's someone from your work. I told him you didn't want to speak to anyone right now, but he insists that it's very important."

"That's okay, Nancy, I can talk," he said, getting up.

"Jon," came his boss' voice on the other end of the line, "I know this is a hard time for you, but something just came up. If you are at all interested in doing something outside the norm, I just heard about a job that will definitely interest you."

"Please go on," Jon said.

"Now, I'll understand if you don't want to go, but a group of paleontology students just uncovered a complete fossil of an unidentified dinosaur species in Wyoming. There's going to be a conference, and we have been invited to send a representative."

"When can I leave?" Jon asked, a smile on his face for the first time in weeks.

***

Near Shell, Wyoming

Nik made his way out to the lobby of the tiny airport. Just beyond the security gate, he saw Professor Bourne, and hurried to meet him.

"Nik, I'm so glad you made it. You're going to love this."

They took a long drive away from the small city to the town of Shell, Professor Bourne pointing out some of the local landmarks that, to Nik, were remarkably unremarkable.

Nik checked into one of the few hotels in the tiny town—despite its size, it was apparently a popular tourist site, due to the number of paleontological sites nearby—then went with Professor Bourne for another long drive out to the dig site.

Professor Bourne explained the purpose of the trip as they drove. "The team from the university was working on this dig. At first, they thought it was an over-sized Deinonychus, but then they discovered what appeared to be bone spurs, which actually turned out to be wings."

The SUV bumped over the washboard road, bouncing Nik in his seat. "Wings? Like a pterodactyl or something?"

Professor Bourne shook his head. "Not quite. They're still doing tests, but it seems our university team has discovered an entirely new species. The team invited several of the professors from the university, as well as other experts and specialists in the field, not to mention the press, for a conference on Monday. Up until now, this has been a closed site, while they tried to figure out what they were dealing with, but now they're opening it for public viewing. They'll show pictures and explain their findings and so on at the conference."

"Wow—a new species? That's… that's huge."

Professor Bourne glanced sideways at him. "It seems like there's more you want to say."

"Well, I just don't understand why you invited me. Don't get me wrong, I mean, I'm really honored, but I don't know why I'm on the A-list."

Professor Bourne chuckled. "Well, you're a promising young biologist, for one thing. One of my best—and favorite—students. I felt that you'd not only enjoy this conference, but you'd contribute to the discussion."

"Thank you, sir. I appreciate your confidence in me." Nik warmed at the praise, but something didn't quite seem right. *One* of his best, *one* of his favorites—but he was not at all qualified for this. What other motive did Professor Bourne have in bringing him all the way out here?

His thoughts were interrupted as the SUV jolted to a stop.

Professor Bourne smiled. "We're here."

Professor Bourne led Nik to the edge of the rope that sectioned off the dig site, then up the small rise that overlooked the dig itself.

Nik could hardly believe what he saw. In an instant, all anger and resentment toward Randi was washed away by one overwhelming thought.

She had to see this.

Professor Bourne grinned. "Come this way." He led Nik toward the pavilion where all the equipment was set up.

"Administrator Schweitzer, this is one of my brightest students, Nik Gary."

Administrator Schweitzer looked up and nodded slightly before going back to whatever he was working on.

A young man came up to them and stuck out his hand. "I'm José Chavira. Obviously, Administrator Schweitzer is a little preoccupied. Let me show you around."

"Thank you," Professor Bourne said.

José showed them the aerial pictures and the ultrasound pictures that gave a fuller, clearer picture of the fossil.

"What's that?" Nik pointed to something that looked as if it were inside the stomach cavity.

"We're still trying to determine that. Bones of some kind. We've almost got it uncovered enough to extract them. Then we'll be able to determine what kind of bones they are."

He showed them some close-up shots. "At this point we're not sure whether it is something the creature ate or whether it is another completely different fossil that just happened to be superimposed in the same rock layer."

Nik peered closer at the picture.

José grinned. "Some of us are suspecting—and, I have to admit, hoping—it belongs to something the creature ate just before it died. If that's the case, it will go a long way toward determining exactly when this creature lived, what the environment was like at that time, and so on."

José finished showing them around the equipment, explaining what various instruments were for and what conclusions the team had reached.

Finally, late in the afternoon, Professor Bourne led Nik back to the SUV and drove him back into Shell.

Nik had a thousand thoughts, all bouncing around in his head, but all of them seemed trite and obvious in the scope of the find, so he rode in silence, thinking about what he needed to say to Randi.

At last, the SUV pulled up in front of the hotel.

Professor Bourne turned to him. "Start formulating some questions you'd like to ask. This conference is going to be huge, and I'd really like to see you be a part of the discussion. It will look really good for you later to have been in on this."

Nik stepped from the SUV. "Thank you, I will."

As soon as he was in his room, he picked up the phone.

Randi didn't answer, so he left a message. "Randi, it's Nik. I'm in Wyoming. Professor Bourne called and invited me out for a special conference. I can't even describe what I've seen—all I can say is, you have to get out here."

He paused, wanting to say more, not knowing what to say. "So, the conference is going to be Monday afternoon. I'll see if I can get you a pass to get into the conference, but just get out here. Call me at the hotel. My cell doesn't get good reception out here."

He left the number and hung up, hoping she'd get the message in time to get a flight out before the conference.

Chapter Twenty-Three

Los Angeles, California

Randi and Carole went out for dinner after work Friday night.

"This has been the longest week of my life," Randi sighed as she slid into the booth at the restaurant.

"Me too."

Randi smiled. "It's been fun, though. Who would have dreamed we'd get so much attention from one tiny little news spot?" It felt both strange and completely natural to say *we*, and to really mean it. She hadn't realized how good it felt to be part of something—a team, that was doing amazing work.

"Seriously. I can't tell you how many creepers have asked for my personal number after that." Carole shuddered.

The waitress came by with water and explained the specials. "I'll be back in a minute to get your orders." She scurried away.

Randi's phone beeped and she pulled it out of her purse. When had she missed a call? "Excuse me a sec."

Randi listened to the message three times. Nik didn't say anything about their fight, but he sounded urgent when he demanded she come to Wyoming. What in the world was going on? And why did Nik sound like the world might end if she didn't get to Wyoming immediately?

"I need to call Dr. Lengel," Randi told Carole.

"Tonight? What for?"

Randi put the phone on speaker and played the message for her.

"Who's Nik?" Carole asked.

"A friend of mine from college. The thing is, we had an argument and he hasn't been speaking to me for days. Now, all of a sudden, he calls me with *this*."

She dialed Dr. Lengel's number. "Hi, Dr. Lengel, it's Randi. I'm sorry to call so late, but I just got the strangest message from my friend Nik. He's in Wyoming. He said I need to get out there right away, but didn't say why. I—I know we're super busy right now, but I may need to take some time off."

"Hold that thought—I got a message from a friend of mine who is participating in a conference of some sort. Let me look into it—it may be something that the Society wants to be part of. I'll call you back."

Dr. Lengel hung up, and Randi picked nervously at her food while she waited for him to call back.

When Dr. Lengel called Randi back a short while later, he didn't waste any time. "I just talked to my friend Steve Henley. He's an ultrasound technician that works on the equipment used for archaeology and paleontology sites. He wrangled an invitation for the Cryptozoological Society to send a representative to some important conference in Wyoming."

"That's great!"

"What I wouldn't give to go. Of course, I can't afford to right now, just when the Society is gaining some publicity. How soon can you be ready to leave?"

"Um… whenever, I guess."

"Great. I'll get you on the first flight I can find."

"Okay—let me know. I'll go home and pack."

Randi hung up the phone and exhaled. Nik had been pretty emphatic about her coming, and despite their fight, he sounded genuinely sincere about her coming.

Whatever it was, it had to be pretty monumental to get Nik to drop a grudge that quickly.

***

Shell, Wyoming

Late Saturday night, Randi finally arrived in Shell, Wyoming. The driver that Dr. Lengel had arranged to pick her up from the airport dropped her off at the hotel where Nik told her he was staying. She wandered around the hotel looking for Nik, but didn't see him.

When she was unable to reach him by calling his room that morning to let him know she was coming, and none of her calls or texts to his cell went through, she decided she would just see him when she got there, but she still couldn't get in touch with him.

"Can I help you find something?" a voice behind her asked.

She turned. A man in his early twenties with dark hair and eyes smiled.

"Maybe. I'm looking for a friend of mine, Nik Gary. Tall, red hair—he's here for the conference."

"I've met him, but I couldn't tell you where he is now. Are you here for the conference, too?"

Randi nodded. "I'm Randi Ross."

"José Chavira. I'm one of the paleontology students on the dig. Have you had a chance to check out the site?"

"No, I just got into town a little bit ago."

"Well, if you'd like, I'd be happy to take you down there tomorrow."

"That would be great, thanks," she grinned.

"My pleasure. Meet me here around noon?"

"I'll be here."

After another glance around without seeing Nik, she decided to go back up to her room for the night.

The next morning, she put on a comfortable dress and walked around town, but still didn't find Nik. The town reminded her of a backdrop from an old Western movie, with its board sidewalks and quaint wooden buildings. She was having so much fun exploring the scenery, she lost track of the time until it was after when she was supposed to meet José.

She hurried back to the hotel.

José was sitting in one of the plush chairs in the hotel lobby when she came in.

"I'm so sorry, I lost track of time!"

He jumped up and grinned at her. "No worries. You ready to go?"

"Can I have five minutes to change clothes?"

His eyes scanned the flowing dress she wore. "You look great to me, but I guess you might be more comfortable in something else."

Fire warmed her cheeks at his compliment and she lowered her eyes. "I'll be right back."

She returned a few moments later in a pair of shorts and a T-shirt.

José led her to a Jeep parked outside.

"So, are you in the paleontology program, too?" José asked as they bumped down the dirt road toward the site.

"No, actually. I'm a historian."

"Really? Then what brings you out here?"

"Special interest. From what I've heard, this seems to fall into my area of expertise."

"What area is that?"

"Dragons."

"Really? That's an interesting area of expertise for a historian."

Randi laughed. "That's about how most people react. They tend to think I should be in mythology, not history, but I happen to believe that, in many cases, those two topics are very closely intertwined."

"What kinds of cases?"

"Well, pretty much all of them, if you think about it. Think of any myth you know and there's probably some sort of historical basis to it."

José cocked his head to the side as if pondering that idea.

Randi went on, not wanting him to think she was completely crazy. "Granted, many times the truth has been so blown out of proportion you can hardly tell it's the same story, but there's usually some sort of historical fact at the beginning of nearly all the stories we now think of as myths."

"That's an interesting theory, but it would be more interesting if you could prove it."

"What do you think I'm doing here?" Randi grinned.

"Good point. Let me know how that works out for you."

Upon arriving at the dig site, José helped Randi out of the Jeep and led her to where she could look down on the excavation.

Randi could hardly believe her eyes. There it was. Living—or, rather, fossilized—proof of the existence of dragons. The shape was unmistakable—it was what the mythological community would call a Western European dragon. The curve of the head, the wings folded behind it, the front legs reaching out as if grasping or clawing at something—all perfectly preserved.

Amazing. And it was real.

She glanced up and caught José looking at her. Heat rose to her cheeks. "What?"

"Nothing. It's just I've led dozens of people around this site and showed them everything there is to see. I've gotten every reaction, from disbelief, to those who said they knew it all along, to sheer awe. You're the first person I've seen take such delight in this find. You're looking at those dried-up old bones like you're in love."

Randi smiled. "In a way, I think I am. I've been dreaming of this moment for years, and now that it's finally in front of me, I don't quite know what to make of it."

"I'm glad you feel that way. That's how I see it. Everyone else is excited about being famous and about putting another species into the textbooks, but I'm just so amazed by it all, looking at it and working on it makes me happy."

"I know exactly what you mean."

She browsed through the collection of casts and pictures of the creature. "Look at that jaw. Its teeth are huge. Like snake fangs."

"Come here. Let me show you this." José held out his hand.

"What is it?" She took his hand and allowed him to help her down the incline to another tent pavilion.

"Bones. We found them inside the stomach cavity. At first we thought they must have been from something the thing ate. We were really excited about that, because it would have given us some very exciting insight into what the creature's diet was like, how it lived, and what the environment was like at the time." He smiled and his eyes danced. "However, we've discovered that that explanation is impossible."

"Why?"

"Because the bones are from a human arm."

Randi gasped. "How odd." She tried not to let the school-girl grin take over her face. "How do you suppose they got there?"

"We're still trying to figure that out. As best we can figure, the human probably died during a period when this area was covered in a swamp or bog and sank through the moist earth. Eventually, he ended up there, just by some odd coincidence."

"How did the bones get *inside* the stomach cavity, then?" she asked.

José shrugged. "The spaces between the bones must have been wider apart at that point."

"Wouldn't the thing have already been fossilized by the time humans came along?"

"Well, originally we would have thought so, but it must not have been."

"Then why hadn't the bones just rotted away?"

José looked at her quizzically.

She had to be careful. She was treading on very thin ice.

"This is not an exact science," José said finally. "We're still trying to figure out exactly how everything happened. It's difficult to determine in a few days what happened over the last several million years."

Randi didn't know much about geology or paleontology, but the explanation sounded weak. Occam's Razor—the simplest explanation was usually the correct one—so why was it so hard to believe that this dragon was alive at the same time as humans, and that it really had taken a bite out of one?

She didn't say what was on her mind. José was being very generous with his time in bringing her out here and showing her all this, and she didn't want to make him angry with her. Besides, she needed as much information from him as she could get so she could plan out what she'd ask at the conference the next day.

The thought of speaking out at the conference caused goose bumps to pop on her arm and the back of her neck, despite the heat. That's why she needed this information. She couldn't risk being made fun of in front of the entire conference.

Randi nodded. "What about the human bones, then? Were they fossilized, too?"

José nodded.

"Have they been carbon-dated yet?"

"Yes. We're waiting for the results."

"Will you let me know what they find?"

"It would be my pleasure," José said. "Of course, it would be easier if I had your direct number."

Randi blinked. Was he… was he asking for her phone number in a not-strictly-professional way? Guys didn't usually flirt with her, so she wasn't quite sure how to interpret his words. "Oh—um… yeah, of course. Remind me when we get back to the hotel to write it down for you."

"I'll hold you to that," José grinned.

Her cheeks flamed, and she quickly turned away to read the detailed notes attached to each of the fossils in the pavilion.

José led her around to the various locations around the site, explaining everything as they went along, until they finally ended up back where they'd started.

"Well, I don't want to take up your whole day," Randi smiled at him. "I really appreciate you bringing me out here, giving me the grand tour and all."

José smiled and led her back to the Jeep. "My pleasure. I mean that."

Randi smiled and turned her head to hide her blush. Despite the good-looking man giving her his undivided attention, however, she couldn't wait to get back to the hotel to write down what she'd learned.

Randi jumped from the Jeep as soon as they got back. "Thanks again. I really appreciate you taking the time to show me around. See you tomorrow?"

"Of course. Perk of being on the original team."

"As it should be," Randi grinned. "After all, you're making history."

"Wait—you forgot to give me your number," José chided.

He handed her a piece of paper from a bag in the back of the Jeep. She quickly jotted her number down, waved goodbye, and hurried inside.

She looked around the hotel one more time for Nik, but, not seeing him, went to her room. She tried calling him again, but still nothing.

She'd be sure to see him at the conference the next day, and in the meantime, she had a lot of work to do.

Chapter Twenty-Four

Los Angeles, California

Jeremiah was late to the office Monday morning. He'd been up late researching and decided to take a couple of hours to refresh before heading in.

Maria sat busily clacking away at the computer, inputting all the information of the new subscribers for the magazine. She gave him a coy smile as he entered. He tried not to look annoyed as he nodded in acknowledgment.

Frank's office door was propped open, as was Randi's.

"Morning, Frank. Morning, Carole, Rand—"

He took a second glance into Randi's office to make sure he hadn't missed anything.

He hadn't. Randi wasn't there. Carole sat behind the desk.

"Where's Randi?"

Carole glanced up. "She's still in Wyoming."

"Wyoming? Why is she in Wyoming?"

"She's covering the conference," Carole said, as if he were supposed to have some idea what she was talking about.

"What conference?" Jeremiah moved down the hall to Frank's office. "Frank, what's Randi doing in Wyoming?"

Dr. Lengel looked up with an annoyed expression. "I sent her to the conference."

"What are you talking about? What conference?"

Frank scratched his protruding belly. "Don't you watch the news? Some paleontology group from the university uncovered a new fossil, complete and in good condition. They're holding a conference to reveal their findings, and I sent Randi to represent us."

"You sent her as our official representative? As new as she is? With no training?" Jeremiah realized after the words were out that his tone might have been a touch louder than it needed to be, but he didn't regret letting Frank know his feelings. Randi shouldn't have been sent off on her own. It wasn't like her going to Europe. That was in search of her own personal quest, not on official Society business.

"Jeremiah, relax. She's just sitting in on a conference. The only training she needs is in taking notes. I think she's got it covered."

"Well, you should have at least called me. I could have gone."

"There wasn't really time. We only found out about it Friday night, and the conference is today. There are no flights directly into the town, so she had to fly out and then I sent a car to pick her up and drive the couple hours to get where she was going. We had to jump on the opportunity or we would've missed it."

"I still should have been a part of the decision-making process."

"I don't get it, Jeremiah. I make decisions like this all the time and you've never once mentioned it bothered you. I'm sorry. I didn't realize it was going to be a big deal."

"Well, you should have at least told me she was going to be gone," Jeremiah scowled, his voice softening.

"I'm really sorry. I didn't realize you'd miss her so much."

"I don't miss her. It's just… I'm a partner here, and I'd like to have some input once in a while."

Stalking into his office, he shut his door a little harder than he needed to. He had a valid complaint, after all. He was an equal partner, but Frank acted as if he owned the place.

Filling his lungs, he forced himself to calm down.

Why did this irritate him so much? He'd never minded before. In fact, he'd preferred it that way.

Frank made all the decisions and took care of the business side of things, and he could concentrate on what he liked best, the research and fieldwork.

Their partnership had worked well for several years. So, why did it bother him so much this time?

Well, it certainly wasn't because he missed Randi. The idea was both preposterous and annoying. Sure, she was a nice girl, and who wouldn't appreciate her positive attitude and pretty face?

Sure, it was nice to have another person in the office, but only because it had been so awkward with just himself, Frank, and Maria.

Of course, it was also nice to have someone who could hold her own in a conversation. Even at church there were few people who could carry on any sort of lively debate with him.

Moreover, Randi didn't obsess about her appearance. She always looked nice and wore a little bit of makeup, but she didn't cake it on her face. A refreshing change from most women.

Jeremiah stared across the hall in the direction of Randi's office. She dressed to flatter her figure, not draw attention. Unlike Maria, who seemed to go out of her way to wear clothes calculated to make a man's heart race and his mind wander in unholy directions. Or Carole, whose clothes always seemed to be two sizes too small, though she didn't seem to even notice.

He toyed with his pen as his mind wandered to Randi's healthy curves. If she ever actually tried to show off her figure, he was sure he wouldn't be the only one sorely tempted.

Then there was her manner—no self-consciousness at all. She didn't let anyone talk down to her, and no one intimidated her. And she—

Jeremiah wasn't sure which was more annoying, the realization that he *did* miss Randi, or the fact that Frank had pointed it out.

***

The Rainforest near Ouesso, in the Sangha region of Congo, Africa

Naomi watched the trail in case Albert reappeared, but he didn't. At last, she got up and set about gathering some herbs and things to make herself dinner.

It would be a long summer, up at the top of the mountain by herself, waiting for him to return. Well, not completely by herself. She had the egg.

She walked over to where she'd hidden it and rolled it out of the nest she'd made, up toward the front of the hut where she could keep a closer eye on it.

Day after day she stared at it, sometimes until long after night had fallen. The creatures roared as they flew out at dusk, hunting. Every time, a chill ran up her spine. What would happen if the egg hatched? Would a monster emerge, ready to devour her? Or would it not hatch at all, since it was away from its mother?

Many times she resisted the temptation to throw the egg in the water, or leave it by the shore for the creatures to find, or to smash it with a rock and destroy it, but despite her better judgment, she couldn't help feeling a little curious.

She settled the egg near the fire, covering it with grass and leaves, and sat to wait for Albert's return, or for something else to happen.

During the day, when she knew the creatures were sleeping, she went swimming or hunting. In the evening, she nestled quietly in the forest behind her shelter of trees.

Out of sheer boredom one day, she began sewing together the skins of the animals she killed for food. She didn't yet know what she'd make out of them, but whatever it turned out to be, it would be big.

***

Shell, Wyoming

Randi dressed in her most professional-looking suit and went to the conference room at the other, larger hotel in town, long before the conference was to begin. She went immediately to the table that held the soundboard and smiled at the man sitting there. "Good morning. I'm Randi Ross, with the American Cryptozoological Society. I wonder if I could ask you a huge favor?"

"Sure." The man's voice was pleasant, friendly.

"Could you by any chance make me a copy of the recording from today?"

The man shook his head. "Copies will be available tomorrow."

"I know, but they banned phones and devices so I can't make my own recording, and I'm going to have to leave right after the conference to make my flight back to L.A., and I'd really like to be able to go over it again on the

200

plane. Please?"

The man sighed but gave her an indulgent smile. "All right, but don't tell anyone."

Randi grinned. "Thanks. I really appreciate it."

"No problem."

Randi found a seat next to José, about halfway back on the left side of the room. She tried not to fidget as she waited for the rest of the crowd to file in and the conference to begin.

It surprised her how many people she recognized as they drifted in and found their seats. Several professors from the university she knew by sight, although Dean Palmer and Professor Bourne were the only ones she knew by name.

She also noticed Dr. Lengel's friend, Mr. Chevalet. It shouldn't have been a surprise to see him—after all, he was the head of the paleontology department at the museum. Still, Dr. Lengel mentioned that Mrs. Chevalet passed away recently, so Randi hadn't expected him to come. She'd try to catch him after the conference to say hello.

As seats filled, Randi glanced up. Nik's unmistakable shock of red hair stood out where he sat in the front row on the right. She wished he had come over to talk to her, but he probably didn't have time. The conference would start any moment. She'd have to catch him afterward.

She smiled at José, realizing she'd only been half listening to what he said. She jumped back into their conversation and continued chatting until a squat, balding man strutted up to the podium.

Conversation rustled to a halt, all eyes landing expectantly on the speaker.

"Welcome, everyone. I'm Administrator Schweitzer. I'm glad you could all make it today. I have some exciting new discoveries to share with you. I'm going to begin by telling you a little about the work we've done here, and then about the fossil we've uncovered, as well as our findings and beliefs about it. There will be a question and answer session at the end, so please save all questions and comments until then."

He paused and gave a long, sweeping glance over the audience.

His speech lasted almost an hour and was complete with a slide show featuring pictures of the dig site, the fossil, and the ultrasound pictures that revealed a better picture of what the fossil would look like when it was completely uncovered.

He completely left out anything about the finding of the bones inside the creature's stomach cavity.

Randi frowned. Weren't they even going to mention them? That detail must come out sooner or later. If no one else asked about it, she would.

Finally, Administrator Schweitzer finished speaking and opened the floor for questions, leaving a fantastic picture—made up of the aerial shots superimposed over one of the ultrasound shots, to give a clearer idea of what the fossil looked like—on the screen.

Randi stood up immediately, as did several others. The room buzzed as people tried to be the first to get their questions answered.

Beaming, Administrator Schweitzer pointed to a reporter near the front.

Randi scratched down notes on a pad of hotel paper from her room and waited patiently for Administrator Schweitzer to answer several more questions before he turned to acknowledge her.

"Yes, Ms.—" He nodded in her direction.

"Ross."

"Ms. Ross. Your question?"

"Can you explain again how you arrived at your conclusion regarding the fossil's age?"

"Certainly. Based on other fossils found in similar rock layers in this same region, we have determined this creature lived during the Cretaceous period."

"What other fossils?"

Administrator Schweitzer ran through a list so quickly Randi couldn't write them all down.

"Have these fossils been carbon-dated yet?"

"Yes, but we're still waiting for the results."

"Is there any chance, based on other fossils found around the area or on any other evidence that these fossils could be from a different era? Perhaps much more recent than is projected?" She desperately hoped he would bring up the bones in the stomach cavity and his theory about that. She had her own theories, but didn't want to bring them up without any actual evidence other than her deep desire to believe dragon-like creatures existed within the timeframe of human history.

"We have no reason to believe that our current hypothesis is incorrect,"

Administrator Schweitzer said, sounding annoyed.

"I've heard a theory that this area was once a swamp, and some of the fossils may have gotten interposed with fossils from other eras," she said quickly. "Can you speak to that?"

"I feel quite certain that when the carbon dating results come back, that will answer more of those questions."

"Thank you, Administrator Schweitzer." Randi's neck and cheeks grew warm and uncomfortable boiling started in her stomach as every eye focused on her. She sat quickly.

She caught Nik's eye as she sat and gave him a quick wink. After a brief smile that didn't reach his eyes, he turned to face the front of the room where Administrator Schweitzer was answering another question by pointing to something in the picture.

José looked at her, eyes seeming too large for his face. His ears turned red and his mouth was drawn in a hard line. She couldn't tell if he was stifling anger or laughter. The look seemed somewhat bemused, somewhat aghast, and somewhat admiring, she thought. Or hoped.

She kept her eyes on Administrator Schweitzer, pretending not to notice the curious glances that darted her way by some and ignoring the hard glares aimed at her by others.

Several more people asked questions, but the answers were mostly things José had already told her.

Someone then asked a question about where the fossil fit on the fossil record.

"We believe this creature may be the missing link between theropods and modern day birds."

Randi practically jumped to her feet, hand reaching for the ceiling, staring hard at Administrator Schweitzer.

Administrator Schweitzer pointedly ignored her and gestured toward a woman at the back of the room.

"This creature is much larger than a Deinonychus, which you say this is evolved from, but according to evolutionary theory, it should have gotten smaller, as it evolved into a bird. Why is that?"

"Ah, good question. We are still looking into that. Our current hypothesis is that this creature may have had some sort of bone disease that caused it to grow excessively. Or, perhaps, like a snake, it continued to grow as long as it was alive and this particular specimen just lived for an absurdly long time compared to its relatives. We will know more when we have completely uncovered the fossil and are able to study it more closely."

The woman seemed satisfied with that answer and sat down.

Randi was standing alone.

Chapter Twenty-Five

Administrator Schweitzer looked out over the crowd, avoiding Randi's gaze.

Finally, after a moment that seemed like an eternity, someone else stood up.

"Yes, sir?" Administrator Schweitzer said.

"What do you make of the protrusion on the end of its tail?"

"Again, it will require further study. It may just be a bone spur—which is most likely, especially if we discover it had some sort of bone disease—or it may be an adaptation it developed as a self-defense mechanism."

The man sat down.

No one else stood, and Randi could feel the sidelong glances that darted between herself and Administrator Schweitzer. She half-suspected no one else stood, just out of curiosity for what she would ask next.

Administrator Schweitzer apparently realized he couldn't keep ignoring her. "Yes, Ms. Ross?"

"I'm confused." She tried to sound as if she genuinely were. "According to evolutionary theory, as dinosaurs evolved into birds, they stopped using their front limbs, and those limbs then evolved into wings, is that right?"

Administrator Schweitzer shifted, his shoulders twitching. "Yes, that's correct."

"How, then, is it possible for this specimen to have both fully formed front limbs *and* fully formed wings?"

A sea of heads swung from attention to Randi to stare at Administrator Schweitzer.

Administrator Schweitzer faltered only a moment. "Until the fossil is completely uncovered, we can't be certain what is what, or whether we're seeing what we think we're seeing."

"Do you honestly think a room full of the most brilliant scientists, paleontologists, and biologists won't recognize both front limbs *and* wings on a picture as clear as that one?" Randi gestured toward the image on the projector screen.

Randi had never seen a face quite that shade of burgundy. Administrator Schweitzer sputtered a moment. "The fossil record, while it does give us valuable clues to the order of the prehistoric earth, does not tell us everything, and scientists must take that information and decipher the clues to come up with a clear picture. With each new piece of evidence found, scientists must reevaluate what they know to find where that piece fits."

"But isn't it possible that this particular specimen is something else entirely? Something that doesn't fit into the fossil record as we know it? Something, maybe, new?"

The looks on the faces around the room were far more angry and annoyed than admiring or even curious by that point, but Randi couldn't concern herself with that. She'd come this far. She had to go all the way.

"We just don't have all the information yet," Administrator Schweitzer bellowed.

"So, since we don't have all the information, isn't it possible this is an as-yet undiscovered species? Something that the casual observer might describe as a dragon? And if it is, in fact, what legend describes as a dragon, isn't it possible those legends were based on first-hand accounts, and it was, therefore, in existence during human history?"

Administrator Schweitzer's bald head glistened, and a vein in his temple throbbed. "There are always adjustments being made, in every venue of science, and we will probably never have all the pieces to put together a perfect picture of the evolutionary tree, but we have come to the most accurate conclusions based on the evidence that we possibly can."

Nods from around the room seemed to calm him.

"Thank you, sir. You've been very helpful." Randi tried to make her tone as patronizing as his, though she couldn't be sure how successful she'd been.

Administrator Schweitzer looked furtively around the audience for another question. After a slight lull, somebody raised a hand.

Administrator Schweitzer's lips split in an obsequious smile. "Yes?"

Randi only half-listened to the next few questions. Based on the sneers and glares shot her direction, Randi guessed she'd won the Disruptive Jerk award for the conference. Professor Bourne shot daggers at her, and even Dean Palmer's usually placid expression carried a frosty disdain.

Randi knew her chance of getting any more questions answered resembled a snowball's chance of survival in L.A. right then. Perhaps if she formulated a new plan of attack…

She waited for a few more questions. As the pauses between queries got longer, she leaned over toward José. She spoke in just above a murmur, but loudly enough for the people sitting beside her and directly behind her to hear.

"He didn't say anything about the human arm bones found in the stomach. Do you think he's going to? You can see them pretty clearly in that picture. I wonder if anyone else has noticed them."

***

Nik stared straight ahead, unable to concentrate. He glanced at Professor Bourne through the corner of his eye. The professor's teeth clenched, his knuckles were white from gripping his cane, and his eyes looked as if they would pop out of their sockets.

He knew what Professor Bourne must be thinking. This was a scientific informational meeting, not a debate, and Randi had treated the whole thing like her personal soapbox. He, more than anyone, knew how much she wanted to prove that dragons existed within the scope of human history, but she didn't seem to grasp that this was neither the time nor the place.

His emotions jumped back and forth between annoyance with her for making a mockery of the conference and pride in her courage and intelligence.

Embarrassment won out. The entire room sat entranced by her, but not in a good way. She was a laughingstock. Hopefully, when this was over, he could talk some sense into her.

Administrator Schweitzer put her in her place, so to speak. For Randi, that humiliation could cripple. He snuck a look back at her. She still sat in calm composure, looking collected and professional, but he'd be willing to bet she was devastated inside. On the other hand, not everyone looked appalled.

Some looked as if her words had started a series of wheels turning in their heads.

He turned his attention back to Administrator Schweitzer.

"Yes, sir?" Administrator Schweitzer pointed, and Nik turned to see him indicate the man seated directly behind Randi. Nik recognized him, but couldn't quite place him.

Randi bit her lip, the way she did when she was holding in a smile. What had she done now? Nik caught her eyes and raised his eyebrows in question.

Her lips quirked in a half-smile, and her eyes twinkled mischievously. A slight tilt of her head told him to pay attention to the question being asked.

"I was just wondering," the man behind her began. "What it is we can see there in the middle? It looks like it's inside the stomach cavity, and it looks like bones. Is that correct?"

"Yes. However, they are unrelated to the fossil. We have concluded that sometime, much after the remains of this creature were fossilized, the wet, swampy conditions of this area caused the fossils to separate slightly, and these bones worked their way into the midst of the fossil."

"Ah, the theory that Ms. Ross conjectured about?"

Administrator Schweitzer coughed.

Someone else stood. "So, these bones are entirely separate? They're not fossilized as well?"

"Well, they are fossilized, but they were fossilized at a later date."

"How?" someone else asked.

"This area was covered in marshland for much of history," Administrator Schweitzer said. "Our belief is that the bones inside the body sank down at a much later date and just happened to land in the same area."

"Have they been carbon tested yet? Did the carbon testing affirm your conclusions?"

Nik had lost track of who was bouncing questions toward the front, as everyone seemed to be talking over one another.

"We're still waiting for the carbon dating results, but we're confident they'll prove our hypothesis," Administrator Schweitzer said.

"So they're not the bones of something the creature ate? That's what it looks like," another voice piped up.

"No, certainly not," Administrator Schweitzer insisted. "Again, when the

208

carbon tests come back, we'll know more.

"But what are they?" the first man, the one behind Randi, demanded. "What kind of creature are they from?

Administrator Schweitzer's head began to glisten again. "Well, from what we can tell so far, they appear to be the bones from a human arm."

The room buzzed with questions, much like at the beginning, before Randi spoke the first time.

The man behind Randi spoke out above the din. "If the bones inside traveled down through the marshland and are not as old as the layer of earth they're in, then how can we know for sure that the dragon fossil didn't do the same thing?"

Chapter Twenty-Six

Randi just sat and smiled. Nik picked his jaw up from where it had dropped. No wonder she sounded so sure of herself! She had inside information—he should've known she wouldn't risk saying something unless she had reason to believe she could be right. He shot a grin her way, even though she wasn't looking at him anymore.

Each answer Administrator Schweitzer gave brought up more questions. People wanted to know more about the fossilized bones, how they got into the dinosaur stomach cavity, whether or not the findings might be suspect, and how they could be corroborated.

Administrator Schweitzer finally resorted to the same answer for every question. "We won't know more until we've had a chance to study it further."

He quickly closed the conference and disappeared out the door behind where he stood.

Immediately the room filled with humming as people stood and began talking with one another, discussing what they'd learned and speculating on every possibility Nik could think of, plus plenty he couldn't regarding the strange, dragon-like dinosaur.

***

The Director stood at the edge of the room, staring at Randi Ross, seething. That girl was really beginning to get annoying. The other invitees to the conference had begun to mill about, conversing with one another, and more than one of them looked in Randi's direction, as though deliberating whether or not to engage her in conversation.

She could not be allowed to continue meddling with everything.

It was becoming clear that it was because of her that Carole McCray had kept her Bigfoot discovery from Seth. Maria said they were close friends, so it stood to reason that she had been the one to convince Carole to leave Seth and come to L.A.

And now she was here. Why had none of the agents informed the Director that she was coming? Her behavior during the conference was unpardonable.

The American Cryptozoological Society had never been a threat—just something the Syndicate kept its eyes on—that is, until Randi Ross had started working there. Even Jeremiah Bryant hadn't done this much damage, and he'd been working against them for years. Now, suddenly, Randi was uncovering things the Syndicate had spent countless hours—and dollars—to keep a handle on.

Rob was supposed to be watching her. He should have been the first to notify the Director that Randi was coming here. He would have to step up his dedication to the cause before Randi did something irreparable.

Who knew what she would do next?

***

The man sitting behind Randi tapped her shoulder. "That was pretty slick there, getting me to ask your question for you."

Randi turned. He was a tall, well-built man in his early thirties with sandy hair and blue-green eyes.

"Why, whatever do you mean?" Randi grinned.

"You know exactly what I mean. You figured Schweitzer wouldn't answer anything else you asked, so you made that cryptic statement about the bones, loud enough for me to hear, knowing full well a reporter like me wouldn't be able to resist knowing what you meant."

"Actually, I had no idea you were a reporter. I just hoped *somebody* would hear and be curious enough to ask."

The man blinked at her, looking a little shocked and vaguely insulted. "You didn't know I was a reporter? Didn't you recognize me?"

Randi stared at him for a moment, trying to remember if she'd ever seen him before. "Should I?"

"Scott Teagan, *Live at the Site*? The world's top independent news source?"

Randi shook her head. "Sorry."

Confusion warred with curiosity across his handsome features. "Wow. That's... new. You've really never seen my show?"

"Sorry, no. I don't really watch anything."

"At all?"

"Hardly ever."

"Why not?"

Randi shrugged. "I have better things to do with my time."

Scott laughed. "Well, I covered your news spot—the Bigfoot thing."

"Did you? What did you think of it?"

"Well, based on what I saw of you then, I never would have picked you out to be so confrontational. I wouldn't have thought you had it in you to attack Schweitzer the way you did."

"I didn't attack him. I just wanted to make sure all the points were covered, and he wasn't leaving anything out."

Scott laughed. "Don't get me wrong, I thought you did great. I enjoyed the little show you put on."

"I wouldn't exactly call it putting on a show," Randi scowled.

"Quit being offended by everything I say. I was impressed! I always appreciate an honest investigation of the truth. Which you'd know if you ever watched my show. In fact, I was impressed enough to want to do a solo interview with you."

Randi brightened immediately. "Really?"

"Very much so. Do you have time this afternoon, after all the conference stuff is over?"

Randi shook her head. "No, unfortunately I have to leave almost right away to catch my flight back to L.A. Once I'm home, I'd be happy to set up an interview anytime."

"Great. Let me get your card and I'll call you later this week."

"Okay." Suddenly grateful for the business cards Dr. Lengel had printed up, she dug one out of her purse and handed it to him.

"Do you have a cell phone or anything, in case I can't get a hold of you at the office?"

Randi quickly jotted her cell phone number on the back.

"Thanks. I'll call you when I'm back in L.A."

Randi nodded. "Great. Hey, I've got to run—there's someone I need to speak to."

With another quick smile, she turned and headed toward where she saw Nik's bright hair towering above the crowd. She couldn't catch his eye, so she pushed her way as politely as she could through the crowd toward him.

"Miss Ross?"

She turned and smiled at the man who stood beside her. It was Dr. Lengel's friend. "Mr. Chevalet, it's good to see you." She took the hand he extended and clasped it warmly. "I'm very sorry for your loss. How are you doing?"

His eyes filled with tears, and he held her hand more tightly. "I don't know. It helps when I can be here, working and not thinking about it. Every time I think of her, I—" He choked, clearly unable to finish his sentence.

Randi nodded, still holding his hand and looking at him with concern. "Do you want to talk about it?"

Jon shook his head and released her hand. "No, not yet. Thank you, though. I'd rather just talk about this conference. Some find, eh?"

"I think so. Would you care to revise the answer you gave me last time we spoke, about not having dragons in the fossil record?" She gave him a sly grin.

Jon chuckled. "Well, my dear, it does seem as if you may have had a point."

"What's your opinion about the human arm bones found in the stomach cavity? Do you agree with Administrator Schweitzer's hypothesis that the bones sank down through a swampy layer and just mysteriously ended up in the stomach cavity? Or would you say it's more likely that the creature ingested the human arm shortly before its death?"

"Fossils ending up in the wrong layer is hardly unprecedented. Certainly it has happened before, and certainly we will find such things again. The bones ending up in the stomach cavity is what gives it the appearance of being something that it's not, but I have no doubt that science will win on this one." A twinkle came into his eyes, and he said, in a surprisingly good impression of Schweitzer, "However, we won't know more until we've had a chance to study it further.'"

Randi laughed. "That excuse will only last for so long, you know. Eventually people are going to want some real answers."

"Which they'll get when the carbon dating is complete."

"Tell you what," Randi said. "I still contend that that dragon was alive at the same time as humans, and it ate that person's arm. The fossil isn't as old as they're saying. If I'm right, you have to publish a paper stating the facts exactly."

Jon chuckled. "And if you're wrong?"

"Then you get to pick my punishment."

"Deal. I have faith in scientific techniques. I'm sure with enough study the truth can be found."

Randi cocked her head slightly. "You really believe that?"

"Miss Ross, I've been studying paleontology for longer than you've been alive. I have yet to see anything that will convince me this is all made-up, or that the hypotheses presented aren't the most likely scenario."

"What would it take to convince you?"

"I'm not sure anything could at this point."

Was there a note of wistfulness in his tone when he said that?

An idea struck her. "What if you saw a real, live dinosaur? A relic from the past, still alive today?"

Jon's eyes widened. "What are you suggesting?"

"Go with my team on a dragon-hunting trip to Africa."

He stared at her for a long moment. "You can't be serious."

"I am completely serious. We're planning to leave at the beginning of next month. So far, it's me, Dr. Bryant, and Carole, our photographer. We could really use someone with your expertise. If you have any other people you'd like to suggest, we'd love to have them along, as well. Dr. Lengel would prefer we have a team of at least six or seven, but we'll take whatever we get."

"You're serious."

Randi nodded. "Completely. Come on," she grinned. "You could use the break. Besides, who wouldn't want a free trip to Africa?"

Well, besides her.

Jon gaped at her, speechless.

"You don't have to decide right now. Think about it awhile. When you get back to L.A., give Dr. Lengel a call and—"

"No," Jon said.

Randi's face fell. "Well, I understand if that's the way you feel."

"No—I mean, I don't need to think about it or call Frank. I'll go."

Randi's jaw dropped. "Really?"

"Really."

"That's excellent!" Randi grabbed his hand and pumped it up and down a few times. "It's great to have you on the team. I hate to rush off, but would you please excuse me? There's someone I need to speak with."

She couldn't see Nik anymore. Pushing through the crowd, she made her way toward the last place she'd seen his red-topped head.

No Nik.

A solid mass of flesh stopped her when she tried to turn. "Oh, I'm sorry," she muttered. "I didn't see you."

The human wall was José Chavira. "That's okay. You can run into me anytime."

Heat rose to her cheeks as she caught the appreciative gleam in his eyes.

José quickly covered her embarrassment. "Hey, I just wanted to let you know I really enjoyed talking to you yesterday and hearing your perspective during the conference today. I was thinking, maybe when I get back to L.A., we could do it again."

"Sure." She didn't realize until after she'd said it that she'd just agreed to what might be a date. Embarrassment rose to her cheeks again, but she pushed it aside.

"Can I get your number so I can contact you?"

"Oh, of course. Sorry. Here." She pulled a business card out of her purse. "My e-mail is there, and I'll put my cell on the back." She scribbled on the back of the card. Then, as politely as she could she said, "I have to run— there's someone I need to speak to before I leave."

"Okay, I'll talk to you later."

Randi smiled then turned away and scanning the crowd, but she still didn't see Nik.

"Miss Ross," said yet another voice.

Randi turned.

The man from the sound booth stood there, a grin on his face, holding out a flash drive. "No wonder you wanted that."

Randi smiled. "Thank you. I can't tell you how much I appreciate it."

"I can imagine. Don't worry about it. Listening to you make those guys sweat was worth the trouble."

"Thanks," Randi grinned.

"One thing I have to know—did you know all that was going to happen before you started?"

Randi shrugged. "I knew the questions I wanted out there and what I wanted people to be thinking about. I didn't know exactly what would happen, but I did know it would cause some controversy."

The man smiled. "But Administrator Schweitzer pretty well slammed your arguments into the ground."

"Perhaps, in a manner of speaking. Everyone here saw his face turn red, though, and there are at least some that aren't completely satisfied with the answers he gave. That's all that really matters. As long as people are questioning what they're being told, and finding out the truth for themselves, I've done my job."

The man gave her an admiring glance. "Well, then, I guess you've done your job pretty well. Congratulations."

"Thank you."

"You're going to make a name for yourself very soon. I'm honored to have met you, Randi Ross."

He turned and walked away without even giving her his name.

Randi watched him a moment then turned around again, searching in vain for Nik.

She scanned the lobby. No luck.

Maybe in his room? She made her way to the front desk. The woman behind the counter dialed his room, but Nik didn't answer.

Finally, she couldn't wait any longer or she'd miss her flight. The driver of the car Dr. Lengel had arranged had already texted her three times.

She'd just have to talk to Nik when they both got home.

Chapter Twenty-Seven

As soon as the conference ended, Nik tried to walk toward Randi, but Professor Bourne took him by the arm and maneuvered him away.

"There are so many important people here that you must meet," he said.

Nik glanced toward Randi, trying to catch her eye, to signal her in some way to wait because he wanted to talk to her.

Absorbed in conversation with the good-looking man who sat behind her during the conference, Randi didn't notice him.

Brows furrowed, Nik followed Professor Bourne, absently shaking hands with people as the professor introduced them. He tried to concentrate, but his eyes kept darting back to Randi. He suppressed a sigh of irritation.

Now she stood in another part of the room, her eyes locked on yet another good-looking guy, as if he were the only person in the room. Nik couldn't seem to get her attention for even a moment.

He glanced at Professor Bourne.

The professor scowled in Randi's direction, then nudged Nik with the end of his cane and pointed out into the lobby of the hotel.

"I don't think it's a good idea for you to be seen with her here," he muttered once they were out of the crowd. "You don't want people to think you're associated with her, Nik. You're a *real* scientist, and you have the potential to really make a difference, but if you attach yourself to the wrong people, you'll lose credibility."

"I'm going to lose credibility just saying hi?"

Professor Bourne tapped his cane on the floor. "Listen, Nik, I invited you out here for more than just to show you something interesting. I've had a conversation with the Information Advancement Fellowship, and they're prepared to offer you a job as soon as you've completed your internship at the Palmer Lab. That's why you're here—to introduce yourself to one of the most respected scientific communities in the world. Unfortunately, that means leaving behind things that will stunt your career. That girl," he nodded his head toward the conference room, "is one of them. Especially after what she pulled in there today, you can't be labeled as an associate of hers."

"I can't even talk to her? So, I have to decide, here and now, whether to have a decent career or a best friend?"

"Welcome to adulthood," Professor Bourne laughed dryly. He started down the hallway in the opposite direction. "In all seriousness, though, essentially that's what it comes down to. You're an intelligent fellow, and you have a bright future ahead of you. This is not the time to chase schoolboy crushes. Now, we have a lunch with Administrator Schweitzer and a few others, so go upstairs and get ready. I'll meet you back down here in half an hour."

Nik considered Professor Bourne's words.

He'd warned Randi about this very thing. He'd tried to tell her that her choices would have consequences, that if she wanted to get ahead in her career, she'd have to play by the rules. He still cared about her—that would never change—but he couldn't very well balk at Professor Bourne's advice, when it was the exact advice he'd given out. He hated being put in this position. When he'd said the same things to Randi, it hadn't occurred to him that, at some point, he'd have to make the same decisions himself.

But here he was, and the choice lay before him.

Follow Randi down a path toward obscurity, or take the opportunities that were handed to him and really make something of himself.

He waited until Professor Bourne was out of sight, then went outside to where he had a little phone reception and left a message on Randi's voicemail. "Listen, I'm sorry I have to say this, but I'm sorry I invited you out here. It was a mistake that could cost me a huge career. I'm going to have to step back and reevaluate my future, and as long as you're making a fool of yourself at important conventions, I can't have you in it."

***

Randi got off the plane and turned on her phone. Finally, decent reception! She had a message.

"Hey, Randi, it's Nik."

Her heart skipped a beat. Until she heard the rest of the message. Then, it plummeted through the floor.

So, that was it. Any potential future, including friendship, was over between them.

She knew it. She knew it would come to this. Thank God she had resisted his pressure to get back together. First, a busty blonde, and now a career in science. There would always be a reason for him to break her heart, but at least it wasn't worse. At least they weren't together, so he couldn't dump her again.

When she got home, she took the plush dragon he'd won at the fair and stuffed it in the farthest top corner of her closet, away from sight.

She went to bed early, wanting to be well-rested for work the next morning.

At least there, she was appreciated.

***

Rob Keane heard the buzzing of his cell phone as it vibrated on the bedside table at two in the morning.

He grabbed it, pressing the silent button, and rolled over to look at Jan. She appeared to be sleeping soundly. He scrambled out of bed and went to the bathroom, shutting the door behind him.

"It's me," said The Director.

"I thought as much," Rob answered. "What is it?"

"Randi Ross. She has become too much of a liability. I want you to take care of her."

"Do you want me to just incapacitate her or do you want her out of the picture completely?"

"Out of the picture." The Director's voice was tight, barely controlled.

"Consider it done," Rob said, keeping his voice calm.

221

There was a click as the Director disconnected. Rob didn't even hesitate before making the next call. Long ago, he had learned to disconnect his emotions from his job.

"Collins," said a groggy voice on the other end.

"It's me. We have an assignment. We have to work together on this one—the Director wants this done right."

"Right," said Collins, "The regular meeting place, then, to go over the plan?"

"Yes. 0700."

"See you then," Collins said.

***

Randi walked into the office with her head held high, proud of her accomplishment at the conference, no matter what Nik thought.

Jeremiah came out of his office, his dark hair slightly tousled and out of place, his green eyes bright. "Welcome back." He sounded eager. "How did it go?"

"Great," Randi grinned.

She held out the flash drive with the recording of the conference to him. "We're going to want copies of that. Also, we're going to need another ticket to Africa, under the name of Jon Chevalet."

Jeremiah took the drive from her, eyes widening. "I'll listen to it right away. Care to join me?"

"Sure." Randi followed him into his office.

She lounged in one of the chairs across from his desk as he inserted the drive.

Carole came in about halfway through Administrator Schweitzer's introduction—she'd dropped Randi off in front of the building before going to park. Randi waved her into the other chair, barely taking her eyes from Jeremiah's face, absorbing the few changes that crossed his features. She was pretty sure the occasional raising of his brows and pursing of his lips meant he was curious about where this was going.

Dr. Lengel sauntered into Dr. Bryant's office just as Administrator Schweitzer neared the end of his speech. "Is this from the conference?"

Randi nodded. "We're almost to the good part."

She stood so he could sit and perched herself on the edge of Jeremiah's

222

desk.

Jeremiah sucked in his breath. Did she smell funny or something? She raised an eyebrow at him, but he didn't look at her.

Maybe it wasn't her. Carol crossed her legs. Her tiny skirt rode up a little higher. Randi caught Dr. Lengel indulging in a long glance before turning away. Carole didn't seem to have any notion of how pretty and sexy she was.

Dr. Lengel's eyes focused on Jeremiah. "What have I missed?"

"Just the introduction," Randi said. "It's not that important. You can listen to it later."

Administrator Schweitzer invited questions and Randi's smile grew wider.

When it got to Randi's question about the fossil having limbs in addition to the wings, Carole looked awed, Jeremiah looked impressed, and Dr. Lengel's eyes narrowed.

All three sat in stunned silence until Administrator Schweitzer sputtered out his response and called on the next person.

"What was that?" Dr. Lengel cursed.

Randi crossed her arms in front of her chest. "What was what? I asked a legitimate question."

"You interrupted an important scientific conference to push your own agenda!" Dr. Lengel shouted.

She glared at him. "I did no such thing. I simply tried to bring to light the holes in his theory."

"That was neither the time nor the place," Dr. Lengel hissed. "You were only there to observe and gather information. I trusted you to give a positive impression of the Society to the scientific community!"

"Well, I guess you should have specified that before you sent me," Randi snapped. "I didn't realize we were only out to make a good impression. I was going on the belief that our purpose was to seek the truth."

"Shh!" Jeremiah hissed as Randi's voice came over the speaker again.

Randi glared at Dr. Lengel.

His face turned a deep shade of red, a vein in his neck pulsed, and his nostrils flared.

Randi turned, scowling, and looked at Jeremiah.

He didn't look angry, but she couldn't interpret the expression he wore.

A man's voice asked a question, and Randi spoke softly to Jeremiah, although she knew the others could hear. "That one was mine, too, but I got him to ask it for me."

A smile tugged at the corners of Jeremiah's mouth as Scott Teagan, *Live at the Site*, asked about the bones in the stomach cavity.

At last, the recording ended. For a moment there was silence.

"I can't believe you!" Dr. Lengel jumped to his feet, looking down at her. "You have made a mockery of everything this Society stands for. We're supposed to be legitimate scientists, and you made us look like a bunch of whackos."

She stood, glaring him in the eyes. "I did not. The man was standing up there making up lies, spouting them out and pretending they were science. He didn't have a clue what he was talking about. All I did was point that out. The man has an actual dragon fossil, with very convincing evidence that it was alive in tandem with humans, and the only argument he could come up with is 'we need to study it more.' I didn't make a fool out of cryptozoology—Administrator Schweitzer made a fool out of science."

She took a step closer, staring at him. "I made people think, while he was trying to feed them a pile of fiction. I portrayed your precious Society as a group of free-thinking individuals who aren't going to take whatever they hand us without looking at all the facts."

"You *ruined* the conference," Dr. Lengel spat. "Worse, you put our grant funding at risk. We can't have you making waves like that!"

Randi clenched her teeth. "What bothers you more—that I made a scene, or that I was right?"

Dr. Lengel sputtered for a moment before sputtering, "You're fired!"

Randi raised her voice in return. "You can't fire me. You've already financed an expedition to Africa."

"I can fire you, and I can cancel your trip!"

"*Enough*," Jeremiah shouted above them both.

Both Randi and Dr. Lengel stepped back from one another and looked at him.

Jeremiah's voice lowered to its normal pitch. "Frank, as I'm an equal partner in this company, you can't fire her without my consent. Please go back to your office and we'll talk about it later. Carole, go to Randi's office and do whatever you need to do. Randi, please stay here a moment. I'd like to have a word with you."

Amazingly, Dr. Lengel obeyed his partner without another word.

"For what it's worth, I thought you were great," Carole whispered as she left.

"Thanks," Randi muttered. When Carole was out of earshot, she turned and scowled at Jeremiah. "I'm not wrong. I did well at that conference."

"I agree."

Randi fell into a chair, stunned. "Really? You don't think I made us sound like a bunch of whackos?"

Jeremiah chuckled. "I'm sure there are plenty who will choose to have that opinion of you, but it isn't because of you personally. Like Frank, they will choose to believe whatever they want about whomever they want, to avoid having to face the reality there just might something they don't already know."

He leaned forward and put his arms on the desk.

"Now, I'd like to talk to you about this more, but I need to talk with Frank first, and I'd like to listen to the recording again. I'd also prefer to talk where we won't be interrupted. Would you be willing to discuss it after work? How about over dinner?"

"Sure." Randi breathed a sigh of relief. He wasn't going to allow her to be fired.

"All right, then, after work it is. I'll take you home after, so you can tell Carole you have a ride. You may go back to your office now."

"Guys, come here," Carole burst into Jeremiah's office. "There's clips of the conference already going viral, linking to national news."

Randi followed Carole out to the lobby where the TV showed Administrator Schweitzer speaking to the camera.

"Of course, we're still working, but we've determined that our initial, inconclusive findings were not accurate."

The camera cut to a clip of Schweitzer at the press conference, discussing the possibility that the fossil was a missing link, then back to him. "We now believe that this fossil is younger than we could have anticipated. It is not a missing link, but a *new* link. A new animal, possibly the next step in the evolution of certain types of lizard. In fact, top biologists and scientists from the Information Advancement Fellowship speculate that we may see more of these types of creatures developing in the near future."

Randi stared at the screen. "What was that? That wasn't at all what he said! How did he change his story so much? And so quickly? That doesn't make sense."

She glanced around the room at the others. Maria sat by her desk, chewing her nails, Dr. Lengel and Carole both looked as confused as she was, and Jeremiah looked…

What was that look? Anger? Why was he angry? And why did she feel like there was so much she was missing?

"What's going on?" she asked again.

"They're getting ahead of the story. Doing damage control. There were enough people at that conference that some of them were bound to share their observations as soon as possible. Most of them probably already have."

"But how does that help?" Randi asked.

Jeremiah's gaze never left the screen. "They know they can't keep your words from coming out in the open, so rather than having to backtrack later, they're coming out with the story first. Changing the narrative. Retroactively making it sound like they're the ones who made the discovery."

Randi shook her head. "But there's the recording!"

"The full recording will never be heard by anyone. Any clips will be completely altered to make it sound like you said the opposite of what you said, and they were the ones acting as the voice of reason."

"Who are *they*?" Randi asked. "Schweitzer?"

Jeremiah didn't answer. Instead, he turned and looked sharply at her. "Does anyone besides you know that you have an original copy of the recording?"

Randi shook her head. "I don't think so—just the tech who gave it to me."

"Good. Keep it that way. For his sake, I hope he didn't tell anyone." With that, he turned and stalked back to his office.

Chapter Twenty-Eight

Nik tried to make sense of the news report. What were they saying? Randi and her questions hadn't made it onto the news clip, but the content was reflective of the questions she'd raised.

Did that mean they'd reevaluated? Would Randi be honored for her contribution?

Did that change things?

Surely Professor Bourne couldn't object to him associating with Randi when they'd almost admitted she could be right. Could they?

The last day had been hell. He'd regretted sending that voicemail since the moment he hung up. He'd have to call her back and make things right, but he'd have to really think through how to do that—and he wouldn't blame her if she didn't give him another chance after what he'd said.

He was miserable thinking that things were over between him and Randi. Even if it cost him a job, he couldn't stand the thought of her not being in his life. One way or another, he had to get her back. And if he still had an internship and the possibility of a job after, well, bonus.

***

Jeremiah sat back in his chair and took a deep breath.

Perhaps, over dinner, he'd be able to discuss with Randi his true mission. He'd almost let too much slip in front of the others, who he definitely wasn't ready to confide in. He hadn't yet decided how much to tell Randi, but he had to tell her something. She needed to know what she was up against.

He filed a little bit of paperwork, hoping to give Frank a little time cool down before going to talk to him. Frank hadn't joined them to watch the news, but if he hadn't seen it yet, he soon would, and Jeremiah wanted to work out what happened with Randi before Frank got any more irritated.

So rarely did he assert his authority as a joint partner—usually he let Frank call all the shots—that when he did, Frank took notice. However, he didn't want to go too long before smoothing things over, either.

Shortly before lunch, he knocked on the older man's door.

"Come in." Frank's voice was gruff.

Jeremiah sat across from his partner but said nothing.

Frank looked at him but continued to work, apparently waiting for Jeremiah to speak first.

He didn't.

They sat there, Jeremiah staring as Frank tried to ignore him.

Finally, Frank broke the silence. "I don't know what I was thinking when I hired her. I should have known she'd be trouble."

"I thought that was *why* you hired her."

Frank shot him a dark look. "What do you mean by that?"

"If I recall, you liked her because she wasn't afraid to go against the flow—to seek out ideas that went against everything mainstream science considers truth. You've said plenty of times that's what makes a good cryptozoologist."

"Maybe so, but I didn't think she'd use it against me."

"What makes you think she did?"

Frank's face darkened.

"Look, Frank, you're only upset because she made the difference between us and other scientists obvious. You want to seek out the unusual and the bizarre, but you still want to be accepted by the regular scientific community."

Jeremiah leaned back, locking his fingers behind his head. "All Randi did was prove it can't be done. You can't challenge science and still be accepted by it. Randi challenged science. Yesterday she proved she is everything a cryptozoologist should be. Maybe you should follow her example instead of getting angry with her because of it. Besides, what she said seems to fit with the supposed new findings they talked about."

"What new findings?" Frank asked, suddenly interested.

Jeremiah waved him off. "There are clips of the conference starting to surface, and some of what they're saying seems to align with what Randi said.

Looks like maybe she made a difference after all and they reevaluated what they thought they knew."

The edges of Frank's scowl started to soften. "What about our grants? What if our funding gets cut because of her?"

"In the unlikely event that something happens, we still have plenty of funding from donors and subscribers. Besides, you know I won't let us crumble financially. If it comes to that, I'll cover it."

Frank sighed and rubbed his temples. "Maybe you're right."

"I'm always right," Jeremiah joked. "One of these days you'll figure that out."

Frank tried to scowl, but failed beneath the smile that surfaced.

"Think about it." Jeremiah stood. "I'm going to get some lunch. Want anything?"

"Oh, sure, just grab me one of whatever you're getting."

Jeremiah nodded and headed back down the hall. Just before he reached his office, the bell on the front door jingled.

"May I help you?" Maria asked.

"Is Miss Ross in?" a woman's voice queried.

"Just a moment."

"I'll get her," Jeremiah called down the hall to Maria. He knocked on Randi's office door. "Someone is here to see you, Randi."

***

Randi looked up, confused.

Who would come to see her?

She walked out of the office, down the hall, and opened the door to the lobby.

What in the world? "Dr. Peterson?"

What could her former professor want with her, especially after getting her kicked out of school?

"I need to have a word with you. Is there somewhere private we can talk?"

Randi's eyebrows shot up. "What?"

Dr. Peterson tapped her foot. "Please?"

"Sure." Whatever it was must be urgent for her to come here. "Come into my office."

229

Randi led her down the hall and into her office. "Carole, will you give us a minute?"

Carole jumped up and went toward the lobby, and Randi closed the door. "How can I help you?"

"Actually, I'm hoping to help you." Dr. Peterson shuffled her feet and glanced around, as if looking for someone.

"What's going on?"

"I know we've had our differences…"

Randi narrowed her eyes. That was an understatement.

"…but I just can't sit by and not do anything."

Randi snapped back to attention. "I'm not sure what you're talking about."

Dr. Peterson looked at her with a mixture of scorn and pity. "You've angered some very powerful people."

A shiver ran down Randi's spine. "What do you mean?"

Dr. Peterson sighed. "There is an organization—very closed, very secret. Nobody really knows who they are except themselves."

"And you."

"And me, but even I know very little. I have no idea who is in charge or what their agenda is. I just know they refer to themselves as the Syndicate, and they're largely responsible for all of the information that gets published and fed to the press." Dr. Peterson's gaze darted around again, and she wrung her hands together. "They are very good at making sure that the public hears only what they want it to hear, how and when they want us to hear it."

Randi raised an eyebrow. It sounded a little made-up—and yet, it was eerily similar to what Jeremiah had said.

"Somehow you managed to slip through their defenses. You managed to get a spot on live news with your Bigfoot thing, and—"

Randi tried to interrupt and say she had had nothing to do with the Bigfoot news conference, but Dr. Peterson didn't let her get a word in.

"Then you managed to not only get into the conference yesterday, but to embarrass the presiding scientist. Of course, they managed to edit the content of the conference to their liking before it got out to the general public, but there were enough people there—including the press—that it will be hard to keep a lid on everything you said."

"Who are *they*? I don't really understand any of this."

"Aren't you listening? *They* are the people in charge of the information the world hears. *They* are the ones running the show. *They* put politicians in power and tear down anyone who opposes them. They're behind every major event in history, guiding the world as they see fit. And *they* are the ones who will destroy you if you don't stop spouting your dragon theories and anti-scientific propaganda."

"I'm not going to stop searching for the truth just because of a conspiracy theory."

"Pay attention, you stupid girl," Dr. Peterson hissed. "They will *kill* you for the information you're going after. They won't let anything come to light that they haven't already figured out how to use to further their causes. It doesn't matter if it's the truth—they'll stop you long before you uncover anything of importance. Trust me, no truth is worth dying for!"

Randi cocked her head to one side. "If not truth, then what in the world *is* worth dying for?"

Dr. Peterson threw her hands up in exasperation. "Don't say I didn't warn you."

"You did. Thank you," Randi said sincerely. "I know how difficult it must have been for you. I appreciate it. I'll be careful."

Dr. Peterson gave her a long look before turning away. "Careful might not be good enough."

***

The Director glanced at the Caller ID, then quickly snatched up the phone.

"It's Maria."

"I know. What is it? More about Bigfoot?"

"Nothing out of the ordinary. We've been swamped with calls all week, but that's to be expected. The trip to Africa to search for dragons is official, though. I'm supposed to make travel arrangements as soon as I have time. The influx of new subscriptions is primarily financing the trip."

"If they're actually planning the trip, they must have a solid lead. What did they tell you?"

"Not much. So far it's Randi, the photographer, Carole, Jeremiah, and some friend of Dr. Lengel's named Chevalet. They're flying into Ouesso,

Congo, and from there, I'm not sure."

The Director's knuckles turned white from gripping the chair's arms so tightly. "When is this trip happening?"

"As soon as we can arrange flights."

"Fine. Keep me informed on that. What else?"

"A few interesting things happened today. First, Dr. Lengel tried to fire Randi and Jeremiah wouldn't let him."

"Go on," the Director urged when Maria paused. "Did they see the news spot about the conference? How did they react?"

"Randi just looked confused. Jeremiah looked upset and hinted toward what he knows about the Syndicate, but he didn't actually say anything to anyone."

"Typical. Keep a close eye on him and let me know if he contacts anyone I should know about. And keep me up to date on whether they're going to try to arrange any more press conferences of their own and what they're putting in the magazine." The Director started to hang up, but stopped when Maria spoke again.

"This may or may not be important, but I thought you'd want to know. Randi received a visit today from a woman I didn't recognize, but Randi seemed surprised to see her. She called the woman Dr. Peterson."

The Director stared at the phone, unable to speak for a moment.

"Director? Are you there?"

"Dr. Peterson. You're sure she said it was Dr. Peterson?"

"Yes. I made a note of it. Is everything okay?"

"No. No, it isn't, but I'll take care of it. Is there anything else I should know?"

"I don't think so."

"Nothing at all? With any of them?"

"Not that I can think of."

"Good. There's a bonus coming your way. Thank you for your dedication."

The Director ended the call with a curse, but after a few deep breaths, picked it up again and dialed Rob.

"What is it?" Rob asked, clearly knowing it must be urgent for the Director to call him.

"It has to be done tonight. I want Randi Ross gone!"

"It's being taken care of."

"Good. I'm out of patience."

"Don't worry. It's as good as done."

"Good. Oh, and Rob? You had better get control of that woman of yours, or I will."

Chapter Twenty-Nine

Nik went by Randi's apartment as soon as he got off work at the lab. He'd decided talking to her in person would be better than calling or texting.

She wasn't there.

"Hi, Nik," Kelly said. "Come on in."

"So. Got any idea when Randi is coming home?"

"Not a clue. Sometimes she and Carole go out after work."

"Who is Carole?"

Kelly handed him a Coke from the fridge. "Coworker of hers who is staying with us until she can find her own place."

Nik opened his drink and took a sip. "Do you mind if I hang out a little while just in case she comes back?"

"Not at all. Make yourself at home. I thought you guys weren't talking right now?"

"That's why I came by. I need to apologize. Does she stay out late a lot?"

Kelly shrugged. "Kinda. She and Carole usually have dinner and then come home. I hardly see her anymore, since she got this job."

"Yeah, about that. How does she seem? Does she want to keep doing it, or could she be convinced to move on?"

Kelly tilted her head to one side and smiled. "I think you're out of luck on that one. She loves it."

"I was afraid of that." He sat on the couch and sipped his drink while Kelly sat at the dining room table working on paperwork. "What are you doing? I thought you were on summer break."

"I'm teaching summer school. I need the extra cash."

"Cool." Nik sat in silence for a long while, but Randi didn't show up, and he didn't want to irritate Kelly with the endless questions he wanted to ask about how Randi was spending her time, so he got up to leave. "Will you tell her I stopped by? And that I really need to talk to her?"

Kelly agreed, and Nik decided he'd wait a little while, then, if he didn't hear from her, he'd give her a call.

***

Janice Peterson opened the door to her apartment and carefully hung her purse on the hook in the entryway. She walked toward the kitchen for a drink.

Her head slammed against the wall. She gasped for breath, blinking against the stars that clouded her vision, trying to focus on who had attacked her.

"Rob? What the—"

He pushed her against the wall and spoke through a clenched jaw. "What did you do?"

"What are you talking about?" She tried to push him away.

He shoved her again.

"You know exactly what I'm talking about! The Director knows about whatever it was you did today."

"What I do is none of your business, and certainly none of your Director's." Blood rushed in her ears, pushed through by the heavy pounding of her heart. She tried to bury the fear pulsing through her with a façade of anger. Of all people, she knew what Rob was capable of, but he'd never turned his force against her. She'd never seen him so angry.

Rob glared at her a moment then crushed her to himself in a tight embrace. "Jan, you know what these people can do. You know what will happen if you make them angry. I've tried so hard to protect you, to keep you out of that world, but… I can't keep you safe if you intentionally defy them."

She melted into his arms. "I know, but I couldn't—I had to warn her."

"You don't even like her."

"Despite my personal feelings for her, she doesn't deserve to die. As much as I dislike her, she's still an innocent person."

"I know you feel that way." Rob stroked her hair. "That's why I love you. But you must promise me never to do anything so foolish again."

He pushed her away and held onto her shoulders, looking her deeply in

236

the eyes. "Promise me, Jan."

"Rob, I—"

"Please try to understand the seriousness of this. You know too much. The only reason you've been allowed to stay safe so far is because the Director trusts me. Don't break that trust. If you do, they'll want you gone, and if I get on their bad side, they'll make me do it."

Janice shuddered. Somewhere deep inside, she'd known that if it came to it, he would choose the Syndicate, and now he'd as good as admitted it. They wouldn't let her leave him, either—like he said, she knew too much. Like it or not, she was stuck. She took a deep breath. "I promise."

Rob pulled her into his arms again.

"Thank you." He pressed his lips firmly against hers.

Janice stood there, her emotions warring within her. Once, she would have done anything for Rob. Now, she wasn't so sure.

***

Jeremiah's tap at Randi's door echoed through the otherwise empty office. "We're still getting dinner tonight, right? Are you about ready to go?"

Randi glanced up and smiled. "Almost—I just need to wrap up a couple more things."

"I'll pull the car around."

"Okay. I'll be out in a minute."

Jeremiah left the office. A man loitered on the landing in the stairwell, smoking. He looked familiar, but Jeremiah couldn't place him. Maybe—yes, that must be it. He was the personal injury lawyer who worked at the office two doors down from the Society. An ambulance chaser of the sleaziest sort.

Jeremiah gave him a brief nod, holding his breath through the cloud of smoke, and hurried toward his car. He edged his way around the parking lot in time to see Randi lock the door to the office and head toward the stairs.

Pulling to a stop, he got out, intending to open Randi's door for her.

A scream erupted from the stairwell.

Chapter Thirty

Jeremiah dashed up the steps two at a time.

Randi's shadow danced against the wall in the flickering light of the stairwell. The man held her in place, a glint from a knife flashing in his hand.

Randi fended him away with a knee to his groin, but that didn't keep him from rushing at her again.

Images too horrible to put into words flashed through his mind.

Oh, God, not her.

He tackled the man, shoving him to the ground away from Randi. His fist found the man's cheekbone, cracking it beneath the force of his blow.

The man rolled away, tumbling halfway down the lower flight of stairs.

The two men locked eyes for an instant.

Suddenly, Jeremiah realized where he'd seen the man before.

It wasn't the ambulance chaser from two doors down, it was—

The attacker pushed himself up, then half-rolled and half-ran the rest of the way down the stairs and disappeared into the dark.

Jeremiah turned toward Randi, fearing the worst.

She slumped in the corner of the landing, breathing deeply. She looked at him, clutching her torso. Blood dripped down, staining her clothes and splashing onto the concrete beneath her.

Jeremiah knelt beside her and examined the gash in her side, over her rib cage. It wasn't too deep, and didn't seem to be near any organs.

Thank God.

Stripping off his shirt, leaving him dressed only in his undershirt, he pressed it tightly against the wound. "Did he get you anywhere else?"

Randi shook her head.

"Come on. We need to get you to a hospital. You're going to need stitches."

"I'm okay." Randi's voice caught in her throat.

Her legs crumpled beneath her when she tried to stand.

Jeremiah put his arms around her and pulled her gently to her feet. He put one arm around her back and the other arm under her legs and carried her down the steps.

***

Randi tried to protest when Jeremiah lifted her, but fog shrouded her brain. Her stomach was on fire, her arm throbbed, her head swam. Bile rose in her throat. She took deep breaths to steady herself, but the dizzy, drunken feeling refused to go away.

Jeremiah put her in the passenger seat and belted her in. One thought tickled the edges of her mind, forcing its way through her lips. "She wasn't crazy."

She held her hand where Jeremiah had placed it to hold the shirt in place, and watched the blood slowly seep through as Jeremiah raced her to the ER and helped her inside. She sat propped against the counter at the nurses' station, her head resting against Jeremiah's shoulder. Her head vibrated as he bellowed out orders to someone behind the desk.

"I want a policeman in here, now!" he demanded.

Randi lifted her head groggily.

"Hey, how are you feeling?" Jeremiah gently brushed the hair away from her face.

"I don't know."

"It's okay. A doctor is going to be here to take care of you any minute."

He lifted her off the counter and led her to one of the chairs in the waiting area, casting a stern glance at the attendant behind the desk.

Apparently his six-foot-five-inch frame and well-muscled physique made quite an intimidating impression—or maybe it was the blood that seemed to be getting everywhere? At any rate, few moments later, a doctor rushed out with a gurney.

Jeremiah helped Randi onto it and came along as she was wheeled back to an exam room.

"How are you feeling?" the doctor asked, his voice pleasant, though terse.

"Not great. A little nauseated and really light-headed."

"Well, let's have a look at that cut, shall we?" the doctor clucked.

He asked her a bunch of medical history questions, like when was her last tetanus shot, was she on or allergic to any medications, and the other usual things as he carefully pulled the shirt from the wound. He drew in his breath sharply.

"Well, it's no wonder you're groggy. You've lost a lot of blood from that gash. Good news is, it appears to be superficial. We'll have you patched up in no time. How did you say it happened?"

"She was attacked leaving work tonight," Jeremiah answered for her.

"Please, sir, I asked Miss Ross," the doctor said firmly.

"Yeah," Randi confirmed, "I came down the stairwell, and there was some guy waiting for me, and he pulled a knife."

The doctor looked from Randi to Jeremiah and back again.

"Would you give us a moment, please?" the doctor asked Jeremiah.

Jeremiah looked confused, but left the room.

"Miss, you're safe in here. Anything you tell me stays between us. Do you want to tell me what really happened?"

"What are you talking about?" Randi rubbed her head. "I just told you what happened."

"I know what you said." The doctor's tone was patient and soothing. "But if you want to tell me anything different, now is your chance."

Randi stared at him blankly.

"Miss, did your boyfriend do this? Does he hurt you often?"

Randi almost laughed at the absurdity of the question, but annoyance quickly buried mirth. "He's not my boyfriend. He's my boss, and no, he didn't do it. We're telling the truth. I was coming down the stairs. I had just locked up, and Jeremiah—Dr. Bryant—was bringing the car around to give me a ride."

After the accusation the doctor made, she didn't want to tell him they planned to go to dinner together. No sense in feeding his speculation. "Anyway, I came down the stairs and there was a man on the landing, and he pulled a knife and came at me."

Her throat constricted at the memory, and she clenched her eyes. "I screamed and threw my hand in front of my face, and that's when he slashed me. I fell backwards against the wall, tried to knee him to get him off of me, and the next thing I knew Dr. Bryant was there and the other guy wasn't."

The doctor seemed satisfied and opened the door so Jeremiah could come back inside then gave her a shot of anesthetic. "Okay, I'll be back in a little bit to stitch that up."

Jeremiah sat down on the stool the doctor had vacated.

"What was that all about?" he asked as soon as the doctor was out of earshot.

"Oh." Randi rolled her eyes. "He thought you were my abusive boyfriend."

"Really?"

Randi nodded.

"Huh. Well, don't worry. I won't abuse you."

Randi was too groggy to think very hard about exactly what he meant by that.

A few moments later, voices sounded in the hallway.

"Is the stab victim in there?" a man asked.

"That's right." That was the doctor who'd just examined her.

"What are your impressions, Doctor?"

"I'm not completely convinced the boyfriend didn't do it, but their stories both match pretty well. I'd question them separately, just in case, but she's probably telling the truth."

A moment later, two men pushed into the room.

Jeremiah stood up and extended his hand. "Officers, I'm glad you're here."

The first policeman didn't waste time shaking hands. Instead, he turned immediately to Randi. "Miss Ross, I'm Detective Rondstadt, and this is Officer Wick. I'm just going to ask you a few questions while my partner talks to your friend, okay?"

Randi nodded.

Officer Wick led Jeremiah out into the hallway while Detective Rondstadt seated himself on the stool next to the bed.

"Can you tell me what happened tonight?"

Randi repeated the story.

"Can you give me a description of the mugger?" Detective Rondstadt asked.

"Yeah." Randi rubbed her temples. "Maybe in his forties, balding brown hair, kind of short—but only compared to Dr. Bryant or Nik. He might be taller than Dr. Lengel, I don't know. Short or average, I guess."

"Any distinguishing marks you can remember?"

She shook her head. "Not that I remember. It was dark."

"Okay. Anything else you remember, you let me know, all right?" He stood and turned.

"Wait," Randi said just as he reached the door. "I don't think he was trying to mug me. I think he was trying to kill me."

Rondstadt whirled around. "What makes you think that?"

"Well, he was in that stairwell, like he was waiting for me. As soon as I came toward him, he pulled the knife. It didn't seem like a random mugging. I mean, he didn't try to mug Dr. Bryant."

Detective Rondstadt chuckled. "It would take a very brave thief to try to mug that man."

Randi grinned weakly. "Good point. But there was also what Dr. Peterson said to me earlier today."

"Who is Dr. Peterson?"

"She used to be one of my professors at the university. I haven't seen her since I... since I left school, but she came by the office today. She said she needed to warn me that I had made the wrong people angry. She said to stop searching for the truth, that it wasn't worth dying for, and that they were going to kill me."

"Who is *they*?"

"I don't know—some organization that controls information in this country. She was really vague."

"What organization?"

"*I don't know!* I just said that." Randi slapped a hand over her mouth. "I'm sorry. That was rude. I'm not feeling well. She said they call themselves the Syndicate, that's all I know."

Detective Rondstadt nodded. "No problem. You're doing a lot better than most people in your situation. What did Dr. Peterson think this organization didn't want you to find?"

"Dragons."

Detective Rondstadt stared at her for several seconds, brows furrowed. "Is there anything else that Dr. Peterson told you?"

Randi scrunched up her face, trying to concentrate. "I don't know. I can't think."

"Okay. You just call me if you remember anything else."

She nodded. "I will."

She could still see him when he stepped into the hallway and jerked his head at his partner who stood talking to Jeremiah, scribbling notes in his notebook.

Officer Wick nodded acknowledgement toward Rondstadt and extended his hand to Jeremiah. "Well, thank you, Dr. Bryant. Give us a call if you remember anything else."

Jeremiah nodded and came back into Randi's room.

The door swung closed, but not all the way. Randi could still hear the policemen talking.

"What've you got?" Rondstadt asked.

"Here are my notes."

"Their IDs match up pretty accurately. Looks like their stories check out. We'll need to get them together with a sketch artist in the morning."

"Good call. Anything else interesting I should know about?"

"Yeah, one thing. Ross seemed to think this wasn't a random mugging. She said her old professor came and warned her that some organization was going to kill her to keep her from finding dragons. What do you think? Conspiracy theory, crazy, or just too much blood loss?"

"Huh… that's weird," Wick said.

"What is?"

"Well, Dr. Bryant seemed to think it wasn't just a random mugging, either. He said he thought he remembered seeing that same man several weeks ago. He was in Canada, and he thought the man was watching him. Some things in his hotel room had been messed with."

"You can't be serious," Rondstadt said. "You really think there's some mysterious organization out there that's attacking a bunch of cryptozoologists? What would be the point? Nobody believes those kooks anyway."

"Yeah, I dunno. Weird that they both thought so, though. They sure went to a lot of trouble tearing her up if it's a hoax."

"Maybe." Rondstadt didn't sound convinced.

Their voices faded as they walked away.

Randi looked at Jeremiah. "You saw him in Canada? Is he stalking you? Is that why he attacked me?"

Jeremiah squeezed her hand. "I don't want you to worry about him. I won't let him get near you again. The police have a description. They'll find him."

"It sounds like they're taking us seriously, at least."

"I hope so. We should probably keep from telling our conspiracy theories to too many people, though. At least for now."

Chapter Thirty-One

The Rainforest near Ouesso, in the Sangha region of Congo, Africa

Albert watched as the medicine man changed the dressing on his wound. It was healing nicely. Westerners could say what they wanted about modern medicine, but Albert knew from experience that traditional remedies were as good as or better than anything the city doctors could give him. In just a couple more weeks, he would be well enough to go back up the mountain to his sister.

He wondered what had happened to the egg. Had it rotted? Would his sister still be keeping it safe? Even if it never hatched, he wanted to bring it home as a souvenir. Proof of the existence of the creatures at the top of the mountain.

He hadn't told his mother yet that he was going back. She had been infuriated when he had returned wounded, half-fainting from the exertion of coming down the mountain by himself.

She'd thought Naomi must be dead, and had wailed throughout the entire village before he had a chance to tell her that Naomi was fine, that she had stayed behind. Then, she had cursed him for leaving his sister alone. She began immediately trying to find him a wife, to settle him down.

Fortunately for Albert, most of the other mothers had decided that he must be unreliable, and were reluctant to give their daughters to him. His mother was very persistent, however, and it was only a matter of time until she found a suitable wife for him. He just hoped it wouldn't be before he was well enough to leave again.

There was no way he could leave if he were married. His only chance was to pretend to cooperate, and, when he was well, announce that he was leaving, and just go. Otherwise, his mother would have him married off before he had a chance to do anything about it.

He went to sleep that night wondering what Naomi was doing up in the mountains, alone with his egg.

***

Los Angeles, California

Janice Peterson stood just inside the door, listening to Rob on the phone outside with his Director.

"Let me get this straight," the Director's voice was garbled through voice-altering technology, but the tone was unmistakable. "Not only did you fail, but you allowed both Randi Ross *and* Dr. Bryant to positively identify you?"

"Not me," Rob protested. "I shouldn't have sent Collins. I should have known this was too big for him, but Ross has seen me, so I didn't want to put her on guard. It won't happen again."

"No, it won't. Now, they not only recognize one of our agents, but they suspect us. If another attempt is made on Randi's life, they'll start digging deeper. Bryant already knows too much, and who knows how much he's told Ross. We can't have them looking for more evidence. Do you have any idea how disastrous that would be? Politicians, world leaders, scientists—people all over have been influenced by our work. If they start questioning what we do, it will cause chaos. We can't let that happen."

"I understand."

Janice squeezed her eyes closed and pressed closer to the door. She knew Rob's job, knew what it entailed, but hearing him actually discuss taking someone out… her stomach churned. That wasn't him. Not really. He was better than that, he was just stuck. If only there were a way for him to get out.

The Director yelled again. "Do you understand? Do you really? I sometimes think I'm the only person in this organization who really believes in what we're doing. *Order*, Rob. It's all about order and organization, otherwise we end up with a third-world universe. I will not let that happen. It's time to cut Collins off. Make him look like a lone wolf."

"I can take care of Randi Ross—"

"No. It's too dangerous. I'll come up with another plan to take care of her. You just take care of Collins."

"I will."

Janice breathed a sigh of relief. At least he wouldn't have an innocent girl's blood on his hands.

"One more thing. We need to get someone on Randi's team. We need to know everything she's doing. I'll get an agent in place, and in the meantime, I want you to contact a man named Jon Chevalet. You'll find him at the Los Angeles Museum of Natural History. This is what I want you to do..." The Director's voice trailed off as Rob walked to the other end of the porch.

Janice had heard enough, anyway. She hurried out of the bedroom and into the kitchen so Rob wouldn't know she'd been eavesdropping.

A little while later, Rob joined her in the kitchen. "How much did you hear?"

She should've known he'd figure it out. "Enough. What's going to happen to Miranda Ross?"

"I don't know. The Director has some plan, but I don't know what it is. Nothing here. It's too dangerous. After last night, anything even remotely suspicious would lead to the Syndicate, and we can't let that happen. Something will probably happen on her trip to Africa."

"Rob, can't you get out? Can't you quit this life?" Janice wrapped her arms around his neck and clung to him.

"I wish I could, Jan. I do. The Syndicate has tentacles everywhere. They'd follow me and take me out."

"We could disappear. Between your savings and my stocks, we'd have enough to go somewhere they'd never find us. We could retire in some remote village and be happy."

Rob gazed at her. "What about your career? You're finally getting to where you always wanted to be. You'd give that all up to disappear with me?"

"I'd give it up for you, if you'd give it up for me."

Rob sighed. "Okay."

"Really?"

"Really."

Janice laid her head against his chest. "Thank you."

"It won't happen overnight, you know. It'll take time to plan and to figure out exactly how to escape without being found."

"I know." Janice looked at him. "I don't care how long it takes, as long as I know we're going."

"That's my girl," Rob breathed into her hair. "We'll make it out of this, and live happily ever after. I promise."

Good. It was settled. Now she just needed to do one more thing before she could disappear. She had to warn Randi Ross one more time.

***

Djazani made her way through the labyrinth of hallways beneath the Los Angeles Museum of Natural History with Kinte. "I still can't believe they kicked you off the dig of a lifetime just for being seen with me."

"You were dismissed unfairly, and they did not want me around to remind them of that."

She squeezed his hand. "I'm sorry. I never intended to ruin your career."

"It was not you. You are the one who told me to wait until we were no longer in such a position, and you were correct. And yet it did not matter. Politics always ruin everything."

"Well, I'm still sorry," Djazani said.

"We will get justice. I am confident of it. In the meantime, I will go where you do, and do as you do."

Her face warmed. "You would really follow me anywhere?"

Kinte kissed her. "I will."

She smiled at him, then continued down the hall until she found the curator's door. "I think this is it."

She knocked.

An older man opened it. "Good morning. How may I help you?"

"Are you Mr. Jon Chevalet?"

"I am."

Kinte took charge of the conversation. "My name is Alan Kinte, and this is Djazani Monroe. We are paleontology students at the university. I believe our professor contacted you about us doing an internship with you."

"Ah, yes. We're meeting under some rather odd circumstances. Did your professor tell you I'm taking a leave of absence from the museum, going on a research trip?"

"Yes," Djazani said. "But he seemed to think it would be just as beneficial for us to go along as to stay here at the museum, if that's acceptable to you."

Mr. Chevalet rubbed his chin. "Well, I'm not in charge of the expedition, but I'll see if I can arrange it. Why don't you meet me back here tomorrow morning, and I'll let you know what I'm able to work out."

Chapter Thirty-Two

Randi woke up feeling dizzy and wondering why her whole body hurt. She glanced at the clock by her bed and sat up, suddenly wide awake, the motion sending fire through her body, spreading from her torso.

Another wave of pain and nausea swept over her, and she collapsed back on her bed.

A sense of déjà vu stole over her, and she glanced down.

The snake bite she'd received in Cameroon that spring was a fading scar, but she was injured again.

The guy in the stairwell.

The mugging that was maybe a contract on her.

Carole came in a moment later carrying a plate with scrambled eggs and toast and a glass of orange juice. "I thought I heard you wake up. How are you feeling?"

"Not bad. Why did you let me sleep this late? We're late for work."

Carole looked at her like she was an idiot. "We're not going to work today."

"I can't not go to work just because I got a couple stitches." Randi tried to get out of bed.

Carole gently but firmly pushed her back down. "Don't even think about it. Dr. Bryant will have my head if I even let you get up today, let alone go to work. He won't even let *me* come in, because I'm supposed to make sure you stay put."

"That's the stupidest thing I've ever heard."

Carole gave her a patronizing smile. "You're entitled to your opinion, but it doesn't change anything. You're not going anywhere, so get the idea out of your head. Now, eat. The doctor said the pain meds should be taken with food."

Randi scowled, grudgingly taking the plate. The smell of food reminded her she hadn't eaten since lunch the day before—the attack preempted her dinner plans with Jeremiah.

In moments, the eggs were gone.

Carole watched her eat and then handed her two pills. "Kelly filled your prescriptions this morning."

"Thanks."

"No problem. Now, get some rest. I'll be back in a little bit. Call me if you need anything."

"I will."

"Oh, by the way," Carole paused by the doorway, "Kelly said to tell you Nik came by last night and you should probably call him."

"Nik." Randi leaned her head back against the pillow.

Was he calling to apologize?

She took a few deep breaths to settle herself, then called him, but he didn't answer.

She didn't leave a message.

She didn't know what to say.

***

Nik paced back and forth in his apartment.

He'd forgiven Randi for the fight they'd had, only to be completely ignored by her at the conference *he* told her about in the first place. Yeah, okay, the message he left her after was a little harsh, but he was trying to make it right.

She didn't call when she got home the night before, even though he *knew* Kelly would keep her promise to tell Randi he came by. She should know it wouldn't be too late, no matter what time she got in. He was trying to make amends, and she was ignoring him!

His phone rang.

Randi!

He almost answered, then stopped himself. She'd waited until now to call? Well, he wouldn't give her the satisfaction of being too eager to talk to her,

254

then, either.

He watched the light on his phone flash until it finally stopped ringing. He'd call her back in a few minutes, saying he was busy and couldn't pick up the phone.

He sighed, mentally kicking himself. Who did he think he was kidding?

The sound of her voice as she matched wits with Administrator Schweitzer echoed in his mind.

Visions of her face, the way her eyes twinkled and the sly little wink she gave him when she wanted to be sassy, all taunted him with their refusal to leave his consciousness. He couldn't stop thinking about her, no matter how hard he tried.

Deep down, he knew he didn't want to. Despite how much she frustrated him, despite how many times she told him they would never get back together, and despite how hard he tried not to, he loved her. Completely, head-over-heels, madly.

He needed to talk to her. Right away.

He picked up the phone then set it down again. Too important to do over the phone. He needed to see her. Maybe if he stopped by her office, took her out to lunch…

He sped all the way to Randi's office, ran up the stairs, and threw open the door to the office, breathless.

The woman behind the desk looked up. "Can I help you?"

"I need to see Randi Ross," he panted.

"Miss Ross isn't in today—"

"What? Why not? Where is she?"

"She's taking a personal day," the receptionist said.

"A personal day? What the hell does that mean? Randi doesn't take days off! What's she—"

Dr. Lengel, the man he and Randi had met at the restaurant that one time—her boss—opened the door and stuck his head into the waiting room. "What's going on out here?"

"I need to see Randi. Why isn't she here?"

The other one—the jerk who was hitting on Randi at the library, Dr. Bryant—also appeared in the doorway. "Nik, come into my office."

Nik's heart stopped in his chest.

Dr. Bryant looked way too serious, way too concerned. Wary, he followed Dr. Bryant into his office.

"Have you spoken to Randi since last night?" Dr. Bryant asked.

Nik considered lying, saying something like they spent the night together or something, but instead just shook his head. Despite his intentions, he found himself being honest. "I haven't talked to her since before the conference."

"Randi was attacked last night as she was leaving work—"

"*What?* Who? When? How?" Nik's words tumbled over one another, nearly incoherent.

"Nik, please sit down and be quiet."

Nik obeyed reluctantly, glaring daggers at the other man.

"First, let me assure you, she's all right. She had to have a few stitches put in, but she's not seriously injured, and she's going to be just fine. We were leaving work and there was a man in the stairwell. I left first and drove around to pick her up—"

"Pick her up?"

Dr. Bryant ignored him and went on. "I heard her scream and ran up the stairwell. I jumped on the man who had attacked her. He ran away, and I took Randi to the hospital. We didn't get back to her apartment until early this morning. I told Carole not to let her come to work today."

"You went to pick her up?" Nik demanded again. "Why were you picking her up?"

"I was going to take her out to dinner." Dr. Bryant's voice was terse.

"You were taking her on a *date*?"

"No, we were just going out after work to discuss the conference. We didn't have a chance during the day."

"You were going to discuss the conference," Nik sneered. "I've heard that one before."

"Even if what you are insinuating were true, I fail to see how it would be any business of yours."

Nik opened his mouth to speak, but no words came out.

"The point is, I was there, and everything worked out. Randi's going to be fine."

Nik's head sank against his chest. "I should have been there. I should have been the one to take care of her."

"She's at home." Dr. Bryant's voice softened. "I'm sure she'd appreciate it if you stopped by. I'm sure she'll want to spend as much time with you as possible before we leave for Africa."

"You're going to Africa? She's going? Since when?"

Dr. Bryant crossed his arms in front of his massive chest, highlighting just how much he probably worked out. "She's been putting the team together and planning the details for awhile."

Nik narrowed his eyes. "When is she leaving?"

"We're leaving three weeks from tomorrow."

"*We?* Who all is *we?*"

"There are several of us, including a noted paleontologist and some paleontology interns."

"I'm coming with you."

Dr. Bryant narrowed his eyes. "Excuse me?"

"I'm going." Nik jumped up from his chair. He hurried across the hall and pounded on Dr. Lengel's door, Dr. Bryant following closely behind.

Nik opened the door before Dr. Lengel even had a chance to tell him to come in. "I'm going on the team to Africa."

Dr. Lengel looked up, sputtering. "I don't—that is, um, what exactly are your qualifications?"

"I've nearly completed my doctorate work in biology. I have an internship at Palmer Labs, and a potential job offer with the Information Advancement Fellowship when I'm done. Unless I'm mistaken, your organization could benefit from a collaboration with either of those groups, and besides, you don't yet have a biologist on your team."

"*I'm* a biologist," Dr. Bryant snapped.

Dr. Lengel snorted. "Young man, I don't know who you think you are, but you can't just hop aboard an all-expense-paid trip to Africa with us. Go on, now."

"I don't need you to pay my expenses, and I don't need your permission. If you don't want me as part of your team, I won't go with you, I'll just go... near you."

Dr. Bryant glared at him, and Dr. Lengel's mouth fell open.

Good. That would show them he couldn't be pushed around.

Time to go see Randi.

He shoved past Dr. Bryant and ran down to his car.

Minutes later, he parked in a way that would probably get him a nasty note from someone, and raced up the stairs.

A petite blonde opened the door to Randi's apartment—the photographer from the press conference. Carole, that was her name.

"Hello," she said shyly. "Can I help you?"

"Hi. I need to see Randi."

"Can I tell her who's here?"

"It's Nik."

"Oh, hi, Nik. Come on in."

"So, apparently she talks about me?" Nik's pulse sputtered with hope.

"Wait here." Carole smiled and waved her hand toward a chair in the living room.

She quietly tapped on Randi's door, paused, and poked her head in. "Nik's here. Are you up?"

"Of course." Randi's musical voice wafted from the bedroom.

Carole stepped out. "You can go in."

Nik practically ran into Randi's room. He grabbed her in his arms and hugged her tightly. "How are you feeling?"

Randi moaned. "You just crushed my stab wound, genius. My pain meds aren't that good!"

Nik released her, stumbling back with a curse. "I'm sorry, I didn't realize—I just—I was so happy to see you, and—"

She smiled, that smile that could melt rock. "It's okay. Sit down."

He sat on the edge of her bed and gazed at her. Reaching out his hand, he traced her cheek with his fingertips. "I'm sorry I wasn't there. I'm sorry I couldn't keep you safe."

"Nik, you can't blame yourself. It wasn't your fault. Anyway, it isn't your job to protect me."

He took a deep breath, wishing he could tell her. *It should be my job. I want to be the one to protect you.* "I know. I'm just sorry it happened."

Randi took his hand. "Thanks."

He couldn't help but think how radiant she looked, despite her tangled hair and tired, drawn face.

Words formed on the tip of his tongue, words that wouldn't come out. She looked at him—looked through him. "What's wrong?"

She knew him so well. Too well. He'd never been able to hide anything from her. "Randi, I—Why didn't you tell me you were going to Africa?"

Randi's eyes widened. "I wanted to. I tried to, but we haven't talked since—" she stopped. They both knew since when. "Anyway, I was going to."

"Then why not at the conference? You completely ignored me."

Randi rubbed her arm. "I looked for you after! I kept trying to get to you, but people kept stopping me and talking to me, and I couldn't get away. Then you were gone. I looked around and waited for you. I even called your room, but I couldn't find you. After that, I had to leave or I would've missed my flight. And then you left that stupid message, and—"

He looked into her eyes. As well as she knew him, he knew her even better. She was serious, and almost on the verge of tears. He hated that. Hated every stupid, jealous thing he'd ever said or done. He never wanted her to feel that way again. "I'm sorry. I really am. It won't happen again."

"Oh? And just how can you guarantee that?" The familiar teasing was back in her tone.

"For starters, I'm not letting you go places and leave me alone anymore."

"What do you mean?"

Nik grinned. "I'm coming to Africa with you."

"What? Why?"

"I just told you why."

She shook her head. "That doesn't make sense. I thought you were reevaluating your future and you couldn't have me in it? And don't you have an internship you have to show up for?"

His own words stung when she flung them back at him like that. He tightened his hand on hers. "I did reevaluate my future, and I realized that I don't want one without you in it. I don't know what it will take to prove it to you, but whatever it is, that's what I'm going to do. Starting with coming to Africa with you."

"You're serious?"

"Completely."

"How are you going to go? I mean, I guess I can talk to Dr. Lengel, but I'm not sure how that's going to go."

"I already talked to him this morning. Let's just say I'm not an official part of the team, but I'm coming anyway."

"Oh." Her head snapped up, concern in her gorgeous eyes. "But you'll have to give up your internship—I know how much that means to you."

"I'll figure it out. I'm hoping that they'll let me use this as part of my internship—collaborating on a research trip and possibly bringing back specimens of… something useful."

"You're coming along on a dragon-hunting trip with a bunch of cryptozoologists. Aren't you the one who insisted that sort of thing would ruin my career?"

"I'm pretty sure I can work it out—I have a good relationship with my supervisor, and he's always encouraging us to think outside the box. But even if it does—this is more important. Why, don't you want me to come?"

"I just don't want you to mess up your plans and your future because of me."

You are my plan. It was cheesy, but true. He didn't say it aloud, though. It wasn't time yet. He could see that now. There was so much between them they needed to work out, but he was finally beginning to see things through her eyes.

She couldn't settle for mundane, not when her entire personality was passion and drive. She wouldn't accept being second-best in anything, and he needed to show her he valued her above every other pretty face, even over his reputation.

Her brows furrowed, and concern shone through her gaze.

"What's wrong?" he asked.

"Nothing, it's just—are you sure this is a good idea? We've hardly talked in a year, and things have been so up and down. Do you really think a jungle excursion is the best idea?"

"I know I have a lot to make up for. I've been a jerk. I've been totally self-centered and I haven't supported you at all. But that's going to change. You were right about everything, and I'm really proud of you. And I'm going to stick by you from now on."

She smiled, but it seemed half-hearted.

He understood. He didn't like it, but he knew she just didn't trust him. Yet.

"It's gonna be fantastic, babe. You'll see."

She looked at him through her lashes. "I hope so."

Emotion filled him. He squeezed his eyes so she wouldn't see. Part of him thrilled to know she shared some of his feelings, but a thread of worry wormed its way to the front. It would be okay. *They* would be okay. He would make sure of it.

Standing up to go, he planted a soft kiss on the top of her head. "It's time for me to fly, babe. I'll talk to you soon."

Chapter Thirty-Three

Randi woke to the pleasant aroma of soup and went out to the kitchen.

"Hungry?" Carole asked.

"Starved."

Just as Carole set a steaming bowl of soup in front of her, the doorbell rang.

Carole jumped up to get it. "Hi, Dr. Bryant. Come on in."

"I just came to check on our patient." Jeremiah squeezed Randi's shoulder. "How are you feeling?"

She smiled. "Pretty well. I think I'll be ready to come back to work tomorrow."

"Don't push yourself. Take some more time off."

"Honestly, I don't know how many days I can just sit here resting. It's only been a day and I'm already bored."

"Fine, but don't blame me when you wish you hadn't come in."

"Deal," she laughed. "Do you want to stay for dinner?"

"Sure, if it's not too much trouble." Jeremiah sat and Carole jumped up to grab another bowl.

"Thanks, Carole." Jeremiah turned to Randi. "Did you talk to Nik today?"

She nodded.

"He tell you he's following us to Africa?"

"Yep."

"How do you feel about that?"

Randi thought for a moment. When he'd first announced it, she'd been thrilled. Then she'd had all afternoon to wonder if he was really serious or if something would come up and he'd back out. She'd almost convinced herself that this would end up like so many other things—he'd be excited about it for awhile, and then he'd find a reason to give up. "I don't know," she said at last. "I guess I'll believe it when I see it."

"I see." Jeremiah's lips tightened in a hard line.

Randi studied the crease in his brows. What did that mean?

Before she had a chance to wonder further, Jeremiah's phone rang. "Dr. Jeremiah Bryant."

Even the way he answered the phone sounded pretentious. Randi suppressed a giggle.

"That's good news... Yes, I'm with her now. Right. See you shortly." Jeremiah put away his phone and turned to Randi. "That was the detective from last night. Are you up for a trip to the police station? They have a suspect in custody."

Randi stood and immediately groaned, clutching her side.

Carole handed her a pain pill.

"Thanks." She swallowed it, then turned to Dr. Bryant. "Let's go."

He took her arm and helped her down the stairs to the car. She didn't really need it—after all, her legs hadn't been injured—but it seemed to make him feel useful, so she allowed it.

They reached the parking lot. An odd expression crossed his face. Did she smell funny or something?

Randi turned, and he thrust his hand into his pocket, fumbling for his keys.

She tilted her head to the side and looked at him. "You okay?"

He coughed. "Fine. Let's go." He opened the door and tucked her safely inside.

Weird. But then, Jeremiah was always weird to her. She didn't understand him.

They arrived at the station a short while later and were greeted by Detective Rondstadt.

"Dr. Bryant, Miss Ross, I'm glad you could make it. Come on in."

"Thank you, Detective." Jeremiah shook his hand. "What can you tell us about this suspect? Has he confessed?"

"Not even close." Detective Rondstadt led them down a hallway. "That's one of the reasons I wanted to get you two down here to ID him as soon as possible."

"What do you mean 'not even close'? He either confessed or he didn't."

"He didn't. I've had the suspect in the interrogation room for hours. He matches the description both of you gave. The only problem is, I can't make the man talk. At all. It isn't just him refusing to admit to attacking Miss Ross—he won't say *anything*. He hasn't even asked for a lawyer."

"Is that weird?" Randi asked.

"I'd say so. I've worked with some of the best interrogators at the precinct. They've tried everything, and still not so much as a squeak escaped him."

"That is weird," Randi said.

"If that's the case, how do you know it's him?" Jeremiah asked.

Detective Rondstadt led them down a hallway and stopped outside a door with a placard of his name. "A few blocks from where he attacked Miss Ross, he tried to mug another woman. A police officer heard the woman scream. Lucky break, there."

Something tickled the back of Randi's mind, something that didn't seem to fit, but she couldn't quite get a hold of it.

"I know this is the same man who attacked Miss Ross, only I can't prove it. Usually in an interrogation room the suspect says something—asking for a drink, for a lawyer—anything can give me an opening. From there, cracking him, tricking him into giving a hint, is something I can get over time, but I can't even get this man to make a sound. Makes it harder to get a confession."

"Apparently." Jeremiah's tone was cool, aloof. Or maybe just concerned.

Detective Rondstadt opened the door and ushered them in. "Eventually, I just had to put him in holding until the public defender gets here. If we get a positive ID from both of you, though, we'll be in a good place."

Detective Rondstadt directed Jeremiah to a chair and turned to Randi. "Miss Ross, with me, please."

Randi followed him and two officers, one of whom she was pretty sure was Officer Wick, Detective Rondstadt's partner from the hospital, to a room on the opposite side of a two-way mirror. A line of men filed in and stood under the numbers on the wall.

"Okay, Miss Ross, take your time. I want you to be really sure about this.

We need this if we're going to put this guy away. Look over them carefully and tell me if you see the man who attacked you."

Randi recognized him immediately. She'd never forget those rat-like eyes, that leering smirk on his face. "Number four."

"Are you sure? No doubt in your mind?"

Randi paused, wondering. Was he trying to test her? To make sure she wasn't just making it up? Or was someone else the suspect he brought in? Was he trying to give her a hint?

Not that it mattered. She knew her attacker. "Number four."

Randi couldn't read the expression on his face, but his eye twitched when he looked at her.

"All right, let's get Dr. Bryant in here," Rondstadt said to one of his companions. "Miss Ross, you can wait in my office.

One of the officers—not Officer Wick—led the way.

"Take the men out of there and switch them around," Rondstadt instructed Officer Wick. His voice was low, but not low enough to keep Randi from hearing. "I want to make sure this is completely fool-proof."

She and Jeremiah switched places. It seemed to take an interminable amount of time before Jeremiah was brought back to Rondstadt's office, where they waited in awkward silence for Rondstadt to return.

He was grinning when he opened the door. "We got him. You both identified the same man. Thanks for coming in. I'll let you know when we have more news."

"Something doesn't make sense," Randi said as they walked out of the station. "If he was really after me specifically, how did he get caught mugging someone else?"

"Maybe we'll find out at his trial," Jeremiah said. He didn't make eye contact with her, though.

Why did she get the feeling he was hiding something from her?

***

One week later

Randi sat at her desk. Jeremiah popped his head in.

She'd been back at work for almost a week, and still Jeremiah hovered like a mother hen. He'd insisted on picking her up and dropping her off at work for the first few days, and when she protested that she carpooled with Carole, he started picking them both up. Eventually, he'd let them start coming together again, but he arrived at the office early and waited in the parking lot so he could walk them up the stairs.

"Randi, I have to run out for a little while," he said. "Don't leave until I get back."

She managed to keep her eyes from rolling. "I'll be fine, Jeremiah. You don't have to walk me to my car every night for the rest of my life."

"I'm serious. I don't want you out there by yourself."

"How about a compromise? If Carole and I have to leave before you get back, I'll call you to let you know I got home safely. Deal?"

Jeremiah frowned, his eyes clouding. "Fine. But call me every half hour and don't leave unless you have to. I'll try to get back quickly."

"Fine." She delved into the papers on her desk, refusing to look up until he left.

She finally made eye contact with Carole, who was doing a very poor job at suppressing a giggle.

"It's not funny."

"I agree," Carole said. "It's *adorable*."

Exactly half an hour later, Carole reminded her to call him.

She glared at Carole the whole time. "It's me. I'm still at the office. Everything is fine."

She hung up without giving him a chance to respond.

Less than half an hour after that, she looked up at Carole. "You about ready to go?"

"You sure you don't want to wait for your knight in shining armor to come back?" Carole laughed at the expression on Randi's face. "Yeah, I'm ready."

Randi stuffed her work back into the files and picked up her purse. She pulled out her phone and dialed Jeremiah. "I'm leaving work."

"Call me when you get home. Be careful."

"I will."

She paused at the top of the stairs outside, her pulse suddenly taking off at a gallop.

It's okay. Suddenly Jeremiah's concern seemed comforting. His solid, strong presence by her side, protecting her was more reassuring than she'd realized. Maybe she should call him, so he would know at least know if anything happened.

"Oh, for Pete's sake. Get a grip," she practically shouted at herself. "The guy who attacked you is in jail."

"You okay?" Carole asked.

"Yeah, just… remembering."

"It's okay. I'm here."

Randi gave her friend a grateful smile. She took one determined step down, then another.

At the landing, just around the corner, a shadow moved.

Randi backed up the stairs, clutching the railing. "Who's there?"

A figure stepped out of the shadows and looked at her.

"Dr. Peterson!" Relief flooded through her. "What are you doing here?"

Dr. Peterson put a finger to her lips and beckoned Randi toward her.

Randi glanced around and made her way warily down the stairs toward the other woman, Carole at her side. "What's going on?" Her voice came out as a hoarse whisper.

"Can we talk alone?" Dr. Peterson asked, glancing at Carole.

"Absolutely not," Carole said.

Dr. Peterson paused, then said, "It's not over. The attack was not a random mugging, and it wasn't a coincidence. They're trying to kill you."

Randi nodded. "I know."

"They won't try again. Not yet. It would be too obvious. But something is going to happen on your trip."

"What can they do? Our team is already confirmed, hand-picked by Dr. Lengel and myself. Besides, Jeremiah and Nik are both going to be with me all the time."

"All I know is, the Director has a plan. Something is going to happen while you're overseas. Watch yourself."

"I will."

Dr. Peterson disappeared down the stairs, leaving Randi and Carole staring after her.

***

Janice parked in her covered spot, feeling content. She'd done all she could. Now she and Rob would be free. Their assets were liquidated, their plans laid out to the smallest detail. In less than a week, they'd disappear together, out of the Syndicate's reach.

Her heels clicked on the sidewalk, a light, even rhythm.

A breeze stirred the leaves on the trees that lined the walkway.

The light between the buildings flickered.

A sharp, burning pain filled her stomach. The world went out of focus.

She glanced down at the thing that protruded through her stomach from behind, at the red stain that spread across her white blouse and down onto her gray pencil skirt.

It wasn't true what they said about your life flashing before your eyes. All she saw were her regrets—regret at not leaving Rob years ago when she'd first found out. Regret at not standing up for the truth long ago. Regret for… so very many things.

Except for one. She'd done the right thing by Randi.

The last thought through her mind, as the sharp metal withdrew from her abdomen, was that Randi Ross was right about one thing.

Truth *was* the only thing worth dying for.

Chapter Thirty-Four

The next two weeks flew by in a flurry of getting things ready for the trip. Dr. Jon Chevalet, along with his two assistants, Djazani Monroe and Alan Kinte, came by the office often to help prepare, as did Nik.

At last it was time to leave.

The whole team met at the airport, along with Randi's roommate Kelly, her mom, a few family members and friends of each of the teammates, and Dr. Lengel and Maria to see them off.

"You ready for this?" Nik asked Randi. He'd managed to get on the same flight as her team, a fact he couldn't help gloating over whenever he was around Dr. Bryant.

"I swear I'm forgetting something. What is it?" Randi raked her hands through her hair.

"You're cute when you're in panic mode. There's nothing we can't get later or do without."

Her heart warmed. "I still can't believe this is really happening—and you're really coming."

"I meant what I said. I'm with you. No matter what. So, say good-bye, and let's get moving."

Randi hugged Kelly, her mom, and even Dr. Lengel before stepping into the security line next to Nik.

He took her hand. "You good?"

"Little late to change my mind," she grinned.

He nodded toward Randi's mom, who was wiping away tears as she watched Randi snake her way through the security line. "How'd your mom take it?"

"She freaked out, of course, but it's not like it's the first time I've gone on an international trip. Anyway, I think she's finally starting to accept the fact that I'm a grown-up."

"Yeah, I'm still trying to remember that, too. How's your wound?"

"Pretty good. I got my stitches out a few days ago, and Carole made me a salve with coconut oil and vitamin E to help reduce the scarring. It's still pretty tender, but it's not too bad if I keep it wrapped."

"Just make sure you take care of it while we're gone. We're going to be pretty far away from modern technology."

"I'm fine, Nicky. Stop worrying."

Less than two hours later, they boarded the plane.

They made their way to their seats. Nik was in the same row as Carole, and Randi sat next to the window, Jeremiah beside her, a couple rows ahead of them.

She thought about seeing if Carole wanted to switch places, but the flight attendants started bustling everyone into their seats so they could get moving.

It was going to be a long flight—she could get up and switch later.

***

Nik craned his neck to see if he could see Randi. He thought about asking someone if they wanted to switch so he could sit next to her, but Dr. Bryant already looked at him like he had scales. He didn't want to make it worse.

Instead, he just glared at the back of Dr. Bryant's head for awhile, until Carole started talking to him. "This is going to be a long flight."

Nik turned to face her, grateful for the distraction. "Yeah. And these planes were not designed for tall people."

Carole gave a sympathetic smile at his knees crunched up behind the seat in front of him. "Sorry. I can't help with that."

Nik grinned at her. "It's okay, I'll live. So, I have a couple of books to help pass the time. Do you want to read one?"

"No, thanks," Carole groaned. "Just thinking about it is making me sick. I get motion sickness really easily."

"Do you want to switch seats in case you need to get out?"

"Sure. Thanks. Seth always took the aisle seat. He said the inside made him claustrophobic." They swapped spots, and Carole angled to face him.

"What made you decide to come on this trip? Are you on board with the dragon hunt, or are you just trying to keep an eye on Randi?"

Nik chuckled. Maybe he was more obvious than he realized. "After she got hurt, I kind of panicked. I couldn't stand the thought of her being so far away and me not having any idea whether or not she was okay. I needed to be with her."

"To protect her?"

Nik didn't answer.

Carole gazed at him. A smile quirked the corners of her mouth. "Where were the guys like you when I dated Seth?"

Nik snorted. "Where were the girls like you when I fell in love with someone who doesn't want me?"

"Well, it's her loss if she can't see what's right in front of her."

"Yeah. Great. Nice that she knows what she's missing." He stared at Randi and Dr. Bryant through the cracks between the seats.

Randi read a book for several hours then leaned up against the window, nestled into her seat, and eventually dozed off.

At some point in her sleep, she rolled over, her head lolling between her chair and Dr. Bryant's, and Dr. Bryant placed her head on his shoulder.

Nik glared daggers at the back of Dr. Bryant's head.

Carole shot a sympathetic glance his way. "What do you think we'll find? When we get there, I mean."

He smiled, again grateful to her for distracting him. "I don't know. Even if she's right and there *is* something to find, the chances of us actually finding it are pretty slim. I mean, suppose her sources *are* accurate. There's no guarantee the information isn't outdated or we'll find anyone who can take us to the right spot. Even if we do make it to the right spot, there are no guarantees we'll see anything. I mean, these creatures, if they exist, have remained hidden for thousands of years. What are the chances they'll come out of hiding just for us?"

"Good point. I hope we do find something—that would be epic. But I'm not going to be surprised if it doesn't happen."

Carole drifted off to sleep. Blonde hair fell in a soft frame around her smooth face. She was really pretty, and nice. If he'd met her six months ago… no, make that six years ago, maybe they could've been a thing.

But he'd made that mistake once. There was only one girl for him.

His gaze traveled back up to Randi and Dr. Bryant. Dr. Bryant looked way too comfortable with Randi leaning on him. Why couldn't he be interested in Carole, instead of trying to weasel his way into Randi's affections?

Somewhat out of spite, he transferred Carole's head to his shoulder. Not that it mattered. Randi couldn't see them. Still, though, he wished it were a head of soft, light brown hair with gold highlights that smelled of lavender, rather than a sleek blonde one.

***

Randi pulled away from Jeremiah's shoulder, her eyes scratchy from poor sleep.

"Sorry," she mumbled around a dry tongue.

"It's no problem."

"Excuse me." She squeezed out into the aisle to stretch her legs. Nik and Carole were sleeping against one another. A pang of jealousy shot through her.

It's not like you want him. Are you going to begrudge him finding someone who does? They'd make a really cute couple. She's exactly his type.

She knew Nik was here for her. Knew he was trying to make up for the past and get her back. She wasn't ready to trust him yet—and he and Carole really *would* be cute together. But that thought filled her with an uncomfortable level of anger. She made her way back to her seat, but glanced back several times, feeling more frustrated and jealous each time.

She finally managed to distract herself by reading her book, but the knowledge that Nik and Carole snuggled just behind her pricked at her like a cactus behind her back. How many more hours did she have to endure this torturous flight?

Too many.

***

Albert sat behind the hut, listening to the muted voices coming from inside. His mother had gone to the mother of an eligible young woman, Marie, to arrange their marriage.

"Nonsense," he heard his mother huff. "All he needs is a good woman to help keep him steady. He's a bright boy and will make an excellent husband."

"Well, I don't know," the other woman countered. "Marie is young yet. And she's not lacking for suitors. There are several young men in our village alone, not to mention in the other villages."

Albert knew it was a lie.

When Marie was little, she'd been following her mother down by the river, picking herbs, when a crocodile snapped at her leg.

Somehow, her mother had managed to grab her and pull her free, but it had left her leg mauled for life.

This, unfortunately, made her less than an ideal wife for many of the young men in the village.

Albert wasn't opposed to the idea of marrying Marie—she was smart and funny and pretty, despite her leg—but he wasn't ready to get married yet.

Leaning his head against the wall of the hut, he listened as his mother spouted his good characteristics and fine qualities. He knew she would wear down the other woman eventually—he just hoped that Marie's mother would hold her ground long enough for him to get away.

It had been over three months since he'd come down from the mountain, and every day since, he'd wanted to go back. The village elders had forced him to go into Ouesso to receive medical treatment. The doctors had insisted he stay for several weeks until they could safely remove his cast, and then they sent stern instructions about what he could and could not do, and how to rehabilitate it.

But now, his shoulder was almost completely better. It was certainly good enough for him to leave. He itched to get back to his sister, not only to check on her, but also to find out if she'd kept her promise, and what had come of his egg.

There were only a few more things needed to get ready, but he should be ready to leave before the end of the week.

If only there were some way to keep his mother from making anything official yet, he could leave, and then they couldn't do anything until he got back…

At the sound of a twig snapping, he stiffened and looked toward the sound.

Marie was coming around the side of the hut, eyes darting around, dragging her almost-useless leg behind her.

A gasp escaped her lips when she saw him.

He smiled. "Did you come to listen to our futures being planned, too?" he whispered.

Marie nodded and giggled.

"Have a seat," he offered.

Marie gingerly lowered herself to the ground beside him.

"So, who are you hoping wins?" Albert asked.

"What do you mean?"

"Do you want your mother to say it will never happen, or do you hope my mother convinces yours that I am a worthy match?"

Marie tilted her chin up, looking down her nose at him. "I plan on telling my mother that I have no intention of marrying you or anyone anytime soon."

Albert breathed a sigh of relief. "Thank goodness!"

Marie turned a glare on him. "Well, I'm glad to know how you feel before it's too late!" she snapped. "I'd hate for you to be stuck with me."

"I didn't mean that! I just meant—well, I'd be just as happy to marry you as anyone…"

"You're hardly in a position to be choosy yourself, you know," Marie spat.

Albert grabbed her shoulders and looked her in the eye. "Would you stop that?" he hissed, trying to keep his voice low. "I like you. I can't think of anyone else I'd rather marry, when I get married. But I'm not ready to get married yet. I… I have things I need to do first."

Marie's lips turned up in a smile, her beautiful dark eyes softening. "Really? You… you'd want to marry me? Even with…" she nodded toward her leg.

"What about it? That has nothing to do with why I like you. In fact, I admire you more because you've overcome that. You're the strongest girl I've ever known."

She smiled even more widely. "All right, then, I forgive you. So what do you have to do before you can get married?"

"You have to swear you won't tell anyone, especially either of our mothers," he said.

"I won't," Marie promised.

"I'm going back up the mountain."

"Why?"

Albert considered just using the excuse that he needed to find Naomi, but something in the sincere way Marie looked at him made him want to trust her. "There's something up there. My father—the Westerners—they…"

He couldn't say it. His father had died insisting to everyone outside Albert and Naomi that the Westerners had made it all up.

But Marie seemed to understand. "You have to know," she said.

He did know—but he just found himself nodding in agreement.

Marie shook her head, but she was still smiling. "You're as crazy as everyone thinks you are."

"Thanks," Albert grinned. "What about you?"

"What about me what?"

"You said you had no intention of getting married yet. What are you going to do?"

"I want to see Europe. Maybe America. Don't get me wrong, I love our people and our way of life, but I would like to see some of the world before I return to live the same life that my mother and every other woman we have ever known has lived."

Albert nodded. "I don't blame you. Good luck."

"You, too," Marie said.

They looked at each other for a moment, and then realized that the voices inside the hut had stopped.

Albert stood, and held out his hand to help Marie up. "I'd better get going before my mother wonders where I am." His hand still clasped hers.

"Me, too," Marie said.

They stood there, holding hands for a moment, just smiling at one another before letting go and disappearing around the house in opposite directions.

Albert began packing that evening. Along with clothes and food, he also packed his bow and a spear. He wasn't exactly sure what he expected to happen, but he wanted to be prepared.

Somewhere in the back of his mind was a picture of him arriving at the last moment and rescuing Naomi from the jaws of one of the creatures at the top of the mountain.

He should be ready to leave in two or three days.

Chapter Thirty-Five

Ouesso, Sangha, Congo

Randi thought the flight would never end, but at long last, the cryptozoology team got off the plane at their final destination.

Carole yawned. "I swear, my body is never going to recover from this jet lag."

Randi squeezed her hands together. "I can't believe we're here."

Despite the fuzz coating her mind and the stiff aching joints in every part of her body, the excitement of arriving at their destination overwhelmed her. It wouldn't be long now until they were really on the search.

It took quite some time to get through customs—some sort of problem with Kinte's suitcase held them up—but eventually they escaped the airport and hailed taxis to take them to their hotel.

After one night in the city, they planned to head out to the village Dr. Rosenbaum and Dr. Schleppenbach had visited.

Jeremiah fiddled with his watch. "It's still early, local time. I'm going to see what I can do about finding a guide to take us to the village tomorrow."

"I'll come, too," Randi volunteered.

Nik stepped up next to her, so close he almost toppled her over. "Me, too."

A slight crease lined Jeremiah's forehead. "Fine. Everyone else, either stay here and rest or do some sightseeing, but be back here in time for dinner."

Randi took a step sideways so Nik wasn't right on top of her and followed Jeremiah to the information desk in the hotel lobby. The clerk directed them to a storefront down the street advertising bus and walking tours of the city.

They found their way to the storefront, and Jeremiah took over inquiring about getting a guide to the village.

The man, in broken English, explained he only gave tours in and around the city, and they would have to find someone else to take them that far out into the rainforest.

He pointed them in the direction of someone else, a couple streets over, who also denied their request, and sent them to find a third person.

Evening was drawing near by the time they found the building they sought. Darkness shrouded the interior and a heavy lock barred the door.

Jeremiah's heavy sigh echoed Randi's. "We'll come back first thing in the morning. Let's go back and get some dinner."

"Good idea," Randi said. "I'm starving."

Nik linked her arm in his and headed back toward the hotel.

Jeremiah looked almost as if he wanted to start a round of tug-of-war with Nik, but settled for walking close by Randi's other side until they got back to the hotel lobby. "Why don't you two get us a table. I'll round up the rest of the team, and then we can all discuss our plans for tomorrow."

Over dinner, Jeremiah explained to the others about their lack of success in finding a guide. "First thing tomorrow, I'll go back to the other guide's building. If all else fails, we can rent an SUV and try to find it ourselves, although obviously that's a last resort. Randi, I assume since this trip is your project, you'll want to come along?"

Randi nodded eagerly.

"Very well. I'll meet you in the lobby at seven. Everyone, try to get some rest. We still have a long journey ahead of us."

***

The next morning, Randi woke early and showered. Though it was still a couple of minutes before seven when she got down to the lobby, Jeremiah was already waiting for her.

"Are you ready to go? We want to get there before anyone else, even if we have to wait for him, so we don't risk him being engaged elsewhere."

She nodded. "All set."

He handed her an apple and a blueberry muffin. "I thought you might get hungry before we got back."

"Thank you." Randi bit into the apple and almost choked on it when Nik swaggered into the lobby with a local man.

"I got us transportation."

Jeremiah narrowed his eyes. "Who is this?"

"This is William. He has two Jeeps that he's willing to use to haul us up to the village."

"Where did you meet him? Does he know where to go?"

"He's a merchant. He's got a store down the street. He goes out into the remote areas to trade with local tribes all the time. He can get us where we need to go.

Jeremiah narrowed his eyes at Nik. He exchanged a few words with William in French before eventually agreeing to hire him. "We'll be ready to go in half an hour," he said at last.

"You're welcome," Nik said.

Jeremiah gave him a grudging smile. "Thank you. This was a good idea. I'll go get everyone else and make sure they're ready to go."

Randi ran up to her room to grab her suitcase.

Nik was waiting outside the hotel room that Randi, Carole, and Djazani shared when they emerged. He took Randi's bag. "Hey, babe, I'll get that for you."

Randi couldn't help but notice the look that Carole and Djazani exchanged. They must have done some gossiping last night, she reasoned.

Outside the hotel, the guide waited with two large, open-top Jeeps with oversized tires.

The guide sat in the driver's seat of the first, and Jeremiah climbed into the second.

"Randi, you ride with me so we can go over our schedule."

Nik jumped into Jeremiah's Jeep and held out his hand to Randi to help her up.

She was torn between being amused and being irritated. Jeremiah just wanted to make efficient use of their time and get as much work done as possible on the road, and Nik just wanted to be near her, but he could be so possessive! And Jeremiah seemed to enjoy antagonizing him, while Nik enjoyed rubbing it in Jeremiah's face that he and Randi were close. Both of them were acting like children, which was both flattering and annoying to be in the middle of.

After everyone piled into the two vehicles—Carole joining Randi and Nik with Jeremiah, and Djazani, Kinte, and Jon Chevalet with the guide—they set off down the road and out of the city to a dirt track that wound toward the distant mountains.

The farther they traveled into the interior of the country, the worse the climate became. The air felt heavy with heat and moisture, and only a liberal coating of insect repellent, reapplied every few hours, kept the swarms of mosquitoes from gnawing Randi's flesh.

Sweat leaked from every pore, leaving her skin sticky.

They bounced and jostled over the rutted path, and after an hour, Randi's head pounded so hard she could hardly think. At one point, the road became so water-logged, they had to get out and put boards under the tires so they wouldn't get bogged down.

Another two hours passed before they finally stopped for lunch.

"Hang on, babe." Nik leapt from the back of the Jeep and held out his arms to help Randi down. She accepted his assistance, holding tightly to his hands and jumping to the ground. She landed in front of him, less than an inch away from collapsing into his chest.

He grinned at her, his quirky, affectionate smile sending her heart skittering. "Good thing I'm here. You probably wouldn't survive without me around."

Hiding the girlish giggle that wanted to bubble up with a mock scowl, she pushed away from him. "I just let you think that to build up your self-esteem."

She sauntered to a space near the Jeep and sat down. Broad leaves sheltered her from the sun, if not the muggy heat, and she sat under the canopy, gazing fascinated into the branches at the wildlife moving around above her head while she ate.

Finally, the guide stood and jabbered something to Jeremiah in French.

"All right, everybody," Jeremiah said, "he says if we want to get there before dark, and he assures me we do, then we need to get moving."

With groans all around, the team stood and stretched one last time before getting into the vehicles.

They traveled deeper into the forest, the track becoming more ragged and the trees growing closer together, filtering out the sunlight until they were bathed in an eerie green glow.

"It's a little creepy in here," Carole shuddered.

"Oh, come on," Nik teased. "You were face-to-face with Bigfoot, and this scares you?"

"Oh, believe me, I was terrified then, too," Carole grinned.

They laughed, but conversation didn't last. Randi suspected lack of sleep and sore, tense muscles affected the others as much as they did her.

As the sun turned orange, the light through the branches turned a muddy brown. In the car ahead, the guide examined the sky and slowed his vehicle to a stop. He jumped out and trotted back to Jeremiah, jabbering at him in French.

"He says the village we're looking for is about half a mile away. This is where we'll camp. We don't want to invade their privacy too much, and there is a clearing here that will be suitable for setting up our tents."

The guide set to work immediately building a fire, while the team made camp.

"Remember, nobody goes anywhere alone, even if it's just to—take care of personal business," Jeremiah reminded them as they circled around the fire for a dinner of hot dogs and beans.

Earlier than she ever would at home, Randi crawled into her sleeping bag in the women's tent.

Djazani came in a moment later, carefully zipping the mosquito net closed behind her. "I hope we don't all die from malaria."

Randi giggled. "I'm more worried about giant baboons and wild cats eating us in our sleep."

"Oh, great, thanks for *that* mental image."

"Sorry." Randi wracked her brain for a good subject change. "Kinte seems nice. How long have you been together?"

"Officially a couple months, but we've been friends and colleagues for a couple years. I've always thought that close friendships make the best relationships." The way she inclined her head toward where the men's voices could be heard left no doubt in Randi's mind that she was referring to Nik.

"Nik and I are good friends, but we already tried the dating thing. It's not happening again."

"You sure about that? Because from where I'm standing, it looks like that man is completely in love with you."

Randi curled up tighter in her sleeping bag, despite the hot, muggy weather. "We're just friends." But she knew she wasn't convincing anyone, least of all herself.

She woke early the next morning and followed Jeremiah and the guide into the village.

The villagers didn't seem surprised to see them. A camp their size would be no secret to natives.

The guide spoke to a woman in the native dialect.

"He's explaining that we're looking for Kudabah," Jeremiah told Randi.

The woman pointed to a hut in the center of the village and hurried away.

The guide led them toward the hut. A woman came out, arms crossed in front of her chest and a scowl on her face.

The guide again said something in the native language, and the woman replied in French.

"She says her husband is dead," Jeremiah translated.

"Is there anyone else who could help us? We're looking for a guide who will take us to the last place your husband went." The guide spoke to the woman, translating into French for Jeremiah who, in turn, kept Randi informed of what passed between them.

"I'm afraid that is impossible. There is no one here who can help you." She turned abruptly and disappeared into the hut.

"What now?" Randi asked.

"We go back to the camp and try again later. Word will get around, and someone may be more willing to talk to us when we return."

***

Albert, flattened against the side of the hut, crept slowly away around the back. This was the chance he'd been waiting for. As long as he could get away without his mother knowing, the rest would be easy.

He had suspected that the Westerners would come into the village that morning. A group that size wasn't wandering around the jungle by accident.

Not wanting his mother to know how curious he was, he'd left at dawn with his bow and arrow, hoping she would assume he was hunting.

Instead of hunting, however, he waited on the outskirts of the village for the Westerners to appear. He'd seen one of the women point toward his mother's hut, and had crept quietly around to listen as the Westerners told his mother what they had wanted.

It was perfect. He had planned to leave the next morning to return to find Naomi anyway, and now he would have the chance to make some money while he was at it.

In search of an alibi to allay his mother's suspicions, he slipped into the forest and shot the first animal he saw, a wild boar, and dragged it toward the village.

Dragging the boar to within view of his mother's hut, he began the work of skinning.

She came out a little while later, as he had expected she would, her hands on her hips. "Where have you been?"

He gave her a confused look, gesturing toward the boar.

Apparently satisfied that he was too occupied to go talk to the Westerners, she turned and walked back toward the hut.

She watched him like a hawk the rest of the day, however.

Several times, he tried to sneak out to the Westerner's camp, but every time, just as he was nearing the edge of the forest, his mother's shrill voice called out to him, and he had to make up some sort of innocent excuse for where he had been going.

Finally, by afternoon, he was getting desperate. "I'm going to go see Marie," he announced.

He and Marie had seen quite a bit of each other since their meeting behind Marie's house, and his mother was well pleased to let him.

He could still feel her eyes boring into his back as he stood outside Marie's door.

Marie came outside.

"Hello, Marie," he said loudly. Then, in a murmur, "I need your help."

"What is it?" she asked softly.

"Would you care to take a walk with me?" he asked, again loudly enough to be heard.

"I would love to," Marie answered.

Taking her arm, he helped to support her as she hobbled along on her one good leg. He led her to the forest in the opposite direction of the Westerners' camp.

"What's going on?" Marie asked as soon as they were out of earshot.

"The Westerners are looking for a guide to take them to the last place my father went," Albert explained.

"I know. The whole village is buzzing about it. Your mother put them in their place, though."

"Well, she thinks she did. I'm going to go offer to take them. The only problem is, every time I try to escape to go talk to them, my mother is watching me."

Marie giggled. "Is that why she's been screaming at you all day?"

Albert grinned. "I need to get over there to talk to them, and the only way I'll manage it is if my mother thinks I'm with you. She's so anxious for us to get married, she's willing to overlook the obvious. That's why I need your help."

"Well, here I am," she said.

"Thank you. You're wonderful," Albert smiled.

Marie ducked her head, looking shyly up at him through her lashes.

He squeezed her hand. "We're just going to circle around the village and head back toward the Westerners' camp," he explained, trying to save her from her embarrassment. "Then we'll have to come back the same way so my mother doesn't suspect anything."

They soon came to the edge of the camp.

"Wait here," Albert instructed.

He boldly went toward the fire in the center of the camp.

Chapter Thirty-Six

Randi sat with Nik, Jeremiah, and the guide by the fire later that evening.

They'd gone back to the village later in the afternoon. The guide had brought some items to trade, which made some of the villagers a little more willing to engage with them, but still, no one was willing to discuss leading them up the mountain.

Now, they were discussing what they could use to incentivize them, besides the considerable amount of money they'd already offered.

"We could try to go on our own," Randi suggested. "Dr. Schleppenbach said they went northwest and they were near a river."

The guide jabbered something, and Jeremiah chattered back. The guide's hands raised in the air, gesturing emphatically.

"I told him your suggestion. He says he wouldn't recommend that. He can't stay to come with us—he has to get back to his store. And even if he could, he wouldn't. Even the natives can get lost in this jungle, and he doesn't have the proper equipment or training to make it, especially since he doesn't know where we're headed. We need someone who knows where they're going."

"That woman said there wasn't anyone," Randi protested.

"Yes, but that doesn't mean we can't ask someone else who would be willing to bargain. We just need to find the right incentive. I suggest we wait until tomorrow. By then, the entire village will know exactly who we are and what we want, and there's a good chance someone will be jumping at the chance to make some money, or will come with a demand that we can try to meet."

Nik's head jerked up and he stared across the clearing.

Randi followed his gaze to the young native man who approached.

Hands on his hips, he stood straight, drawing himself up as if to make himself taller than he was. No more than five feet, Randi estimated. Maybe even shorter.

The boy spoke in French.

Jeremiah's eyes widened. "He says he'll take us where we want to go."

Nik scowled. "So. That's pretty convenient. Who is he, and how do we know this isn't just a scam to make a quick buck?"

"Does it matter?" Randi said. "This is exactly what we're looking for."

"This young man's name is Albert," Jeremiah said. "He says he's Kudabah's son."

"But his mother said—"

The native boy spoke again.

"He says he knows where to go and how to get there."

"How much is he going to charge us?" Nik grumbled.

After another brief exchange, Jeremiah nodded. "A fair enough price for what we want. We leave at dawn."

***

"It's about time. Where have you been?" the Director demanded.

"Believe it or not, it's not exactly the easiest thing to sneak away for a satellite call in the middle of the jungle when I'm with a whole group of people," the agent replied dryly.

"I thought you had better training than this."

"I'm calling now, aren't I?"

The Director didn't appreciate the sass, but at the moment, more important things were at stake. "Any news?"

"Not yet. We found a guide to take us up the mountain. We're leaving first thing in the morning."

"Is everything in place?"

"Yes. All contingencies accounted for."

"You're sure?" the Director asked.

"Positive. I'll call you when I have any news."

***

Albert's mother stirred as he crept from his bed. Holding his breath, he froze until his mother stopped moving. He carefully tiptoed out, not releasing his breath until he was safely outside.

A shadow moved toward him and he stopped, thinking he had been found out, until he realized it was Marie.

He held out his hand to her and led her out of the village. It wasn't until they were well out of earshot that he finally spoke. "Thank you for coming."

She squeezed his hand. "I didn't want you to go without being able to say goodbye."

He thought he heard her sniff slightly.

In all too short a time, they arrived at the Westerners' campsite, where there was a flurry of activity as the camp was being packed up.

"You'd better get back before anybody wakes up," Albert whispered.

Marie nodded and started to turn away.

"Marie, wait…"

She stopped and looked up at him in the soft light of dawn.

"I was thinking… about you going to Europe." He pulled the wad of cash the leader of the Westerners had given him out of his pocket and stuffed it into her hand. "I want you to have that."

Marie looked at it and gasped. "Albert, I couldn't."

"I want you to have it," he said again.

Marie's eyes were wide as she looked up at him. She flung her arms around his neck in a tight hug.

He returned the hug a little shyly. "Anyway, I figure it's a good investment. You'll get all that traveling out of your system, so you won't always be asking me to take you places when we're married."

He felt a splash of tears against his neck. Marie's body shook, but he soon realized she was laughing. "I'll still make you take me places."

"Anywhere you want to go," he said. "But take this and go do the things you want to do for yourself."

"This is too generous," Marie feebly protested.

"They're going to give me more when I bring them back safely. Besides, I thought that maybe…" he stammered, "maybe if you're gone at the same time that I am, I won't miss you so much."

Marie hugged him again. "Thank you," she whispered into his ear. "I'll miss you, too."

She pulled away and wiped the tears from her eyes.

They looked at each other for another moment, then Albert glanced over at the camp.

"I should go," he whispered.

Marie nodded.

"Well, goodbye, then," he said.

"Goodbye."

He took a deep breath and turned toward the camp. Then he stopped.

Turning, he gathered Marie in his arms and kissed her thoroughly on the mouth.

Marie's arms snaked around his neck, and she returned his kiss.

They both pulled away, suddenly shy, but both grinning.

"Goodbye," they both said again, then quickly turned away from each other, Marie back toward the village and Albert toward the camp.

**

Early morning sunlight had just begun to lighten the jungle gloom when Randi emerged from her tent. They packed up their tents and divided the gear among everyone, so each person had a share of the camping equipment in a giant pack. Randi finished strapping her backpack on and went to stand by Jeremiah.

A few moments later, Albert, their new guide, sauntered into the camp.

The guide who brought them from the city accepted payment from Jeremiah and returned to his Jeep. He'd leave the second Jeep here until their return from the excursion, at which point he'd lead the way back to the city. The Jeep was security for the team that he'd come back, as well as security for the guide that he'd get the rest of the payment promised to him.

Albert tapped his feet and gazed around the camp.

What was his hurry? Randi looked around the camp at the others as they finished packing and tying shoes and gobbling down their breakfasts. A few short minutes later, they all lined up behind Albert, ready to begin their trek.

Albert started walking, setting a pace Randi found hard to match, despite his being several inches shorter than either her or Carole, who were the shortest of the group.

A hot rain began to fall, soaking through Randi's clothes and making the slick ground sticky. Mud sucked at her boots, so every step felt like she was dragging weights on her ankles.

They reached the base of the mountain, and the path grew steeper. If it could even be called a path.

Albert bounded ahead, his energy seemingly endless as he urged them onward.

Jeremiah kept close behind him, his long legs stretching over distances nearly twice as long as any Randi's could boast.

Randi gasped for breath. She paused with her hand on a tree. The others passed her, except Jon.

"Are you all right?" he asked.

"Yeah, I'm fine. Go on, I'll catch up."

He stood and waited. "I needed a break anyway."

She smiled at him. "Thanks." She took just a few moments to breathe and drink from her water bottle. "Okay, I think I'm good."

Ahead, Carole screamed. A sound like thunder followed her voice.

Jon pushed Randi off the path just as an avalanche of muddy rocks and debris tumbled past.

"Carole!" Nik shouted.

Randi stood and helped Jon to his feet, and looked to where the others were gathered.

Carole lay half-buried in mud, eyes closed.

Randi hurried to join the others at Carole's side, and began digging through the mud with her hands.

Carole woke up and tried to fight her way out, as well.

The slick, wet sludge stuck to Carole's body, and for every scoop that they removed, more slid down from the mudslide that still seeped down from higher on the mountain, making it seem like she was getting more buried rather than less.

"This isn't working," Jeremiah said after a little while. "Nik, help me get her shoulders."

The two men grabbed Carole and pulled.

A sucking sound accompanied the groan that escaped Carole's lips, but after a few moments, they pulled her free of the quicksand-like mud.

She lay on the thick foliage to the side of the path for a few moments, catching her breath, as Jeremiah hovered over her, checking her for injuries.

"I'm okay," she said. "But I'd like to get some of this mud off before we go on."

Nik helped her to her feet and threw his arms around her in an impulsive hug. "You really had us worried for a second, there."

A pang shot through Randi as she watched Carole linger in Nik's embrace for a moment. *Stop that*, she chided herself. *Carole almost died. You can't begrudge her a hug.*

Albert led Carole to the river, and she splashed the majority of the mud away. Finally, they were on their way again. After that, Albert seemed to be trying to make up for lost time. He pushed them along, scarcely seeming to take any care, even after the mudslide.

Hours later, he finally began to slow his pace, but he still only allowed them one short break for lunch.

Randi sank wearily down on a log and took a swig of water from her bottle.

Nik plopped down beside her. "So. How are you holding up?"

She shrugged. "I'm okay."

It wasn't entirely true, but she didn't want to admit how much the hike wore on her. She wasn't the one who got buried in a mudslide, after all. Besides, she might not have Carole or Djazani's fantastic figures, but she didn't want it to be too obvious she was in so much worse shape than everyone else, either. If sheer force of will could get her up this mountain, she'd make it.

"Do you want me to carry something for you?"

"No." He was just trying to be helpful, but it took effort to keep an annoyed tone out of her voice. Did he really think she was that weak? "I can get it. You have your own load to carry."

"Are you sure? I—"

"I'm fine." There was a little snap to her voice.

Chapter Thirty-Seven

Nik, looking a little hurt, walked away and sat down on the ground, facing away from her.

She tried to ignore the guilt gnawing at her as she took another drink of water.

Carole sat down beside her. "That wasn't very fair. He was only trying to be gentlemanly."

"He thinks I can't do it."

"That's not true."

"I didn't see him offering to take your load," Randi grumbled.

"Of course not. He's not in love with me." A note of bitterness touched Carole's voice.

Randi shot her a look. "Well, it's still not very flattering to be the only one in the group who's in such bad shape. Even Jon is keeping up better than I am. You don't know what I would give to have your body right now."

"Believe me, I'm not exactly bursting with energy at this point, either."

"It's not just that. It's everything. The way you move and look like you're always comfortable in your body, and the way everybody thinks you're beautiful—" she stopped, not wanting to sound too jealous.

"Well, when it comes down to it, it really hasn't done me much good. There's apparently more to being attractive than looks."

"What do you mean?"

"It's obvious, isn't it? My boyfriend cheated on me, while you have two great guys falling all over themselves for you."

Randi stared at her. "What are you talking about?"

Carole cocked her head. "Oh, come on."

"No, I'm serious. What are you talking about? *Two* guys?"

"Well, there's Nik."

"Yeah, of course. I know Nik."

"And Dr. Bryant." Carole's tone made it sound as if it should've been obvious.

"*Jeremiah?*" Randi gaped.

"You can't tell me you didn't know."

Randi continued to stare at her, eyes wide and mouth open.

"You seriously never noticed? The way he stares at you, the way he goes out of his way to do things with you?"

Randi shook her head. "He's my boss. And he feels guilty about the mugging. And this is my expedition, so he's deferring to me because I'm the one who read all the—" She trailed off at the look of incredulity that Carole wore.

"How about the fact you're the only one who gets to call him Jeremiah instead of *Doctor* Bryant? Or way he's constantly glaring at Nik when the two of you are together, or the way he was at your side taking care of you when you were attacked? Or the way—"

"Okay, everyone, it's time to get moving," Jeremiah said. He came over to where Randi sat. "How's your wound?"

Out of the corner of her eye, Randi saw the significant glance Carole gave her.

"It's fine."

He held out a hand to help her up. "Good. Let me know if you need anything."

"Thanks."

He nodded and took his place behind Albert as they began the next leg of the trip.

It was too difficult to talk while they pushed their way through the dense growth, the mud sucking at their feet as they slowly made it up the mountain, which was just fine with Randi. She didn't know what to say. She didn't even know what to think.

"Don't move," Jeremiah said, putting a hand on her shoulder.

Randi stood still. When had he fallen back to walk near her?

"Albert?" Jeremiah said, his voice just loud enough to be heard.

Randi followed his gaze to the ground near her feet and nearly jumped, despite Jeremiah's warning.

Inches away, a snake as long as she was tall slithered along the ground beside the trail.

Albert laughed and said something in French.

Jeremiah inhaled deeply. "Apparently that one is a constrictor, not a venomous one, and it's not big enough to be interested in eating us. But watch out for the little ones that hang from trees."

Jeremiah left his hand on her shoulder until she stepped away.

Was it possible Carole was right about his feelings for her? If so, how could she have missed it? Did Nik know? Was that why he didn't get along with Dr. Bryant? Why he came on this trip—to stake his claim and make sure Jeremiah didn't do anything to get between them?

Her eyes darted back and forth between the two men as they walked, growing more and more confused each time one or the other of them looked back at her and smiled, which was far more often than she'd previously realized.

When they stopped for lunch, Randi sat next to Carole, her back to the rest of the group, avoiding looking at either man. She couldn't help but wonder what was going through their heads every time she looked at or spoke to either of them.

It wasn't Nik she concerned herself with, however. She'd known for a long time how he felt about her. They'd been over their relationship—or lack thereof—a hundred times. Nothing new there. Except that now he really was following through with his promise. And she was beginning to believe he meant it—beginning to think maybe they could get past their history and try again at a real relationship.

Really, though, *Jeremiah?* Worse, Nik apparently knew, and they had some sort of rivalry going on without her knowledge. She thought it was just petty man-squabbles, both trying to be the alpha-male in the group, but, if Carole was right, it wasn't just that, it was personal.

Now she had no idea how to react to Jeremiah. She didn't dislike him anymore, as she had when she'd first met him, but he wasn't someone she would ever have considered romantically.

Of course, just because he was interested in her didn't mean she had to be interested in him. But now she wasn't sure she could look at him or talk to him the same way as she had before. Would it be strange to work for him, knowing how he felt about her?

Maybe she was worrying too much. Carole could be wrong. After all, Jeremiah had never said anything to make her think he was interested. She, of course, had never done anything to encourage him. Yes, she was just overreacting. She needed to stop worrying.

She jumped at the voice beside her.

"You awake in there?" Carole asked.

"Sorry. Just thinking."

"About?"

"Just stuff."

"About how to act around Dr. B now that you know how he feels?"

"Since when are you psychic?" Randi frowned.

"What are you worried about? Nothing has to change. Just act the way you always have."

"Yeah, but he's my boss. It's weird."

"No, it's not. The weirdness is just in your head."

"Maybe it's all in *your* head. I mean, Jeremiah's never given me any reason to think anything—"

A hand settled on her shoulder and Jeremiah asked, "Are you feeling okay?"

Randi stiffened, jerking out from under his grasp. "I'm fine."

She couldn't help noticing Carole's grin.

"Let me know if you need anything." Jeremiah walked away.

She didn't miss the angry glare Nik shot his direction.

A few minutes later, Albert began walking again. Randi stretched and pulled her backpack on, hurrying to catch up. He was walking fast again, and soon Randi ran out of breath. Her legs burned from the exertion. She wasn't sure how much longer she could make it.

Glancing up, she saw Carole walking next to Nik. She made it look easy, keeping her stride in line with his, smiling and laughing. A pang of jealousy tore through her.

Was this how Nik felt when Jeremiah talked to her?

What right did she have to be jealous? After all the times she turned him down, she ought to be glad for him. Carole was a great girl. He was lucky to have someone like her interested in him.

She ought to be glad Carole was there to take Nik's attention away from her—it would prove what she'd known all along, that Nik wasn't ready for a serious relationship. Better this, now, than after they got together and she trusted him again and history repeated itself.

She ought to be glad—but she wasn't. Jealously, as hot as the flames from a dragon's mouth, seared her. Seeing the two of them walking together made her eyes burn with tears she didn't dare shed.

It was almost dusk when they stopped for the night and began to build their campfire. The women set up the tents while the men gathered firewood. Albert took his spear and went hunting. He came back a short time later with a wild boar, which they roasted over the fire.

Randi thought she wouldn't be able to eat after watching him kill and skin it, but as the aroma from the freshly cooked meat began to fill the air, her growling stomach overcame the nausea she felt watching the animal be prepared.

Carole laughed at something Nik said. A pang of jealously shot through Randi.

When Nik walked away, Randi went to talk to Carole. "Why didn't you tell me you were interested in him?" She tried to keep the hurt out of her voice.

"I'm sorry," Carole wrung her shirt in her hands. "I didn't mean to be. Honestly, I just started talking to him and getting to know him. I couldn't help comparing him to Seth. I mean, Nik is so… honest and trustworthy and faithful. He's everything Seth wasn't. He's a really great guy, you know?"

"I know," Randi sighed.

"I don't get you." Annoyance tainted Carole's voice. "You like him, you admit he's a great guy, and yet you refuse to do anything about it, even though he clearly returns your feelings."

"It's… complicated." Randi wasn't really in the mood to discuss the dynamics of her relationship with Nik.

"What's complicated? You either want to be with him or you don't, but you won't make it that simple. You won't date him, but you keep leading him on. You don't want him, but you don't want anyone else to have him, either. You need to make up your mind, Randi. Either take him or set him free."

She stalked off, leaving Randi staring after her, tears welling up in her eyes. Not because what Carole said had hurt her, but because it was true.

***

Randi approached Nik while the food was cooking and sat down beside him. "Hi."

"Hey." His voice was gruff, and he wouldn't look at her.

"I'm sorry I snapped at you before. I didn't mean to."

"It's fine." There was still an edge to his voice.

"I'm really sorry, Nik. I had no right to be rude to you. I was just frustrated because I felt like you thought I wasn't in as good of shape as Carole and you only offered to help because you felt sorry for me. In reality, I was feeling sorry for myself, and I had no right to take it out on you."

He turned to look at her then. "Don't you understand that doesn't matter to me? It's you I—I care about. If I offer to do something for you, it's because I care, not because I feel sorry for you. I have never felt sorry for you in all the years we've known each other."

"You're a good friend, Nik."

He gave her a sidelong glance that was equal parts longing and annoyed. "You too."

"Carole likes you, you know."

She knew she was pushing the issue, but she wanted to make it clear she was not only okay with him seeing someone else, but she wanted him to.

No longer would she let him cling to false hope or give him the impression there was more to their relationship than there was. No longer would she be guilty of the things Carole accused her of.

Maybe, just maybe, if she knew he had moved on, for good this time, she could, too.

Nik looked at her, his eyes pleading. "You don't get it. This has nothing to do with Carole. Even if I were attracted to her, there would never be anything there." He reached out and grasped her hand. "She still wouldn't be you. Do you really think that I would go to this much effort if I wasn't completely sure about my feelings? I made that mistake once, and now I know better. There isn't anyone else in the world for me. No matter what you say, I can't move on. I don't want to move on."

Randi tried to pull her hand away, but he wouldn't let go.

"I appreciate you trying to let me down easy, but you're the only one I want."

Randi's eyes filled. "I'm sorry."

His fingertips brushed the tears from her face. "You don't have to be. You haven't done anything wrong. You haven't led me on or given me false impressions. You've always told me exactly where you stand." Dropping her hand, he turned his eyes toward the fire. "I'm not giving up. I know I don't deserve a second chance. I don't blame you for that, and I don't want you to have to wait for me, either. You have a life and a calling that, at least right now, doesn't include me." His gaze swept back to her face for an instant before returning to the dancing flames. "I want you to do what you're supposed to do, without me holding you back. It doesn't mean I care about you any less—it just goes to show how much I *do* care about you. I want what's best for you, even if I'm not part of it. But I'm not going anywhere. I'll still be here waiting. No matter what."

Randi wiped the tears from her cheeks with the back of her hand. She wanted to trust him. She wanted to give in to the feelings she'd been holding in check for all these years. But part of her still clung to the agony she'd endured when he'd broken up with her the first time. She couldn't go through that again. She just couldn't.

"Let's not talk about this," Nik said. "All we ever do is talk about it, and nothing ever changes. What do you think we'll find at the top? Albert seems really determined to get us there in record time—do you think he's just eager to earn a paycheck, or do you think he knows something about what we're after?"

Chapter Thirty-Eight

Jeremiah stared across the fire at Randi and Nik, imagining all the possible conversations they might be having right now. At any rate, it looked like they had made up from whatever spat they'd had earlier, because they were both smiling and Randi's face was animated as she talked.

Carole came and sat down beside him. A sideways glance at her told him she knew exactly how he felt.

"It's like living in a soap opera," Carole said after a moment. "The way they go back and forth. I tried to talk to her earlier, but I don't think anything I said mattered to her. She's still over there flirting with him like nothing happened. I just wish she'd make up her mind."

Jeremiah nodded. "At least then we'd know if either of us stood a chance."

"You've never told her how you feel." It was more a statement than a question.

"What would be the point? She doesn't even like me. Besides, as much as she says they're just friends, it's obvious how she feels about Nik."

"And he about her." Carole's voice held the same amount of wistfulness he felt.

Jeremiah met Carole's eyes and they shared a moment of common ground, both knowing how the other felt, before looking away.

"What I don't understand is how a guy like you hasn't already been snatched up," Carole said after a few moments. It wasn't flirty, exactly—more curious.

Jeremiah shrugged. "I just haven't found the right one, I guess."

"Do you ever really know if it's the right one? I mean, I thought Seth was the right one. We had everything in common, we had a lot of fun together, the sex was *great*. How do you have all that and still not be right for each other?"

"I wouldn't know."

"You've had relationships, right?"

"Yes. I was even engaged. Clearly, however, since I'm not married, I can't comment on the methods one would use to maintain a relationship."

"Do you think if Nik were out of the picture you could have a relationship with Randi?"

"I don't know. As long as he is, I won't intrude. I won't be the one to pull them apart and ruin whatever it is they have."

Carole frowned. "You're right. I just wish he'd stop wasting time on someone who doesn't appreciate him and take a look at what's right in front of him."

Jeremiah didn't answer. There was nothing else to say.

***

Djazani followed at the back of the group the next day, and Kinte walked with her. The further they went into the jungle, the more the stress got to her. She couldn't help wishing she were back under the Wyoming sun, dusting off bones. It seemed to affect Kinte even more. His brow furrowed, and he spoke even less than usual.

The second day passed much like the first, although Albert did ease up slightly on the pace.

Djazani squeezed Kinte's hand as they sat before the fire that night. "Why don't you sit with the guys?"

"That's not why I'm here."

"Dr. Bryant seems nice. And smart. He'd probably—"

"I am here to do a job," Kinte snapped. "I must go on with this and complete my apprenticeship so I can go back to being a real scientist."

She stroked his hand. "This is my fault. I should've done something—talked to someone—so you could stay in Wyoming."

He turned to her. "No, this is not your fault. None of this is. I know it has not been easy for you, either. We both had other plans for our lives, and this is…" He sighed and straightened his back. "This is a detour. Nothing more.

302

We will do what we have said we would do, and then we will work our way back and make our lives what they were meant to be."

"You think so?" Djazani asked.

"Yes. But you are correct in one thing. We ought to integrate ourselves more into this group. I have had difficulty getting to know Nik and Dr. Bryant, but I will try harder to make friendships."

"If you can do it, I guess I can, too," Djazani said.

"Yes, this is the attitude we must have. We were given a task. But it is hard to bear, knowing when we finish we will have to start over and find another paleontologist to work with."

Djazani slapped at a mosquito. "True. Administrator Schweitzer won't let us anywhere near the dig in Wyoming. But Mr. Chevalet is a respected paleontologist. He knows people. If we work well with him, he may be able to help us."

"Mr. Chevalet belongs in the museum, not just working in one."

Djazani giggled. "No argument here. But Mr. Chevalet is our best hope right now of moving on later."

Kinte frowned. "Very well, I will try to make the best of it. But I do not promise to like the old man any better."

***

They started out again after a short lunch break. By now, even Jeremiah was beginning to feel the exhaustion settle in.

He tramped along behind Albert, asking him about his father.

"He used to take Westerners on expeditions. Your people always expect to be the first to make a discovery." Albert laughed, but it was good-natured. "They wanted to capture the evidence of a mysterious creature, Mokele-Mbembe."

"Yes, I've heard of that. It's supposed to look like a dinosaur. Have you ever seen it?"

Albert nodded. "Only a few times, from a distance. But I know him to be real. The other creature is the one he thought was only legend."

"The dragon."

Albert nodded. "Just before he died, he told my sister and me the truth. They went to the lake to look for Mokele-mbembe, but he did not appear. My father thought he was migrating away, trying to stay out of reach of civilization. The Westerners promised more money if my father would take them deeper into the jungle."

Jeremiah glanced back at the group to make sure everyone was still accounted for. He worried about Jon, but the older man seemed to be keeping up without trouble. He turned back to Albert. "Go on."

"They went higher into the mountains than our people usually go and came to another lake. They kept their eyes on the mouth of the lake, when they should have been watching the sky. At first, my father thought it was an owl. The thing was nearly on top of them when my father realized it was a creature from his ancestors' legends."

"Look out!"

Jeremiah turned around in time to see Nik leaping toward him. They tumbled to the ground, rolling to the side of the path, just as a leopard jumped from a tree onto the spot where Jeremiah had been standing a moment before.

Albert whirled and thrust his spear into the leopard's chest. He grinned at Jeremiah. "Guess what we're having for dinner tonight?"

Nik rolled away and lay on the lush carpet of undergrowth to catch his breath.

Jeremiah looked over at him. His hands shook. The encounter rattled him more than he wanted to admit. "Thanks."

"Any time," Nik grinned. He stood and held out a hand to help Jeremiah up.

Maybe he wasn't such a self-centered child, after all.

Albert looked around. "This is as good a place as any to set up camp. It is not as far as I wished to go, but we can make up the time tomorrow."

As they had the previous nights, the women set up the tents while Jeremiah and the rest of the men gathered firewood and helped Albert with the meal.

The least Jeremiah could do was be friendly, after Nik had saved his life that afternoon. After that incident, he and Nik seemed to have reached a sort of grudging respect for one another.

"What do you suppose they can talk about all day that's so interesting?" Jeremiah asked Nik, nodding toward Randi and Carole, who laughed hysterically as they pounded tent pegs into the ground.

"Us. What else could possibly be so funny?"

Jeremiah chuckled. "I didn't think we were that interesting."

"Speak for yourself. I'm definitely that interesting."

Jeremiah smiled. "Well, at least they can't stop thinking about us."

"Right. Negative attention is better than no attention, huh?" Nik laughed.

"Sure. You know, they're probably not even saying anything. They're probably just pretending—to make us wonder. We could do the same thing to them. Then they'd really have something to talk about."

"Careful, Doc," Nik grinned. "At this rate, we might end up friends."

Jeremiah gave him a serious stare. "I never wanted us not to be."

"Please." Nik's tone was joking, but his body was tense. "You're as bad as I am—when it comes to Randi, we just can't think straight."

Jeremiah didn't deny it. "Fair enough."

Nik sighed. "You know what the worst part is? It's just all so stupid and juvenile. I feel like we've been running around in circles for years, acting like children. Ever since her dad died, it's like the only thing she can think about is vindicating his work. She says it's because she can't get past how our relationship ended before..." Nik threw a piece of wood on the fire. "And yeah, okay, I kinda broke her heart, but it boils down to the fact that she can't move on with her own life until she wraps up her father's. We should have this thing between us figured out by now. Either we care enough about each other to make it work, or we don't."

"It's not always as easy as just wanting to make it work."

"Meaning?"

I should tell him about Megan.

No. Jeremiah's entire being revolted against the idea. *No, I can't share this with him. Megan is my own private torture—I'm not going to tell him about her. He won't understand.*

"Nothing."

"If it was nothing, you wouldn't have brought it up."

"I just meant, sometimes people's lives take different paths, and there's no working that out."

"If you care about each other enough, then there's nothing you can't work out." Nik looked at him, his brows furrowed. "What?"

"Nothing. I just—" He took a deep breath. "I was just thinking how I used to have those exact thoughts."

"Yeah?"

"A few years ago I was engaged. Her name was Megan. She was beautiful. Gorgeous, actually. Smart. Funny." A smile crept over his face as he thought of her. "She had a doctorate in archaeology. The only problem was, she was called to be a missionary, and I wasn't."

"So, you broke up with her because you didn't want to be a missionary?"

"Actually, no. I had every intention of being a missionary. I would have followed her to the ends of the earth."

"I know the feeling." Nik cast a glance Randi's direction. "So, what happened?"

"She changed her mind. Got asked to be part of a major archaeology group, and when I accused her of giving up our dream, she left me."

"You're not a missionary. So, didn't you sell out, too?"

"No. I tried to follow through, but one thing after another cropped up, and it prevented my going. However, it was her dream, not mine, so eventually I realized trying to make it happen would never work. I would've been miserable and totally ineffective in my work."

"Why didn't you get back together with her after that?"

"It was too late by then. She was with someone else."

"So you ended up here. Are you fulfilled, even without Megan?"

"When Megan and I were still together, I discovered something. Something of vital importance to the world. I didn't pursue it then, because of Megan, but after we separated, I began to delve into it. This"—Jeremiah gestured toward the camp and the others seated around—"is a means to an end."

"What's the end? What is your ultimate goal?"

"I can't talk about it right now. Perhaps at some point, but this is not that point. You're not ready to know."

"Wow. Okay, then. Just when I thought we were in a good spot."

"I didn't mean—"

"It's fine. I'm sorry your life took a different path from Megan's, but I'm not going to let that happen to Randi and me."

Chapter Thirty-Nine

Randi glanced across the camp at where Nik and Jeremiah sat in earnest conversation. "I wonder what they're talking about."

She wasn't really talking to anyone in particular, but Jon Chevalet stood near enough to hear. "Just be grateful they're talking," Jon said. "At least they're not, for the moment, competing."

"You know about that, too?"

Jon chuckled. "I think it's been obvious to everyone but you from the beginning."

"I didn't ask for them to bicker over me like children."

"We rarely ask for the things life gives us."

Randi instantly regretted her words. How selfish it must seem to him, for her to be complaining about her two suitors, when he'd so recently lost the love of his life. "I'm sorry. How are you holding up?"

"Oh, I'm fine. I used to be quite active in my younger days."

"I didn't mean physically, I meant…" Randi trailed off, not sure how to bring up the subject.

"You mean after losing my wife?"

She nodded.

"There's not a day that I don't miss her. The ache is always present, the hole never filled. Shelly and I were together for twenty-seven years. I held the same hand, kissed the same lips, every day for all those years, and now, to wake up alone… I'm sorry, you don't want to hear all this."

Randi smiled. "I don't mind. Talk about her all you want."

"You're a sweet girl. Shelly would've liked you. She had that same sweet, soft-spoken nature and optimism. She always saw the good in everyone. We always wanted kids, but… well, like I said, life rarely gives us the things we ask for. I think, though, if we'd had a daughter, she might have been something like you."

Tears stung Randi's eyes at the compliment. "Thank you."

Jon nodded toward Nik and Jeremiah. "Those are both fine young men. Either would be a good match for you. Don't wait too long to decide. Even twenty-seven years isn't long enough."

Jon stretched and went to help Djazani and Kinte get water from the river.

Carole came up behind Randi. "Nik and Jeremiah talking? That's new."

"I know. It's weird. At least when they couldn't stand each other, I knew where they each stood. This is like some twisted alternate universe."

Carole laughed. "Yeah. I hate those creepy places where everyone learns to get along."

"You know what I mean."

"Yeah. Just don't jinx yourself. We're only halfway to our destination, and we still have to go all the way back down. Do you know how difficult it is for this many people in this close proximity to get along for that amount of time? Enjoy the fact that everyone is being nice to each other while you can."

"Good point," Randi smiled. "I will."

A short while later, the fire roared and Albert had the meat roasting on a spit. A stack of firewood was in place, and Jon and Kinte purified the water.

Randi, Carole, and Djazani finished placing everyone's packs into the tents, and Randi stretched, ready to rest for the evening.

"Here." Carole handed a granola bar to Randi and one to Djazani. "To tide us over until the meat is done."

"Thanks." Randi started to unwrap hers but was interrupted when a pair of arms slipped around her waist.

Turning, she put her hands on Nik's chest, starting to push him away. "Nik, what are you—"

He silenced her by putting his mouth on hers.

For an instant she melted into his embrace, enjoying the warmth of his kiss, the strength of his arms around her, before she pulled back with a gasp, too shocked to say anything.

"We need to talk." Nik half-led, half-carried her to the edge of the woods.

"I lied before. I'm not willing to let you move on without me. The worst mistake I ever made was breaking up with you, and I've spent the last three years trying to get you back. Even if nothing ever happens between us, I'll always be waiting for you. I can't help myself. You're the only one for me. Hell, I followed you to the other side of the world, and I'd do it again a thousand times, just to be near you. You think I don't want to break out of the mold and do important work, but it's not true. I want to make discoveries and uncover the truth just as much as you do, and I'm okay with not playing it safe. There's I want to do that is more important than you. I don't want to move on with my life if you're not in it."

"Nik, I—"

"No. No more excuses. I know I hurt you and I'm sorry. But I also know you feel the same about me. I'm not going to make the same mistake twice, and I'm not going to let you go. Let's get back together."

Randi answered almost without thought. This was everything she wanted. It was time to choose. And she wanted to choose Nik.

It was time to trust that he meant what he said—to stop dancing around the issue, to stop wavering. "Okay. Yes."

"Really?" Nik looked like he might burst.

"Yes. Let's get back together," Randi said.

He kissed her again, deeply, fully, making up for three years of lost time in that one moment.

***

Three days later, Randi's legs burned with every step. Her breath came in short, quick spurts. Three days of hiking, as the terrain became steeper and more rugged, had taken their toll, making it harder than ever to go on, each moment of this fourth day more agonizing than the last.

Grasping Nik's hand for support, she pulled herself along.

Jon leaned heavily on a branch he'd acquired as a walking stick. He smiled at Randi, glanced at her hand clasped in Nik's, and gave her an approving nod.

Even Jeremiah and Carole, who appeared to be in excellent shape, seemed to struggle as the altitude increased.

Even so, Albert pushed them mercilessly onward. Their morning break was shorter than usual, and their lunch break was almost nonexistent.

"We can be there by afternoon if we hurry," Albert told Jeremiah, who translated for the rest of the group.

With the end in sight, Randi gathered a second wind and pushed onward.

Shortly after, when their afternoon break should have been, Albert began talking excitedly and making wild gestures with his arms.

Jeremiah turned to face Randi. "Apparently we're here."

After a few more steps they came upon a little hut nestled in among the trees.

"Naomi!" Albert called out. "Naomi!"

"*Qui est Naomi?*" Jeremiah asked.

Albert answered him and poked his head into the hut. "Naomi?"

"What did he say?"

"Naomi is his sister." Jeremiah followed Albert into the one-room hut, and Randi trailed along behind.

Albert pawed around as if searching for something, muttering in his native tongue. "Naomi!" he called out again.

"I don't think she's here," Jeremiah said. "We might as well set up camp."

"Why not out by the lake? It looks like there's plenty of wide, flat space out there," Randi suggested.

Albert turned sharply and said something in a firm voice.

"He says we don't want to be out on the lake after dark. Find a space to set up the tents under the cover of the trees."

"Why?"

"I don't know, but I'm not inclined to disregard his advice."

A short while later, Nik came to where Randi worked. "Are you almost done?" He stroked her hair with his fingertips.

"Yeah, just have to finish getting the tent set up." Randi smiled.

She pounded the last tent stake into the ground and stood.

Her hand slid easily into Nik's, like a puzzle piece finding its proper place, and she walked with him toward the lake.

Stark cliffs rose on three sides, framing a sparkling lake. Blue sky and wispy clouds reflected in the water, unbroken on the smooth surface. Behind them, the jungle stretched out in verdant leaves blanketing the mountain as far as she could see.

Randi gasped at the sight. "It is so beautiful up here. It almost makes that hike worth it."

Nik stroked the top of her hand with his thumb as they sat down on the ground in front of the lake.

"I wonder what's in all those caves up there." He nodded toward the steep walls of the cliff.

"Buried treasure," Randi laughed.

"Good. At least we'll have some money to start off with when we get married."

"Nik," Randi chided. "It's a little too soon to be talking like that."

"I didn't say it had to be tomorrow, but is there really any point in pretending it's not going to happen eventually? What purpose could that possibly serve? I fully intend to marry you, Randi. I love you."

Her mouth dropped open. It was the first time he'd said the words. "Nik, I—" she couldn't continue.

"I intended it to be a little more romantic than that." Nik chuckled. "But I do. I have since forever, and I've been waiting to tell you for a long time. I love you, Randi."

Tears stung her eyes, but she didn't speak.

Nik brushed the tears away with his hand, then slipped his arm around her waist. "You don't have to say it. When you're ready."

She smiled.

They sat in silence awhile, Randi enjoying the rest, the completion of their journey, and the beauty of the day. Warmth spread through her from Nik's arm around her.

"I'm starving. I'm going to go grab a snack. You want anything?" Nik asked after a while.

"Sure, thanks."

She continued gazing over the calm lake, watching the reflection of the sparse white clouds drifting over the surface and disappearing into the shadows of the rocks.

The warm sun low in the sky, the peaceful air, and the three days of exertion all contributed to making her drowsy. She yawned and blinked a few times.

Albert said they'd arrived at their destination, but he was clearly more interested in finding his sister than anything. But if this was where she was, then they had to be close. Maybe the next day he would take them to the nesting grounds or wherever they could watch for the creatures described by Dr. Schleppenbach.

She grew excited just thinking about it, although she reminded herself to be realistic. It could take days of watching and waiting before they saw anything, if, indeed, they ever saw anything at all. She tried not to get her hopes up too high. Jeremiah had told her about countless monster hunting excursions where he'd come back disappointed, and even Carole said she'd searched for years before finally seeing Bigfoot.

Rubbing her eyes, she glanced back to see if Nik was returning yet, but didn't see him. She turned back toward the lake and froze.

The reflection of an enormous flying creature bounced off the water.

The thought flashed through her mind she was dreaming, seeing things, or perhaps just going crazy. She looked up.

Her heart seemed to stop beating and her mouth went dry.

Streaking toward her, a black splotch against the setting sun, flew a creature like none she'd ever seen.

Its head looked similar to a dinosaur's in shape, but its ridges were more pronounced, sticking out almost like spikes from its head.

It had a long neck and a short, powerful body. Two short, arm-like limbs, adorned with long claws, were curled up under its chest, and it had two majestic wings that seemed as if they could have almost spanned the size of a village as they stretched, unfurled, out to either side.

A long tail, a small spike on the end like an arrowhead, lashed out behind it. What had once been a fantasy, a dream, a wish in her mind, loomed in front of her.

She froze, unable to move, as the terrifying reality of scales and claws, yellow eyes, and fangs glistening with saliva swooped straight toward her.

Chapter Forty

A few months earlier

It started a little more than a week after Albert left Naomi alone on the mountaintop with the egg.

A strange scratching sound outside disturbed her sleep.

She yawned and went outside. The scratching stopped, so she stood very still at the door of the hut, listening. After several moments, she heard it again.

The sound came from over near the fire pit. She crept toward it. Perhaps there was a wounded bird or something.

The scratching stopped again, and she looked around the fire. She didn't see anything. Even pawing through the grasses and leaves littering the ground, she found nothing.

What made that sound? A loud crack behind her made her jump.

When she turned, her eyes landed on the egg.

A line in the side lengthened until it stretched from one end to the other.

With a gasp, she stepped a little closer. The crack in the egg widened, and a tiny chip of the eggshell fell away.

She knelt down and peered as the crack became a spiderweb of cracks forming on the outside of the egg.

Even though she knew she should be more careful, knew what was inside and how much damage it could do, she couldn't help giving in to the curiosity that overtook her.

She sucked in her breath as the cracks grew wider and bigger chunks were pushed away, until suddenly a large piece popped off the top and a small, spiny head appeared.

Naomi fell back and landed hard on her backside. The hole cracked open wider as the head pushed forward, and two little claws grasped the edge of the egg. The creature scraped against the edge of the egg, pulling itself out a little at a time.

The egg rocked and tipped, sending the creature toppling over onto its face. It gave a grunt, then clung to the grass to pull itself out. Soon, it slithered out of the egg and uncoiled its body, about a meter in length, from the top of its horned little head to its narrow, spiked tail.

Rough, scaly skin, a dark brownish green color, covered its body.

It stood on the grass on all fours and stretched. First back, like a cat, stretching its front legs and shoulders, then pushing its back legs out behind it and craning its neck. Finally, it unfurled little wings on its back. Naomi could see the veins and bones through the thin, papery skin.

The animal gave a piteous little squawk and looked around. Naomi reached out to touch it. It saw her finger, and with surprising speed, struck at it and clamped onto it with sharp little teeth.

Naomi yelped in pain and yanked her finger away. She smacked the creature on the nose with her other hand.

It gave a surprised howl then began hissing like an angry cat.

Naomi laughed as the little creature stuck its head out, spitting. "I'm sorry, little fellow. I probably look like breakfast to you. I'll get you something to eat. You just stay here."

It stopped hissing and looked up at the sound of her voice, cocking its little head to one side as if studying her.

"I'll be right back."

A net of vines in the stream kept her with a steady supply of fish, so she ran quickly to the bank and reached her hand in.

It wasn't an easy task to reach in and grasp one of the slippery, wriggling fish, but Naomi had plenty of practice. In a few moments, she was carrying a fresh fish back to where the little dragon lay pacing around the nest of grass and leaves by the egg.

"Here you go, little one." Naomi tossed the fish down next to the creature's head.

It sniffed the fish a moment, then tore into it with little fangs, ripping up bits of flesh and gobbling them down.

Naomi grimaced at the sight, suddenly grateful her finger hadn't gotten more than a few punctures. "We're going to have to do something about that if you expect me to keep feeding you."

The creature glanced at her when she spoke, but continued tearing at the fish until it had eaten about half of it. It then stretched again and turned in a circle like a dog before settling into the grass nest and promptly falling asleep.

Naomi sat and watched it for a long time. She still couldn't believe it, even though it was right in front of her. She watched its body rise up and down as it breathed, saw the intricate detail of its scales as they overlapped, creating a protective armor. It was beautiful and majestic, and at the same time terrifying, because it wouldn't always be small enough to pick up. What would happen when it grew up? Would it be a mindless hunter, relying only on instinct? Would it try to eat her as soon as it was big enough? Or would it remember her and know she cared for it as a baby?

If it grew up at all. She had no idea how to raise a baby dragon. What if she inadvertently killed it? A poor, defenseless baby, robbed from its mother, its home. A wave of guilt swept over her at the thought that she might accidentally be the cause of its death, not because she was protecting herself and not because she needed food, but simply because she was incompetent.

"What am I going to do with you?" she asked aloud.

The thing woke up several hours later and finished off the rest of the fish before settling back to sleep.

She stood, hands on her hips. "I'm going to need to get you more food before you wake up."

She came back a few hours later with a small tree monkey.

Her little monster was already awake, mewling impatiently. It crawled to the edge of the grass nest and looked out.

"I'm coming, I'm coming."

At the sound of her voice, it stood up on its hind legs and grunted, pawing and snapping at the air impatiently.

"I know you're hungry."

She started to toss the monkey over but changed her mind. She had an idea. "Let's see if you can learn something."

She held out her hand.

The creature reached out and snapped at it, but Naomi withdrew her hand before it was bitten. She smacked it on its snout.

"No!" she said sharply, tossing her head.

The creature drew back in surprise and looked up at her.

She reached out her hand again. The creature reached toward her hand again, more slowly this time, looking her in the eye.

Gingerly, it put its mouth on her hand but didn't bite down.

Naomi drew her hand away and smacked the creature's nose. "No."

The creature drew back and observed her. She put her hand out again. The creature leaned toward it but didn't put its mouth on it.

"Good boy!" Naomi rubbed its head.

The creature looked at her and cocked its head to one side.

She scratched under its chin, which it seemed to enjoy, because it stretched out its neck and made a soft grunting sound. She scratched a little while longer, then tossed the creature the dead monkey.

The creature looked at it and sniffed it a moment but didn't eat it. It looked at Naomi.

"You may eat it. Go on."

The creature gingerly took it in its mouth and looked again at Naomi.

She grinned. "What a smart fellow you are. Go on and eat."

The creature waited another moment, and when it didn't get reprimanded, tore eagerly into the monkey.

She laughed, and the creature looked up at her as it ate. "It seems I'm going to be doing nothing but hunting to keep you fed."

The creature grunted and continued eating, then promptly fell asleep again.

Naomi knew she would have to get more food for herself, as well as her new companion. She already thought of it as hers. So, once it was back asleep, she went hunting again. She returned with a deer just before dusk.

Her foot crunched on a patch of dry leaves, and her creature raised its head and grunted.

She set to work building a fire as the little creature watched her curiously. She put a chunk of meat on the spit over the fire for her dinner, then got another chunk to feed the creature his.

"Let's see if you remember your lesson." She held out her hand toward his face.

The creature sniffed it then nuzzled it with its nose.

"Good boy! If you are a boy. I have no idea, and I don't know how to find out. Well, I think of you as a boy, anyway, so we'll just assume that's the case, shall we?"

The creature grunted and nuzzled her hand. She scratched under its chin, and it stretched out contentedly.

She sat near it and began to skin and dress the deer, tossing it some chunks of meat, which it hungrily gobbled down.

"I need to think of something to call you. How about Kudabah? After all, he's the reason I'm here."

The creature looked up at her and grunted.

Naomi giggled. "Kudabah it is. It's time to sleep, Little Kudabah."

Out over the lake, the creatures called to one another as they swooped out of their caves.

The little one by her side heard it, too, and stood on its hind legs, whimpering and pawing the air with its front feet. Its wings flapped wildly, but apparently it was too small to fly.

Naomi looked at the little creature.

He looked back and forth from her to the edge of the forest.

Briefly, she considered letting him free to return to his own kind, but changed her mind.

For one thing, she couldn't take him out there without risking getting attacked. For another, she didn't know whether his mother would come to claim him, or if he'd end up on the beach all night. Or worse, get killed by the other animals Some animals killed their young if they smelled human scent on them. Maybe his mother would reject him or kill him.

Suddenly, she realized she didn't want to let the creature go. All her reasons were just excuses—almost without realizing it, she'd selfishly decided she wanted to keep him.

Kudabah looked at her and whined.

She tossed him a piece of deer meat, which he ignored. He lowered himself to all four feet, scrambled over the edge of the nest, and walked toward the edge of the forest.

She wanted to grab him, to scoop him up and carry him back with her, force him to remain. But even as she considered it, she knew she couldn't do it.

If he wanted to be free, to return to his own kind, she had to let him.

She picked up the meat again and held it in front of his mouth, but he just kept going until he emerged from the tree line onto the lake's shore.

He cried out, that sweet, piteous, mewling sound echoing out into the night. In the distance, she heard the cries of the other creatures of its kind. It called out to them, but they didn't come near.

All through the night, Kudabah continued to cry. Finally, near dawn, he crawled back. Instead of climbing into his nest he climbed up into her lap and curled into her. He whined for a little bit, then ate a little of the meat she offed him. At last, the little creature fell asleep, and Naomi went into the hut to catch a few hours of sleep herself.

Chapter Forty-One

After nearly a week of staying up through most of the night with Kudabah, exhaustion claimed her. After the first few nights, he stopped crying, but he still went out to the lakeshore to prowl around. She knew he was nocturnal by nature, but she couldn't help wondering if she could change his habits.

Perhaps she could train him to be awake during the day. He'd proven how smart and easy to train he could be from the first day he understood not to bite her and to wait for her command before he ate.

He recognized the word *no*, and seemed to understand what she meant when she said *come*. She even though he recognized the name Kudabah.

Once she got him onto a decent schedule, perhaps she could train him to do more. Until then, though, she needed to get some rest.

She took a nap in the morning while Kudabah slept. When she woke, she went hunting. Then she woke Kudabah and made him stay awake with her by taking him for a walk and playing with him before she fed him.

Cutting a strip of animal hide, she waved it in front of Kudabah's nose until he grabbed it. Soon Kudabah understood the game of tug-of-war.

"You're getting so strong," Naomi laughed, scratching the underside of his stomach.

He nuzzled her hand with his head.

"You're a good boy, Kudabah," she smiled.

Next, she wrapped a piece of hide around a stick and, after letting him smell it, tossed it.

Kudabah looked at her with his head cocked and sauntered over toward it. He sniffed it and picked it up in his teeth.

"Good boy, Kudabah. Come."

With the stick still in his mouth, he returned to her. After rewarding him with a small piece of meat, she took the stick and threw it again. Almost immediately he understood the point of the game, and from then on wanted to play until Naomi's arm ached and she refused to throw it any more.

Kudabah had been awake for several hours by then and was looking quite sleepy, so she didn't object when he curled up in his nest. It was a good start.

She took a nap, too, but woke him before long and played again, so by dusk, when normally he would be ready to be awake for a while, he was tired.

She fed him and scratched under his chin until he dozed off.

Kudabah woke in the middle of the night, bright-eyed and playful, but Naomi refused to play. She fed him and went back into her hut.

A soft moaning noise kept her up for over an hour, but she didn't get up. At last, Kudabah quieted. With a sigh, Naomi rolled over and went to sleep.

***

After Kudabah fell asleep for his morning nap, she got out the animal hides she'd saved and began to work.

It took several days of working in between training Kudabah and hunting, but at last she'd woven a leash and halter from long, thin strips of leather.

She fitted the halter carefully over Kudabah's head and around its front legs. He woke as she was putting it on him and whined at her, so she gave him more meat.

He seemed annoyed by the leather strapped across his back, but couldn't reach his head back far enough to examine it. He paced and whined, but finally became interested in his food. Naomi adjusted it slightly, until she could take it on and off of him easily and appraised it proudly.

The next morning, Naomi led Kudabah by his leash when she went hunting.

He scared off much of the game with his eager shrieks, but Naomi thought it would be a good lesson.

Each time he made noise, she said, "No. Quiet."

His eyes were wide, his head cocked, as if wondering what he had done wrong, but soon he made the connection between the noise and her command and was quiet.

Before long, Naomi shot a monkey from a tree.

Kudabah glanced eagerly from her to the monkey.

"Go ahead."

He pounced on it and gobbled it up. She hunted a little more, finding her own dinner, before walking back to her camp.

Once there, they played tug-of-war again before she allowed him to sleep.

Each day, she kept Kudabah awake a little longer, and at night left him alone. She heard him wander to the lakeshore, and eventually back to his nest.

A couple nights later, when he returned in the night, he'd brought back a small rodent he'd hunted.

Naomi smiled in satisfaction the first morning she wasn't awakened during the night. Kudabah was becoming more and more independent, but he always returned to her. He spent about half the night awake, and half the day awake with her.

But now she had other problems to deal with.

"You're getting too big."

He must have more than tripled in size already, his body almost as long as she was tall, and his wings spread out equally as long.

She'd sewn two new harnesses as he outgrew them, though he hardly needed one at all anymore. When she went hunting, he came along willingly, and more often than not, he was the one to bring down prey.

But he also began to have trouble moving around through the dense undergrowth. Before long, he'd be too big to hunt in the confines of the forest.

Moreover, he'd begun stretching his wings, furling, unfurling, and flapping them.

"I suppose it's time you learned to fly," she told him one evening. "We'll go out tomorrow to practice."

The next morning, she led Kudabah out to the clearing by the lake. She took a deep breath. This could be an interesting experiment.

She patted his rump. "Go."

With the open air and the nearness of other creatures of his kind—once he figured out he could join them, he might not come back.

It was a risk she needed to take, and it was probably better now, when he still depended on her, than later when he could care for himself.

Kudabah cocked his head and looked at her.

"Go."

After a moment, he left her side and began walking along the edge of the shore.

Stretching his wings and finding they didn't hit trees or shrubs, he unfurled them all the way and flapped them.

An eager grunt bellowed from his chest as his wings stretched wider and flapped harder. Then, in one graceful movement, he lunged, launching himself into the air.

That first flight awed Naomi. Kudabah soared over her head, diving and twisting, and stretching out to his full length.

Of course, he could've done this at any time during the night while she slept, but perhaps he hadn't known how, without others of his kind to show him, or without her there to encourage him.

Naomi suspected if he'd grown up with his mother, he'd have learned long ago. A pang of remorse tugged at her, but instinct apparently superseded training, because he flew as if he'd done it hundreds of times.

She let him fly for a few more moments before trying her experiment.

She cupped her hands around her mouth. "Come, Kudabah."

He turned his head to look at her and immediately soared toward her. He landed awkwardly, skidding to a halt in front of her.

Naomi grinned. "Good boy." She handed him a chunk of dried meat.

Kudabah eagerly gobbled it down, then stood on his hind legs, wings twitching.

"Go."

Turning, he sprang once again into the air. Somewhere high on the mountain he must have spotted a small animal, for, with a graceful turn, he swooped down and grabbed something in the talons of his hind feet.

He landed on the side of the mountain to devour his prey, then soared into the air again, flying a little farther with each circle around the lake.

Finally, Naomi decided it was time for a rest. As Kudabah soared overhead, she called out. "Come, Kudabah!"

He soared down to her, his landing much more graceful and steady than it had been before.

"Good boy." Naomi scratched under his neck again.

She didn't fasten the leash to the harness. Instead, she just walked calmly toward the forest. "Come."

To her delight, Kudabah followed. She walked back to her *mongulu*, Kudabah close at her heels.

They both took a short nap, then went hunting in the afternoon. Kudabah stayed close by her side, waiting for her command before chasing after his prey and returning immediately to her side.

The first few small animals Kudabah caught, he ate, but when Naomi gave him the command, he caught an animal and brought it back to her.

After Kudabah caught a few more animals and brought them back to her, Naomi led him back to their camp for the night.

She fell asleep, planning what she would teach him the next day.

*****

Naomi fell into bed, exhausted. Another long day spent training Kudabah, and every muscle in her body ached. Kudabah came on command, and he knew to retrieve things she threw—sticks, animal skins, even rocks. She'd taught him tricks, also.

She'd developed a series of whistles, and when he did a particular maneuver in the air, she used a whistle, until he began to associate each different move, dive, turn, and flip, with a different sound.

A sense of pride filled her, both for her ability to train and for Kudabah's ability to learn—pride akin to a mother's over her child.

She rolled over on her soft mattress of dried grasses and leaves and was almost instantly asleep.

It occurred to her, as her consciousness drifted away, she'd become careless with her village of one while working so hard with Kudabah. She'd need to spend a good portion of the next day burning the animal bones and making the campsite less attractive to predators.

She woke with a start sometime in the early hours of the morning. It took her a few minutes to realize what awakened her—something was shuffling around outside.

Creeping outside, she peered out into the darkness. A dark shape rummaged through her pile of discarded animal remains, but darkness clouded her view, making it impossible to tell what kind of animal it was.

"Kudabah?" she whispered hopefully.

With a roar, the thing—not Kudabah—turned and lunged toward her. She still couldn't tell exactly what it was, but bared fangs dripping with saliva reflected the dim light of the embers in the fire.

A scream escaped her lips.

In a second that lasted an hour, the thing came toward her.

A different type of roar split the night.

From the side, flames appeared, engulfing the attacking animal. It howled in pain, and the odor of singed fur and flesh filled the air. The thing turned and fled, disappearing into the forest.

Naomi collapsed, coughing.

Something cold and moist touched her forehead and she looked up.

Kudabah's tongue, flicking in and out, licked her face.

"Thank you, boy," she whispered, scratching under its chin. "You saved my life."

Kudabah nuzzled her with his head, as if he understood what she was saying.

She looked into his eyes. She almost felt like she could understand him. *I'm here to protect you. I won't let anything harm you.*

"I know you won't. We're a team now, Kudabah. We'll take care of each other."

Kudabah seemed to have doubled in size again just in the last couple weeks. He ate a large animal every few days, so Naomi shouldn't be surprised at how fast he grew, but she was. He now stretched twice as long as she was tall, not including his tail, and his wings stretched out beyond that.

The small clearing under the trees was nearly impossible for him to reach, crawling through the thick growth back and forth to the lake. Naomi made a nest for him on the edge of the forest, using leaves and grass from his old nest so it bore his familiar scent.

"I hope you don't decide to leave me." She sat with him in his new nest. "Being around others of your kind around will be tempting, especially now that you're so good at flying."

Every morning she walked from the safety of the trees to the shore to greet Kudabah. She scratched his chin and played with him. They spent most of the day together playing, except when Kudabah flew away to hunt.

One day, he disappeared for several hours.

Naomi hadn't realized how much she depended on his company until he left for so long.

Sitting by the edge of the lake, she stared up at the sky, waiting for him to return. She couldn't keep him by her side all the time—he needed to exercise and hunt—but she wished there was a way to keep from being alone so long.

That's it. I know what to do with all of those animal hides I've been saving.

After fashioning a needle from an animal bone, she cut long, thin strips of leather and sewed together a large blanket.

Within a few days, she finished.

She walked out toward the lake where Kudabah lay in his nest. "Kudabah, come."

He followed her to the edge of the lake, and Naomi scratched under his chin. He let out a low, contented growl, stretching his neck toward her.

"Okay, boy, we're going to try something."

She tossed the blanket on his back, above his shoulder blades, below the spikes on his neck but above his wings. A strap around his neck, and another around his chest, behind his front legs, held it securely in place.

Kudabah kept his yellow eyes on her but didn't object, ignoring the blanket after one glance.

"Well, what do you think?"

Kudabah grunted.

"Go." she commanded.

He launched himself into the sky, soaring and tumbling to her whistled commands until she called him back.

"All right, boy, let's do this," she muttered, half to herself.

Grabbing hold of a strip of leather on the blanket, she put her foot in a loop sewn on the side. With one swift movement, she pulled herself up, swinging her leg over, and sat astride his back.

A snort escaped his nostrils as he turned to look at her.

"It's okay. It's just me." She scratched behind his ears.

She sat there for a while, just letting him get used to the feel of her on his back. After a few moments, he turned his head away, walking to the lake and leaning down to take a drink.

"Ready for the next step?"

Wrapping her hands around the leather handle on the blanket, she gave the order. "Go."

His body underneath her shifted, his shoulders rotating as he pulled his forelimbs close to his body, his haunches coiling and compacting. An instant later, he launched into the air, his wings stretching out to either side.

A rush of wind stung her eyes, and her breath escaped her completely as they rose into the sky.

He banked sharply, and she almost fell off. The leather strap cut into the palms of her hands, and a sharp burning spread throughout her legs from clinging to his back.

Kudabah seemed to understand the tenacity of her hold and flew in slow, deliberate circles above the mountain top.

The jungle looked just like satellite photos she remembered from school—the glassy lake, the lush green trees, the sparkling river as it cut a swath through the verdant valley far away.

The wind whipped at her like tiny claws grasping at her clothes and face.

Kudabah's muscles tightened and relaxed with every flap of his wings. Tense, release, tense, release—over and over in a thrumming rhythm as they soared, king and queen of the air.

For over an hour, they glided through the air, before Kudabah turned around and returned to the lake.

Every day after that, and sometimes several times a day, Naomi rode Kudabah as he flew.

She grew more comfortable, and Kudabah became more accustomed to having her on his back. Soon, she began to try some of the tricks she'd taught him. She nearly fell off the first time he dove, and she spent most of the next day making improvements in the blanket she used as a saddle, sewing another harness to keep it in place better, and sewing leg holds, in addition to the foot holds, and arm straps to keep her in place.

After enough improvement, she signaled him to flip and do some other tricks while she rode him.

The ground floated above her head as she soared, upside down, on his back. Turning over and over, diving, swooping, shooting up into the sky, they flew together, one with the air.

He soon began to hunt with her on his back, as well, swooping down and clutching his prey in his talons and landing to eat it. She dismounted and went

326

to find food, while Kudabah contentedly ate his meal, before returning to her hut each evening.

They came back from an unsuccessful hunt late one afternoon. At one point, Kudabah spotted something, although from behind his neck Naomi never got a very good view of what was in front of them. The animal must have looked up at just the right moment, seen him coming, and run into the safety of the forest. They searched for a while more, but no more animals came into view. Finally, toward evening, they headed home.

As they neared the lake, Naomi nestled in closer to Kudabah's neck, preparing for the long glide that would end with a thud on the ground below.

Suddenly, Kudabah shot forward, wings flapping silently, diving the way he did when he hunted.

Strange. Animals scarcely ever came near her *mongulu* or the area of the lake where she spent most of her time. The animals smelled her, and she suspected they also sensed the proximity of Kudabah and instinctively knew to stay away.

She craned her neck and peered around his head, trying to see what he dove toward.

The air left her lungs. Kudabah's prey was human.

A Western woman sat on the ground by the lake. She looked up but froze as Kudabah streaked across the distance between them.

Naomi only had a split second to gather her wits and give the command. "*No!*"

Chapter Forty-Two

Time seemed to slow down as the last several years of research flashed through Randi's mind. So many days waiting for this moment, and now, suddenly, it was upon her. All her dreams of finding a dragon were realized.

She'd been right all along. All her theories, her hypotheses, her conjectures about what might be, were completely accurate. More than accurate, for she'd supposed all the dragons had died off.

She'd said they were very real, historical creatures, alive during the ancient and even medieval times, but even when she set out on this trip, full of ambition and hope for finding evidence, she hadn't expected to actually see a live dragon.

She expected to find anecdotal evidence, perhaps cave paintings or stories passed down among the natives. Even if the natives still believed the creatures were alive, she presumed that, like Mokele-mbembe, sightings would be few and far between, tales scarcely believed even by those who told them.

If she were really lucky, she hoped she might even be able to find some sort of fossil or ancient native relic to confirm her beliefs. In her wildest dreams and hopes, she imagined what it would be like to really find a dragon, to see her obsession with her own eyes. She never truly believed it would happen, though—never really thought it possible.

Yet here it was. Just like a picture out of a medieval painting, or the monster out of a fantasy novel, the creature swept toward her. Her dream come true, and she wouldn't live long enough to enjoy it.

From the moment she locked eyes with the creature, she knew it was coming for her. In the split second it took for the thought to cross her mind, she imagined it snatching her up in its powerful talons, ripping her apart and feasting on her flesh.

It bore down on her, every instant bringing it closer. She didn't have time to move or run away, or even scream. The creature was almost upon her now, mouth gaping, talons outstretched.

The dragon swooped down with its hind legs extended, reaching for her.

Squeezing her eyes shut, she waited for the feel of its claws ripping into her flesh.

She heard a shout.

"No!"

Her eyes opened in surprise.

The creature veered sharply away, missing Randi by only inches, its tail screaming past her face. It turned sharply again and landed on the shore of the lake, only a few yards away, facing her, its mouth still gaping open.

Randi screamed, the sound echoing against the cliffs that surrounded the lake, bouncing back at her in a hundred fragments.

The thing looked exactly like she'd imagined it: a giant lizard with a serpentine head and neck, except with stegosaurus-like plates jutting out from the back of its neck. It looked at her with yellow eyes and clawed at the ground with enormous, taloned feet.

A young woman slid from the dragon's back, landing gracefully in the sand by its side.

A moment later, the shore flooded with people. Randi's scream brought the entire team out to see what happened.

They all rushed out into the open and then stopped short, staring at the monster that stood before them.

Randi looked from the girl to the dragon and back again, unable to think or move. The girl stared back, one hand on the dragon's neck.

For a long moment, no one moved or spoke.

A shout broke the silence. "Naomi!"

The girl looked away from Randi and up toward the forest. A grin spread over her face. She said something to the dragon and ran to meet Albert, smothering him in a tight embrace.

Randi stood by as the two chattered back and forth in their native language. Naomi swept her hands in broad gestures toward Randi and the

330

group of dragon hunters, curiosity plain on her face. They went back and forth for several minutes before Naomi gave a command to the dragon and walked toward them.

Albert stepped forward, and Randi followed close behind.

Naomi spoke soothingly to the dragon, scratching his chin, and motioned her brother forward.

As he drew near, a low growl rumbled in the monster's throat.

Naomi continued to scratch his chin and speak in low tones.

The dragon looked at Albert, yellow eyes rolling, but allowed him to approach.

Naomi continued to scratch under his neck with one hand and beckoned Randi forward with the other.

The dragon didn't growl this time.

Behind Randi, Carole snapped picture after picture on her camera.

Randi stood for a few moments, near the dragon's nose, letting him smell her. Then, with slow, steady movements, she reached her hand out and scratched under his chin.

He let out a rumbling growl that seemed something akin to a purr.

Naomi turned and grinned at her, and she grinned back.

A few moments later, Naomi glanced up at the sky. Her brows creased, and she gestured toward the jungle.

Randi looked back at the dragon. She could spend months just watching it, and years after that studying it, but there would be time tomorrow. She followed as Naomi herded everyone back toward the little hut.

Naomi said something in French.

"They said we need to get in under the trees," Jeremiah told the group.

"Why?" Randi asked.

Naomi spoke again, her hands on her hips, and tossed her head in a way that suggested she was used to being obeyed.

Jeremiah repeated her words. "Because the rest of them will eat you."

"The rest of them?" Randi gaped.

She followed the group into the forest and looked back. The dragon settled into a nest of leaves and grasses by the stream that flowed out of the lake.

Naomi said something and pointed over toward where the dragon lay.

"She said Mokele-mbembe comes out there to feed and to get water, sometimes, too," Jeremiah translated. "If you watch you may catch a glimpse of him, but he is more shy than Kudabah's kind, and with this many humans around, he might not show up."

Randi hurried to the tent and grabbed her notebook to start writing down everything that had happened since arriving at the top of the mountain. "Come on, Carole, bring your camera. Maybe we can get some good pictures of Mokele-mbembe while we're here, too."

Carole grinned. "I've already got it. I got a bunch of shots of you with that dragon back there."

They found a spot well protected by trees, but out of which they could still see the stream and the lake, and sat quietly to wait.

The sun disappeared behind the cliffs, leaving the valley in twilight.

The dragon, named Kudabah, Randi learned, lifted his head and looked over at them, but soon settled back down, his head curving around to rest on his back, under his wing, like a bird.

Movement caught Randi's eye. She grabbed Carole's arm with one hand and pointed to the sky with the other.

Over above the lake, barely visible against the dark sky, a cloud of black shapes rose up from the cliffs that surrounded the lake.

Carole positioned her camera, snapping several shots in rapid succession.

The flashing light attracted a few of the creatures, which soared and dove toward the trees.

Carole continued shooting pictures as the creatures got closer and closer, until Randi yanked her arm and dragged her deeper into the forest, ducking down behind a clump of bushes.

Only seconds later, one of the creatures landed just on the outside of the forest. With an earth-shaking roar, it sent a jet of flame into the trees.

The grove where they'd stood only moments before erupted in flames that quickly died out, unable to take hold of the soggy foliage. As close as an arm's-length away, leaves and branches were singed, crackling in the night.

Randi and Carole sat, hunched over, panting, watching through the leaves as the dragon turned and launched itself into the sky, in search of better hunting grounds.

Jeremiah and Nik burst upon them. "What happened?" they demanded in unison.

"We almost got eaten," Randi said lightly.

"What? Are you okay?" Nik looked her up and down as if searching for missing limbs.

"We're fine. We got out of the way in plenty of time. Plus, we got some really great shots."

Carole showed them the pictures she took. "Most didn't turn out well, but there are a few you can distinguish. This one's really good."

She pulled up a picture. The dragon's wings outstretched, mouth gaping, flying straight toward them, close enough that the flash caught it, glaring off its eyes and outlining its form, it looked like something out of a movie.

Nik pulled Randi close, rubbing his hands up and down her back. "Don't scare me like that."

Randi nestled into his enveloping arms and drank in his scent. Shivers ran up her spine at the renewed sense of wonder accompanying the knowledge that her relationship with him was no longer just friendship. "Sorry. Just to warn you, though, I'm going to stay up tonight and try to track their habits."

Jeremiah opened his mouth as if to say something, but snapped it shut when Nik spoke.

"I'll stay up with you."

After the rest of the team went to bed, Nik and Randi sat down at the edge of the forest. The sky was empty, the creatures off on their hunt. Randi pulled out her notebook and started writing down what she had observed and learned about the creatures so far—their size, diet, where they lived.

Nik brought his own notebook and, using their flashlights, they sat contentedly next to one another, each doing their own work.

"I don't understand how they survived all this time when dinosaurs didn't," Nik said after a while.

"The climate here is very similar to what it was back when dinosaurs were alive. I mean, that's the whole theory behind Mokele-mbembe. Just the right conditions in small, uninhabited pockets of the rainforest, and dinosaurs could still be alive." Randi leaned a little closer to him. "Same thing with dragons. Even if only a few survived, it would take several generations for the population to build back up to the point where there are significant numbers again, like what we're seeing here. There are probably other colonies like this in nearby areas that are far enough from villages that no one—at least no one with access to technology—saw them."

Nik squeezed her hand.

"I wish I knew how far they go each night. They can't go far enough to reach any of the villages, let alone the cities, or there would be more stories about them. But based on how many of them there are, they'd have to spread out pretty far to find enough food."

She kept her voice low, not wanting to attract unnecessary attention from whatever jungle creatures might be roaming the night. She pushed her glasses up on her nose. "That raises other problems, too. For their survival, I mean. With deforestation and pollution, they're either going to die out because they can't find food, or they're going to have to travel farther, which will make them vulnerable to attack."

"Or make people vulnerable to them."

Only half-listening, Randi tapped her pen against her teeth. "My guess is, hundreds of years ago, maybe even a thousand, around the time of the dragon legends, they were killed off to the point that people assumed they were all gone."

She scribbled in her notebook while she talked. "The survivors retreated away from places of human habitation and have survived in relatively small numbers ever since. The jungle is so dense here, they could live for years without ever being sighted by a human."

Pausing, she looked over at Nik. "The problem is, it would be hard to declare something that isn't supposed to exist as an endangered species. Even if we can prove their existence—which could be difficult, because there will be plenty of people who will try to write our findings off as a hoax—then it will be hard to tell farmers they can't kill the thing hunting their livestock, or tell the natives they can't kill the thing that carries off their children. It's not like you can keep something like this in a zoo."

Rambling thoughts overtook her tongue. "Sorry. I know I'm babbling. It just helps me to say all this out loud."

Nik scooted a little closer and put his arm around her waist. "You're adorable when you babble."

"Thanks, Nicky." Bending over her notebook, she scribbled down the thoughts she'd voiced.

It would take some work to create a coherent report from her jumbled writings, but she'd have plenty of time for that once they got back home. Right now, she just wanted to get as much information and as many of her first impressions written down as she could.

Nik tickled her, sending a shiver up her spine.

She giggled and elbowed him in the stomach.

His lips touched her hair in a soft kiss before he released her.

"Do you know what this means?" Randi asked after a while.

"What what means?"

Randi waved at the sky. "This. It means I did it. My dad was right, and I just proved it. I got on a plane and I flew to *Africa*, and I did it. I justified everything he ever did. It wasn't all for nothing."

Nik pulled her close and kissed her cheek. "You did. And I couldn't be more proud."

"Why don't you get some rest?" Randi suggested.

"You mean leave you alone out here? Not a chance."

"Well, just go grab your sleeping bag and lie down right here. I'll wake you in a couple of hours when I need a rest."

"Okay. Deal."

He soon returned and stretched out on the ground beside her.

With one hand, she ran her fingers through his hair, while she continued to write with the other.

Periodically, she scanned the sky. Sometime after midnight, a form, slightly darker black than the deep blue of the sky, appeared in the distance. Shutting off her flashlight, she watched as one of the dragons returned, carrying something in its talons.

It was hard to make out what it might be, limp and flopped over as it was, but it looked like some sort of deer. The dragon and its prey disappeared into a cave at the far end of the lake. A high-pitched growl echoed off the walls of the cliffs.

Was that a mother, bringing home a meal to her baby?

She jotted down some notes about the dragon feeding her children, like a bird, rather than the young being on their own from the beginning like many reptiles.

It was another half hour or so until another dragon appeared, this one also carrying something in its talons. Its arrival in a cave sent forth another distant wave of growls echoing across the water.

Over the next couple hours, several more of the dragons returned, each carrying some sort of animal. At last, the trickle of dragons returning to their caves dwindled, and the night returned to stillness, broken only by the babbling of the river and the chittering of night animals.

Randi knew she'd seen far fewer return than leave, so she remained awake, watching and waiting, writing down ideas and theories.

It wasn't until nearly dawn that the rest of the dragons returned.

Chapter Forty-Three

One, then two, and then two more right at the same time, but from different directions. None of these carried food with them. Soon, a few at a time, and more as morning grew nearer, the dragons returned to their dens. Only about half the beasts returning so close to morning carried anything in their talons.

Randi made a note to study that phenomenon further. She did a quick tally—by her estimation, the herd, if it could be called that, was made up of somewhere between thirty and fifty dragons. She nudged Nik. "They're coming back," she whispered.

Nik sat up, rubbed his eyes, and looked out over the horizon as the last of the dragons returned. One flew directly over their heads, just above the treetops.

Randi peered at it as it passed over them, heading toward its cave.

They were easier to see now, with the sky beginning to lighten. Randi grabbed Nik's hand, squeezing it in her excitement.

The sun glanced off the cliffs as it climbed up in the sky. They waited several minutes, but no more dragons appeared. It soon became evident none would.

"You should try to get a little sleep," Nik said.

Randi yawned. "Good idea."

She tried to stand, but joints, stiff and sore from overuse and under-rest, tightened, and she crumpled back down.

"Apparently I'm not taking good enough care of you." Nik stood and pulled her up. Wrapping one arm around her waist, he walked her back to the tent. "I don't want to see you up for at least six hours."

Randi kissed him lightly. "Yes, dear."

***

Low voices chattering, soft laughter, and feet shuffling through leaves and grass woke Randi. A glance at her watch told her she'd only slept a few hours, but she got up anyway.

Humid jungle air greeted her when she climbed from the tent.

Nik jumped up from his seat near the fire and slipped his arms around her. "You shouldn't be up yet."

"Like I could sleep."

"Yeah, I know." He kissed the top of her head. "I saved you some oatmeal for breakfast."

She shoveled the food down and she and Nik joined Jeremiah and Naomi out by the lake.

With Jeremiah acting as translator, she asked Naomi everything she knew about the dragon.

Why wasn't he nocturnal like the rest of his kind? How had she gone about training him? How quickly did he learn, and how intelligent was he? Did she know for certain whether he was male or female? What did he eat, and how often?

Randi wrote everything down in her notebook.

The creatures seem to have amazing intelligence, possibly on the same level as porpoises and porcine. Naomi says Kudabah can almost anticipate what she is going to tell him. This level of intelligence could account for some of the legends that claimed dragons could read people's minds. Creatures with this cunning certainly would have been reported to have magical powers.

After a break from her interrogation for lunch, Randi set about examining the dragon—his size, the texture of his scaly skin, the shape of his forefeet and how they differed from his hind feet, and the ridges on his head and neck. She mused aloud while Nik took notes for her.

Naomi held the dragon's head while Randi examined his mouth. "I wonder where the fire comes from."

Jeremiah snorted. "That's something we'll probably have a hard time figuring out without an internal examination, and I, for one, don't have any interest in a firsthand look."

"I wonder," Jon said. "We make all sorts of suppositions about dinosaur defense mechanisms, based on everything from nostril position to fossilized plants in the same area. We compare dinosaur skeletons to living creatures to make educated guesses about their functions, but without living tissue, we really have no way of knowing certain things."

Randi smiled at him. Her father would've said much the same thing, had he lived to make this discovery with her.

Randi only half listened. Saliva from the dragon's fangs dripped on her hand, where her bite was now a pair of fading pink blotches, making her skin itch.

"I think it's a chemical thing. His saliva is giving me an allergic reaction, almost like a mild venom."

She yanked her hand out and stared at the scar, then back at the dragon. "Look at his teeth—the shape of his bite pattern."

"What? What is it?" Jeremiah asked.

"I think this is what bit me. Over spring break, I was working on an archaeological dig. I got what I thought was a snake bite, but now I wonder if it was a baby dragon. It would make sense. I was just a few hundred miles north of here. Maybe this isn't the only pocket of these creatures still in existence."

She would have to make a note of that and go back over the notes she took in Cameroon.

Naomi tapped her shoulder and asked her something.

Randi looked expectantly at Jeremiah, waiting for a translation. He wasn't looking at her. His green eyes pierced through Naomi and he rattled off something in French. Randi couldn't understand what he said, but the word "no" was clear. Several times over.

Naomi planted her hands on her hips and jabbered back at him.

"What's going on?" Nik asked.

Jeremiah whirled on him. "She wants to let Randi ride the dragon."

Nik's glare joined Jeremiah's in an apparent attempt to intimidate Naomi away from ever suggesting such a thing again. Both men managed to position themselves between Randi and the beast, as if they could keep her from considering the offer by standing in her way.

Randi pushed through them and stood by Naomi, nodding her head.

Naomi grinned and helped hoist her into the saddle on Kudabah's back.

"Miranda Leigh Ross, get down from there," Nik ordered.

She glared at him. "Since when are you my father?"

Jeremiah snorted. "For once, I have to agree with Nik."

Randi turned her glare his direction. "I'm riding this dragon, so the two of you can be supportive or you can go pout in the tent like children, but you're not stopping me."

Kudabah pranced back and forth, rolling his yellow eyes and snorting at Randi. Naomi muttered soothing words and scratched under his chin, calming him down.

Naomi showed Randi how to hold on and how to position her legs in the straps. It took a bit of adjusting, because Randi was a good deal taller and heavier than Naomi, but soon she sat comfortably astride Kudabah's back.

At a word from Naomi, Kudabah sprang into the sky and soared close to the lake.

Wind whipped around her, filling her nostrils with the scents of lake and forest and clean mountain air. Below her, the lake sparkled in a dozen shades of shimmering blue, from a pale, almost white reflection of the clouds, to a deep midnight in the shadows of the cliffs. Tall, brilliant trees, with their lush branches reaching heavenward, stretched out in an endless canopy to every side.

Every sense Randi possessed seemed heightened as she took in her surroundings. Rough scales shifted beneath her legs, chafing and rubbing them raw through her jeans, as the dragon's heavy muscles contracted up and down. An eternity—and yet only moments—later, a whistle from Naomi brought Kudabah back to the lake shore, landing with a graceful thud on the ground.

Nik grinned at her, relief at her safe return evident on his face. "How was it?" He lifted her into his arms.

"Amazing! It was better than anything you can imagine. Better than anyone in any fantasy novel could have described it. I could see everything, and the wind whisked past my face, and—it was amazing!"

Nik laughed, sharing her joy, and planted a kiss on her lips. "I'm glad you enjoyed it. Don't think I'm not still mad at you, though."

"I'll make it up to you." She grabbed her notebook to write down her experience.

Naomi said something to Kudabah and he launched into the air again, disappearing from sight.

"Where is he going?" Randi asked.

Jeremiah asked Naomi, then translated. "Hunting." He turned to Nik. "About how fast do you think he was flying?"

Nik shrugged. "It's really hard to measure just by watching. I'd guess between forty and fifty miles per hour, probably."

Jeremiah nodded. "I was thinking at least fifty." He called Mr. Chevalet and Kinte, who were busy examining the rock formations along the edges of the cliffs, and asked them the same question.

Mr. Chevalet agreed, as well.

"How about you, Kinte?"

Kinte shook his head. "That is not really my area of expertise."

Jeremiah pushed a few buttons on his watch. "Naomi," He asked her something, then turned to Randi and the others. "I asked her to tell me as soon as he returns. I'd like to get a rough idea of how far he travels."

Randi sat down next to Djazani and Kinte. "Do you believe these creatures are similar to the one you uncovered in Wyoming?"

Djazani just shrugged.

"It is hard to determine," Kinte said. "We were only just starting to uncover it when Djazani and I left. We had not come to any definite conclusions. Also, they look much different with skin and muscle on them. My best guess would be yes, this is the same or a very similar creature within the same family as the one in Wyoming."

"That would explain how human bones got in the stomach cavity. That creature existed at the same time as humans."

Djazani's eyes narrowed a little. "Maybe. We really can't tell yet if this is the same thing. There are so many little details to look at when you're examining fossils, and we didn't get a chance to do any of those things, nor can we compare those findings with one of these creatures, short of killing one and dragging its body all the way down the mountain."

"I got some pretty good shots, though," Carole walked over from where she'd been taking pictures of the lake and the caves. "I'll bet by comparing these pictures to the pictures of your fossil we could come up with a pretty good idea. I mean, artists depict what dinosaurs would have looked like by adding flesh to what they know of existing fossils. Why can't we do the same thing in reverse?"

"That is a possibility," Kinte nodded.

They talked for a while longer, until Kudabah returned, a fat deer clutched in the talons of his hind feet. Ignoring the humans, he dragged the animal to his nest and began to eat.

Jeremiah checked his stopwatch and asked Naomi a series of questions.

He took notes on her answers then turned toward the group. "I think we can safely estimate these creatures have a range of fifty to sixty miles they travel for food, staying mainly near waterways, such as rivers and lakes, where there's more room for them to maneuver when they hunt and where they're more likely to find adequate prey."

Nik's eyes widened. "Thirty to forty miles? That's a long way to go for food."

"True, but if you consider each of these creatures—and from what we saw last night there could easily be a couple dozen or more—hunts every night, even a sixty-mile radius in each direction has to be divided pretty thinly for each to get well fed."

"Didn't Naomi say Kudabah doesn't have to eat every day?" Randi asked. "Even though they hunt every night, it doesn't mean they each find food every night."

"Good point. Also, a sixty-mile radius is a pretty conservative estimate. It's entirely possible they travel farther than that. Randi, you said most of the creatures didn't return until morning."

Randi nodded.

"Now, why Kudabah doesn't travel farther, I don't know." Jeremiah rubbed at the stubble on his chin. "Perhaps because he's domesticated or because he's carrying a rider."

"Or maybe he just doesn't need to." Randi suggested. "Since he hunts during the day, and the others hunt at night, maybe he has a greater variety to choose from in a smaller area."

"Good call." Nik squeezed her hand.

"It's worth looking into," Jeremiah agreed. "We have a few more days before we need to head back down the mountain. We'll spend the time

342

tracking and recording as much data as we can."

***

The Director answered the call on the first ring.

"It's me," the agent said.

"Of course it's you. I was expecting to hear from you days ago."

"This is the first time I've been able to sneak away from the group long enough to call."

"What's going on out there?"

"She found what she was looking for."

The Director sucked in a breath. It couldn't be. Despite all the precautions, sending the agent and planning for all contingencies, the Director hadn't really believed Randi would succeed in her quest. "Are you sure? Does she have proof?"

"Yes. Plenty of it."

The plan was not ideal. The Director had hoped to have more time before deciding on an endgame. There was too much at stake, however, to let Randi succeed. "Get me everything you can. Notes, pictures—everything. It is absolutely imperative that we have that information first. As for Randi—you know what to do."

"It will be taken care of."

"I want it done tonight."

"That is impossible. I can't right now. Don't worry, though, I'll do it."

"You'd better not fail me."

"I haven't yet," the agent said smoothly. "Don't forget about my compensation. I'll be expecting what we talked about when I get back."

"If you succeed, you'll get all you want and more."

"I'll see you when I get back, then."

The Director hung up. A contingency plan for the agent might not be too far in the future, either.

Chapter Forty-Four

Randi spent the next several days charting everything she learned from Naomi and from her own observations.

She examined Kudabah several times, each time coming up with new observations.

And each night, she sat just inside the safety of the trees and watched the dragons come and go.

It never ceased to amaze her—every majestic beast that soared out from its cave and returned from the hunt was a fresh joy.

Randi sat with Jeremiah one morning just before dawn, watching the sky and charting the dragons.

"I'm thinking these are all the males, coming back in the morning, and the ones who return around midnight every night are the females bringing food to their young," Randi said.

"That sounds plausible. Of course, there's no way to prove it at this point, but I'd go so far as to hypothesize the males of the species intentionally travel farther to find food, leaving the closer hunting grounds for the females."

"Interesting. That would suggest some sort of group identity. A pack mentality, of sorts."

"I don't think most reptiles travel in packs, but I suppose it's possible."

Randi leaned her head against her knees. "There's so much to know, so much to find out about these creatures. I wish we could stay up here forever."

"I understand. That's not possible, though. We've been here two weeks already, and that's not even counting the time we took getting up the mountain or the time it will take getting down."

Randi sighed. "I know."

"I'd like to come back and put GPS trackers on some of them, if at all possible."

"I want to be here to watch that," Randi teased.

"Very funny. I've got some thoughts on that. I think Naomi and Kudabah might be able to help us get close enough to tranquilize and tag a couple of them while they're sleeping. But even if not, we can set up some trail cameras with night vision capabilities. In the meantime, at least we have enough to make a pretty detailed report. It's time to wrap this up. I think we have all the information we can reasonably get in one trip."

Randi breathed deeply. "Okay. I guess I've gotten all I can without actually feeding myself to one. Can we stay a few more days at least?"

Jeremiah put a hand on her shoulder. "Two days. Then we need to head home."

***

Randi and the others spent the next two days cleaning up the camp, following up a few questions and details with Naomi, and detailing all they could about the terrain.

Jon and Kinte had discovered some fossils in the rocks along the sides of the cliffs, and along with Djazani, they spent the better part of the days photographing and charting his discoveries.

After several excursions into the air on Kudabah's back, Randi felt almost confident in her ability to control the creature. Naomi taught her some of the whistled commands she used, and Kudabah obeyed her almost as well as he did Naomi.

The day before they planned to leave, she climbed on his back for one final ride. She grinned down at Nik as the dragon leapt into the air and soared away.

Soaring through the air on the back of a dragon, it suddenly struck her that she'd won.

She'd found proof of something everyone said was just a myth, discovered something no one before her had. She had a whole book's worth of notes about how dragons really lived and speculations about how the legends must have grown from things she knew to be fact.

Moreover, she'd beaten the mysterious Syndicate Dr. Peterson had warned her about, not to mention the skeptics who scoffed and laughed at her theories. Her theories were fact, and she could now prove it. Her father would be vindicated, once and for all. And there would be no way the university could deny her her degree now. She'd appeal the moment she got home, and they would have to rescind her expulsion.

And, like icing on the proverbial cake, the man of her dreams, her best friend, loved her, and she loved him back.

She threw her head back and laughed aloud at the sheer joy of her life at that moment.

It was almost sunset when she returned to the shore of the lake. She hurried to the camp and glanced around.

Everyone seemed to be present. Except—

"Where's Jon?"

Kinte looked up. "Last time I saw him he said he was going to collect some samples of the local flora. He said there were some species of plants he recognized only because they resembled fossils he'd seen over the years and he thought he might have discovered a living specimen of a plant thought to be extinct."

"That doesn't sound like him. He knows better than to be out there at dusk."

Kinte folded his hands in front of him. "I know only what he told me."

Randi hurried to the edge of the forest and scanned the open area. Jon was on the far side of the shore, collecting plants and sticking them in a bag, not seeming to notice how far away he was. Each step took him a little farther around the curve of the lake until he was almost to the opposite ridge, where the cliff rose sharply, black against the orange glow of the setting sun.

Straightening, he glanced at the sky and seemed to realize just how late it was. He put the last of his gleanings into his bag and began to trudge back around the marshy shore toward camp.

Randi waved at him, but he didn't seem to see her. He hurried his steps, making his way toward the forest that, on his side of the stream, lay even farther back than on the side where the camp sat.

His leg caught in something. He tugged at it, but it didn't come loose. "Jon!" Randi called.

He didn't seem to hear. He bent over and fiddled with his shoe. A moment later, he started again, one foot wearing only a sock.

The first dark shape appeared in the sky, an inky blot against the deepening velvet backdrop of twilight.

Randi's stomach churned. He was too far from the edge of the forest.

Jon looked up.

The dragon circled.

Jon tried to run, but now his other foot seemed to be stuck in the marshy ground.

What was wrong with his shoes? How was he getting trapped there?

Randi urged him silently along.

The dragon swooped down, searching the edge of the lake, followed closely by several more of its kind.

Randi broke from the tree line and started toward him. "Jon!"

He turned toward the sound of her voice.

She reached for him but was jerked back into the forest. She landed on her backside, staring up at a dragon that rocketed toward where she had been standing a moment ago.

She looked beyond, to where Jon stood.

A dragon swooped down and dug its talons into Jon's shoulders, uprooting him from the sludge that had held him and now dripped from his stockinged feet.

Randi watched in horror as Mr. Chevalet's body whipped like a rag doll being shaken in the dragon's talons. His bag flew from his hand that now hung as limply as the rest of his body.

She rolled to her knees in the tall grass just inside the tree line, retching. Her whole body shook with violent spasms as she emptied her insides.

Strong hands held her shoulders, steadying her until she finished. She looked up. Jeremiah knelt beside her.

She wiped her face with her sleeve and sat back. Jeremiah pulled her into an embrace and held her as she trembled.

"I talked him into coming. I shouldn't have. He's too old. I brought him up here and now he—"

"You can't blame yourself. Jon knew what he was signing up for."

"No, he didn't. He didn't even believe. He had no way of knowing he'd get eaten."

"What happened is horrible, but it's not your fault."

"This was my trip, and I'm responsible for the people on it."

"Randi, look at me."

Randi blinked at him through her tears.

"This was not your fault. It's a tragedy, but there's nothing you could've done. If you'd gone out there, you would've been killed, as well."

***

The next morning dawned foggy and humid. Naomi stood by the edge of the lake with her brother while the Westerners packed up their gear and prepared to leave.

"Please come with us," Albert pleaded.

Naomi shook her head. "I have nothing down there. Besides, I can't leave Kudabah alone. He wouldn't know what to do. I'm his only family. He's only beginning to understand there are others of his kind, family other than me. Now that he understands there are other humans—and he's not supposed to eat them—he's been more curious about socializing with the other dragons. I know Randi has been tracking him, but I don't know if she realizes what he's been doing. There's one specific dragon that he follows when it leaves. He's trying to make friends, and if he's friends with other dragons, maybe they'll learn to be friendly to me—to us, as well. I have a purpose now. Something that gives my life meaning. I have to stay."

Albert sighed. As much as he missed his sister and hated to leave her behind, he knew where his purpose was, as well. "I understand. Well, if you're sure you won't change your mind." He looked at her hopefully.

She shook her head sadly. "My home is here now."

"I'll come back to see you soon."

"I'll be waiting," she smiled.

"Maybe next time I'll bring my wife," he grinned.

Naomi stared at him, uncomprehending for a moment. He hadn't said anything about that before. "Who is she?"

"Well, she isn't yet, but she will be Marie."

Naomi's mouth gaped open. "You're going to marry Marie?"

Albert nodded proudly.

"But, she could never make it up here—not with her leg."

349

Albert scowled. "Of course she could. It may take a little longer, but there's nothing she can't do when she puts her mind to it."

Naomi smiled and hugged her brother. "Well, then, I look forward to meeting your wife."

They embraced one last time, then Albert hurried to the head of the column of scientists snaking along the trail.

Randi trotted over and hugged Naomi. She didn't understand most of Randi's words, but the warm embrace and tears in her blue eyes conveyed her appreciation.

Naomi squeezed Randi's hand and said in halting English, "One day we will meet again."

The group made their way down the side of the mountain, toward their homes, their lives. Naomi waited until they were long out of sight before turning to her closest friend.

"Shall we go hunting, Kudabah?"

***

Subdued silence reigned around the campfire.

They'd gotten back to their starting point late the night before, and had hired a messenger from the village to run to the nearest village with a telephone to contact the guide, who'd arrived earlier in the evening with the second Jeep, back to pick them up.

Randi sat in front of Nik, using his legs as a backrest. Her stomach still churned as images of Jon Chevalet, disappearing into the dark sky as he dangled from the dragon's talons, flashed through her mind.

She'd lost count of the number of times she'd vomited in the three days it took to travel down from the mountain lake.

She forced her thoughts away from the gruesome vision of the past and onto the future.

"I can't believe we're going back to civilization tomorrow," she said. "It hardly seems real."

Nik's long fingers combed through her hair in slow, soothing repetition. "I'm just glad we made good time coming down. There were times I didn't think I could walk another step."

"Tell me about it."

With the adrenaline from the trip waning and the reality of leaving without one member of the team settling on her, the effects of days of hiking and weeks of being away from home draped a weariness around Randi she couldn't shake. Now it was almost over. She was anxious to get home to rest and mourn the loss of a friend, but also to rejoice in her discovery and the culmination of all her work.

Jeremiah stood and glanced around the group. His eyes lingered a little longer on Randi than on the others, but he quickly jerked his gaze away. "Don't stay up too late. We want to get an early start." He turned and walked into the forest. He stayed close—Randi heard twigs snapping occasionally as he passed—but far enough out of sight she couldn't see him. He wasn't heading to bed, despite what he'd suggested to the rest of them, but was walking around, just out of sight.

A twinge of guilt flicked at her, but she pushed it aside. She couldn't help his feelings, and she'd waited for Nik long enough. She didn't want anything to interfere with that bliss.

Nik leaned forward so his face was only inches from hers. "I think you should take some time off when we get back. I want you to come home with me and meet my family."

"I've met your family before, Nicky."

"I know, but that was before we dated the first time. Back then, you were just a friend I knew from school. It's different now. I want to take you home to meet my family and spend time with them as my girlfriend."

Randi frowned. "Your mom didn't seem to like me when I was just a friend. She's going to hate me now."

"She's not going to hate you. She'll be glad someone finally came along to settle me down."

"This is you settled?"

"You know I am." He turned her face toward him so their foreheads touched. "Please come?"

"You know I will."

"Thank you."

His lips met hers, drawing her in. Even now, kissing him thrilled her. Lips tingling, body warming, she drew closer to him, trying to fill an aching need for him that only grew, the closer they became. Grams and Papa always said they loved each other more after sixty-two years of marriage than they did when they got married. Randi wondered if this growing infatuation was anything like what they felt.

She had to tell him. After years of denying her feelings, the words didn't want to come, but she loved him, and she wanted him to know. *Needed* him to know.

Pulling away, she cradled his cheek in her hand. "Nicky, I—"

"Randi, can you come here for a minute? I need to show you something." Djazani towered over her, solemn-faced, though Randi didn't ever remember her smiling.

"Sure." Randi stood and followed her toward the edge of the forest, around the back of the Jeeps.

"Right over here."

"What is it?"

"I'd rather you see for yourself."

They walked a little farther, and Djazani pointed. "Right over there."

Randi took a few steps and looked where Djazani indicated. "I don't see anything."

Turning, she looked at Djazani and froze.

The moonlight glinted off the barrel of a gun pointed straight at her.

Chapter Forty-Five

"Djazani, what is this?"

"I'm sorry, Randi. You seem like a nice enough person. In another life we might even have been friends, but I have a job to do and a career to get back."

"Djazani, no—"

Everything happened in an instant, rushing together in an incoherent blur.

Nik leapt out of the forest by Randi's side and lunged toward her. A shot rang out, echoing against the night sky.

The last thing Randi heard before crumpling to the ground was her own scream.

***

Something heavy pinned Randi down. Shouting came at her from every direction.

She struggled to sit up, pushing against the oppressive weight. A sharp pain in her shoulder stopped her. She couldn't feel her hand—was it missing or just numb? Her head throbbed.

Where am I? What's going on?

The thing pressing on her suppressed her ability to breathe. She shoved it with her other arm.

Nik's red head flopped to the side as she pushed, his eyes half closed, his breath coming in shallow gasps.

Warm, sticky blood flowed out, spurting from a yawning hole in his chest. Each gasping breath sent another eruption of blood flowing out.

She screamed and pushed herself onto her knees. She pressed her hands against the wound. Sticky red warmth oozed out from between her fingers.

She screamed again. "Help!"

Her voice didn't sound like her own, shrill and eerie, screeching and panicking, reverberating against the walls of the forest.

Violent sobs wracked her body. "Hold on, Nicky. Hold on."

He looked at her through glazed eyes. "Randi."

"I'm here, Nicky." Panic edged her voice.

"Randi," he rasped. His eyes fluttered closed.

"Nicky, don't do that. Open your eyes, Nik!"

He didn't move.

Wetness flowed down her face. She couldn't see through the tears spilling from her eyes. "I love you. I love you, Nik. Just stay with me. I love you!"

He blinked once, slowly, then again. His eyes found her face. "It's time for me to fly. I love you."

With one last gasp, he closed his eyes. His chest stopped moving.

She cradled his head, stroked his face and hair and kissed his lips. "No, no, no—no, don't do this. Come back, Nicky. I love you. Come back."

***

Jeremiah stopped walking and stood by a tree.

He'd prayed until he had no more words, and now just stood still, eyes closed, listening to the voice inside that spoke wisdom and comfort to his heart.

Deep breaths, in and out, helped to calm him as he stood silently, trying to accept what would never be.

Someone rustled the leaves near where he stood. He opened his eyes.

Randi and Djazani walked into the forest, away from the tents, more or less in the direction of the Jeeps.

That was odd. Where were they going?

He started to follow, but Nik followed them. With Nik close by, they'd be safe, at least. Still, he wondered where they were going and what they were doing. He followed along at a little bit of a distance.

Djazani said something he couldn't hear, so he walked a little closer.

Nik circled around nearer Randi, though as far as Jeremiah could tell, the women hadn't noticed Nik or himself.

Randi turned to look at something, and Jeremiah saw the quick movement of Djazani's hand pulling something out of her belt.

The moon glinted off something shining in her hand.

Why did Djazani have a gun?

He crashed through the trees toward her. At the same time, Nik dove out of the trees toward Randi.

A deafening crash accompanied a blinding flash from the gun.

Djazani turned and dashed toward the Jeep just a few yards away.

Jeremiah intercepted her, grabbing her around the middle and pulling her to the ground beside him, wrestling the gun out of her hand.

She grunted and struggled, impotent beneath his superior size and strength.

"Somebody help me!" he called out.

Kinte, Carole, and the guide burst through the trees.

"Help me with her. She just shot Randi—or maybe Nik. I'm not sure."

He grunted and panted as Carole and Kinte each grabbed one of Djazani's arms and pulled her up. Anger painted a mask across her face. Her eyes narrowed to fierce slits.

"Djazani, what's going on?" Kinte looked hurt and confused.

She tossed a scornful glance his direction, but didn't answer.

"Tie her up with something and keep an eye on her. I'm going to check on the others." Jeremiah jogged toward the sound of Randi's wails.

In a moment he came upon her, sitting with Nik's head in her lap, running her fingers through his hair and telling him she loved him.

She didn't look up when he knelt down beside her.

One glance told him all he needed to know. Even if he'd gotten there sooner, he couldn't have done anything.

He sat beside Randi and touched her shoulder.

She screamed out.

Jeremiah looked down. The blood on her arm was her own.

Her eyes fell on him, her expression blank. She looked at Nik, then back at him.

"Randi, listen to me," he said gently. "We have to take care of your arm."

She stared at him—no, through him. Her eyes darted around, unfocused, not seeming to even see him.

"Randi, you're hurt. We need to take care of your arm. Do you

355

understand what I'm saying?"

She looked back at Nik, and a fresh wave of sobs shook her.

Going to her other side, he put her good arm around his neck and pulled her out from under Nik's body.

"Can you stand?"

She didn't acknowledge him, but her legs seemed steady enough.

"Come on."

Her scream rent the air as she pulled away from him and clawed for Nik's body.

"We'll get Nik in a minute, Randi. Right now you have to come with me." Sliding his arm around her waist, he dragged her along back to the camp.

Carole rushed to meet them, sucking in a breath when she saw the blood liberally staining Randi's body. "What happened?"

"She's in shock. Her arm is wounded. Nik is dead."

Carole staggered back, half-falling into the trunk of a tree.

Jeremiah didn't give her time to think about it. "Where is Djazani?"

"She's secure. Tied up by a tree next to the fire. Kinte and the guide are watching her."

"Good. Run get the medical kit and meet me there."

Carole sprinted away, and Jeremiah pulled Randi to the camp. Carole returned a moment later and handed him a box.

From inside, he retrieved a bottle of pain relievers. It wouldn't do much, but maybe it would help some. He pushed a pill into her mouth and gave her some water, which she took, coughing and spluttering.

"Kinte, come help me hold her still."

Kinte got up from where he sat glaring at Djazani and stood over Jeremiah as he struggled with Randi's writhing form.

"Hold her down so I can take care of her shoulder."

Kinte sat, and Jeremiah placed Randi in his arms. He put Randi's good arm around Kinte's back and helped him to wrap his arms around her chest and pin her legs down with his own.

"Carole, hold her arm out like this. She's delirious, but we need to take care of it before she makes it worse. This is going to hurt her and she's probably going to scream, but I need to clean out the wound."

Carole obeyed, flinching and squeezing her eyes shut.

"That's good," Jeremiah murmured, tearing Randi's sleeve from around the wound in her arm.

He opened a bottle of disinfectant and poured it freely over the hole in Randi's arm, causing another round of agonized yelps from her.

He bandaged her arm tightly then took her from Kinte. "That's all we can do for now. She needs to get to a hospital. You and the guide take a tarp and go get Nik's body. Put it in the backseat of one of the Jeeps so we can take it home."

Kinte nodded solemnly as Jeremiah repeated the instructions in French for the guide. The two men disappeared into the forest, and Jeremiah held Randi close to his chest, keeping her arms still so she couldn't thrash around and injure herself more. Little by little, she began to settle down, as exhaustion overtook her.

He directed the others until all the preparations were made.

Kinte came and sat beside him. "It does not make sense, what you say happened."

Jeremiah glanced over at Djazani, who glared at him. She hadn't explained herself, nor made any excuse or defense for her actions.

"I don't know what to tell you. I saw what I saw."

"She is not acting like the woman I know. The woman I love."

Jeremiah didn't answer. What could he say?

"There is something else at work, some other factor, some interpretation of events that will come out," Kinte insisted.

"What explanation could there be for her shooting someone?"

"I do not know, but I cannot believe Djazani capable of what you said."

"You saw the body."

Kinte nodded. "Yes. I will never forget it, how he lay there covered in blood, his mouth open."

Jeremiah pulled the gun from his pocket and showed it to Kinte. He hadn't paid attention to it before, but now he could see it was 3D printed.

Kinte gasped. "That is Djazani's gun. She bought it in Wyoming. For protection, she said, against the snakes and things that infested the dig site. I did not dream she would ever use it on a person."

"Well, she did. She killed Nik."

Jeremiah watched as hurt and confusion on Kinte's face quickly morphed to fury. "She seduced me. She deceived and betrayed me."

"So it would seem."

Kinte's eyes darted to where Djazani sat. Jeremiah had tamped down the temptation to use the thing on her, and he imagined Kinte was doing the same. He put the gun back in his belt, just in case. He wouldn't risk another murder, even if Djazani deserved it.

"I will not let her get away with this," Kinte vowed. "I will see to it she is in prison for the rest of her life."

Jeremiah nodded. He would see to it, as well.

He called out to the group. "Get some sleep. We're leaving as soon as it gets light. Kinte, you take first watch guarding the prisoner. In two hours, wake up the guide. I'm going to stay with Randi and make sure she makes it through the night."

Kinte lashed Djazani to the tree with another layer of rope taken from their packs, and sat down in front of her with a cup coffee.

Jeremiah pulled his sleeping bag out of his tent and lay down, holding Randi's now-sleeping form against him.

All those times I wished to hold her in my arms—this isn't how I wanted it to be.

Jeremiah fell asleep, his breathing keeping time with the half-sob breaths of the woman beside him.

Kinte woke him up a couple hours later, and a couple hours after that, he woke Carole.

Everyone except Randi woke long before dawn. In the dim light of the fire that lingered in the fire pit and the gray light of the sky, they packed up the tents and their few remaining tools and utensils.

When they were finished breaking camp, Kinte and the guide untied Djazani from the tree and tied her arms behind her back and hobbled her legs.

Jeremiah directed the work in low tones, watching out for Randi who still slept on his sleeping bag. "Is everyone ready to go?" he asked.

Kinte held on to one of Djazani's arms. "Yes." He seemed to have taken Djazani's betrayal as a personal attack and stood vigilantly guarding her.

Carole gave a cursory glance around the campsite and nodded. "Looks like we're ready."

Jeremiah carefully picked Randi up and instructed Carole to get his sleeping bag. "Carole, you'll drive the second Jeep, and Kinte, you'll sit in the back and guard Djazani."

Djazani didn't protest as Kinte led her to the Jeep and helped her in. He tied another rope around her, securing her to the roll bar so she couldn't try to jump out and escape, buckled her in, and sat down beside her.

Carole sat in the front, her eyes narrowed at Djazani. "Don't let her do anything that will make me crash."

Jeremiah lifted Randi into the other Jeep, holding her in his lap in the front seat next to the guide.

With a roar of engines, they set off for the city.

Chapter Forty-Six

Randi's arm felt like it was on fire. Worse pain than when she'd gotten bitten, worse even than when she was stabbed.

Bumping and jostling finally drew her out of a haze of semi-consciousness.

She blinked a few times, not sure where she was or what was happening. One of her arms—the one that sent convulsions of misery spasming through her—was strapped to her body. Strong arms held her. A muscled chest pillowed her head.

"Nik?"

"It's Jeremiah," came the gentle reply.

She pulled away and looked at him, confused. "Where are we? Where's Nik?"

"We're on our way back to Ouesso. Do you remember anything that happened last night?"

Randi shook her head.

Jeremiah took a deep breath. "Last night you were attacked. By Djazani. Nik saved your life."

"Nik, is he—"

"I'm sorry, Randi. He—he didn't make it."

Randi stared at him, not comprehending for a moment, before the memories rushed back to her.

Her throat constricted. She clutched at Jeremiah's shirt, unable to breathe. "Nik, no!"

She rested her head against Jeremiah's shoulder and let the tears come.

Not the hysterical screams of the night before, but the overwhelming grief that accompanied full comprehension.

Jeremiah put his arms around her and held her close, gently stroking her hair with his fingers as her body shook with tears. "We're going to the city as quickly as possible. I think the bullet is still lodged in your shoulder, and we're going to need to get it out. Try to rest as much as you can."

Jeremiah said something to the driver who slowed the Jeep to a stop. "We're going to take a break for lunch."

Carole jumped from the other vehicle and ran toward them. "You're awake. How are you feeling?"

Randi allowed Jeremiah to lift her from the Jeep, then pushed away from him and clung to Carole. "It hurts so badly. I feel like I'm going to die." Her eyes landed on the tarp-wrapped bundle lying across the back seat. Despite tightly squeezed eyes, tears rolled down her cheeks.

"I'm so sorry." Carole led her to a tree and helped her lower herself to the ground. "Try to eat something. You need to keep up your strength."

The thought of food tightened Randi's throat, and a dizzying nausea accompanied the throbbing in her arm, but she nibbled a few bites.

Jeremiah handed her a few pills. "It's not much, but it should take the edge off the pain. Let's get going. We want to get you to the hospital as soon as possible."

Jeremiah sat in the back for the rest of the trip, allowing Randi to sit up front by herself.

She stared out at the passing scenery without really seeing it. The cavern in her chest deadened her senses and her ability to respond to anything else.

***

Late in the afternoon, they finally arrived in Ouesso.

The guide took Jeremiah and Randi straight to the hospital, while Kinte and Carole delivered Djazani to the local authorities.

Jeremiah poured himself a cup of coffee and sat to wait for news.

A short while later, Carole called. "We explained what happened and left her with the authorities. They'll work out with the American authorities what to do with her."

"Good. Thank you. She's no longer the responsibility of the American Cryptozoological Society."

"We're on our way to return the Jeep to the guide's store. Then we'll head back to the hotel to wait for you."

"Thanks again, Carole. When you get back, please contact Dr. Lengel. Fill him in on everything, and work with him to look up flights to the U.S. leaving over the next couple of days."

"Sure thing. Let me know when you find out anything about Randi."

"I will. Thank you. I appreciate it."

Over an hour later, he still had no news of Randi's condition. He paced the hospital halls, played games on his phone, and browsed through a couple of magazines. He even called Dr. Lengel.

"Jeremiah! Carole told me what happened." Dr. Lengel cursed. "Is she all right?"

"I don't know. She's still in surgery."

"You should've brought her home to an American hospital."

"There's no way she would've lasted that long. Her arm was already starting to get infected, and the bullet was still lodged in there."

"Why would Djazani do something like that?"

"I wish I knew. I tried questioning her a few times, but she refused to speak. The only explanation that makes any sense is she was trying to keep Randi quiet."

"Quiet? So you found something? Carole hung up before I had a chance to ask."

"Oh, yes. Everything we could want and more. I'll show you when we get home."

"Great! I'll get everything set up and ready for our next press conference. See you in a few days."

Jeremiah hung up, a little irritated that both Jon Chevalet's and Nik's deaths could so easily be swept aside for Dr. Lengel's fame and fortune. His annoyance at Dr. Lengel, however, paled in comparison to his agitation at not hearing anything about Randi.

At last, a doctor emerged. "We retrieved the bullet, but extensive damage was done to the muscles and tissues in her shoulder."

"What does that mean?"

"It's probable she'll lose some, maybe even most of her function in that arm, even with physical therapy. How much is hard to say, but with luck,

363

she'll recover some use."

Jeremiah nodded. At least she'd live. "May I see her?"

The doctor nodded. "This way." He led Jeremiah to a room lined with beds separated only by torn, thin curtains.

Randi lay in a bed near the middle of the room, still unconscious from the anesthesia.

"How long until we can take her home?"

"If she recovers well from the surgery, she could be moved to a hospital in the States soon—a few days at most."

Jeremiah called Carole to update her, then slumped into the chair by Randi's bed. For a long time, he sat next to her, just watching her sleep, but he knew he couldn't put off the inevitable.

Picking up the phone, he dialed Randi's mom.

"Hello, Mrs. Ross? This is Dr. Jeremiah Bryant. I'm the scientist in charge of the research trip your daughter went on."

"Oh, hello, honey." Randi's mother's voice radiated joy and exuberance. "I'm so glad you're back in telephone range. Randi said you'd be out for a while. How did it go? Where is she? Can I talk to her?"

"Actually, that's why I'm calling. There's been… an accident."

"What happened? Is she all right?" Terror tainted her voice.

"She's going to be fine, but she's in the hospital right now. She was hurt pretty badly, but we expect her to recover."

"What hospital? We'll drive out there tonight."

"Actually, we're still in Africa. I'll phone you as soon as I know when we're heading home." He ended the call quickly, before he had to listen to her cry.

The next call was infinitely more difficult. He had to tell Jon Chevalet's sister that her brother had died overseas.

But the last phone call was the worst of all. Telling Nik's parents their son died—torture in a third world country would've been preferable.

At last he hung up, the devastated wails of Nik's mother echoing in his ears. He leaned back in the wobbly chair by Randi's bed.

***

Morning light filtered in through the window. Jeremiah sat up and glanced around. He must have fallen asleep.

Randi still slept in the blissful coma of medication. Convinced she would be all right for a while, Jeremiah went to take care of the other things. First, he arranged to have Nik's body cared for and transported back to the United States.

He called Nik's family again. "Nik's body is being transported to a funeral home in L.A. I've given them your numbers. Here's the number for the funeral home, so you can make arrangements to retrieve him."

He felt very cold and clinical sharing these details, but he didn't know anything to say that would comfort them. He gave them as much information as he could and hung up.

A doctor came into the room. "Everything looks like it is healing well. She should be able to travel in a couple of days, as long as she gets immediate medical attention when she gets home."

As soon as the doctor moved on to the next patient, Jeremiah called Dr. Lengel. He'd arranged flights for them, on the assumption that Randi would be well enough to travel. That confirmed, he called Carole. "I'm on my way back to the hotel. We're leaving in three days."

"I didn't want to call you, because I wasn't sure how Randi was doing, but—there's something you need to see."

"I'll be there soon."

Back at the hotel, Jeremiah pounded on Carole's door. "What is it?" he demanded when she opened it.

"I went through Randi's notes, trying to put them back in order, and I realized some of the pages were missing."

"Missing? Or just misplaced in all the hurry?"

"Missing. And—more than just some. Most of them. I looked everywhere, but I couldn't find them. Then I remembered something. The other night, before—everything—Djazani was looking through the pictures on my camera. At the time I had no reason to suspect her of anything, so I didn't think anything of it, but then just now, I realized my memory card is missing, too."

Jeremiah slumped against the wall. "What do you mean missing?"

"Stolen. There's nothing left. I've looked through all of Djazani's things, but I can't find it. For all I know, it's in lying on the ground in the jungle somewhere. I had a second card, but I don't think there's anything valuable on it. I had filled it up with pictures along the way, but I switched it out shortly after we got to the top of the mountain, before…"

He sat heavily on the bed. "Everything's gone?"

"As far as I can tell. Did she get anything of yours?"

Jeremiah went to his room and dug through his notes, returning a few minutes later. "She got to mine, too. Bits and pieces are still here—enough so I wouldn't notice everything was gone, I suspect, but all the facts and measurements and other work is taken out. I should be able to duplicate most of my research, but most of the key points are gone."

Carole sat beside him. "What are we going to do?"

"Let's see what's on the first memory card—maybe there will be something we can use."

Carole stuck the card in the camera and handed it to him.

He browsed through the digital pictures, frowning.

The remaining pictures were virtually useless.

Pictures of the terrain—the lake, the caves in the cliffs, the stream flowing out, trees and foliage, pictures of the animals they saw drinking from the stream and in the surrounding woods, pictures of the campsite and of the team members hard at work—pictures that would have filled in the gaps and helped with the details that would have created a clear understanding of the lives of the dragons were all intact. Without pictures of the dragons themselves, however, they were just pictures of a remote mountain lake in Africa.

He kept browsing, frustration growing deeper and deeper.

He stopped. A smile spread over his face. "She missed one."

Carole grabbed for the camera.

A clear and beautiful shot of Randi standing next to Nik, grinning at him, one hand reaching up to scratch under Kudabah's neck, remained.

"This is from the first day. After the shock wore off and Naomi let them come close. I didn't remember that this one was on this card!" Carole threw her arms around him in an impulsive hug.

Jeremiah extricated himself but smiled. "It's not what we had, but at least we still have some proof."

Their notes they could be put back together, and they had a usable picture. Mission accomplished.

Randi stared out the window of the plane as the land rushed by beneath her. This should have been a happy moment. She'd vindicated her father's research—his entire life, really. She'd fulfilled her dream of proving the existence of dragons and seen a live dragon with her own eyes. She even rode on his back.

Yet, at what cost? Was it worth it? She would have gladly traded all the dragons in the world for one more moment with Nik.

Nik was gone.

She'd spent so long trying to prove she was right—trying to prove her father was right—that she'd neglected the most important things in life. Her ambition had gotten Nik killed. And she had the rest of her life to live with the knowledge it was her fault.

***

Djazani called the Director as soon as she got back to L.A. and was given a phone call.

"It's me," she said. "And I'm ready to get out of jail."

"You failed me," the Director spat.

"I think not." Djazani kept her voice cool. "I got all the information you wanted. The memory card with all the pictures Carole took, plus most of the notes from the rest of the team are in Mr. Chevalet's things. All you have to do is send one of your people to retrieve his effects. You'll have plenty of time to come forward with your findings before they can come up with anything. As you well know, the first story is the one people believe. Get ahead of the story and publish your own findings. And then you will get me out of here."

"You allowed them to come back with information, and you let Randi live."

Djazani twirled the phone cord around her fingers. "I not only sabotaged the trip and deleted all of the proof they gathered, but now Randi Ross knows she doesn't want to cross the Syndicate."

"You were supposed to kill *her*."

"It's a minor detail. One I think will prove to be more useful in the end."

A snort echoed on the other end.

Djazani ignored it. "Remember our deal. You're going to have

Administrator Schweitzer fired, or at the very least relocated, and his job given to me. I'll continue to work for the Syndicate and to do as you ask, if it doesn't interfere with my other duties."

The Director's heavy breathing echoed through the phone for several long seconds. Finally, "Consider it done. And get ready to work when you get back. With the evidence you're bringing, we've got quite a story to tell."

Chapter Forty-Seven

Los Angeles, California

Jeremiah sat by Randi's bed at the hospital in L.A. His eyes were scratchy and his back ached from sitting so long, but he wouldn't leave her.

They'd done a second surgery, with a lot of reconstructive work on the damaged tissue.

She was still being medicated pretty heavily. She'd woken up a few times—long enough to get her bearings and understand where she was and why—but she hadn't stayed awake long enough for him to really have a conversation with her.

It couldn't wait any longer, though. He needed to have her with him before she got caught up in her regular life.

The next time she woke up, he took her hand. "How are you feeling?"

"How do you think I'm feeling?"

He considered waiting—giving her more time to process—but he didn't know how much time they had. If he knew anything about the Syndicate, they'd want to get in front of the story, spin their own narrative before the Society had a chance to make their announcements at the press conference.

He was running out of options, and he had to do this now. "I know this probably doesn't seem like the best time, but there's something I've been waiting to talk with you about for a long time."

"What?"

"Dr. Peterson was right about the Syndicate."

"I have no idea what that means. Dr. Peterson warned me about them, but she never said *why* they want to keep things quiet. Or what they have against me personally. Or what proving the existence of dragons could possibly do to compromise their mission or whatever. What exactly is the Syndicate?"

Jeremiah pulled his chair a little closer and put a hand on her good arm. "They're an old organization dedicated to controlling the flow of information in the world."

"Classic secret society. Why?"

"Money. Power. The oldest reasons in the book."

"So you're telling me an ancient secret society is trying to hide the truth? Could they be any more clichéd?"

Jeremiah chuckled. "Where do you think those clichés come from? They make good fiction because they're based in the truth. There are actually many ancient secret societies, all with their own little corner of their own little markets. The Syndicate rules many of them. Many divisions, many Directors, many channels. The one that's after you deals mainly in science and technology. Until now, they've been content to run things from the shadows, but I believe they're planning to make their presence public."

The nurse popped her head in the door. "You doing okay in here?"

Randi nodded. "Could I get some water, by any chance?"

"Sure. I'll be right back," the nurse said.

Randi turned back to Jeremiah. "You were saying you think they're going public? Why?"

"Because anonymous power only goes so far. They've been building up the organization for years, but to obtain true power, they need people to believe in them."

"Okay, assuming you're right about that, what do they want with me?"

"You just made a major discovery. The kind of discovery that is world-changing. Even more than Carole's discovery of Bigfoot. Something like this changes everything from science to history to politics. They want—no, *need*—to be the ones to declare it. That kind of knowledge comes with incredible power. To control that power, they have to control the knowledge. You have forced their hand by getting proof, and now they have to take control before they lose the ground they've gained."

The nurse returned with Randi's water and promptly left again.

Randi took a sip. "How do you know so much about them?"

"They destroyed my family."

Randi choked, spitting the water all over her lap. "Wait, *what?*"

"My parents were scientists. My mother was recruited into the Syndicate when I was a baby. Her job was to report any findings she and my father came up with. When I was in college, my father invented a way to harness the natural energy—sun, wind, rain—and use it for electricity. Naturally, my mother shared this information with the Syndicate. They told her to make sure that information never got out."

"What happened?"

"My father recorded his findings, and tried to patent the technology. The next thing I knew, the house I grew up in burned down. Two bodies were found inside."

"The Syndicate had them both killed?" Randi gasped.

Jeremiah swallowed. "They stole his research. Much of modern solar power technology is based on my father's work, but the Syndicate is making money from it."

"I'm so sorry."

Jeremiah smiled, but he wasn't telling her this for sympathy. "When my father realized their lives were in danger, he sent me all the information he had on the Syndicate and its dealings."

Randi shifted and winced when she moved her arm. "So why hasn't the Syndicate killed you yet?"

"I know too much. They know I have information on them that could harm them, but they don't know how much or where I keep it. They can't risk that if something happens to me, an investigation into my death will lead authorities right to them."

"If you have this information, why haven't you used it to shut them down?"

"It's not enough. Not yet. I know some of the key players, and I know some of what they're planning over the next few decades, but I don't have nearly enough proof. I can't take them out until I have enough to destroy the whole organization from the roots. But that doesn't mean they won't hurt the people I'm close to. Randi, as long as you're working with me, your life is in danger. You need to understand that. If you want to go work somewhere else,

I won't blame you."

A look of concentration crossed Randi's face. "Do they do this a lot? Kill people whose research they don't want coming out?"

"All the time."

Randi looked at him, tears in her eyes. "Dr. Schleppenbach. His whole team was killed or institutionalized, and he was in hiding. And... he sounded surprised when I said my dad committed suicide. Do you think... did the Syndicate kill my father?"

"I don't know. But it's entirely plausible."

"And then they tried to kill me, but got Nik instead."

"Yes. But it's not too late, if you want to get out. You could go live a quiet, peaceful life somewhere."

"In a remote village in Switzerland?" she asked dryly. "I think I'll risk it. Besides, it's too late for me to go anywhere else."

"Are you absolutely sure? They're everywhere. They have spies infiltrating everything, and I believe they will do whatever it takes to keep us quiet."

"So, what are you saying? I should give up and shut up?"

"Not at all. Quite the opposite, in fact. I just wanted to make sure you're completely aware of what's at stake and the danger involved before we move on."

"Meaning?"

Jeremiah took a deep breath. "I am the head of a counter organization, one that works to prove both the existence and the agenda of the Syndicate. I would like you to be a part of it."

"What would I have to do?"

"The same things you're already doing for the Cryptozoological Society and for your own research, but with a higher purpose and one very specific goal."

Randi raised an eyebrow. "What goal is that?"

"We're going to take down the people who killed Nik."

Randi's jaw tightened, and her knuckles turned white as she gripped the blanket covering her legs. She looked at Jeremiah, blue eyes icy. "I'm in."

To be continued...

Other Books by Avily Jerome

Jack Davidson Case Files

The Breeding

The Possessing

The Haunting

The Infecting

Fairly Dark Tales

Swimmer

The Amulet Saga

The Heir

The Defector

The Silver Shores

The Prophecy

The Sorceress

The Beginning

The End

Acknowledgements

Special thanks to everyone who has ever read any version of this story. This is a heart story—one that I began so many years ago I can't even count that far back. It has seen innumerable iterations, has been through multiple attempts at publication, and has been turned inside-out and put back together. So if you ever gave me any feedback on this, thank you! I appreciate you!

Thank you to my Wonder Women—Lindsay, Catherine, and Sarah, my dear and wonderful friends, whose support is what keeps me going.

Thanks to my husband, for all he is and all he does.

Thanks to Robert, my amazing cover designer, for making this beautiful cover that completely captures Randi and the overall vibe of this story.

About the Author

 Avily Jerome is a writer and freelance editor. She spent five years as the Editor of *Havok Magazine*, now *Havok Publishing*. Her short stories have been published in multiple magazines, both print and digital. She has judged several writing contests, both for short stories and novels, was a book reviewer for Lorehaven Magazine, and is a copy editor for Enclave Publishing.

She is also a writing conference teacher and presenter, and she enjoys speaking to local writers' groups and going to SFF cons.

She loves all things SpecFic, and writes across multiple genres. Her writing heroes include Joss Whedon, Robert Jordan, and J.K. Rowling, among others.

She is a wife and the mom of five kids. She loves living in the desert in Phoenix, AZ, and when she's not writing, she loves reading, spending time with friends, and experimenting with different art forms.